DIANE DE REUCK

*To dear Nathan &
With my love
Diane de Reuck
(16th September 2018).*

'WOLMUNSTER'

William Ropert at the Cape 1839

By Diane Grace de Reuck

William Ropert, 35 yrs. old, embarks on a voyage to the Cape Colony in 1839, leaving England and his former life in Dublin behind. He is forced to desert his only true love, Fanny McBride. She had been financially responsible for his studies and his achievement of becoming a barrister and a Whig supporter. Their love remains a secret and social norms complicate their relationship. Appointed by the Whig Government under Earl Grey, William takes up the post of Attorney General in Cape Town. His ability to influence others and to deliver solutions for the difficult political problems found at the Cape, result in his popularity as a liberal politician. His life is exciting and new acquaintances enrich his life. He meets a young woman Nerina and falls in love with her. William proposes to her, a merchant's daughter, but their relationship is fraught with problems especially as the memory of Fanny still haunts him. In the meantime Cape Town grows in importance as an exporter of wool, some metals and wood from the Eastern Cape. Issues such as drafting a Constitution for the Colony and fine tuning the taxation of individuals, William's belief in the equality of all men brings concepts of a civilised society to the Cape.

As we meet Capetonians, Christian and Malay, Black and White one is rapidly transported into the milieu of colonialism and the seeds of racial inequality are beginning to take root. From the San Bushmen to the British and Boer, the various elements of Cape Society are unveiled. This novel is a magic carpet with different skeins of many colours woven together to delight you.

Introduction

When I learnt from my cousin, Colleen, that William Porter, Attorney General at the Cape from 1839 to 1874, was our great, great uncle she persuaded me to work alongside her to research the life of William who had never married nor had fathered any children. Both of us took time over more than thirty years to piece together some semblance of his character; but, it was I who decided to write about him. Once I had made a conscious pledge to myself to create his character from my notes and imagination, my desk would groan under heaps of dusty journals, letters, 19th Century newspapers and articles from the Government Archives. At last I was ready to begin but, first I would write to my cousin who had left her beloved Zimbabwe to reside in Ireland, for her to share my excitement and enthusiasm for the task ahead.

Dear Colleen,

You must be wondering where my research relating to Great, Great Uncle William has taken me following your visit to Manchester recently. You shared information of where William was born, went to school and finally practised as a barrister and where he lived in Dublin. You opened up his world in a very personal way. Since then I have read about his public life in the archive material of South African Government records as well as those of the South African Military Historical Society. In order to learn more about the times in which he lived at the Cape I have studied dissertations about the Cape from 1488 to 1854 i.e. **The Age of Exploration** *by Professor Maurice Boucher; the* **Occupations of the Cape 1795 to 1854** *by Professor Basil A le*

*Cordeu; **The Settlers 1820 to 1824** by John Bailie and **The Cape Colony 1854 to 1881** by J, Benyon and many more..*

All these describe the shaping of the new Society at the Cape. To immerse oneself in the images that these scholars present to us is both enjoyable and informative. I have read letters of all sorts including those of David Livingstone, Robert Moffat and then to the other extreme one from a little girl who is a border at school in the 19ᵗʰ Century, from where she writes to her 'Mama' and 'Papa' about an outing in which she wishes to participate. The design of clothing and hats and the richness of fabrics used for both is fascinating as was the means with which they used to travel around the Colony in wagons, Hansom cabs and phaeton carriages among some of them. My imagination is full of delightful pictures about a generation that has passed away nearly two hundred years ago. I have studied architecture and town plans, photographs and the paintings and drawings of the period. I even learnt how balls, shooting parties and picnics were amongst some of the events which everyone enjoyed.

*You were so kind to introduce me to J. L. McCracken and his biography of William, **A New Light at the Cape of Good Hope.** I was delighted that you could meet him in person and that he is pleased with the research we are conducting. You have mentioned how he wishes he could write about William's thoughts, loves, hates, dreams and desires. To obtain such an excellent time-line and details of William's career from him has been so useful. Of course, I would have liked to have had more descriptions of his personality, intimate life of the men and women he loved and more of his letters and speeches. I have already begun to form his character and have created his relationships with women, family and friends relying on my imagination.*

*I have managed to find a couple of speeches at my own endeavour. I have also discovered a scholar from a university in the USA who obtained a doctorate for his studies about **Prize Negroes**. The young man, R. L. Watson had discovered the entire debate about the problems with labour at the Cape and I am delighted with the speeches William delivered on the subject. There was also Tennant's **The Rotary Manual** which has an article that William wrote about **Prosecute not persecute**. These verbatim accounts are extremely interesting, shedding light on William's daily diary which was full of things to do and people to see. I have researched the 'who's who' of the day and will introduce some of those people into my novel by researching their lives. I have imagined how they and William would interact e.g. newspaper editors, pioneers, explorers, merchants and politicians. Such characters! Of course, to offset them I have found information about infamous robbers and men of ill repute and have created William's fictitious and most hated enemy from their unsavoury melange of characteristics!*

I have learnt so much about the country in all its aspects e.g. geography, geology, zoology, botany and even anthropology. The scene is set and I can now write a novel from what I have gleaned on my paper trail and where I have found a mere hint of an underlying meaning or oblique suggestion I can then expand the thread to weave a fascinating story. I also hope I can create an imaginative consciousness for William bearing in mind that I have to use poetic licence to make the novel come to life I intend to use Ropert as William's surname being the anagram for Porter in the same way that I have changed our names to Kathleen and Disa for the sake of the novels. The title "Wolmunster" is the name of William's residence and means 'wool sack' Dutch for a quantity measure.

The politics of the day require the intervention of a liberal mind and William had the metal to fight to defend truth and bring the Eighteenth Century ideals of liberty, equality and fraternity to a country which was still a melting pot of men set on making their personal fortunes. These adventurers more often than not took advantage of the wilderness of Africa by exploiting its people and resources. I will start where William sets out on his journey to the Cape where he begins his quest to create a modern, perfect society based on sound western values.

We are truly blessed to have such a famous Great, Great Uncle, well known for his philanthropy and agile mind.

With love,

Diane

I folded the letter and addressed an envelope. I now had all the ingredients for a good story and I hoped Colleen would approve of her portrait of their great, great uncle. I felt immersed in his world, Cape Town, then a small town below Table Mountain with streets of sand, buildings of various continental styles, wealthy men and women from the west and the east including the workers who were either slight of build like the Khoikhoi and the men and women from Malaysia and Indonesia or the physically strong and muscular West African prize negroes. It was a world I could learn to love and I knew my love for William would grow as I grew familiar to his personality as it was gradually revealing itself to me and his good nature to which I hoped I could do justice. I already admired his language and skills as a raconteur. I licked the stamp and placed the envelope that would go to Ireland in my handbag. The journey had begun.

PROLOGUE

Winter 1870

Bally Gally Castle, County Antrim

A chill wind blew and the leafless branches of trees were black etchings against the sombre sky. William was in his brother, Robert's study writing while a fire spat and spluttered with the draught from a poorly fitting door.

As William finished writing notes in his journal for 1870 he looked back over some of the entries in his journals dating back twenty years or so. So much had happened and how he longed for the Cape. To recapture each moment, to savour the industrious energy of a budding colony.

He flicked through the pages of his journals and stopped to read excerpts. There was the time there had been the demonstration when the convict ship arrived in Table Bay but the people of Cape Town refused to allow the convicts ashore fearing they would be a bad influence on Cape society. The ship was forced to sail on to Australia.

The journalist and newspaper owner, John Fairbairn's home had been stoned by the demonstrators as he had expressed sympathy for the convicts. The sound of their yells was heard from afar. William had been put into an awkward situation as the stance of the Government was still against importing British workers and the convicts would upset the delicate balance at the Cape. He had been most alarmed when he eavesdropped on a large gathering of men and women who were against allowing the convicts to land and live amongst them. A man with a mane of red hair streaked with grey and a distinct limp which required him to use a crutch, took to the stand and began shouting his views on the matter. My goodness, William had thought, Roland Craven!

"You are far from home!" William had raised his voice to make his point.

"I'm in town on other business and wanted to make my allegiance to John Fairbairn known. At least he believes in the milk of human kindness," Roland had not recognised William.

"What do you hope to achieve by offering convicts the chance to live here?" William asked again.

"I ask that the convict ship be allowed to sail to Port Elizabeth. We, at the Eastern Frontier, need able workers and won't look down on them like you lot. Call yourselves Christians, you are no better than those you are depriving of a new life. Convicts aren't all murderers or highwaymen. These days in England you get arrested for stealing a loaf of bread and then sent to the Colonies. I ask you, for a loaf of bread!"

"Those convicts have done a lot more than just steal a loaf of bread. You would have been a convict if you had committed your crime in today's Great Britain! If you were on that ship, I would have made sure you never landed on these shores," William couldn't resist bringing his old enemy down a peg or two.

"Ah, it's the mighty Attorney General. I need more citizens for the Eastern Frontier and we will soon have our own government at Graham's Town. How are you going to stop us from fighting for our independence?"

"The rule of law will stop you. You cannot take on the whole of the British Empire even with your self-aggrandizement!" William began to walk away.

"Don't forget, Ropert, we've unfinished business, you and I!" Roland was enraged by his arch-enemy's cool self-confidence.

William continued to page through his journal and from time to time wished he had read some of the entries to Fanny. After all, it was she who gave him his very first journal. But, now she was gone.

A little later he read what he had written quite recently about how a steamship service had begun and now fruit especially oranges could be exported to England and mail would now only take forty seven days. Water reservoirs were built below Camp Street. The first Cape Parliament had sat in Cape Town, a pinnacle of history. The Cape Commercial Bank had opened. Wooden street paving had been introduced. An earthquake had occurred with fortunately no loss of human life but damage was done to buildings. Boating and boat races began to take place on the Vlei. Strand Street had been macadamized. So many improvements...

A memorable event for him was Albert, the young Prince of Wales' visit. He remembered the occasion vividly as he had taken it upon himself to accompany the teenage Prince wherever he went. Perhaps his meeting with Queen Victoria in 1839 had bestowed in William a sense of awe in his regard of the Royal Family. Queen Victoria was a comely young woman when he met her. He remembered her fine features, large eyes and small rosebud mouth and how dainty she was in her voluminous gown and corseted waist. 'The Commercial Advertiser' had remarked on his friendship with the Prince since he had seen fit to set aside his official duties as attorney general in favour of the Prince's wellbeing. William chuckled looking back. John Fairbairn enjoyed teasing him but it was with the camaraderie of old friends. He also remembered meeting Dr Livingstone and his explorations had filled him with the desire to venture inland where no white man had gone before.

He continued to page through his later journals. The first railway had been built between Cape Town and Wellington, followed by a line to Wynberg. A great occasion was the visit of the American privateer, "Alabama" to Table Bay. Trade could now take place with the United States. A new form of power became available and the noonday gun could now be fired by electricity. The first telegraph service came into being and penny postage was introduced for letters within the City. A horse-tram service was also introduced between Cape Town and Sea Point. Docks were at last built to handle the growing import and export trade. He remembered the awful storm the year before when sixty people died and eighteen ships were lost in Table Bay. The Cape of Storms had lived up to its name. The Cape had been renamed the Cape of Good Hope in the vain hope that by changing its name, it would miraculously remove the danger of sailing in those seas. And, of course, gold had been discovered in the Transvaal and diamonds in the Free State, a fact that would yet again turn the country on its head.

He had witnessed the making of two Boer republics that comprised of farmers of Dutch descent who had moved away from the Cape Colony into the vast virgin lands beyond the Orange River. The Republic of the Orange Free State which lay between the Orange and Vaal Rivers stretching to the eastern mountains of the Basotho kingdom of Moshweshwe, came into being after the signing of the Bloemfontein Convention. The Transvaal Republic occupied the land north of the Vaal River and the Republic was founded after the signing of the Sand River Convention after the Boers had conquered the Ndebele warriors of Moselikatse and sent them northwards over the Limpopo River. The Boer Republic of Lydenberg soon followed until it amalgamated with the Transvaal Republic forming the South African Republic with M. W. Pretorius as president. All formidable neighbours. The thought of thousands of Boer trekkers leaving the Colony in the 1830's and streaming over the land had been a sincere regret in his heart. The British had driven them out by refusing to allow them to have the same rights as British citizens even denying them the right to use their dialect of Dutch as their own language for legal purposes and for personal expression.

William remembered how Herman Merivale the under-secretary of the Colonial Office, his erstwhile companion on his first Circuit Court, had sung his praises in order to secure for him the position of chief justice.

He had written, Mr Ropert "is one of the ablest perhaps first among the ablest legal officers under this department. His reports …on important constitutional affairs connected with South African affairs have been many times printed for Parliament and referred to as high authorities in the discussions which have taken place both in and out of Parliament. He was substantially (under Lord Grey's direction) the framer of the present Cape Constitution and it was a task of no common difficulty…..I have thought it right to minute at once my own opinion of Mr Ropert's eminent qualifications and claims on Government."

William was not proud of his achievement, he thought to himself, but rather had the satisfaction of doing a job well. It was after all his Protestant work ethic. He had been touched by his brother, John Scott's support when he lobbied for him to be made chief justice. His elder brother hadn't been prepared for William's refusal to accept such an office. William recalled while reading from his Journal how he had declined the position as he strongly felt the need to carry out and on occasions make the law rather than become a figurehead with little action in the legal processes.

He had written "The attorney general has more power for good and evil and more serious responsibilities than even the chief justice."

Besides he wasn't a ruthlessly ambitious man to need to have a grandiose title. He remembered events that made him feel a sense of achievement. He wanted to show prisoners fairness and he had been praised for his liberal treatment of Andries Botha, an Afrikaner who was arrested for treason.

He also spoke out against Coloured people who committed murder as in the case when San cattle thieves were murdered by Hottentots "who had returned home after the raid with consciences as clear as if they had been out on a hunting party for exterminating wolves and had met with good success." He had endeavoured to try to instil in the Hottentots a sense of shame and impressed on them that any killing no matter what the circumstances was illegal.

He had also stated that Black peoples in the frontier wars should be treated "not as enemies entitled to the rights of enemies but as in law, thieves and pirates." The distinction between the two types of enemies was a fine line but living in those times made him reluctant to set free so called prisoners of war who would immediately resume their nefarious activities, killing farmers and their families for a herd of cattle.

The Eastern Frontier was still a dangerous part of the Colony but the numbers of settlers in the area had increased after more young people were drafted in from Holland and Ireland. He remembered voting for three thousand Crimean War veterans, the German Legionnaires as well as two thousand seven hundred German civilians to be offered land in Kaffraria. He had also been involved in the assisted immigration schemes which brought in another twelve thousand British settlers over and above the number of settlers that had arrived in the Colony in 1820. The Colony had been strengthened by such projects and agriculture and commerce had prospered. He had always been aware that the Eastern Frontier would press for autonomy and vote for their own Parliament which would be based in Graham's Town. Until now they had always failed. The new colony of Natal had fared better and been allowed to govern itself.

Thinking of the Xhosa tribes that infiltrated the Eastern Frontier, he had never ceased to be shocked by witchcraft crimes "as the perpetrators didn't regard themselves guilty of any crime". As far as he was concerned all were equal under the law. There had been many such memories and anecdotes in his scribbling. He knew his work was far from done and kept in mind the possibility that he would return to the Cape where he knew his niche in society.

He sighed and closed the last journal. He turned down the gas light and used a candlestick to light his way to his bedroom. He had to admit to himself that age was catching up with him but he would not be alone that night as his one true love was waiting for him there. He was truly blessed.

CHAPTER 1

Dublin

1817

The elegant Georgian home of Dr David McBride stood with others of its kind in the Glasnevin part of Dublin where men of distinction in legal circles and in medicine bought their families to live in admirable surroundings. Fanny McBride aged twenty two and her sister Eliza who was two years older prepared for the wake of their mother, Mary, who had died at such a young age from a fever brought on after a miscarriage. The two girls tearfully washed her cold lifeless body and dressed her in her wedding dress and bought flowers which they arranged into a posy and placed them in her hands.

"There, there Dearest," Eliza whispered in her mother's ear, "You always were the fairest in this Town." Her voice broke and Fanny dissolved into tears. Both girls brushed away the wetness on their cheeks, straightened each other's shawls and flicked their ringlets back into order.

"Father's waiting in the study for us," Eliza reminded her younger sister. They were in awe of their father and to be fair he always had their interests at heart allowing them to study under a governess with their brothers before the young men went off to Trinity College and a seminary in Scotland respectively.

"Come in and sit down there's much I need to discuss with you," David McBride buttoned a cuff of his shirt, "We need to find out what to do with the two of you now that your dear Mother has passed on, God bless her soul. Eliza, you are a very intelligent young woman and I believe you could be a governess so that you can put all your learning to good use and Fanny – ah - Fanny, my girl, you have been well schooled by your Mother in housekeeping, sewing and music so we must prepare you for marriage. A young teacher, you know him well,

Matthew O Connor, has asked for your hand in matrimony. Do you have feelings for this likeable young man?"

Both girls sat transfixed as their father dispatched their futures with a clap of his hands. Eliza had expected to have been married by now and her father's words encouraged her to feel like an old spinster and she only twenty four years old! Not that the idea of teaching young children didn't appeal to her, on the contrary perhaps she would meet her future husband if she left Dublin and moved to new surroundings, new acquaintances.

Fanny found the news of her imminent marriage somewhat of a shock coming so soon after her mother's death. She was numb when she should have been feeling elated. The timing wasn't right.

-o0o-

It was six weeks later that Eliza moved up north to Limavady to take on the role of governess to the Minister's younger two children as their mother was unwell and suffering from a wasting disease. The boys, John Scott and William went to the Artillery Lane School in Londonderry but returned home for weekends. Eliza felt welcome in their home and soon prepared a full timetable of lessons and activities for the children. Fanny's wedding was to be in the spring and Eliza promised to be there on the day and before she left, she and Fanny made the wedding dress and set the menu for the festivities as well as the guest list.

Matthew and Fanny went through the etiquette of courtship and their love was a delight to them both and onlookers would smile and look wistful remembering such a time in their own lives.

On a wet and windy afternoon, Matthew called for Fanny to take her to the theatre to see Oliver Goldsmith's play, "She stoops to conquer". They huddled closely together under an umbrella and Fanny lifted her skirts when they splashed through puddles. Laughing light-heartedly they crossed the road just when a sudden crack of thunder sent a team of six horses clattering down the avenue, without a driver, the carriage darting left to right and back again. Matthew just had enough time to push Fanny out of harm's way but he fell under the hooves of the terrified animals.

It was so sudden. Fanny tried to catch her breath and then ran over to Matthew's broken body, fell down beside him and lifted his head onto her lap. He lapsed in and out of consciousness as she whispered endearments and comforted him.

He was taken back to his home and his doctor, mother and Fanny hovered around his bed. When the doctor shook his head regretfully, his mother screamed out in pain but Fanny felt numb. The fairy-tale couldn't end this way. But it had.

A month later, Eliza invited Fanny to Limavady as she needed her sister to be with her to help her arrange the Minister's wife, Mary's wake. With so many children, an extra pair of hands was most welcome and Fanny was so gentle and understanding. The children aged between eight and fourteen hovered around her as she tried to lighten their pain with games and stories.

The one boy, William, just twelve, approached her at quiet times of the day and he seemed to recognise her own unspoken grief. They would go to the little church where no one could eavesdrop and were like two souls stranded on an unknown beach where there was no one but themselves and as they prayed the chapel surrounded them like a warm womb. During the first of such meetings, he took her hand and played with her engagement ring. "Miss McBride told me that your fiancé died tragically. What was it like, to see him die? They wouldn't let me see my mother when she was dying. Did she suffer too?"

They discussed life and death and how no one could escape from the inevitable shocking end of consciousness, one's mortal 'human-ness' ending and one's soul living on eternally. How did the soul live on without the body? The thought of meeting their loved ones after their deaths comforted them as they imagined how wonderful Heaven must be like when life on Earth was so unbearable.

For Eliza and Fanny another blow soon followed when their father died very suddenly in his sleep. Fanny went to live with her brother, John who was a bachelor and was too engrossed in running his newspaper to consider taking on a wife. It was an ideal situation to have Fanny look after the housekeeping in return for her board and lodging. But, Fanny fretted, longing for affection and the love of a husband and children…

-o0o-

CHAPTER 2

Dublin

September 1834

The courtroom was hushed except for a trapped sparrow fluttering inside at the windows while outside torrential rain poured down with large drops stoning the window panes. For a moment, the storm clouds parted and a shaft of sunlight fell upon the Judge in his carmine robes. He was perfectly lit like a portrait where the artist has used the technique of chiaroscuro. His face was lined and his thin lips parted.

"Roland Craven, I sentence you to five years in prison for having maliciously and intentionally caused grievous bodily harm to James O'Hagan on the 7th July 1834 and for raping his wife, Siobhan, before setting alight their family home in Kirkpatrick," Judge O'Toole looked fiercely at the prisoner in the dock, "You will be required to make financial reparation to your victims and you'll now be taken down to await transfer to Dublin Jail."

Roland stood up, all six foot four inches of him knotted with anger, and his upper class good looks had been soured by cynicism and debased by fornication. He passed a hand through his unruly auburn hair.

"All rise," the Sheriff of the Court ordered those present. The floorboards of the old courthouse creaked as the spectators got to their feet, talking in whispers, their thumb-print faces smudged in the gloom.

As he passed the Prosecutor who was standing serenely like an acolyte of some holy order, Roland hissed at him, "I'll have you for this, William Ropert. I promise you that once out of prison I'll hunt you down and there'll be no place to hide. You have had your revenge but you'll pay the price of crossing swords with me!"

Roland's face was flushed with anger and humiliation and his thick red hair seemed to stand on end. He never believed that he was morally weak and as a son of Lord Craven, he believed he was invincible.

William Ropert, in his stock, black gown and stiff white collar stared into the angry eyes of his erstwhile tormentor, "I will cherish the memory of today, of seeing you cut down in size and no wealthy father even with all his connections can help you now. Do your worst when you come out of jail. You may not find me here but wherever I am, I'll be waiting for you!" William Ropert was tall but more slender than Roland with curly hair that was bleached blond by the sun in summer and his face was finely carved with high cheekbones, a straight nose and full lips. His light blue eyes did not waver.

William's words were measured with an outward calm as he remembered the constant jibes, the bullying and prods in his ribs and the many times Roland had tripped him up sending him flying to the ground in the school yard.

Yes, he did feel the warm rush of satisfaction that he had finally evened the score with his old enemy. When he had prepared for the trial, he hadn't been surprised to learn that the spoilt heir of the Craven dynasty had hounded James O'Hagan for money he owed Roland after gambling away all his savings in a game of poker in one of the smoke-filled back rooms of the Black Swan Hotel in Dublin. O'Hagan had innocently entered the domain of the most ruthless gambler on the Emerald Isle...

William believed that he could now bury the boy within himself and the memory of the torments and violence meted out to him in the school yard. He shuffled his papers, put them into his briefcase and looked around for the last time musing how very much he would miss the old courtroom with its dark wooden panelling and the embossed coat of arms above the austere chairs where the chief justice sat. His black gown billowing William rushed out of the courthouse through the tall pillars below the triangular Greco-Roman façade and down the stone steps. The dome supported by the rectangle of the Four Courts was lit with white light, a beacon on the skyline and the ebbing away of the grey pall of falling rain made Dublin's cobbled streets glisten. He strode along the embankment of the Liffey which was alive with a flotilla of dancing wavelets drenched by the clouds' tears and those in the centre of the river seemed tethered like sailing boats to the retreating storm and water rushed away down river.

A new life was beckoning but he would always love Dublin town where there were so many friends he held so dear.

-o0o-

As he walked home William revisited the case just closed and remembered how in December 1834, The Black Swan was heaving with drunk patrons as usual and in a room tucked away at the rear of the building, six men sat hunched over the green card table smoking and drinking ale. Hearts, diamonds, clubs and spades hidden face-down under red cards were sent flying to the players who scooped them up, fanning them out in their fingers to look at them, sucking in their breath nervously. The game that the town's gamblers had been waiting for had begun.

Hours later with dawn breaking over the rooftops of the city and swirls of smoke growing as the town awoke and women stoked glowing embers in the grate setting alight new logs or coals, the men had been playing for eighteen hours and were bleary eyed and stale from acrid fumes of their pastime which left overflowing ashtrays and empty glasses. The room stank like a urinal. Hunched in a corner, James O'Hagan was barely conscious as yet again he had to fold his hand and see his whole life go up in smoke. He had bet his last savings and had signed several IOUs to the winning player, Roland Craven who laughed loudly as the young broken farmer staggered out into the sunlight, "I'll get every last penny from you, O'Hagan!" Roland Craven snorted. His shock of red hair made him look demonic above his laconic grin. He was in his thirties and ignoring the bloodshot blue eyes and dark rings under them, he regarded himself as handsome.

Months later when James O'Hagan failed to meet his debts, Roland found him at his farm and knocked him down into the mud of the yard allowing his horse to rise up and kick out with its hooves.

"I told you not to cross me, O'Hagan. You owe me a damn fortune. But no, you go all mealy-mouthed about paying me "next month", well, "next month" is here now!" Roland snarled.

"I can explain. The potatoes are ready for harvesting…" James whimpered but his tormentor pressed his horse forward knocking James to the ground where he lay still, already unconscious from the wound gushing blood from his forehead. Roland dismounted and tethered the black stallion to a fence before walking purposefully to the door of his tenant's cottage. Unaware of what was happening in the yard, Siobhan shrunk back from bread-making as his tall frame blocked out the view of the hills from the doorway. She was a bride only six months ago and the bloom of her beauty was fresh with her lustrous black locks, dewy ivory skin and blushing cheeks. Her irises were clear green glass in youthful flawlessness.

Quickly Roland had Siobhan's hands pinned behind her back as he pushed her onto the bed in the corner of the living-room. He tore her spotlessly clean faded dress from her breasts and ripped it right down to its hem.

She screamed, "Let me go! I beg you, please let me go!"

She started to whimper but he was ready as he pushed into her, hurting her and not stopping but making it go on and on and on. She was being torn by his assault and half unconscious she could feel his teeth biting at her nipples and yet not breaking the tender skin. He had her in a vicelike grip, one hand rendering her flailing arms useless.

He climaxed and lay on top of her panting, "You were one helluva ride, my beauty. Oh shame, you're not so snow-white now," He traced her lips with his finger and pressed open her bruised mouth. His tongue licked hers and penetrated further and she squirmed and then the assault began all over again. In the end, he raped her until she fell unconscious and then he lifted her up and took her outside and dropped her body on top of her husband's. He swaggered back to the ordinary little home and lit a match, dropped it on the bed and watched as the cottage was soon on fire with the thatch quickly catching alight. He escaped into the fresh morning light, untied his horse, wasting no time by leaping onto its back and with a flick of his riding crop the lively animal raced out of the farmyard with its mane and tail flying.

William had the details of the case emblazoned on his mind and his despair about the two young lives being so violated, made deep anger fester inside him. He would be happy to meet Roland Craven again. If legal justice hadn't chastened the coward and bully or given him clarity about his own depravity, then William knew he would take him on, man to man and may the best man win…

-o0o-

CHAPTER 3

Dublin

November 1838

Early winter in Dublin was a damp, cold-to-the-bones experience but indoors in John McBride's home a fire spluttered its red ribbons up the chimney and the coals spat as they cracked with the heat.

Neither William nor Fanny had ever mentioned their love for one another. It would never be consummated as she was his stepmother's sister, although only ten years his senior. William sighed as he drew on his pipe, inhaling the sweet unctuous smoke that relaxed his pent-up emotions. He smiled at Fanny who was reading contentedly and they fell silent, happy to be in each other's company, a blessing that was soon to be denied them.

When he was twelve Eliza now pregnant had the idea of sending William to live with Fanny and John with the idea that he could serve his apprenticeship in accountancy. Eliza knew Fanny loved William as though he were her own child. Fanny was elated and welcomed William warmly. As time passed William had found keeping the books for John tedious and frighteningly boring and Fanny took John to one side and fought for William's future.

"The boy has spirit and intelligence and there he's locked away in a stuffy old office. He deserves to go far but at the moment he's miserable and as a result his work's poor as his heart just isn't in it, John."

"The young man worries me as he hasn't tried to apply himself," grumbled John.

"You could do something about it and sponsor him. Do that, for me," she begged, "Send him back to school to be prepared for London to study for the Bar."

"What makes you think that he has the ability," Her brother began pacing around the room, cornered.

"You know how he speaks very well and he has a sound mind. You should hear what he says about the articles he reads in your paper."

John McBride already myopic and set in his ways, had been taken off guard, "Fanny, you're asking me to commit myself to educating a young man who isn't even my kin? You're aware of the expense," John knew his defences were crumbling as he spoke as he, too, had been impressed with the intense, likeable youngster.

"Very well. Anything to get you off my back. If you weren't my sister, I wouldn't deal with William so kindly. However, you're right about his talent for speaking his mind."

"Thank you, oh, thank you, darling John! You won't regret it, I promise!" Fanny rushed out of the drawing room to find her young protégé and break the news to him.

John settled down again to read the latest press of "*The Northern Whig*" using a magnifying glass. He was proud of his publication. It supported the liberalism that was spreading through intellectual and political circles. In fact, in 1830, the Tories had been ousted by the Whigs. John remembered how bonfires were lit throughout Ireland in celebration. Lord Grey had become prime minister and Lord Melbourne was given the responsibility for Ireland. He remembered that William had been enthusiastic, to say the least, about their belief in 'perfect equality of rights, laws and liberties'. The Irish could at long last be liberated.

-o0o-

Years later, William remembered the good fortune that had come his way with the kindness of his stepmother's family. He felt at home in the drawing room of their Dublin home. It was bright with sunshine pouring onto the claret damask drapes bleaching them pink while the prisms of an ornament danced colourfully around the room. Brass hearth furniture gleamed and the black green fronds of a fern were emblazoned with a golden hue. The smoke rose in a white wisp that spiralled around the room. He tapped his pipe, "I've you to thank for reaching this pinnacle of my life, Fanny. If it weren't for you I would still be doing bookkeeping and would have become a grumpy, bitter, old bore!"

In the amiable silence of the drawing room, Fanny was assessing the William of the present with pride. He was a handsome, tall, witty, intelligent man with a positive outlook on life. He was sociable, moderately religious and wanted to be known to have great tenacity in his forensic search for truth in court. He was an avid and eclectic reader, an athlete, a lover of nature and an empathetic humanitarian. However she felt he was still lacking in total self-knowledge and also needed to discover his ultimate goal in life.

William sat lost in thought, too. He felt from deep within himself a longing for something he could not put into words despite which he was generally happy. One of his main disappointments was that he was about to leave behind his relatives in Ireland, particularly his father and Fanny who loved him unconditionally. He thought of how Fanny and he had lived together with John for all those years. They had all the familiarity of husband and wife without the nuptials or children. They were both destined to be childless.

Back in the present, his reverie was interrupted when they were called into dinner by Hayes, the butler and William took Fanny's hand affectionately kissing the back of her fingers before tucking it into the crook of his arm, and led her to the dining room. He saw her cheeks turn rosy and she smiled up at him with her eyes brimming with love and he patted her hand, wishing with all his heart that he could court her and one day make her his wife but their circumstances were such that society would regard them erroneously as too closely connected as kin and the disparity of their ages would make people disapprove.

At dinner he looked at her face as she sat opposite him. She had her hair parted in four sections with chestnut locks dropping down her back with curls around her face and a row of laurel wreath-shaped plaits over the crown of her head. Her neck was swanlike and had a satin ivory gleam reaching down to her bodice. Her face was quite long with a patrician nose and her eyes were opalescent with irises the colour of old sherry and they glistened with the tears of laughter or sadness. Her lips were painted with a rose-madder coloured cream and her cheeks bloomed naturally with soft pale rose. The shadows on her face were jade green and raw sienna. She was a work of art, he thought

"If only's" filled them both with longing and their love remained fettered and untried. Now there would never be the next step, the next level of love, or would there? Would there be a day people wouldn't criticise and look askance at them after all they weren't related by blood ties? Life was relentlessly cruel. William wondered if Fanny realised that he had never bought his own home because it would have meant they would be separated. He couldn't have borne an existence without having Fanny to come home to every evening.

Life's course was now taking him away from her to another country so far away that any relationship would be tested to the limit. Would she follow him or would he send for her? He didn't want her to be exposed to the dangers of the arduous sea journey or the unexpected hazards of an alien continent with its inhabitants who were governed by very different norms to those she was accustomed to. He drew her chair out for her and pushed it safely under her as she sat down to dinner. The light of the many candles in the candelabra bathed them all with the comfort of gentry living… In a week he would leave his beloved Ireland for an undefined time. His heart constricted and Fanny's eyebrows flew upwards as she sensed his pain.

Later that evening as they sat in front of the hearth, William watched Fanny with affection. Her features were etched with shadows in the flickering light but her delicate lips as soft as rose-petals with their two peaks of her upper lid so tempting. Her mouth was always turned upwards always smiling and her brown eyes flashed with wit as he related the momentous outcome of the latest court-case with all its twists and turns. He had never related the evil and vindictive cruelty of the defendants he prosecuted in detail in deference to Fanny's innocence.

"Well done, William!" Fanny clapped her hands and wished she could throw herself onto his lap and embrace him as a wife would - so strong were her feelings.

She was wearing a powder-blue velvet gown with gold thread woven through the material with a decollate neckline and the flush that flew across her face and down to her breasts didn't escape William's attention. How he longed to kiss her smiling lips and hold her close to him finding the floral scent of her perfume quite intoxicating. He longed to unpin her long hair to allow it to fall in locks around her shoulders.

He turned to business matters and opened his mail with a finely carved ivory letter opener. A couple of invitations to soirees and balls in London fell onto the table. He laughed, "I've been invited to the Queen's Court and Lord Grey has arranged various functions."

Fanny immediately leapt up folding her sewing away, "I've news for you William Ropert! It's time you learned to dance!"

"For heaven's sake, Fanny, not now!" He grimaced, put out.

Just at that moment, Hugh Arnly, William's life-long friend, was shown into the parlour and Fanny took hold of his arm and led him to the piano. "You can play the piano, not so? We will give William his first lesson in performing fashionable dance routines." She pushed the furniture and carpets back against the walls with Hugh's help.

"Come on, William. I need a good laugh so don't be a coward and back down! Let the lady have her way," Hugh was filled with devilment as he struck up a chord.

Fanny showed William all the movements and the complicated sign language between partners. They danced and it became an act of romantic courtly love. The troubadour wooing the maiden was a foreign experience for William.

"We'll practise again until you master the steps!" Fanny collapsed eventually into a chair with her cheeks turning scarlet from the exertion. She picked up a fan and waved it disarmingly to cool the moisture glistening on her brow. William believed that that was the way she would look after lovemaking and his heart contracted painfully. Perhaps neither of them would ever enjoy such delights.

William was silent for the rest of the evening. The dances set something free inside them both. For a moment they had been in dangerous, forbidden territory.

-o0o-

Before turning in for the night, William sat at the stout oak desk in his room and paged through his documents in the lamp-light. His grand designs of being involved in politics at Westminster had taken surprising turn when he was offered the position at the Cape of Good Hope. This would be a far cry from speeches in Dublin's law courts. Could he still entertain the politicians at the Cape in the same way? He loved words and used them with such dexterity as to leave an adversary tongue-tied. His father's oratory on Sundays had no doubt rubbed off on him.

After being called to the Bar in Dublin, William had become friendly with other barristers who held the same beliefs as he did. He knew Robert Holmes, who once took part in a duel and ended up in prison and as a result couldn't take silk. There were also Louis Perrin and Maziere Bradley and another was Curry, the MP for Armagh. These men were responsible for putting William's name forward for the position of attorney general at the Cape, based on his good character and because his views and most cherished beliefs could mitigate the views and prejudices of Cape society as there were already issues coming out of the Cape that were raising eyebrows.

Unlike some of his fellow barristers he had travelled far and wide in Ireland practising in his legal capacity and had therefore gained much experience and with that expertise he would deliver equal justice that would be impartial regarding race, colour or even language in the Cape and his Unitarian philosophy would also make him respect all creeds. William had not known the extent to which his friends enjoyed his Irish wit and humour which was charged to the brim with Bar anecdotes and they also thought his oratory was masterful and at a dinner held in honour of his appointment, his friends told the guests of his heartfelt hatred of injustice and as they drank their toasts to him they knew that William would not dishonour the Irish Bar in his new position.

During the dinner, William remembered how he had met Daniel O'Connor, the stalwart supporter of the Irish cause in Dublin. The Irish situation was similar to the Cape one. Ireland was ruled by the British on the other side of the Irish Sea. The flagrant unfairness of the Irish losing their autonomy was aggravated by British coming over to Ireland, seizing land for themselves and inflicting on the poor an outdated feudalism.

O'Connor said to him celebrating, "*The Whigs have muzzled the ferocious tiger and drawn the fangs of the persecuting wolves.*"

William was delighted that the Orange Order had been outlawed and that the first Catholic judge had been appointed and as they talked he found it sobering to think that his own people were originally English and had followed the government of the time's call for settlers to buy land in Ireland to establish an English presence there. So by rights, he could only claim to being half-Irish and torn between serving two masters. He could feel a thrill of adventure course through him as he prepared for bed. He was on the brink of changing his life forever....

-o0o-

It had all begun when William had completed his studies and he had been called to the Irish Bar at King's Inn. Rev. William Ropert had been adamant that his studies should take place in an atmosphere of Enlightenment which the English philosophy was adopting. A strange coincidence, William mused, as his grandfather had done the same thing to his father and sent him to a seminary in Edinburgh where he came into contact with revolutionary theories about religion there. His father had held rational beliefs thereafter about the natural rights of man. Rev. William had instilled in William a deep and abiding love for the Fatherhood of God, the Brotherhood of Man, the Leadership of Jesus, and above all the belief that man can obtain salvation by his own good character and that would ensure the progress of mankind onward and upward forever. This belief that man has a part to play in his own destiny while travelling along his path in life and would not to be led astray by talk of predestination was something that William held dear.

It was almost dawn and soon the carriage would arrive to take him to the harbour to board a ship preparing to set sail for England. Pull yourself together man, he silently urged himself. Fanny was already up and he could see that she had slept fitfully as well. They looked at one another helplessly. Fate was relentless. It was taking him away from her.

"You will write, William? As soon as you get to London, do please scribble a few lines and tell me what the Queen is like? I would love to hear what people in her court were wearing, why they were there!" She loved such gossip and would read his letters with enjoyment. It would be some comfort. In just thirty minutes he would be leaving.

She wanted him to kiss her passionately like a husband but propriety would not allow it. His gaze locked with hers as his belongings were hauled onto the carriage. John was fussing and giving William fatherly advice. William shook John's hand and then turned to Fanny and lifted hers so small and scented with rosewater, to his lips. Their secret was sealed. From now on they would live in different worlds and their lives would be shared in their correspondence. A small consolation.

The carriage door slammed shut and the horses were eager to leave. William looked pained as the farewell became drawn out only to end as the horses pulled away and clattered down the street. He didn't look back.

Fanny ran up the stairs to her bedroom and flung herself on her bed and silently cried into her pillow. After an hour she collected herself and sat down at the small writing bureau and composed a letter.

My dearest William,

I will miss you more than words can describe. We have had a lifetime together with many roles in our theatre. At first, I was your mother and then several years later we became brother and sister and now…now I feel like your friend – no, it's more than friendship, my Love. How I have wished you would make me your wife. Here I am, imagining how we could proudly announce our betrothal and then we'll have the ultimate delight on our wedding night to know each other in the biblical sense. I long for you to call me 'Wife' and 'Love' and I would articulate the same honour to you, 'Husband' and 'Dearest'.

Of course, the letter would never be sent but lie hidden away in a secret drawer in the Davenport.

-o0o-

William's first letter arrived after he had been in London just a week.

"The Queen is a mere girl but good-looking with a petite figure. I remember having my nose at the Queen's wrist when kneeling and I then kissed her hand. I am sure you want to know about the women? Well the ladies at the opera disappointed me. They were all beautiful butterflies lacking often in substance and none of them had a sensible thought in their heads. I enjoyed the balls and your coaching me to dance paid off handsomely. You would've put the women here to shame with your elegance and femininity. I also felt let down by the members of Parliament as I found their speeches deadly boring and had to concentrate so as not to fall asleep during them. Another thing disappointed me too. My greatest desire was to speak to Macaulay – you know, the writer and orator, but it wasn't to be. You see this plain man before you has this compulsion to speak well so any help I can get, I most appreciate."

He had then gossiped shamelessly about the relationships of the upper classes. Fanny would laugh and he shook visibly with the pain of being cut off from her physical presence. He would have to dream about what could have been had they not been such different ages and related by a cruel twist of fate.

Before he left, Fanny had given him a vellum-covered journal to keep. Inside the cover of the Journal was an inscription:

"To my dearest William,

Inscribe those wonderful words of your thoughts and observations herein. Their spirit and beauty deserve to be preserved for posterity.

In writing, you'll perchance pen a quick letter to your family left behind in Ireland. The absence of your presence will be a deep sadness to those who love you.

Your ever loving Fanny."

He now remembered standing on the jetty at Gravesend in the fog feeling every painful beat of his heart as the wrench from loved ones was unbearable. In the Journal, the first entry was this emotional outpouring of feeling, *"The land where live the living and lie the dead who love me as I shall not again be loved, was hidden from my sight and the cloud that descended upon it, settled cold on my heart."* Yes, he was homesick from the very first moments of departure.

The morning of the 28th December William's ship finally set off and Fanny received another letter from him and she felt comforted by the fact he was so wrapped up in the melee of social obligations before leaving for the Cape he was able to leave without too much regret. She drank in his words.

"I was invited to Joseph Chamberlain's home before leaving for the Cape. I was also asked to sit for a portrait, and there is no doubt in my mind that the artist was talented as he portrayed me very much as a gentleman of some importance. Me, an Irish cad! I can't believe I was talked into it," William remembered laughing with embarrassment at the whole event. *"Another highlight of my time in London was to attend Queen Victoria's levee and the Marquis of Normandy introduced me to her. I remember that especially. My friends, O' Loughlin, Pigot and Kelly were with me and Kelly taught me how to behave. I had to kneel in the proper manner of performing my kow-tow!"*

He wrote how his friends had embarked on the trader with him including Hugh, who was accompanying him as his clerk. It had been a cold, drizzly day and dreary which dampened the spirits of the leaving party. William had handed his friends letters of farewell to be delivered to his family and close acquaintances.

His final message to Fanny was "*Farewell. The record of old times is written in my heart and can never be obliterated. Farewell.*"

Suddenly, they had all left and he and Hugh were alone and finally at three in the afternoon, the ship got underway. Both were the worst for wear and admitted to being more than just a little drunk! William sighed. The dye was cast. He could not go back to his old life now. He then turned his mind towards the future and what it would hold. Soon land dropped out of sight and the trader unfurled its sails and the wind took them onward across the green swells….the Cape beckoned.

-o0o-

CHAPTER 4

February 1839

En route to Cape Town

"What's waiting for us just across the horizon, Hugh?" The words were snatched out of William Ropert's mouth by the brisk south-easterly wind. His hair was blown back from his face as he strained against the elements on board ship. The whipped-up salty spray stung his cheeks.

"Adventure!" Hugh Arnly shouted back. The ship rose and fell on the swell of the Cape Rollers. Many a ship was lost when storms battered wood and snapped masts and they had now just passed the Skeleton Coast, the graveyard of many vessels. The two friends headed towards the prow of the merchant ship running and stepping backwards with the ship's motion as they enjoyed the sensation of being swept along. William cheered when he saw the dolphins riding the prow wave with skill and sheer enjoyment.

Hugh shouted above the thudding sounds of wood on water, "It must be thrilling for them to be propelled forward at such a speed. Remember what a joy it was when we went body-surfing in the sea at Cushendall as boys."

Hugh put an arm around William's shoulders affectionately. His brogue was strong with the musical lilt of the Irish and with bursts of the long and short modulation of vowels and the upward lift in tone at the end of a sentence. William's accent had mellowed into a pleasant and compelling Anglicised accent that often revealed his skills as an orator even in plain talking.

William's eyes strained as he searched the horizon as by now he was tired of ship-board life, after two months at sea and it had left him yearning for hard work and getting to grips with his new colleagues and the new society where he hoped to form lasting relationships as he enjoyed the company of good friends. He was tall, thirty four years old and well-built with short fair hair that curled at the nape of his neck.

"I guess a continent of so called "heathen" awaits you with their customs and way of doing things!" Hugh held onto the ship's rail, "We'll probably find a population totally different to what we are accustomed to!" A large wave hit the ship side-on and they both leapt out of its spray. William's white shirt rippled in the breeze.

"This Dark Continent with its noble savages needs to be enlightened!" Hugh shouted above the crashing waves.

The sails whipped and the ropes squealed as they grew taut and held fast. "We've come a long way together," William laughed, his teeth white in his tanned face while his skin was as brown as honey. He was in his prime and had never felt so alive which was making him laugh out loud from sheer enjoyment.

Later in the shadow of the canvass sails, the two men remembered how they had first met.

"The first time I met you, you were being teased as being the pretty boy of the class and Roland Craven was the worst," said Hugh, "You had pink cheeks and curls like a girl and we all tried to kiss you but you paid us all back by being so damn good academically. I always enjoyed hearing all the Latin idioms and terminology you use when I've watched you in court. At last I could see the purpose of learning declensions and conjugations!" Hugh had never felt inclined to compete with William.

William thought of school. Whenever he felt angry with the other boys particularly Roland with his freckles and red hair and flashing light blue eyes, Hugh would come to his aid and even today the teasing and bullying that he had to endure, made him feel ashamed.

"Do you remember when we became friends?" William spoke more normally as the wind dropped and the sea became calm allowing them to enjoy the gentler somnolent movement of the "Sterling" which they agreed was an excellent ship. "You were such a rude and belligerent individual!"

Once, when the kissing game in the school-yard was getting out of hand, the young Hugh suddenly went to his aid, defending him with flailing fists and gasps of foul language. Hugh was shorter than William and well-muscled even for his age so he dealt Roland a vicious blow and after that William was left in peace.

On another occasion at break time, William joined Hugh who was sitting drawing in the sand with a willow twig but not before William saw the words as Hugh quickly brushed them out. They were "Hate", "Anger", "Kill" and "Suicide". William never let on that he had seen what Hugh had written so poignantly and from that moment on the two became firm friends and William learnt that Hugh was an orphan and was brought up by his guardian so on many occasions he asked if Hugh could be invited home for the holidays. William noticed that Hugh was unaccustomed to women and even with the offers of friendship by Fanny he kept his distance and William thought perhaps Hugh had never forgiven his mother for dying as that had led to his father's suicide.

The boys did everything together and as their puzzlement at life grew they discussed the age-old questions of life and death, good versus evil and the complexities of human nature and relationships. They were inquisitive and liked defending their own views; usually Hugh would take one side of an argument and William the opposite.

Before William and Hugh had set out of the voyage, Fanny wrote to William the first of many letters. "*In Hugh you have the best substitute this world could afford for all you have left behind in Ireland,*" was one of her most astute observations.

"You and I make a great team," Hugh laughed and looked at his friend as he often did, sometimes without William's knowledge. "I appreciate being able to accompany you to Cape Town. People must think we're joined at the hip. 'Whither thou goest, so shalt I go...' He looked away embarrassed. "When will we see land? We have been waiting up here for hours!"

William had light blue eyes and a long nose and his mouth was quite full and proud for a man. Hugh believed that William had the best attributes of Michael Angelo's colossal statue of David and the gaze and tough-minded intelligence of Julius Caesar's marble bust they had once seen at a museum. He also believed that William was as good an orator as Julius Caesar and Cicero and had a lot of the Christian good sense of St. Paul!

When Hugh matured he could have passed for an Irish gypsy with his dark curly hair and the brightest blue eyes which sparkled with wit and humour. In contrast to William's fairness, Hugh had a dark Mediterranean complexion and William thought his surprisingly beautiful hands, were Hugh's best feature. Strangely, his handshake was reassuring rather than menacing and he would often put an arm around William's shoulders in laughter at some shared joke. But to others, he remained aloof as only William was his saviour and he felt he owed everything he had become, to him. His aversion to women became more noticeable as his misogyny grew.

"We should soon get a glimpse of Table Mountain to the south. I bet you I'll see land before you!" Hugh dared.

The hardy trader lurched once more in the huge green swells. The sails whipped as the wind, now more gentle, played with their lax cloth and the ropes as wide as a man's wrist, creaked under the strain. The air was refreshing although William remembered the high humidity and the times they were becalmed at the Equator as then they had longed for a breeze to pick up and end their torture. The Crossing the Line ceremony had ensured they stayed inebriated and didn't notice their discomfort for a while!

"You know I never gamble. I'm half way a Presbyterian, after all!" William replied. Hugh laughed and his teeth flashed. Both men were fit and healthy despite the poor food offered on board.

Later they returned to the others who were occupied in various activities on the top deck which was now empty of the rotting cabbages and onions that had been strung up with string on nails around the trader for the voyage. Provisions were replenished at the two stops at islands along their journey. The barrels of lemons, carrots, potatoes and flour were nearly depleted. Most of the straggly chickens in the coops had served their purpose as meat that was both tough and unappetising. The once stinking enclosure for the pigs was empty as the portly animals had all ended up on the menu as the only tasty dish on board ship. Afterwards, the pens had been hosed down thoroughly.

"What a relief to have clean air to breathe at last," William said to Hugh.

The water barrels were stale and tea tasted rancid and the only potable drinks were gin and wine. The passengers had also almost finished their own provisions of salt meat, hams, potted duck and other such luxuries.

-oOo-

William dropped down onto the deck where he had left his books. He always enjoyed the mental exercise of study which was why his books were all well-thumbed. With his usual enthusiasm he wasn't going to disappoint the Governor at the Cape of Good Hope where he was to take up the post of attorney general. He grinned happily, counting his blessings and he applauded the fact that the Whigs had come to power at Westminster and that Lord Grey was taking an interest in the small British colony at the southern-most tip of Africa where there was a collection of issues that were unique and for which there were few local precedents which left the legal system ripe for development. The medley of nationalities mixed peacefully for most of the time but often disagreements grew and government became a complicated mismatch of political persuasions so just as he could sum up human nature he could also see some good in most people, even the criminals he would prosecute.

Hugh was in deep conversation with their captain, Gabriel Forster, who was telling Hugh about the last close shave he had with a pirate ship. Hugh's eyes widened at the spectacle of Gabriel wielding his sword and delivering a mortal blow to a surprised pirate captain. After escaping from Gabriel's clutches before he finished another story about a confrontation with a slave ship, Hugh sank onto his knees on the deck near William and lay down shading his eyes from the sun.

William kicked him playfully, "Gabriel had you well and truly captive, there. For a moment, I thought I should rescue you!"

Suddenly, the passengers felt a chill in the air and the light faded as a shadow passed over the sea in front of them.

"What's happening?!" one of the women cried in alarm.

"It's a solar eclipse, my dear," Gabriel said excitedly.

An authority on all manner of things in the heavens above, he had been waiting for this moment, "Look, if I use this mirror and direct the image of the sun onto this white card we should see the moon passing over the disc of the sun. If we are lucky we'll see a ring of fire surround the black circle of the moon like a halo when the eclipse is complete."

Symes, a teacher, found a pane of glass and let a candle gutter with black smoke which lightly coated the glass and he offered that around.

"Never look directly at the sun. It can turn you blind. Look through this" He said.

Everyone crowded around and William wondered about the meaning of the eclipse as it wasn't something one witnessed very often and everyone knew it was often considered to be a portent of either good or evil.

"What do you think of such a strange phenomenon, Hugh?" William uttered concentrating on enjoying the rare experience.

"I believe it's perhaps better to regard it at face value. It's merely nature having its way with us, if only to remind one that we're just mere mortals on a very small planet," Hugh was waxing philosophical and that was quite out of character!

After the excitement had died down, they joined Gabriel in his quarters. Maps and compasses, protractors and callipers were strewn around on his desk and he was staring out through his gallery of windows using a large telescope. Without a word he gestured to William to look through it.

William shouted with excitement, "I see land ahead. Land ahoy, my friends!"

He embraced Gabriel and then Hugh and down below they could hear the yells of delight from the rest of their companions. So neither of the friends won the bet! Seeing it first, their captain had turned the tables on them.

Back on deck, William saw the sentinel of the Cape of Good Hope grow steadily nearer and the magnificent Table Mountain appeared to be steaming as the clouds tumbled down its sheer granite face. The waterfall of clouds was like a table-cloth set for the gods of wind and sea. The mountain reared up at great height with awe-inspiring blue crags and gullies to an even summit that was flat and extended for several miles. There was no fairer landmark anywhere else on earth.

William and Hugh returned to the prow. The dolphins of the southern oceans swam with ease around them and welcomed them to the calmer waters of the natural bay. Now as William watched the streamlined bodies of the creatures, he delighted in their strange relationship with man. Another fascinating incident that happened on the journey occurred in the Tropics when a flock of swifts had settled on the ropes of the sails, finding a place to rest before recouping their strength for the final leg of their migratory journey southwards for the southern summer. William pondered on the fact that his journey was a migration, too. Since he was young, he had enjoyed a natural bond with nature and always sought to protect innocent creatures from man's brutality. He swore he would never lift a gun to end the life of a harmless healthy animal in sport.

-o0o-

It was late afternoon when William and Hugh retired to their cabin to pack all their goods and chattels. Soon "The Sterling" dropped anchor in the clear waters of the harbour. The first sight of Cape Town from the ship was reassuring to Hugh and William. Stretching to the bottom of the slopes of the great mountain were houses, churches, shops and what must have been government buildings. William thought how well they decorated the landscape. Their gaze took in the old fort which they noticed was built in a pentagon shape and one of their companions remarked that it had been constructed from the ballast offloaded from ships before they took on board loads of food and naturally occurring raw materials. William believed it to be the "Castle" which was the oldest building in the area and felt the excitement of being freed from the shackles of tedious repetition of the same routines back home. This attractive town which was to be their new home, had met with his approval besides which he had much to look forward to: a Government position, moving in new social circles and exploring the hinterland.

He wondered about meeting the young women at the Cape as he knew that the hope that Fanny could one day be his bride was a forlorn dream. They both knew that their love would never be recognised by Society.

She had whispered to him before leaving, "William, you must marry. I set you free, my Darling," She had taken his head in her hands and kissed his lips. She was giving him the gift of searching for a wife to fulfil his longing for a family of his own.

He had shaken his head, "Don't ask me to stop hoping we can be together. I could send for you. No one at the Cape would know about our relationship back in Dublin." He embraced her holding her so close as to inhale the scent of her dark hair that had escaped the pins holding it in an elegant style.

He never wanted to let go of her but she grappled with her hands and forced him to release her, "Fate will dictate to us how and when our two lives can merge. Perhaps that can only be in Heaven." The moment had been extremely painful for both of them.

Hugh, however, never mentioned having a family and William didn't press him on the subject. But then he remembered the strange eclipse and he felt uneasy. The future would be momentous, of that he was sure but would it be for good or for evil?

-o0o-

William wrote in his Journal how he had taken himself off to read in the shade of the sails. His books were of a different calibre altogether than that of the normal novel. He was studying Justinian's "Institutes" about civil law, Van den Linden's "Koopman's Handbook" which was in Dutch and about Roman Dutch Law, the American Brown's Civil Law, Halifax's "Analysis of Roman Civil Law and de Beaumonts "L Irlande". The law practised in the Cape would be Roman Dutch Law which is governed by precedent rather than the British system of jurors. He was keen to hit the ground running when he arrived to fill his position of attorney general. For lighter reading, he wrote how he preferred Mme de Stael's "Corinne," Robert Hall's "Sermons" and Thomas Brown's "Religio Medici" and finally "Hydrotaphia".

For a moment he turned to the first page, *"You who may one day read this as my wife or son or daughter, or descendants see a plain man who has laid himself bare before you in writing this. I have this compulsion to speak well of those I hold dear so your patience I most appreciate."*

In between the vellum and the card, he gently teased out a missive and read it with sadness before returning it to its hiding place:

"Beloved, you must ask why I allowed my name to be put forward for the position at the Cape. Plainly, my Dearest, I could no longer endure the realisation that sharing our lives the way we did would continue until restraint and unfulfilled desire would make the beauty of our love fade like flowers starved of rain. When the offer of promotion was presented to me and because the climate will be favourable for improving a society it seemed I'm morally obliged to use my powers in an altruistic fashion. Pride is something I abhor but the satisfaction of making a difference is a reward I seek so that I can hand down to my heirs the knowledge that I have not shirked my duties but embraced the demands on a thoughtful and concerned mind."

Another scrap of writing carried the words of a man in love:

"You found me at my mother's funeral and led me away from the huddle of relatives in their black mourning clothes. I remember thinking that they were silent black crows and the open grave with the freshly cut flowers tossed on the coffin was an entrance to Hell. How can one make such a horrific ritual palatable to a twelve year old child or make him see beauty in the illness and suffering leading up to that day? How was I to know that my mother's spirit was more

exquisite in death than in life and had been taken up into the heavens where purity and gentleness would enfold her? I was a babe wrenched away from its mother's breast. Tears coursed down my cheeks and you wiped them away with your scented lace handkerchief which you pressed into my hand. You were twenty two and about to be married to Stephen, the teacher. I was your orphan lamb or the chick fallen from a nest and no one could have wished for more love and tender care than yours."

Another letter kept for perhaps sending one day, continued the same theme:

"You and John gave me a home to ease the burden from the shoulders of Eliza, my stepmother and you sent me to a public school where learning and reading changed the course of my life. I was always mindful of your own grief which was so poignant and I as a youth of twelve was at a loss as how to comfort you in the manner in which you comforted me.

"At my Mother's funeral, I stood stiffly at your side, your pallor and sorrow for a woman unknown to you moved me to hold my grief at bay so as not to cause you further pain.

"I find it difficult to understand why you have never married and had children of your own. It must be an agony you have had to bear each day. You took me with you when John invited us to live with him. He gave me my apprenticeship but my world revolved around you. You were there when I awoke. You were there when loneliness and despair overwhelmed me. You tried to ease my anxiety of not knowing where I belonged. You never knew how much I hid my love for you and the bitterness of futility often clouded my mind.

"When I left you to go to London to study for the Bar the wrench was a physical ache. I joined my friends in public houses to drown my sorrow while they laughed and joked without cares. Sober evenings spent at my brother's manse surrounded with yew trees were the height or depth of bachelor life. The absence of female

company was a dagger in the heart and books were my dearest
companions."

He laughed quietly to himself. Some jottings were a celebration of his
love for Fanny:

*"Dearest, never wear black or grey but adorn yourself in shades of
claret, azure blue and rose. Let the finest lace frame your neck and
pearl earrings embellish your dainty ears. I yearn to touch your
hands, soft and gentle as wings of white doves and to see them folded
in repose as you listen to my meandering mind which as ever seeks
to entertain you with details from my world. How I wish I could
decorate your fingers with my rings. I cannot give you a ring or a
necklace and now so far away I cherish the memories as that is all I
have now to comfort me."*

Just a few lines of concern were on a small scrap of paper. He intended
to send it to Fanny when he arrived in Cape Town:

*"Pet, please adhere to my advice. Do not do your sewing after dark.
Nor should you read by the dim light from the oil lamp. You have
such sensitive eyesight and if you should lose it, you will lose those
pastimes you hold so dear."*

He removed the last torn square of paper and it brought tears to his
eyes which he willed not to flow down his cheeks:

*"Your quick whisper as I left the home I had known for twenty years
has left me confused but sober. You have given your blessing for me
to marry without love but to learn to respect my wife for her
dedication towards creating a home and family. It must have been
like the blade of a knife in your side to utter those words. No other
woman could fill my heart as completely as you. You have a man
accustomed to oratory left speechless with emotion. I feel
unspeakably alone."*

Before Hugh could disturb his reverie, he quickly hid the missives
again in the secrecy of the Journal's cover and then took himself off
to their cabin to occupy himself in the festive packing up of all of his

worldly possessions. What stories could this new town, this new world tell him, tales of adventure, treasures to be found and in his case lives and property to protect and a society to mould? Whatever lay before him he was ready to grab each challenge with both hands.

-o0o-

CHAPTER 5

It was winter of the year 1839 when Castle Maud, a stone fortress positioned on a gently undulating hill sat with imposing grandeur. The architect had complemented the building with a high wall on the upper gradient, which protected a wide herbaceous border only to be reached down stone-hewn steps, flowing down to a knot garden and clipped yew trees which led to a focal point of a fountain reminiscent of Italian vistas in Tuscany. The weather was far from Mediterranean and mist and rain made the stone glisten and the garden was washed out with all the colours on the rich palette running into the green wetness.

Lord Craven sat in the huge hall beside the fireplace which was eight feet high and logs burned on top of the iron dogs where white ash trickled through to the stone underneath. The Craven coat of arms had been carved into the marble surround. Two grey Irish wolfhounds lay at his feet, their bodies stretched out in sheer bliss but Lord Craven who knew he was wasting away, had an austere expression on his lined patrician face and a grey pallor revealed an illness he never mentioned and about which he had bade everyone from making any comment. His hair had turned white when he lost his eldest son in a storm at sea and he was as thin as a mummified Egyptian. Now, he fiddled with a leather pouch, fingering it while his thoughts were far away.

The doors were flung open and the new arrival brought in a gust of cold air with his frame looming large and menacing in the doorway. "Father, I heard you want to speak to me, an honour with which I was hasty to comply. You obviously heard that I am a free man once more!" His face was chiselled as if wooden and no smile or softening of the eye betrayed his pain at being the black sheep of the family. His red hair was shot through with silver.

"Oh, it's you. I won't beat about the bush. I want you to leave immediately for India. Your passage has been paid for and you will be sailing from England a week today on the King's Bride man o' war.

Take this," He flung the pouch which clinked with coins upwards and Roland caught it. "You have disappointed me once too often. I'll have nothing more to do with you. So do us both a favour and make a new life somewhere far from here."

Roland paused, before turning on his heel and leaving, banging the huge doors shut behind him, showing his great strength. His face contorted in rage, self-pity and raw pain. The bully baulked at being bullied… However, his father's will had to be obeyed and furthermore his name was besmirched and no friends were around to save him…No one could be bought this time.

-o0o-

The next few months were busy ones for William and also for Hugh, as there were many cases brought before them. Hugh managed the legal diary, book-keeping and administration with dogged determination. He had heard rumours that the people of repute believed William was particularly suited to solving the internal problems that were arising politically. His liberal and non-conformist views were soon known to all. Word had spread that the new Attorney General wasn't only an English Liberal but an Irish Liberal. He supported anyone who had to flee from their country to find a safe haven elsewhere like the French Huguenots who had found a safe haven at the Cape, especially in the Franschoek Mountains.

He became aware of the dissatisfaction of the Dutch settlers who were known as the Boers. He studied their history and even arranged to have lessons in Dutch in order to read their literary and philosophical works in the language in which they had been written. He had quickly learnt their form of law and its dependence on precedents and it was a change for him to deliver judgements without consulting jurors. He was the chief prosecutor in cases of Boers being violent towards their slaves who, although slavery had been abolished in 1834, had chosen to remain with their former masters as the Boers' paternalism had its benefits. He researched all he could about those accused and on the other extreme saw to it that slaves were brought to book for murdering their masters or stealing their masters' goods and in amongst it all he heard grievances from all groups.

He found his true aim at the Cape was to emancipate the Boers, women of all groups, freed slaves and other "men of colour" which included the growing number of men and women of mixed blood. He was also concerned that the Khoikhoi or Hottentot numbers were in decline as they were being oppressed into leaving the Colony.

William looked a figure of authority in his fine white stock, distinctive bands and silk gown. Hugh called his outfit the "superior article". William drew the line at the wearing of wigs. He often grew frustrated as being Attorney General he had to juggle two jobs as he owed his first allegiance to the Governor as advisor with regard to legislation and he was also a public prosecutor.

He had muttered to Hugh one day, "My two functions in life run hand in hand and although united in the same person should be regarded as distinct and are functions which, were theoretical perfection alone consulted, would never normally be combined." He was concerned that he was spreading his knowledge widely and perhaps thinly, and hoped the wisdom gained with regard to both would grow and not diminish.

He and Hugh had little time for social engagements and times for relaxation were sought outside the town. They decided to rent a cottage in Rondebosch in the countryside for the weekends. It was situated beneath Devil's Peak which was just an hour away by Hansom cab and a couple of feisty horses. In the garden, indigenous flowers of peacock blue irises and white gladioli were intermingled with roses and nasturtiums in a riot of colour as could be found in an English cottage garden, but neither man was nostalgic for his homeland.

The climate and countryside were very much to their liking. They had the sea, mountains, sparkling rivers where they could spend a leisurely afternoon fishing, go for walks or they could harness their horses to their trap and drive to the closest beach at Muizenburg to swim in the warm sea, just an hour away.

William had looked forward to balls and soirees especially as Nerina Smith was sometimes a fellow guest and they spoke often in the gentile reserve of the times. He enjoyed seeing her perfect face and brown eyes where innocence smiled up at him. She would, no doubt, soon be married and he wondered what his true feelings were regarding marriage. Would any woman match up to Fanny? Fanny was his idea of perfect womanhood and she had an allure and good sensibility that he had found disarming. Perhaps he was unfair to Nerina by expecting too much from her.

Sitting on the veranda of the cottage one fine summer's evening in the shadow of the mountain, he mused with Hugh, "Tennyson writes that women should stay at home with their needles whilst men wielded their swords. Women should be innocent, virtuous, biddable, dutiful and ignorant of intellectual opinion," He was stroking the spaniel at his feet.

Hugh, lazing in a hammock, mocked, "What woman – now be honest with me, William – has the brain for law or medicine or to be a merchant?" Hugh had often tried the company of ladies but his clumsiness in the art of courtship, the latter so sadly lacking, that women drifted away. Some were often quite disappointed as Hugh had an Irish flair for the outrageous and they mistook him for a romantic troubadour, and when uttered, his caustic remarks shocked them and they would turn away in alarm.

"What saddens me is that I believe that capability would be there if given half a chance," William wished Nerina had the opportunities he, as a man, had been offered. Sewing and cooking and following a Book of Household Management overflowing with receipts and recipes were undemanding exercises.

"I could be swayed by a magnificent rack of lamb, roast potatoes and fresh vegetables followed by "Apples a la Frangipane" that Mrs Smith's cook had prepared at the dinner for us at last Sunday. "Geseende Huis" was impressive, didn't you think?" William asked.

"I know where this is leading to," Hugh jumped out of the swinging hammock, "You would be prepared to marry Nerina for her cooking! Just think you'll get Epicurean menus and high moral values!" Hugh laughed.

"There is more to Nerina if only you could see it, Hugh. Anyhow, it would be helpful to have a woman to run the home, budget and do the accounts. It would allow us considerably more time for finer pursuits!" William argued.

How could he tell Hugh that he longed for the gentle embrace of a woman, her scent and delicate ways, her whisper of love in his ear and if he were to be honest with himself, he wanted the glorious moments of married bliss; something he could never share with Fanny? He had a longing for children of his own and meanwhile as a substitute he had found a way to help homeless waifs and strays, the flotsam of poverty, living on the streets of Cape Town. He had the innate desire to help those in dire need especially when he remembered the tight-knit extended family of his father and Eliza back in Ireland.

"We'll sample their generosity again next weekend as John Smith has invited us to camp out of doors at a beach south of Saldanha Bay," William told Hugh, "We'll travel to his brother-in-law's home and spend the first night there. I think the homestead is called "Bergendal". It's planned that the next day we'll ride to the shore on horseback and the women and picnic hampers and tents will follow in two wagons. The men will then go hunting after we put up tents and hopefully we'll bring back a buck to roast on hot coals."

"We should make sure we ride this weekend. If what you say is true, we will undoubtedly need the practice. Using cabs and carriages has dulled our riding skills," Hugh warned.

-o0o-

Nerina enjoyed being at "Bergendal" as it was a gracious building in the style of high gables and thatched roof and around the house were verandas with their own flat roofs. It was situated under the jutting mountain that imposed its grandeur on mere humans. Underneath the back veranda were cellars where their cool temperature made apples and pumpkins last for months not to mention their suitability for the storage of wine and provisions for the kitchen.

The garden was arranged to either side of a long formal pool which was fed with mountain water and beds of pansies, stocks and hydrangeas were all edged with flame red and pink pelargoniums which were an added stunning decoration. At the pool, arum lilies grew at the boggy edges and waterlilies floated on the surface, with their stars of cream and pink flowers vibrant with light on the dark green expanse of water.

To the north of the homestead were the vineyards in neat rows. As it was midsummer, the pruned, stunted vines were draped with lush green leaves and the hanging candelabras of grapes were still green. Grapes were the mainstay of the region around Tulbagh, the nearest town.

As the heat was oppressive, Nerina and the other women all wore white muslin dresses. Gone were the fashionable Victorian gowns with their v-shaped waists, layering, crinolines and *engageantes* which were now all the rage in the Colony. What freedom to move about so easily and to enjoy the material that was as light as a feather and quite becoming in its own way.

Preparations for the camp were underway. They were to go to a bay south of Saldanha where there were no shops so they needed to be totally self-sufficient and had to take their goods with them. Two ox-wagons were hitched up to the six strong oxen each and everything needed to survive for three days was loaded onto one of the wagons including cooking ware, dishes and cutlery. A cook and housemaid would travel with the entourage to give the women time to relax and enjoy themselves, too. They would never be expected to prepare the food which always had been the role of servants.

Once they arrived at the small protected bay called The Grotto, William soon found out that the camping and picnicking wasn't to be an indolent affair.

"After our coffee, we'll make our way into the hills," Jan Erasmus spoke with a marked Dutch accent. He was their host for the duration of the adventure.

"I know of a herd of springbuck just north of here." He informed them.

Mr and Mrs Smith didn't accompany the party but remained behind at "Bergendal".

"Show some enthusiasm, William," Hugh muttered under his breath, "Erasmus thinks he is offering us an experience of a lifetime."

William downed a hasty mug of coffee and just managed to have a few brief words with Nerina, who appeared flushed and happy, her hair, loosely braided, escaping into curls around her face. A dew of perspiration made her complexion glow.

Already saddle-sore, William mounted his horse and tried to look as though he was having a most enjoyable experience,

"You'll have to do any shooting," he looked fiercely at the other men, "I prefer my buck walking around on all four legs." The others laughed.

Six hours later, the men-folk returned with two buck flung over the front of Jan's horse and the horse of his brother, Dirk. The gutting had been done in the veldt and William had felt nauseated and struck dumb by the whole affair. The cook would skin and butcher the carcasses. Hugh was in fine fettle and was little perturbed by their expedition.

Soon the racks of venison were roasting on a spit over the coals of a large fire and sosaties that the cook had marinated in wine and spices and strung onto sharpened sticks of wild herbs, were also grilling away.

William and Nerina had been for a walk along the beach enjoying the breath-taking view of Table Mountain and the Twelve Apostles which stretched behind it, to the south. Sea birds floated on the wind and the bay was flecked with suds of spray in the breeze. Robben Island or Seal Island lay in the bay like a floating dead whale, a shadow where the sun was sinking lower. William realised it would soon be dark and they would need to turn back. In the salt breeze the whiff of sizzling meat and smoke was tantalising.

"How is your work developing, Mr Ropert? I hear that you are occupied with the civil cases and no doubt Governor Napier has other plans with which he wishes to engage you. Excuse me such matters are none of my business." Nerina asked politely.

She was happy and content. She felt no threat in the proximity of her companion or that they were without a chaperone.

"I've never worked so hard in my life," William admitted, "The civil cases are many as there is some confusion about people's rights. Slavery has been an iniquitous abomination created by mankind and I'm now seeing the aftermath and to crown it all the Colony is desperately in need of a constitution. On those lines, I'm in consultation with Governor Napier about drafting such a document."

"Do you have cases to do with bankruptcy and infidelity between spouses?" She laughed mischievously, "No, I don't expect you to reveal such matters to me. I'm being foolish."

"There are many of those and ones more serious, such as murders and various types of cruel, unfair treatment of man upon his fellow man. That is what is goading me on to discover ways of tempering this society.

"You know, the one thing that I've found reassuring is that this small corner of the British Empire has no class distinction not in the sense that applies to Britain. In England everyone weighs up another's breeding and where he stands by comparison, for example we have what is called the Upper and Lower Classes and now the Middle Classes are making an appearance with all the businessmen and professional people improving their lot. In the Cape, merchant, governor, teacher, doctor, farmer, shopkeeper, are all equal perhaps because we do not have any lords and ladies who own castles and stately homes as is the case in Britain. But there is something creeping in that worries me and that is the tribal question. The Khoikhoi and the freed slaves are considered somehow to be lazier, more devious and less bright than those of us who have come here from abroad." He wished she would tuck her hand into the crook of his arm like Fanny used to do.

Even though it wasn't quite dark, the light from a distant lighthouse sparked intermittently.

"Have you read any works by St Augustine or Pelagius? I don't know if you know Pelagius was a British monk who lived a few hundred years after Christ?

She shook her head.

William continued, "We should be teaching the natural rights of man. We are all brothers and equal, and we should treat each other so, but, we are also all responsible for our own acts and must progress onward and upward to achieve complete goodness in this life!" William said to her.

He was having difficulty keeping his mind on their conversation. Why did Fanny want to make him communicate with so much honesty with a young woman so many years his junior?

"I do believe that this world is meant for us to achieve happiness instead of needing penance and mourning. I believe education in true values is what's required and if I were not rich and supported by my father, I should have liked to have been a teacher," Nerina commented.

She had failed to persuade her father that she should be sent to college as he felt with his position she wouldn't be expected to work for her living. She had however cajoled him into arranging lessons for her and she had been well taught by governesses, for which she was most thankful.

"I've heard of your work with the homeless children. You're a very kind man, Mr Ropert. I would like to get involved in such charitable acts." She offered.

Nerina was looking forward to having children of her own one day. Would this man be their father?

"I appreciate your kind offer and I'll let you know if you can be of assistance. On second thoughts, perhaps you could find a seamstress who could help by making clothes for the orphans or asking your friends to donate old children's clothing?" He replied.

William was disappointed that they had nearly reached their camp. There was singing and delicious aromas floating on the air.

"Mr Ropert, I'm sure we can tempt you with our fare," Jan Erasmus, beckoned him to the fire and held up a morsel on the end of a long fork, "You do eat meat even if you do not kill the animal it came from?"

Hugh had been keeping an eye on his friend, "He prefers the food of love. Have you noticed he has a way with women?"

The others laughed jovially as the weekend was turning out to be a wonderful break from the daily hubbub of life in the town. Tomorrow, they would go fishing before breakfast and he was told they would no doubt bring back galjoen or Hottentot fish, maybe even rock lobster for breakfast. In the afternoon, they would shoot pheasant and partridges that had been introduced into the area.

William had a lot on his mind as he watched the last embers of the fire die down. Nerina had made a great impression on him but almost at once he remembered the other woman in his life, dearest Fanny. She had been a devoted friend to him. He would need to think carefully about what it was he wanted for his future. With work being all consuming, did he need to make his life more complicated than it already was?

-o0o-

CHAPTER 6

It had been a busy time in Dublin with Fanny mostly preoccupied with the wedding preparations. Her duties as housekeeper and church member were now stretched most uncomfortably. Sewing and embroidering, and making items of clothing for Delilah made her increasingly weary. She was so exhausted that she broke the news to John that she would be travelling to a guest house in Cushendall for two weeks' holiday after the wedding.

The wedding was a success and Delilah with her wild hair tamed into locks with the hot iron tongs looked a picture in a cream silk and lace gown that served to tone down her gregarious personality. There hadn't been time for both women to confide in one another and Fanny realised that she would not find social discourse or companionship with Delilah.

At last, the day came for Fanny to set off on her short holiday. When she was settled her driver cracked a whip above the horse's head and the trap bounced on the cobbles down the street. Soon the horse cantered in front of them through the countryside. It was a summer's day that swallows celebrated in the heavens. Fanny took her little black canine friend along for their visit to Cushendall and he sat between her and her driver. He was William's Scottish terrier and since William's departure, MacDuff had sat on William's chair and fretted. Gradually, the plucky animal turned his affections to Fanny. She had laughed as just before they left and were loading their suitcases onto the carriage, he barked at her, reading her mind and he trotted off to fetch his lead.

They had a lovely ride through the landscapes of Antrim countryside and finally arrived at their destination, a picturesque village with streets that rose and fell with the rolling hills, set amongst tall trees that formed leafy knaves and cupolas above them and blackbirds sang their sweet songs with golden notes that lifted any sad heart. However, from time to time, the rooks in the trees cawed and it grated the nerves and reminded one that there were dark forces about.

They stopped at the top of a lane leading to the beach and Fanny and the little dog with its short legs but dapper attitude walked down to the sand where the waves were just retreating. Each footstep pushed water out in a print and with the next step water erased the last indentation. MacDuff's paw prints were deep and zigzagged alongside. She felt the grey shroud of depression unravel as though caught on a thorny branch and beside her MacDuff was a black scrubbing brush swishing back and forth with a head and tail and four stubby legs.

Fanny felt her pallor filling with a blush of exhilaration as the sea breeze invigorated her. She breathed in deeply and the salty air brought tears to her eyes. She and William had often walked along the beach together on similar summer days allowing MacDuff off his lead to explore the high tide line.

She let the little dog run free and sat down on the sand. As she relaxed she felt her fingers iron out the lines of her face and she breathed deeply, escaping the complications of her life for a while.

-o0o-

The fortnight in Cushendall felt like another life and era and she allowed a different persona to inhabit her body. Casting aside 'Fanny' was such a relief. The landlady of the room she took was a kind soul who was also companion to the lady of the manor. She would share with Fanny tales of Cushendall sometimes veering on the supernatural and her firm belief in fairies soon had its effect on Fanny who would scour the countryside looking for fairy rings or she would sit still at a stream under beeches hoping to see the little people. She lived in the moment enjoying everything her senses brought to her soul washing away the poisons of loneliness and fettered longing. The taste of a wild strawberry, a sip of elderberry wine, marmalade on toast, the scent of aniseed from fennel growing in the vegetable garden, raw carrots and beans, the spellbinding smell of the hairy green stems of tomatoes…

Soon, however, the day came for her to return to Dublin but loath to return she decided to take the coach to Limavady to visit her sister. She needed to unburden herself from "Fanny" even further and Eliza was the best person to give of herself selflessly to strengthen her younger sister. Their sorority was a blessing and to partake of it now was essential before she fell back into the depression of Dublin and the house that was no longer her home.

-oOo-

The coach journey to Limavady was bone shakingly uncomfortable with MacDuff in a wicker basket with the coachman whose song was clipped from his lips by the wind while he drove the horses hard. The countryside was soaked in myths and legends and they passed the decaying ruins of castles and towers, Fanny daydreamed about Finn McCool, and Finn who ate the salmon of knowledge and Cuchulainn who killed Culann's hound. She saw four white Hooper swans flying close to the land over the water of a lake. Her favourite myth was the story of the Children of Lir who had a jealous stepmother who changed them into four swans. She felt like a swan seeking to find its humanity and a prince she would love and above all she needed a resting place somewhere in the future where these dreams could come true.

After hours that seemed like days she finally arrived in Limavady and recognised the tall thin steeple of the church that pricked the speckled sky. She surprised Eliza who was bringing in the washing that had been dried by the strong south westerly wind. Laughing they fell into each other's arms and they crossed the back courtyard where chickens pecked and scratched in the dirt. A basket of warm brown eggs was perched on the top step at the door that was painted a bright blue. Moss covered the roof with splashes of green chlorophyll.

"What a surprise to drop in on me unannounced!" Eliza looked much older than her sister not just in years but weather beaten by life. Looking after two broods of children had mapped out her face with laughter lines around her mouth and worry lines on her forehead. She put the kettle on the range to make a cup of tea to sip as they chatted.

"I'm needing some of your mothering, Eliza. You're so good at finding the right solutions to problems. Oh, my dear sister, I feel like a child that has got itself lost through its own misadventure," Fanny seldom bared her feelings so openly and Eliza took a long look at her sister. She looked like a widow but there was no death she could be mourning. Losing her fiancé was so far in the past. Fanny wanted to tell Eliza everything but she reined in her galloping emotions.

"As a young girl I used to dream of being ravished on my wedding night by a good and honourable man who cherished my body and my mind and soul with his love," she stumbled over the words that were as heavy as rocks.

"What racy books have you been reading!" her sister laughed.

"I'm never going to be married, am I?" Fanny stirred the hot tea hoping her sister would read the tea leaves left in the cup after she had sipped it all.

Eliza felt her own heart contract painfully as she loved her sister not just because they were related but because they were best friends and she had to admit their usual exchange of letters had slowed while she worried about her husband, Bill who was ageing before her eyes and the difference in their ages was fast beginning to show.

"You may yet find a handsome bachelor or widower. You would be an asset to any good man who would share his home with you. You must attend gatherings at church or join committees. With William gone and John wrapped up in his new wife, you really must put in an appearance at social functions." It sounded the way she felt, out of her depth and it pained her to hurt her sister.

"Why don't you think of visiting Jane's American husband, James and his family and get to know your step-niece's children? I still cannot believe she passed away so young but each birth could be one's last. Why we women must carry such a weakness, dear alone knows," Eliza thought to herself perhaps she would make such a journey herself one day.

"I may consider it. To see America would be such an adventure. I'll mull it over." Fanny thought of Jane's children growing up motherless. "What was it like to carry a baby in your womb? John's wife is with child and I envy her but harbour feelings of anger towards myself and self-pity. I often dream of giving birth to a baby but without fail it doesn't thrive and it dies in my arms. Each time I feel labour pains and the sweetness of the end of all the pain when one hears a baby cry. In my dreams, I blame myself for being unsuited to motherhood, feeling I must be cursed. It's so dreadful," Tears were threatening to spill down her cheeks.

"Have you finished drinking your tea? I'll read your future if I can in the leaves. Yes, swirl the last of the tea around and then turn the cup upside down on this paper napkin. Good!" Eliza peered into the bone china piece curiously.

"Do you see anything?" Fanny had cheered up, her mind distracted by the fortune telling.

"I'll go around the top of the teacup and work my way down…Ah, I have found a bell in the area for next month so you should get good news – perhaps a letter from William. That would bring the smile back on your face. Look at this Fanny," she pointed to the mesh of leaves in the shape of a spider-web. "You are keeping a secret! Come on tell me what it is, do tell!"

"If I had a secret it wouldn't be a secret anymore now would it if I told you?" Fanny laughed.

"I also see a crescent moon. That means there'll be changes afoot in your life. I wonder what those could be." Eliza was as good as a gypsy at reading tea leaves.

"I feel change is coming, too," Fanny felt a chill sweep over her like the shadow of a great bird.

"Look here right at the bottom of the cup. See that. It is just the shape of a dog. There is a faithful friend waiting for you in a few years' time. And, next to it is a tree which stands for a new start. So, well done, dear Sister things won't always be as they are now. Your future is mapped out for you and may seem inscrutable now but when the time comes it will all fall into place. Fanny, oh Fanny, what can I say or do to take this cross that you have to bear off your shoulders?" She knelt next to her sister and held her hands. "Come, let's clear the table for making the farls of soda bread for tonight's meal." She busied herself and set to work sieving flour onto the table, adding the bicarbonate of soda, pinch of salt, buttermilk eventually turning the well of ingredients into a clinging mess of wet flour and finally kneading it into a satiny dough.

Fanny took a handful of dough and kneaded it firmly as their mother taught them to do. Back in Dublin they had a cook but Eliza had to be all servants rolled into one at the manse. "When I became a widow before ever becoming a bride I wanted to change my faith and become a nun," Fanny felt like turning her back on the world.

"I remember," Eliza laughed, "I couldn't have you become a Catholic and disown us all. Why else did I give you William but to comfort you?"

"I was out of my depth to start off but later I realised I knew automatically what to say and do for him. He means everything to me, Eliza." She wanted to unburden herself further but something held her back from giving words to her passionate love and the pain and heartache that accompanied her desires.

"My Bill is about to retire," Eliza broke the news to her sister reluctantly not wanting to foist their problems onto her vulnerable sister, "Fanny, I'm worried about him. He has spent all that we have in providing an education and profession for all the boys. Now we aren't sure how to afford to live during our old age. He's looking frail – you'll see what I mean when he arrives home. He used to be a picture of health but he complains of pains in his chest and legs and sometimes his feet feel numb so I rub them with oil and massage the problem away. He's also forgetting parts of his sermons and gets quite agitated and frustrated."

MacDuff lay next to the warm range where the coals burned brightly and the flour on the griddle pan started to brown so they laid the farls now cut into triangles on the black metal ring waiting for the bubbles to form and air to rise up into the dough as the bicarbonate of soda began to do its work.

"Write to William," Fanny inhaled the aroma of baking bread, "Please do, Eliza. From his letters he is making a comfortable living at the Cape and he is buying stock and selling it to make an admirable profit. He is pouring money into developing projects to facilitate the Colony's development. You know how caring he is. He'll never let you or Bill endure any sort of poverty."

"You really believe he'll help?" This time it was Eliza's eyes that filled with tears. "I know you think he walks on water but perhaps I'd be asking too much of him"

"Of course, not. He has no family as yet not that that would make any difference." Fanny wanted to shout out how much she loved him and still Eliza never guessed her guilty secret…

-o0o-

On returning to Dublin, there were letters awaiting her return and there was one from William. She had hidden William's letter in her handbag which was full of all sorts of paraphernalia and the letter would go undetected there. She went out into the garden to read it where there were no prying eyes. She believed that he saw to it that any trader or man o' war leaving the Cape for England would take a letter from him to her. For her, it was less easy and some of her letters took three months to reach him. Even in the bright sunlight her eyes squinted to read what he had written.

Her heart contracted with pain when he wrote about Nerina Smith but she shook her head and lifted her chin, reading on. She looked for hidden messages between the lines and felt all the emotion it took for him to confess to the fact that he was enjoying the social scene at the Cape. He knew she would pine and he could do nothing about it.

When she had been home a few weeks, she sat down at the sturdy desk in the study to write her reply. The oil lamp flickered and she had to press her face close to the paper to see as she dipped the pen into the black ink to form the words of encouragement she wished to convey. She had an important message for him.

"My dearest William, how wonderful it has been to read your interesting news about your day to day courtroom dramas and the frequent dinners spent with dignitaries in Cape Town. Are you still as enamoured with the young woman, Nerina? You have not mentioned her for some time and I have the feeling that you don't wish to break my heart by telling me that you love her. My Darling, I understand that you must find happiness where you can. Life for the two of us can never be the same again. You must follow your heart should you wish to marry her. Don't have any concern for my feelings as I have come to terms with our separate lives," Her forehead puckered into many lines and she put pen to paper again.

"My beloved, there is some news you should know. Roland Craven walked free from Dublin Jail this week. His term of imprisonment has ended and rumours abound but the one that holds most credence

is that his father has sent him to India. He need never cross your path again."

Fanny pressed a handkerchief to her cheeks as tears kept spilling from her eyes. At last, all her news was written down. She folded her letter and melted sealing wax allowing it to drip onto the parchment and as it congealed she used her dainty signet ring to make the seal.

-o0o-

"Take me to the trading ship, the Tudor Rose, porter," Roland Craven slurred while two plump and dishevelled ladies of the night, giggled as they tried to keep him upright. He had his hand over a breast of one of the women. Their long hair looked like straw and the ribbons tying up their locks were faded and dirty.

The vessel loomed up through the fog like a grey ghost-ship and for a moment Roland thought he could see a skeletal apparition at the top of the gangway. He veered away nearly bringing all three of them down onto their knees.

"What haunts this ship? I feel that evil awaits anyone who sails in it," He shivered and drew himself up to his full height.

"Farewell, my lovelies. India awaits me and I will make myself a fortune. Good luck to this God-forsaken England. Goodbye to Ireland, too, and good riddance!"

Betrayed by his feckless friends and disowned by his own father he felt he was suffering more than he ever did in jail. His coldly calculating brain would devise ways to settle those scores. He wasn't one for turning the other cheek…

-o0o-

As the months passed, Fanny felt desolate and was inconsolable. John could see that William's absence was linked to her depression. The ready smile and the spirited flash of her eyes were absent. William was the son she had never had, John thought to himself. In addition, he was unaware that the additional strain of living with Delilah had almost made Fanny ill.

Fanny mourned the loss of William's affection and now regretted she had allowed convention to stand in the way of the happiness William and she deserved. Now she wished they had revealed their feelings in actual word and deed. They had so much to say to each other but it had all gone unspoken. They had lived together in a terrible symbiosis where neither was fulfilled and neither grew in life experience, personality and independence from one another. They were co-dependants holding each other back and satisfied with just companionship on an easy, superficial level. Why had they settled for so little? Why had they become blind, deaf and dumb emotionally?

Now she wanted to speak her mind and she tried to break through the conventions of Victorian language but stumbled and then the words on the page lay inert, failing to sow the seeds of romance. She longed for his arms to embrace her as her body had never been allowed to melt and take on the contours of his physique. Where was her chance to lie between clean, linen sheets with him and feel his body warm as bread cooling after it had been in the oven? The rapture of lovemaking had been denied her and a life without the children they could have had, loomed darkly before her. In any case, she was too old now to ever carry a child or safely give birth to a healthy baby.

John had noticed that letters from William seemed to disappoint Fanny. What declaration was she expecting? He saw her write daily in her diary to the point of obsession and he grew concerned as she battled to write or read even in daylight. He didn't want to countenance that she might be going blind like her mother before her and like her mother's mother before that. He sighed as he contemplated his dear sister's future....

CHAPTER 7

Towards the end of his first year in the Cape, William found there was much to learn about the land that he had chosen to adopt as his home for the foreseeable future.

Although he had discovered that there was no class or caste system in the Cape, the so called Europeans were apt to differentiate between people by nationalities and tribes and the bigotry of the farmers wasn't responsible for that.   William was sad to discover that the enlightenment that had spread throughout Europe years before hadn't yet reached the Cape and hadn't influenced the society apart from the abolition of slavery in 1833 which was later than in England. For the first time at the Cape, now there was a need for democracy. Those ideals had to find a voice and into that dissemination William was prepared to put his heart and soul.

His moment of reverie was soon over as he prepared for his next client. William was conscientious and punctilious. However, some of the laws he had to adhere to weren't to his liking. He was nauseated by questions regarding legitimacy of relationships. The social *mores* left a lot to be desired. The society was, after all, a microcosm of Europe with its current social ills. That very morning he had a case where a little girl had been assaulted. He was almost as distressed as the family, not to mention the shy child.

Fortunately, most cases were less disturbing. Land disputes, families fighting over inheritances, theft, arson, bankruptcy. Crimes against the Government of the day didn't exist. He had liberal ideas about marriage and felt that happiness and sociability were more desirable than what the law had to say about such matters.

The "noble savage" too, had views that clashed with European sensibilities. With regard to punishments employers meted out to their servants, William sought to let employers know that it was now illegal to inflict degrading punishment as in a perfect society employees should be deemed to be equal before God. The fact was that such grievances had to be settled in the courts and not by employers taking the law into their own hands.

William also learnt that Anglicisation of the Cape was never the main objective of the British. This was chiefly done to avoid confrontation with the Afrikaner or Dutch element of the society. However, two governors, Sir John Cradock and Lord Charles Somerset broke away from that unwritten intention the decade before William's arrival. English became the official language in government circles, the civil service and in courts and schools. Even in churches, Somerset attempted to ensure that Dutch clergy made way for clerics from Scotland. Fortunately, that attempt failed. Nevertheless the damage was done and the first emigration of Afrikaners out of the Cape began in 1834 at the time of the Sixth Frontier War with the Xhosas.

Outside William's office, Hugh had made time as usual to read the daily newspapers in order to keep William abreast of social commentary and the latest news of business and political developments. Hugh had become immersed in the growing commercial market and advised William to invest in imports and the establishment of new businesses or Government projects. There were rumblings about a railway system and installing gas lighting in the streets and homes. Hugh himself put a large proportion of his earnings into stocks and shares and soon both men were considerably enriched and more than ever William was a most eligible bachelor.

William still wished to court Nerina, much to Hugh's irritation and after his last client for that day, William put pen to paper:

Dear Nerina,

I trust that you are in good health. Please accept my apologies for the long delay since your last letter. I've been much engrossed in political and legal matters that have dictated how I spend my every moment. I wish to call on you if it's agreeable to your parents. I've much missed our conversations.

Your devoted servant,

Yours sincerely,

William Ropert

It was his last task for the day. The main item on his agenda for the following day was attending a dinner with John Fairbairn, the editor of the *Commercial Advertiser*. They had met at ad hoc meetings of the Council, but this occasion had the potential of cementing an allegiance between the two men. Fairbairn wanted to discuss *sub rosa* the problems of illness among the poor and wanted to find a way to end the poverty being experienced at the Cape.

-o0o-

The morning had become all the more special to Nerina when she was handed an envelope bearing William's seal. She held the letter to her heart and smiled with great tenderness. When she read about his desire to visit, she ran to her mother who was sitting near a window, making lace. The silver weights of the fine threads glinted, throwing reflections of sunlight around the room. Liesbet's eyes were suffering from the strain of myopia which was a sign of the onset of middle age. She looked up at her daughter with great curiosity. So the new Attorney General had unmistakably fallen for Nerina's good looks and charming manner. Her plans were bearing fruit at long last…

"Of course we must invite him, Nerina. You must reply but not too promptly as it would give the impression that you are acting in too much haste through great neediness. I'll dictate a suitable reply." Liesbet's mind was already concocting the nuances and underlying promises of a four-line letter.

Nerina returned to her task of drying flowers. The heathers and other Cape flowers could be dried between the pages of a heavy book and arranging them between blotting paper or silver paper with cotton wool ensured they dried without any signs of decay. She had collected hydrangea florets, pansies, Namaqualand daisies with their gold flowers, pincushion protea, a most unusual flower with its modified petals rolled up to a point like a giant pin, rose petals and the unusual orchid, the *disa* with its three petals, a trinity, of the deepest red and its delicate throat promising nectar to bees. Within days these blooms would have dried and set their colours. The drying process could be enhanced by placing the volume in the sun. Nerina tied string around the old book. She found a heavy marble book-end lain on top, was essential. There it was done.

Nerina enjoyed this time of year. She wasn't without her admirers and recently had enjoyed a dance on board a French man-of-war in Simon's Bay which was a difficult coach ride away from Cape Town but it had been worth the inconvenience and discomfort. Sometimes they shortened the journey by crossing the sandy beaches instead of following the rocky and very bumpy road.

She loved the French with their flamboyant manners and blatant romanticism. It was so daring and she felt the urge to live for the moment and enjoy the pampering. The English were so offhand and hamstrung by convention by comparison.

However, none of these young naval officers would meet with her mother's approval.

The previous weekend was spent at "Groot Constantia", one of the most gracious homes in the whole of the Cape Colony. Their host had invited a gathering of English naval officers and they had all gone riding or for walks up the foot-hills of the mountain. The young people had then returned breathless and with burning cheeks to enjoy the cool evening in the stylish gardens of the grand house.

Nerina loved "Groot Constantia" with its architecture of high gables with sash windows to either side of the entrance. She found the front veranda was most inviting. It was set high up the mountainside and from it she could see the cultivated valley below and behind it the vineyards faced the morning sunshine, ideal for the vines. When she found herself alone, she wandered through the house and found it was tastefully furnished in an almost Quaker-like simplicity but decorated with vases of flowers from the garden. It was lit from the outside, sunlight being reflected inwards with the aid of long mirrors. Family portraits watched the comings and goings with benign frozen smiles. The dining room was also a very long room stretching the full length of the house.

Of all the homes she had visited, Nerina loved this one the best. She daydreamed of one day being the mistress of such a homestead. She sighed when reality came flooding back.

She dipped her pen into the inkpot and did as her mother had suggested and wrote the following message to William Ropert:

"Dear Mr Ropert,

It would be an honour if you would care to dine with me at my parents' home this Saturday evening at seven p.m. It'll be our pleasure to entertain you with our humble hospitality.

I look forward to meeting you again and hope to hear the news of the fruits of your appointment and how you are faring.

Yours sincerely,

Nerina Smith."

Nerina had practised her finest handwriting and eventually was satisfied with the artistry of her hand. She prayed that God and Fate would give her some assistance in her search for a happy marriage with William.

-o0o-

CHAPTER 8

Cape Town,

Summer 1839-40.

A year had passed and besides learning about Roman Dutch Law and the languages of his new country, William had busied himself with learning more of the history of the land where he was now beholden to uphold the law, both civil and political. He found the divisions according to colour and degree of "civilisation" most perturbing.

He read what Craig, the first British Governor at the Cape had written about farmers' appropriation of land and its message: "With what face can you ask me to allow you to occupy lands which belong to other people? What right can I have to give you the property of others? Reflect for a moment on what your own sensations would be, were you to hear that I was even debating on a proposal to turn you out of your farms and give them to others?"

William's primary interest was how, although Roman Dutch Law was retained, a new Charter eliminated the whole existing system of the administration of justice, both legislative and civil. A Supreme Court with a Chief Justice and three judges who were independent from any political persuasion was created. Judges were given lucrative remuneration and were trained as lawyers. William himself was made an advocate of the Supreme Court. He had often considered his future regarding his career and whether he would want to be a judge but finally decided he didn't want to sit in judgment but rather to prosecute or defend clients. He still had his strong desire to help those less fortunate and taken advantage of, or those who were injured by theft, bodily harm, arson and broken contracts. Law meant retribution, returning victims to their former completeness.

Although Roman Dutch law was retained, William discovered that as an attorney general he would be in charge of fiscal matters and use the style and format of British procedures which included trial by jury. He hadn't fully appreciated that. Also, as local magistrates throughout the region couldn't try cases of a complicated nature, both civil and criminal, these would be heard by attorneys from the Cape in the form of a circuit court and these men would travel around the Eastern Province to assist the magistrates or "heemraden" or "landdrosts". The Afrikaners resented this loss of the one form of representation left to them.

Napier had called William to a meeting and briefed him that it was now time for him to travel to the Eastern Cape and to hear the grievances of the Afrikaner or British colonists there. "You'll be my eyes and ears, Ropert. The trials that you'll prosecute or defend are coincidental. We should endeavour to restrain farmers from leaving the Frontier and leaving it undefended."

"I can understand completely, Sir. If that happened, the remaining colonists would be vulnerable to even more attacks from across the border. I've heard that the Xhosa are no longer mollified by glass beads and trinkets. The growing herds of cattle belonging to the settlers, are proving too much of a temptation."

"Correct," Napier nodded, "If the Xhosa continue to infiltrate our land and murder farmers, we won't only have an open rebellion by the Frontier farmers but a whole scale war on our hands with the Xhosa. I also want you to draw up treaties for the Griquas who have now claimed for themselves land across the Orange River, East and West Griqualand." The Griquas were people of mixed race and the progeny of KhoiKhoi and the various nationalities that had occupied the Cape. They were ostracised by both peer groups and had grown in number over the two centuries of occupation. Their leaders were Adam Kok and WaterBoer, each of whom had a substantial number of followers.

This excited William, "What you ask is daunting to say the least, Sir. I'll most certainly do my utmost to assist you in both regards."

"I wouldn't have given you the task had I not believed that you have now fully familiarised yourself with affairs of the colony. I believe you have even been learning Dutch and Afrikaans. You'll be able to put that to good use. You'll no doubt be staying with Afrikaner families from time to time when you are travelling between the main towns." Napier liked the young man with his boyish good looks and his fair hair was almost blond already bleached by the African sun.

The two men discussed the format of the treaties which would define borders. Napier mentioned to William that a further treaty was required along the same lines and would need to be negotiated with Moshweshwe, the chief of the Basutos or Ba Sotho tribe who lived in the mountain kingdom of Basutoland.

William didn't know that Napier had only heard praise for William from his advisors. He became known as being a modest individual both courteous and sympathetic and he inspired respect and those who came into contact with him were impressed with his confidence and generosity. One quote was well-known as William had always maintained that his work was to "prosecute not persecute". Already he was known for his impartiality regarding race, religion or language. He stood up for Coloureds especially as he had learnt much about them from his housekeeper, Fatima, who was Coloured person.

Fairbairn had also added his praise for William when he had the Governor's ear and felt that William, had he been in the Cape in earlier times would have mitigated the view and prejudices of Cape Society. William also had the optimism that the Africans and Coloureds would not overthrow the Europeans. He believed that those groups would "climb the ladder of civilisation," and be drawn into society that would be colour-blind. However, if the black and coloured groups were driven to war with the Colony, a "darkness, thick darkness, rests upon the future".

When William returned home that evening, he couldn't contain his excitement but Hugh was worried, "It'll be dangerous both in terrain and with the local tribes. I should like to travel with you. I can assist in preparing the legal documents." Hugh sighed. William had an increasing load on his shoulders especially juggling his legal position with his political one.

Both men sat down to a dinner of pickle fish which Fatima had prepared from fine steenbras fish. The piquant onions, curry and vinegar turned the fish into a delight to eat. Fatima also looked after the two bachelors' every need with the housekeeping.

"Have you told Nerina that you'll be away for the next few months?" Hugh put down his knife and fork and contemplated what lay ahead for them.

The wild Frontier wasn't a jot like the magnificent Cape or gentle Ireland according to what he had heard. It would be rough dusty terrain on horseback most of the way.

"I'll visit her before we leave," William was growing fond of the young woman but the past few months had been overwhelmingly busy and he realised he had neglected her shamefully. It was, however, a man's lot to work and it was a woman's lot to civilise him in manners and religious devotion and provide maternal caring for the family and dedication for education, nourishment and leisure. A woman was a joy to behold and a promise for the future.

-o0o-

The kitchen was a cosy place at Geseende Huis and Nerina was sewing at the rough-hewn yellowwood table which had been in the family many years. Her ancestors had carved their initials on the wood on the sides. Lily, Leah's daughter, was sitting at the table in front of a very large white, enamelled basin shelling peas. Just then Leah arrived home from Sea Point village where she had delivered messages from Mrs Smith to the butcher, baker and dairy farmer. Liesbet left the choice of vegetables for the day to Leah herself. Nerina used to accompany Leah when she was much younger and she could still smell the fresh meat and sawdust of the butchers, the warm aroma of freshly baked bread and the sweetness of the milk at the dairy. Now it wasn't seemly to do one's grocery shopping oneself. This afternoon, Liesbet had asked for privacy to pray and study her Bible on her own in the parlour. For Nerina it was a moment to escape from her mother's constant scrutiny of everything she did.

A cat sunned itself on a windowsill and dogs lay at Nerina's feet. Petrus, the gardener came through the screen door and deposited before them a basketful of new potatoes he had just dug up and the rich, loamy soil still clung to the swollen root vegetable.

"Good day, Missie," he raised a grimy hat in Nerina's direction and his toothless smile was full of gladness, what for he didn't know! He held out his hand and in his palm lay six golden bulbs, "I dug up these up as the nonnie asked. You want to plant them somewhere? I can do that for you!"

Nerina smiled and greeted him as warmly, "No, I will keep these. I have a plan for them!"

"Leah, you must bring in the washing, rain is on its way," he warned the matronly cook, straightened himself and limped away, his arthritis bothering him which always was a sign of a change in the weather.

Leah, Lily and Nerina rushed outside where the colourful array of clothes billowed in the wind. The washing smelt fresh and the linen was firm with old starch. Far below them, the sea was being whipped up and the waves reached the beach with foam and spray spreading over the sand like fans of lace.

Tea was made and bread and butter for Liesbet was prepared and placed on a silver tray with a starched tray cloth embroidered intricately with geometric designs. Leah poured the tea and everyone grew silent to enjoy the leisure break. "How is your young man, Nerina? You haven't mentioned him for a while," Leah had been taken into Nerina's confidence a long time ago.

"He has been told to go the Frontier on the Governor's business and to act as king prosecutor in the rural courts. Oh, Leah, how can I bear this separation?"

"Now then, Miss, you haven't seen much of him these last few months," Leah was worried that the courtship was on the wane. She hoped that the gentleman wasn't just encroaching on the young madam's goodwill regarding teaching him languages.

"He has written regularly. He has been busy in many court cases. He has said that in the first three months after he arrived here, he had a hundred cases. It's very lucrative business, he has told me. Did you know that he is partially responsible to the slums being cleaned and the sewers built? Running water is now available. He is hoping there'll now be less disease. I heard of some children dying of malaria in the past."

"That garment you are making is for a child, isn't it?" Leah was folding the washing. Tomorrow was ironing day. Leah prayed to Allah in gratitude that she and her family were never that destitute to live in such a place as the slum. She liked the rows of terraced little flat-roofed houses, painted in pastel colours that clung to the Mountain. The Malay people had built those for themselves. She prided herself on keeping her house spotless in the little time she had for looking after it. She had a low wall around the front and often sat in her little flower garden. People's washing would be hung from one house to the one opposite but it was a clean, cheerful place. The Mosque and minaret could be seen against the blue sky.

"I know what you are thinking! No, I believe it's unlucky to make clothes for children for my bottom drawer. It's tempting fate too much. Mr Ropert long ago asked me to make clothes for the orphans. I managed to convince my friends to sew dresses, trousers and shirts, too. We have become a home industry! Mr Ropert has said that the orphans parade around their accommodation now with great pride."

Nerina's "bottom drawer" was an old camphor-wood "kist" and it contained linen, towels, tea towels, crocheted doilies, China items, all her worldly treasures for when she got married and created her own home.

"Miss, it doesn't worry you that this man is sixteen years older than you? What about a nice young man from the army or a merchant's son?" Leah was like a hen fussing around her chicks. Her gaze passed on to her own daughter, Lily who was working away quietly.

The two young women couldn't be more different, Nerina who was so fair with her hair, shiny and straight done up in a stylish knot with tendrils of hair curling down her cheek and neck, and Lily as brown as polished mahogany wood, the sort which her husband crafted into ornate furniture. Lily with her unmanageable hair but oh, the beauty of her daughter, with her high cheekbones and full mouth and perfect white teeth. However, her hands already showed her station in life. They weren't protected by gloves or pampered with lotions so that when a man bends over to kiss a lady's hand, it's as soft as white gladiolus' flowers and perfumed with lavender soap. Rings for ornamentation shone on those pale fingers where the nails were manicured and buffed to shine healthily. Such is the lot of being locked into one's station in life.

"Age doesn't matter, Leah, when two people love each other!" Nerina would still love William even if he were an elderly man. The goodness in him is what she loved. So what if he aged quicker than she would. She would care for him no matter what infirmity came along.

"How long are you going to see this man before he asks you to marry him," Leah had come straight to the point. Nerina had known Mr Ropert for a year now. Mind, she had heard of long engagements but they certainly would put a strain on any woman waiting while her beauty starts to wane and interest from prospective suitors equally diminishes.

"My Mama says he's a man of means and he's successful, attractive – madly so - and we can talk about all sorts of things. Sometimes he seems surprised by my comments. I think he has enjoyed male company for too long and other men have been disparaging about a woman's intellect!"

"When you marry, Lily can become your house-maid. She's a quick learner and like you she has a good brain although unlettered. She would be honest, reliable and would only want to please you. Where would you live?" Leah's talk made Lily uncomfortable.

"He has a house in Rondebosch and he has promised to invite my parents and me there when he returns from the Frontier. It's apparently well suited for his needs. He has a male companion from his school days living with him. I've met him and he's a strange man. I catch him looking at me and it's almost as though he doesn't approve of me," Nerina sighed. Fate would have to take a hand in designing her future.

Leah grew silent. She hid her misgivings well.

-o0o-

CHAPTER 9

In his first year at the Cape it seemed to William the world was spinning too fast but somehow he succeeded in maintaining his punishing work schedule. The new adventure to the Eastern Frontier with Justice Whyle accompanied by Ebden, a merchant and member of the Legislative Council, Van Ryneveld, Edward Wild and Roselt who would act as interpreter on the court circuit, meant considerable preparation and organisation which, thankfully, he could hand over to Hugh. They packed for this trip and tried to keep papers and clothing to the minimum considering they would travel on horseback once reaching Stellenbosch by coach over the sandy plain of the Cape Flats. The courtroom paraphernalia was being transported in an ox wagon sent on ahead some days previously. They would set up the courtroom "stage" in any large room available wherever they went. Landdrosts or magistrates would also be at hand.

At their first destination he and Hugh gratefully booked into a pleasant boarding house in the main street where magnificent oak trees shaded the pavements with splashes of indigo and the white gables of the houses shaped like a hat Dutch women wore were quaint. The buildings were all thatched and the layout of the town was thoughtfully designed. The Judge and the others made their own arrangements for the duration. There were several whitewashed official buildings and a street of colourful shops. The small town of Stellenbosch was surrounded by towering blue mountains where vineyards covered their eastern slopes like a green shawl.

They spent two weeks of court duties before finding fresh horses for the long and gruelling trip to Beaufort West which lay in the semi desert of the interior plateau.

"I'll have that one", the Judge pointed to a lively black stallion, "I like a spirited stallion," The Judge insisted.

He was somewhat portly but was no fool at handling a horse. After accepting offers of help to get him into the saddle, he charged down the main street. Hardly out of town, a storm brewed up and Justice Whyle's horse reared up at the sound of thunder.

"Down you coward!" The Judge shouted, "Who the hell chose this horse? Down, I say!"

William and Hugh tried to keep their own mounts steady and were careful not to laugh at the scene.

"Watch out," William shouted but it was too late. The stallion proceeded to throw the Judge out of his saddle and he ended up "burying his nose for some depth in the soft clay" as William, with great humour, told everyone when they returned to Cape Town.

The Judge was no worse for wear and was even good-humoured about his accident.

The Karoo had its own charm with its flat, sandy vistas with occasional hillocks of stone placed randomly on its dry expanse of the plain. Birds and insects were plentiful and occasionally they saw buck and black-backed jackals which were remarkably similar to foxes back in England. They even witnessed a swarm of locusts like a dark purple cloud in the distance and they could hear the hum of the millions of wings as the insects came closer.

They arrived in Beaufort West a few days later having broken their journey by camping out on the veldt. This proved to be a novel experience for Justice Whyle. Their bodies ached and they were saddle-sore, a result of which meant they didn't look forward to the next day's journey. The pack horses were freed of their load and their Hottentot employees erected several tents and a fire was lit for cooking and brewing strong coffee in a blackened pot that hung from a tripod over the flames.

While they rested William said to the group, "When we return to Cape Town, we must lobby for the development of roads in the mountain passes in order to make these outlying districts more accessible." He had been shocked at the dangerous conditions. In repose, he took out his journal and began sketching the scene of the camp.

The following day they donned their finery and the court was held in an improvised room in a school. The sun outside was harsh washing out the interior of the "court" as eyes adjusted to the gloom. Farmers in this part were wealthy and content and grievances were mainly to do with their labourers. Occasionally family disputes had to be settled in court. William was soon aware that the British merchants in Cape Town had a significant advantage over the local merchants.

The sheep farmers with whom William came into contact, complained vociferously to him about labour problems. Herders weren't reliable.

"Conditions here have been appalling since the abolition of slavery," said one man, "You have no idea how difficult it is to farm without labourers. For a farmer on his own in these regions life is hell. I'm thirty eight and I've lost all my strength."

Another man interrupted, "I haven't enough food for my family as the farm is not yielding its full potential!"

One man cornered William in the street, "The problem is acute and won't go away no matter how hard you officials argue. Our labourers become vagrants and are totally unreliable!"

William mulled over the problem and began formulating a restructure of the current system to enable employers to sue for breach of contract. The farmers needed to be mollified and the labour situation required urgent attention.

The week passed and they soon they were in the saddle again, riding towards Graaff Reinet, the market-town. When they arrived William was pleasantly surprised to find it was a picturesque town, well laid out with neat rows of whitewashed and pastel-coloured cottages and an inn with stables. Shops provided the farmers with all their worldly goods. The citizens of the town were very hospitable and William, Hugh and their travelling companions were invited to spend the night with Hendrik du Toit, a local farmer who was Afrikaans, on his farm, Allemanskraal just outside the town.

The accommodation was first class and their horses were given a wash and allowed fresh hay and oats. The animals drank thirstily and then relaxed into feeding. Hugh and he would be able to rest in comfort after an arduous part of their trip. Mrs du Toit showed them two neat if not Spartan bedrooms and provided each with a basin and urn of warm water so that they could wash and improve their appearance. Their rooms looked out over the courtyard where pots of flowers were arranged on the flagstones. After refreshing themselves they came down to the dining room and sat down at a long wooden table where the family and their other guests were waiting. Family names had been carved on the sides the stinkwood.

Hendrik a tall giant of a man with a black beard and booming voice, stood and read a verse out of the family Bible and then said grace, after which and on cue, the maid brought in a large platter on which sat the cooked, skinned head of a buck. The family had chosen the choicest part of the buck which Hendrik had shot that afternoon, as their special treat for their guests as well as a '*bredie*', tomato stew. Johan offered William an eye from the gruesome head.

"Have you ever tasted this part of an animal?" He laughed, "I can say it's very good, in fact, the best!"

The children giggled before being scolded by their mother.

William smiled politely but the spectacle was too much to bear and his horror was plain for all to see, "If you don't mind, I would rather not."

"I'll try it," said Hugh stepping into the brink, "It's not unlike oysters, slimy and tough", he whispered to William who turned pale.

"I would like to try the tomato *bredie,* Mrs du Toit," William managed a smile. He enjoyed the stew very much indeed, trying hard not to think what the others were tucking into with such relish. Mrs du Toit finished off the meal with a delicious *melktert* or milk custard tart.

Johan began to talk about the Frontier wars and how the last treaty with the Xhosa was constantly flouted by raids across the border. Sometimes the Xhosas would drive off the farmers' cattle and leave the farmhouses and cultivated fields alone but sometimes it was a case of slash and burn. Farmers and their families lived in constant fear. Feelings ran high in this part of the Colony and William had to admit that the tour of the Frontier was opening his eyes to many of the inherent problems the Government at the Cape had to face.

-o0o-

The next week was filled with cases to prosecute with men and women coming to William requesting his help. A farmer who was returning to the Cape asked if he could leave his common-law, Griqua wife and marry a White woman in the Cape instead. William made his disapproval and distaste known. The Griqua woman was his wife and there could be no further argument about the matter.

A widow came to him for help in retrieving her farm which had been stolen from her by her brother-in-law. She had to admit that she couldn't afford her legal fees. William agreed to prosecute the brother-in-law, with no charge being levied. He found himself often waiving his fee when he trusted the provenance of his clients.

William was making enough money personally and he and Hugh were investing money in the mercantile ventures in Cape Town. He had been saddened to receive a moving letter from his father before embarking on this trip. Rev. Ropert was suffering a certain amount of hardship since retiring and wondered if his son could help him and his wife.

William, my son,

It pains me to ask you for your help in a very personal matter. You may know that I have retired from my ministry for eleven months now and with the lowly stipend I am finding I have financial shortfalls. Eliza and two of the boys, McBride and Frank are still living at home so I need to put food on the table and clothe them but I can no longer afford to keep them in the same manner to which they have been accustomed. McBride will soon be leaving for the seminary but Frank insists on becoming a merchant, a rash dream. Eliza has heard from Fanny that you are doing very well and have lucrative investments. If I didn't think you had the means to help me, I would have never have considered sending this begging letter. I know from old that you have the most generous heart and I also know you will not be offended.

I have had the pleasure of being proud of my offspring, particularly you, William. The joy of your success is emblazoned on my heart.

Your loving father.

William had immediately cashed shares and sent the money, distraught at his father's circumstances. He also berated himself for not having the imagination to foresee such a development. He had suggested Frank should sail to the Cape where he could soon glean the harvest of buying and selling goods and sending his wares back to England.

He was grateful for Hugh's company on this trip as in a strange way, being away from the Cape crystallised his current position with regard to those that mattered to him. He promised himself he would send Fanny a long letter once he returned to Rondebosch. He had a longing to see Nerina Smith but in the meantime Hugh's companionship was a salve to his pain.

-o0o-

With sober realisation that they had been on the road around the country for three months both William and Hugh were now tired of the routine cases, the enduring disputes between man and his fellow man. In all the cases, though, William never stinted in obtaining evidence and wielding his fine intellect against the defendants' advocates.

They now visited Cradock. "Someone should have warned us that this town is scruffy and down at heal.   It's a disappointment especially after Graaff Reinet," he muttered to Hugh. "To think how we mustered all our strength to cross that treacherous pass between George and the Longkloof only to reach this mediocre town." William complained grumpily.

He relived the event.

"We started off along the trail up the mountain at sunrise with the deep shadow of the mountain leaving the lee side still in night. By mid-morning the track was a forty five degree angle and we had to urge the pack horses onwards. After hours of straining upwards each foot along the way, we were on a narrow ledge of rock with splinters of stone as sharp as knapped flint stone back home and rocks gleamed like gold and amethyst in the sunlight. Underfoot every step forward fell on material that shifted and the rush of falling shale was like the berg's deep exhalation of breath. We took our lives in our hands and looked down into the gully and saw the wreckage of broken wagons and the bleached bones of oxen. Near the apex of the mountain we joined the wagon train ahead of us and as the team of twelve oxen strained and shook as the animals tried to find footholds, we came in the nick of time to the aid of the anxious farmer. His Hottentot servants pulled at ropes tied to the team of oxen and one cracked a long whip over the heads of the animals whose heads shot up and eyes rolled under their foot long horns. Their nostrils gaped as they sucked in the dusty air. We tied ropes to the wagon and with our horses pulled the wagon away from the edge. It was a miracle we weren't all pulled over the edge to our deaths. The farmer's wife walked along behind us with her children who were as nimble as goats. Aloes grew everywhere like striking candelabras of vermilion flowers and thick leaves that were serrated on their edges. Colourful bejewelled sunbirds like humming birds flew from one living sculpture to the next with their long curved beaks ideal for drinking the nectar from trumpet shaped florets, the colour of red rubies. As we crossed the summit and began the downward journey the scene changed from dusty plateau to a verdant forest and ahead was the next plain to traverse."

William closed his journal and put it away in his writing slope and confided in Hugh, "All I had ever heard or read of this infernal road proved nothing to the horrible reality. It would require a goat of some agility to clamber over it with anything like ease." Their next destination was Cradock where they were given a roof over their heads by the Van Rensbergs. They also stayed with Gilfillan, the magistrate of Cradock who entertained them more lavishly.

"Gilfillan is wanting to get in your good books, William. I'm sure he would like an official appointment at the Cape!" Hugh laughed.

Another town that William was pleased to see the back of was Colesberg. They and the rest of the Circuit Court, proceeded to Somerset East and on to Graham's Town. To reach it, another tortuous track this time through the Gannahoek Pass had to be traversed. William felt they were taking their lives in their own hands. It was rumoured that Graham's Town wanted to be the capital of its own Colony of 1820 British settlers.

Emigrants from Ireland and Scotland who had found themselves hounded off their lands by the English, had answered the Government's call for farmers and tradesmen to create a British colony on the Eastern Frontier of the Cape. Unknown to them they were to be settled in the Suurveld which had been a no man's land at the east end of the Frontier and would be a first line of defence to ward off the marauding Xhosa people to the east of the Great Fish River. When they landed at Algoa Bay, they were met by the Boers would offer to transport the new families to their assigned land. At first they spent the summer months camping in tents while they planted crops and built their small, simple houses of reeds and mud whitewashed to look quite quaint. They had been duped into becoming a ragtag militia to guard their farms. They now wanted their own jurisdiction and their own parliament as they felt the Government at the Cape was too removed by distance and inclination to listen to their problems.

On reaching Graham's Town William offered up a prayer of thanks. It was a lovely town and very English with cottages rendered with plaster and painted white. It was totally different to the towns further to the north-west. The climate was more pleasant, too. The heat on the plateau had been uncomfortable and dusty, the houses brown with glinting corrugated iron roofs.

In Graham's Town, William and Hugh soon got to know the many officials and William formed lasting friendships. Talk of home, made him long for Fanny, his family and the green lush Irish countryside, the rivers, lakes and valleys.

The mayor gave William a welcoming dinner and William admitted to Hugh during the meal, "Who could wish for more kindness. I've been treated like the son of an Irish king!"

Assessing their progress so far, William was pleased that he had made some good personal relationships in various parts of the country.

A butler approached their host, James Bartholomew a portly banker, "Sir, your other special guest has arrived at last and sends his sincere apologies but he was waylaid by a broken wheel."

James threw his napkin on the table and strutted out of the room. When he returned with the mystery guest he said, "I believe you two are friends!"

"That's stretching it a bit," The man replied sardonically.

William felt his heart miss a beat and turned quite pale.

"You!" He could only manage the one syllable.

"Yes, it's me. I always have a habit of turning up like the proverbial bad penny," Roland Craven said with the tone of voice that suggested he knew what outcome his arrival would have on certain of the guests. He and William were obliged to shake hands. William felt he would be dining with the Devil, himself.

Roland was every bit the son of a Lord tonight. He was splendidly dressed with a white tie, a brocade cumber-band, silk shirt and cutaway velvet jacket but his shocking red hair was untamed as usual. His russet eyes flashed and he bent to whisper in William's ear.

"There, there, stop pursing those cupid-bow lips, pretty boy!" He made sure what he said was only for William's ears.

With admirable self-control, William smiled and continued being the entertaining raconteur and the gathering was roaring with guffaws at the end of each punch-line.

When it was time to leave, William saw Roland leave ahead of them as he made his excuses too. William and Hugh breathed in the cold night air as they stepped into the blackness with the stars blinking brightly. A form loomed up in front of them and they were shocked to see the menacing figure of Roland.

"The last time we met you saw fit to threaten me, Ropert." He hissed.

"I seem to recall that it was you who swore you would have me when you were released. You had to travel far to find me!" William whispered back, livid that he had been taken so by surprise.

"You see," Roland pressed his face into his sworn enemy's personal space which everyone respected except Roland.

"I was en route to India," He informed William, "when we chanced to land at Port Elizabeth which by the way is not much of a port. I heard all about the rich pickings to be had in the vicinity so I thought, why go all the way to India to make my fortune and then I heard that you just happened to be in the Cape and my mind was made up. So you see I have crossed oceans to find you by chance. Fortune is kind to me!"

"Fortune is mine," William retorted, "It is better to sniff your prey on the wind and to keep upwind of him in case the opportunity arises to aim and fire before he takes the advantage."

Roland sneered and struck William's cheek with a fine leather glove, "You will defend your honour, Ropert. This has been a long time coming. I have enjoyed the fun of baiting you and seeing you rise to my jibes."

William's anger made him throw caution to the wind, "Pistols at dawn on the banks of the Buffalo River at the new stone bridge on this side of the water," He heard himself say followed by a burst of words which he couldn't recognise were his own, "Craven, name your second."

Roland pushed him and sent him staggering, "It will be a pleasure."

William's face was suffused with blood but around his mouth there was the pallor of steadfastness and pent up aggression.

"William, duels are illegal. What do you think you are doing! Remember who you are. Of all people you are the one who should uphold the law," Hugh rushed to his friend's side.

"No one will know. I swear you to secrecy, Craven," William said.

"I give you my word. However, you won't live beyond the dawn, so your word is worthless to me," Roland jibed.

He turned on his heel, "I'm going to need my beauty sleep if we have to travel so far, so farewell. We will see what the morning brings," Roland bowed and left with a swagger.

-o0o-

As he contemplated the wisdom of the duel, William sat down in the guest house and quickly took out his writing slope and smoothed the paper on the leather mounted on its burred walnut sheen. His heart was racing but he was not afraid. Logic had flown out of the window and excitement, darting thoughts and breathlessness had to be subdued before he could dip his pen into the black inkwell:

My dear Fanny,

I have undertaken a foolhardy mission while antagonised by Roland Craven who, would you believe, is here in Graham's Town. It's a matter of honour and I can see you admonishing me for such male impetuosity and arrogant pride. While out in Africa, ruthless unbridled actions seem to pulse through otherwise sensible men. We are back to ancestral values of the survival of the fittest and I am laying claim to the positive outcome of the duel.

As I take these moments to make my peace with you and with my Maker, I urge you to forgive me should this be the last letter I may ever write. Now with nothing more to lose, I desire to acknowledge my deep and abiding love for you, my beloved companion whom I have so thoughtlessly abandoned for the fruits of a new official position in a land so far away. Sweet Heart, you have been a spirit accompanying me like a guardian angel over the past year through problems and through great happiness and I now in all seriousness wish to have you to hold and cherish throughout both our lives. I honour and worship you with body and soul and love you forever more,

Your humble and passionate,

William.

Not long thereafter, Hugh and William were back in the saddle galloping towards the languorous Buffalo River. William had found another willing second man and a doctor followed some distance behind them in a horse and cart. He would declare death or to tend to the wounded. Both citizens were sworn to secrecy.

 When they arrived at the docile river, the sun was rising and the sandbanks were soon tinged pink and the water reflected the night sky melting away into the early morning turquoise ribbons of the sunrise. The dawn chorus began with red bishop finches and yellow weaver-birds noisily rattling the bulrushes flying from stalk to stalk while black widow birds with their foot-long tail feathers flapped upwards with tortured wing-beats which made their flight dip and lift almost as though the birds were in too much pain to fly.

They arrived ahead of Roland who soon rode in with his horse lathered with foaming saliva and his two seconds in hot pursuit. He jumped out of his stirrups and breathing deeply uttered,

"There's no point in pussyfooting. Let's get this over and done with," He was matter of fact and his blood was pounding with the thrill of it all.

"My desire, too," William couldn't quite believe what he was about to do. The seconds loaded and checked the two pistols and the two adversaries paced out the yards while the doctor held a large white handkerchief aloft which hardly waved as the air was so still. The men turned to face one another. The birds were suddenly silent and the dawn halted with Aurora looking on while pagan gods wagered bets. On the bank, a band of itinerant Xhosas crouched down to watch what a battle between the two men was obviously. Their faces were hidden in the dark silhouette of their bodies…

The doctor dropped the piece of cotton cloth, and both William and Roland fired simultaneously. The blasts echoed in the stillness and both men fell to the ground.

"Oh God," Hugh shouted as he ran to William's motionless body, "I'll never forgive myself if he is dead! William, William," He tried to shake the unconscious man.

He lifted William's torso into his embrace and William roused himself from the shock of feeling the bullet hit his shoulder and travel out the other side of his back, seemingly without harming blood vessels, nerves or bone.

"God, I'm alive! Hugh, I survived!"

The two friends looked at each other's face with sheer relief and William stood up shakily, gingerly trying to protect his left arm. He looked at Roland's body and the seconds fussing over it. Then Roland uncrumpled himself and sat up, crying out with pain.

William could see the red stain flood down Roland's calf. He had shattered his enemy's knee. Roland might never walk again and if he did it would always be with great pain.

The doctor attended to Roland first and worked away to remove the bullet and his patient swore and roared out his annoyance and frustration. Even half a bottle of gin didn't mask the agony.

"Our old scores are settled but make no mistake Ropert, I'll be snapping at your heels, no matter where you go. You'll never know when I'll next strike," Roland glowered up at William's disdainful and cold expression. William didn't deign to reply.

"Get the horses, Hugh," He muttered after the doctor had cleaned and bandaged his shoulder. He followed his friend to where the horses were being untied by the other of his seconds, Major Lilley and he suddenly felt very world-weary.

At the guesthouse back in Graham's Town, William pulled out his portable writing bureau and wrote a second letter to Fanny and a missive to Nerina. He would decide whether to destroy the letter he had hastily written to Fanny the night before and replace it with the new sentiments in the second letter:

My dearest and most precious Fanny,

If you receive this letter it will be with the news that I have survived the duel. To say I have acted foolhardily is probably an understatement but the extreme goading of my loathsome enemy, Roland Craven, turned my common-sense towards courting death with no fear but with an arrogance to challenge Fate to do its worst with me.

I wish again to reveal to you my deepest love for your gracious heart and inquiring mind. I respect, love and cherish you and not a day goes by without my longing for your presence, so feminine and fair. I have been blessed with such friendship for all of my yesterdays but never before been more damned that I am only allowed to desire you from afar. We are hapless lovers like a crusader on a quest and his lady left waiting in a tower for his return.

Farewell, my love, my life.

W.

The second letter was to Nerina. He couldn't tell her that although high in his regard, she had always been second to Fanny.

My dear Nerina,

Please forgive me from the impertinence of almost squandering my life on a silly whim. Pride is man's downfall and I have been a vulnerable servant to that deadly sin. I met my sworn enemy from the past and some unfinished business needed to be conducted. My antagonist's downfall would have freed me from his constant baiting and ending that burden became so all-consuming that I was prepared to offer my life for that opportunity. I beg of you to keep your own counsel about the duel which took place today.

Suddenly, the reality of my relationships with those dear to me, demands that I am more honest with you. I cherish you with my unflinching admiration and my deepest desire is to trust what lies in the future for us which could have lain buried with me, had my life been snuffed out. I am now aware of issues where I must make life-changing decisions. I am learning that one must not put off life but catch it and hold it in one's hand gilding it with every experience that is good and desirable. The sun does rise no matter how hard we would deny it having reason to do so.

I await our reunion sometime soon in the coming weeks.

Yours respectfully

William.

After reading what he had written to both women, he realised he was still torn in different directions by his love for each of them. It was obvious he couldn't decide whom he loved more even after the clarity of emotion and thought that was awakened during his battle with his adversary. Regarding the latter, he would stake his life over and over again as he foresaw that Roland Craven would never disappear from his life while alive. If only, the outcome that morning had been different....

-o0o-

William and Hugh spent a further few days travelling before reaching Port Elizabeth. When they arrived they found a decent boarding house and were soon in their room and William collapsed on the soft mattress to ease the pain in his shoulder. His arm was still quite lame but he had managed to ride his horse. He would consult a doctor and ask him to clean his wound and bind his shoulder with fresh bandages.

As the Court Circuit neared its conclusion, William started to wish he wasn't so popular. His reputation as a prosecutor had gone before him. He had some interesting clients – for instance, the Prussian army captain who wanted advice as to how he could get his wife, who was still in Europe, to join him in the Cape! What law could make that possible? There was also a defamation case about an elderly lady who was supposed to have had a relationship with a young man.

They travelled on to Uitenhage and there at last William felt he was doing what he was paid to do by the British Government. He began working on the treaties for General Napier for making deals with the Griquas and Moshweshwe. He invited the Griqua leaders, Adam Kok whom he found to be a slovenly, sly individual and also WaterBoer whom he liked better, for meetings to discuss the terms of the treaties. Adam Kok arrived at the agreed meeting place near Philipolis on the banks of the Orange River, a mud-baked house with earthen floors and a corrugated iron roof and William's party set out the Treaty on a grimy table. William had donned the official uniform of the Attorney General. Kok and William sat down and the former spoke coarsely, spitting chewed tobacco on the floor, before signing his name below William's signature, his beady eyes darting around the room.

As soon as the ink dried, William's party set out for the last leg of the four month long trek around the Frontier. William, the two clerks, an interpreter and Hugh rode out on horseback to the kingdom of the Ba Sotho people where their king was ensconced on the flat-topped summit of ' the mountain of the night', Thaba Bosiu, which William was to sketch in his Journal. This strategic position was situated in amongst the lofty citadel of peaks which reminded William of paintings of the Cairngorms in Scotland. The mountainside was decorated with the bee hive shaped grass huts much like those of the Hottentots, made with flexible saplings set into the earth in a circle and tied together at the top with string made from plant fibres, interlaced with wickerwork and then covered with woven grass mats making the building warm and dry with a small entrance which could be covered with one of the mats to keep out the chill that was experienced at such a height.

William and his entourage camped at the foot of the mountain and relaxed around a fire as they recovered from their journey, William writing or drawing as usual. Hugh reclined against his saddle and smoked with enjoyment. The plain was virtually unadorned with trees and they counted numerous buck and ostriches, even cheetahs and the blue crane, not unlike the emu and whose feathers Moshweshwe sent to Dingane, chief of the Zulus, their interpreter explained, for his headdress. Moshweshwe whose name was given to him as it was the onomatopoeia of the sound his knife made while in bloody combat as William had learned, finally arrived in all his finery of special feathers from the black Bateleur eagle and a gold headband on his head, a gold necklace with lion fangs and an amulet around his neck, gold arm bracelets and bracelets around each leg. He wore a robe of a sumptuous material that fell in folds around his thighs. He held a carved stick with a knob at one end in the manner of a ceremonial staff. William made a mental note to sketch a portrait of the striking warrior king. Unlike most Africans, William noticed he had a short beard as did many of his warriors. His guards carried shields that were the shape of the silhouette of an eagle soaring in the heavens.

Moshweshwe held himself aloof with the dignity of a man whose reputation was legend and he displayed his strength by showing leniency towards conquered tribes. William found the man before him dignified and highly intelligent. He didn't need the British as he had his own supremacy over all the tribes between the Orange and Vaal rivers and he was rich enough to bestow cattle in herds to friend and enemy alike who were then only required to return offspring of the cattle to him annually thereby strengthening the bonds between the king and his minions, an epitome of an astute politician.

As William in full regalia, explained the Treaty that would allow a peaceful co-existence with the Ba Sotho's and the British, Moshweshwe solemnly put his mark on the document. William sighed with relief. At last, if they all kept their word, the north-eastern Frontier would now be safer. However the east, bordering on the land of the Xhosas, was altogether different. The peace there was wearing thin again as five years had passed since the last Frontier War with them which had kept them at bay but the settlers in the east were being attacked again regularly and time taken to defend their farms prevented them from cultivating their fields and breeding cattle as both could be destroyed or driven away in an attack leaving the colonist little option but to start all over again or to throw in the towel and move into the towns.

-o0o-

At last, he and Hugh arrived back in Cape Town, somewhat older and wiser. They knew they were home when they saw the impressive vista of Table Mountain looking ominous in a thunderstorm. Lightning flashed across the sky. It was almost apocalyptic and it stirred a passion in William. This part of the world wasn't tame, perhaps it never would be. However, it did give him a sense of freedom. The country had more than enough room for vast improvement.

"No people ever ripen till the sun of freedom has begun to shine upon them," he thought to himself. He wanted personal freedom for every individual. Freedom like he had. His education and his beliefs had given him that.

-o0o-

Nerina found herself pining for the man she loved. Her parents were concerned when her appetite disappeared and she lost weight which she could ill afford to do. The circuit William had to make to all the towns must be gruelling, she thought. Sometimes she mused about the man she loved. She hoped when they married and had children that they would have his blue eyes. Sometimes, his humour lit them with a fire and sparkle and at other times, he could show the frustration of not quite meeting his own expectations of himself when she was teaching him.

As he held the books, she would look at his hands. They were neatly manicured. She could imagine them being gentle when they touched her. They could have been musician's hands with their long agile fingers. He talked considerably with his hands in tune with his delivery in an attractive educated Anglo-Irish accent. She longed now to hear his voice. It conveyed so much more than his words.

Liesbet decided that waiting until there was an appropriate time to do things was a waste of time and effort and she began planning for the marriage of her daughter to William. It would occupy Nerina's mind and take her thoughts off the pain of separation that she was feeling, so they spent a couple of months visiting shops in Cape Town. There wasn't just the wedding dress that had to be made, but undergarments, petticoats, new daywear.

After weeks of indecision, finally the materials were purchased. Liesbet knew of an excellent seamstress from the Continent whose creations were regarded as beautifully cut and sewn together. The dresses would take many months to complete but her stitching was the finest in Cape Town. The fittings came and went and Liesbet's intuition proved correct, Nerina's spirits lifted and the happiness flooded back into her eyes. Soon William would be back in his rightful place in the Cape and she longed to be at his side forever. If he ever went away again, she would accompany him rather than wilt in the absence of his being.

At dinner, Liesbet would relate what they had bought or her plans for the next step of the wedding. John Smith, a portly man with a neat beard and a reddened face where his eyes smiled good-naturedly in the folds of his eyelids under bushy eyebrows, would nod his approval and rarely uttered a word to contradict his wife.

"William will have to move from that small house in Rondebosch," Liesbet said to him.

She was in charge as usual, "I've heard that St James, that new seaside village next to Muizenberg, is now the place to reside or else he should look for a suitable house in the Constantia valley. I know you love the Constantia area, Nerina. You never stopped talking about "Groot Constantia" after your visit there."

"Liesbet, don't you think you are being too presumptuous about this wedding and now you are going so far as trying to find a house for your prospective son-in-law?" John said wiping his moustache carefully with a napkin and immediately Liesbet was on the defensive, "We must let Nerina have some say in the matter, John. Besides, see what fun it's for her to make all these plans".

"Mama, these are your plans, not mine," Nerina smiled but nevertheless knew that she was enjoying making preparations for a wedding, "I've heard talk in Town that William has arrived back from his trip to the Frontier. I'm so looking forward to hearing all about his exploits. He loves telling a good story, doesn't he, Father?"

"Yes, my dear, he can hold the attention of everyone in a room when he speaks. The man is a born orator. When I start in my bumbling bursts of trying to explain myself, I wish had been gifted in the same way as William."

Liesbet had an issue that needed attention. She had to have her say about William's friendship with Hugh as she didn't like the fact that their friendship was so deep that it could affect his relationship with her daughter. Nerina must come first in William's affections,

She looked thoughtful and then spoke her mind, "I hope William will see less of Hugh. He won't need Hugh so much once he has you. They can remain good friends but not live in such intimate circumstances as they do now." Liesbet frowned on the friendship of the two men. It was "unnatural".

"But, Mama, they have been together since they were boys. I cannot ask William to put his friend out on the street."

"Hugh has some sort of hold on William. Mark my words no good can come of it." Liesbet rang a silver bell and the maid appeared, to take away their plates and to bring through the dessert, a steamed marmalade pudding and custard sauce.

Nerina's thoughts were about William. How she longed for him to take her in his arms and press his lips on hers. What joy to be embraced and to laugh and dance around a room spontaneously! What would it be like to lie with a man, with William? She would wear a white muslin nightgown, drawn up to the neck with lace and ribbon and he would unbutton it like untying a gift, a precious gift.

-oOo-

CHAPTER 10

Dublin

Once Fanny returned to Dublin, revitalised and more optimistic about her future, life at 2 Blackhall Place in Dublin with its plain dark brick façade, began to reach dizzying heights as John, Delilah and Fanny prepared for the new baby, soon to be born. Delilah took to fainting rather than wearing appropriate clothing for her condition and Fanny often had to bring her round with smelling salts. Eventually Delilah capitulated and behaved with good sense and waddled around the house in housecoats, her two favourites were one of emerald green silk with a paisley pattern with a fringe of black tassels and black embroidery and another of purple satin decorated with a floral pattern of padded satin stitch and seeding edged with geometric patterns and added to these she wore loose-fitting patterned skirts. Her hair had been tamed but was still her crowning glory.

She began spending many hours in the nursery and had ordered an ebony cradle that hung on a simple stand and they made sheets and blankets and a small pillow, all in white and trimmed with satin. They pasted wallpaper with a fairy motif on the walls and arranged toys on shelves and Fanny placed a wooden rocking horse in the corner of the room, her present for her niece or nephew and already Delilah had bought a doll's house, wooden farm animal pieces and a stick horse.

Fanny was making clothes for the baby, that would suit either sex, and the bonnets and dresses of fine muslin took her many hours to stitch. She enjoyed doing 'white-work' for the bonnets and covered the cotton batiste with the finest hand embroidery. An exquisite Christening robe with a high bodice comprising of Valenciennes lace bands sewn together and further embellished with hand embroidery was her favourite as it fell in a cascade of Valenciennes ruffles. Delilah tried to do her part by knitting little white jackets and stockings but she was painstakingly slow and Fanny would nod approval when a garment was completed which delighted the younger woman who would dance clumsily around the drawing room. The two women had become closer the more Delilah needed Fanny's skills and Fanny felt more relaxed than she had done for a long time. It augured well for the future. Her heart-ache for William was now overtaken by the excitement of the imminent arrival of the baby.

-o0o-

They say that babies more often than not arrive during the night and this seemed indeed so when Delilah was awoken by the sudden cramp engulfing her abdomen with such force that she cried out loud. "John, I think you're going to be a father today," She laughed and lit the candle on the bedside table while John struggled to wake up at the God-forsaken hour of two a.m.

"I'll get dressed and go for the doctor," He gave Delilah an affectionate kiss and stroked her stomach that had become still again, "We will make sure that no harm comes to you both," He was frantically worried by what lay ahead in the next few hours and he prayed that his child would be safely delivered with no harm to his lovely wife and their new baby.

He knocked on Fanny's door while still in his nightshirt and holding the candlestick and strange shadows turned his usually benign expression into a theatrical mask. Fanny gasped and realised that the moment they had all been waiting for had come.

"It's time, isn't it?" She yawned pulling her nightgown tighter around her, "I'll sit with Delilah. Do hurry, John. She'll be more at ease if she feels the doctor is in control of the labour." Her lustrous dark brown locks fell around her shoulders and she looked vulnerable and feminine as she caught her reflection in one of the mirrors. She put her hands on her flat stomach and tried to imagine the physical changes

Page | 96

that were happening in Delilah's body. Putting aside her daydreaming and pulling on her gown, she quickly went to sit with Delilah.

"This is it?" Delilah looked at her, flushed with excitement making her green eyes sparkle and their whites shone like pearls in the semi-darkness. She bit her bottom lip to stop it from trembling.

"Yes. You can do this. It's a woman's instinct to know what to do!" Fanny whispered. However, within minutes, another contraction made Delilah cry out and she instinctively panted to ride out the wave of pain. The sequence of calm and storm raged in the sea of the young woman's body, great breakers of agony curled and fell with loud crescendos of demented rage and pleading.

Fanny held Delilah's wet hand and grasped it firmly when another paroxysm of labour contorted her body and she mopped her brow with a damp cloth. She had placed the Chinese screen in front of the fireplace to ward off the heat from the fire which was still flickering like a scene from Dante's Inferno. Fanny watched the coals turn into skulls and demons. The walls of the room depicted a pageant of spirits. The four poster bed with its swags became a ship in a storm. Where was John and the doctor? This baby wanted to be born and wouldn't wait much longer.

"Where is John?" Delilah appealed to Fanny.

"I don't know," Fanny admitted reluctantly, not wanting to distress Delilah any further. She took a tentative look at the young woman's under the covers and could see she was fully dilated, "Delilah, the top of the baby's head is showing. Maybe you should push with the next contraction so that the head can crown then it will be simply a matter of one last push and the baby will be born." Delilah's body lay on the crushed snow white sheets with her arms and legs in unnatural positions and her nightdress was soaked through and her full breasts shone through the muslin. Her chest heaved with exhaustion. "The baby is killing me, Fanny. I want it to come out but it's fighting me. Why doesn't it want to be born?"

At last the doctor, his face lined and his hands veined and arthritic, and John arrived. "We were held up as the river has flooded the roads," John explained.

It was only then that Fanny realised a storm was blowing outside. The doctor took control. Only ten minutes passed when John and Fanny who were waiting outside the bedroom door, could hear the cries of a new born infant. The doctor rushed out with the baby wrapped in a towel, "Take her while I deal with Mama," He placed the new born child in Fanny's arms, "Mr McBride, your wife is bleeding badly." Then he returned to the room using reassuring words to allay the fears of the almost comatose new mother.

"Hello, little one," Fanny whispered to the baby whose eyes were trying to focus on her face, its little fists tightly closed, "You are going to be loved so very much indeed. We'll all take care of you."

In a short time the doctor arrived and hurried to Delilah's side and gave her something to help the placenta to come away. He then staunched the flow of blood with wads of cotton-wool and after some time the bleeding stopped and Delilah fell into a deep sleep. John was afraid she would never wake up again. The bed was stripped of the bloody sheets and towels and fresh bedding arranged around and under the sleeping woman and a fresh sheet was pulled over her to her neck and her arms were arranged as though in prayer on her chest.

"Make sure she doesn't have another confinement for some years," The doctor warned John, "Her body has been badly damaged. She should recover this time but next time, who knows?"

"I will do nothing to harm her in any way. She's my reason for living. Both she and the new baby," John looked across at Fanny who was rocking the little mite backwards and forwards, totally captivated by the small being that had thrust itself into their midst.

"As long as I'm alive, you will be safe. I will make sure that no harm ever comes to you", Fanny breathed the words over the child, inhaling its sweet perfume. The world had suddenly become a place of fairies, magical tales, playing with toys and learning, oh, learning ever so much from the moment of her birth. Fanny prayed that God would always look after this little baby so like one that so nearly, so very nearly could have been hers if life had been different, if she had married and Matthew hadn't been killed. The one person whose baby she would have sold her soul to carry inside her, William, would never know the sacrifice she had made to stay a spinster so that she could be with him. It was more than any woman could bear but she had made the choice herself. So I must blame myself, she chided herself quietly, feeling the peace that holding a baby bestows, wipe away any regrets or blame.

-oOo-

Dawn broke and dispelled the velvet night with its shafts of silvery light making the dew shimmer under the clouds of mist. The rooftops were wet and windows dropped tears staining brick and slate. Fanny aroused herself after only a few hours' sleep to see to the baby. She washed and dressed with a light heart and found herself singing a joyful song when suddenly John burst into her bedroom looking demented.

"Please excuse me bursting in on you like this. It's Delilah – she's taken a turn for the worse. I've asked Jim to prepare Shadow so that I can ride out into the storm to fetch a wet nurse. There's also the baby to see to; she needs you," He stood there with his hands outstretched, beseeching her to come to his aid, "Shouldn't it have had a feed by now?"

"Yes, if Delilah can manage to focus her attention on the little mite," Fanny replied feeling her brother's anxiety transfer itself to her. She didn't know what to expect when she walked into the room where Delilah lay soaked to the skin with fever and thrashing around barely conscious.

"Fanny, promise me you will look after my baby," Delilah grasped Fanny's hand and drew it to her lips to kiss, "Promise me, promise me!" She insisted.

"Of course, Delilah, but you're going to recover. You must believe you will overcome this. Even when there's little hope, faith will conquer all," Fanny bathed the young woman's forehead and wiped away the tears of a mother distraught about her child. She felt salty water well up in her own eyes and spill over as she heard the muffling mews of a little soul becoming aware of its body, clenched fists escaping from the swaddling clothes.

Dr McAllister kept the family at bay. He took one look at the sick woman and immediately knew it was puerperal fever, blood poisoning of the worst kind. It had taken hold and was raging through Delilah's body. Already her breathing was shallow and with a sigh of grim capitulation, he administered a potion that would provide some sense of peace to the dying woman. Childbirth was responsible for the death of so many women and it never ceased to dismay him. His calling was to do the very best for his patients but he felt so ill equipped and ineffectual.

He washed his hands in the basin pouring the water over them and he splashed his face, shaking his head to dispel the horror of death.

He opened the door and let John and Fanny fall on their knees next to the bed, an open coffin. The fire in the hearth was dead and the smell of ash filled the room. The house maid silently entered and went over to the fire to clean out the grate and relight the coals.

"The baby is hungry. I see you have fetched the wet nurse" the Doctor lifted the baby out of the cradle and handed her to Fanny.

A few hours later, they knew it would soon be over and after holding John's gaze for the last time, Delilah's eyes rolled back in her head and her spirit left her body which sank back into the bedding lifeless, liberated from the pain and fear. John sobbed as he placed his head on her chest and Fanny nuzzled the top of the baby's head, wondering what the future would hold. We should call her Amber, she thought, saddened by the thought that Delilah was deprived of even that small act. Just a few hours earlier Fanny had envied Delilah, regretting being unmarried and childless and now a baby was handed to her for safekeeping, cherishing and nurturing, qualities she had in abundance. In the mist of his tears, John noticed in Fanny the adoration a woman feels when she falls in love with her baby. He felt his heart contract and then fill with hope again, hope that he would be the best possible father to his little daughter and together with Fanny, they would still be a family.

After settling the infant down after the wet nurse had left and preparing for bed that night, Fanny sat down to write to William.

"Dearest William,

"We're told that life's a ball of string. Today, I found it has knots that can be untied and those that can't. The ones I couldn't loosen are those forecasting and witnessing Delilah's death in childbirth today, a terrifying and tragic event affecting us all. Another knot that remains firm is John's devotion to her and with the healing of time to his daughter.

One knot I managed to untie was in my own heart when I allowed Delilah's baby to shine into it and banish its darkness. I wish to name her Amber Marigold McBride if John agrees, as I can foretell that she'll have hair the colour of that resin and her personality will be as cheerful as the summer flower. Her dependence on me now for all her needs makes me a mother and this little cherub almost fills the emptiness left inside me following your departure.

"Each baby has the key to our hearts by pouring love into us, creating in us a love of innocence, an adoration for God's creation and for the unequivocal binding of a knot of mother to child. The infant soul has escaped from heaven, a spark from God's fiery radiance, and my receptive spirit is about to be reborn into my golden

age as she sets me free. I need to pour my love for her into an overflowing well of happiness inside her and nurture her as if she were my own.

"Love of my life, share this experiment of love creating love with me.

With my devotion,

Fanny."

Before snuffing out the candle she reached into the cradle next to her bed and felt the slight movement of the baby breathing. Reassured she curled up into a foetal position, hugging herself with contentment.

-oOo-

CHAPTER 11

Spring 1840

Cape Town

When William and Hugh returned to Cape Town, they needed time to recover from the ordeal of the court circuit. They packed a wagon with a tent as well as all the utensils and bedding required for a week at Cape Point, the very tip of the Peninsula. They took their fishing rods and hoped to live off their daily catch. They also packed a wicker basket with rusks, essence of coffee, baking powder and wholemeal flour which when mixed and kneaded could apparently be taken to the lighthouse keeper to be baked in his oven, fresh butter; apples as well as potatoes which could be baked in the fire and cold *frikaddels*, made from shredded steak combined with egg and breadcrumbs, nutmeg, pepper, a little onion and some parsley and hard boiled eggs mixed and fried, were delicious and added to those, a chicken pie was Fatima's contribution to the holiday. Apparently milk could be bought from nomadic Hottentot families who eke out a living on the hills, herding their cattle to fresh pastures.

They made sure they had a kettle and an ample supply of water. Once there they would find enough dry pieces of wood for making a fire. The idea of freedom in the solitary simple life of just living for the day was already boosting their flagging spirits.

"*Carpe diem*!" William rejoiced, "This was a capital plan. I can already taste the salt spray in the air." He cracked a whip and their horses set off at a satisfactory trot.

"On a day like today, I can almost imagine myself in Antrim. It's hard not to miss Ireland with all its complexities. I never thought that the Cape would harbour similar discrepancies. But, both have such beauty that we Irish believed were only reserved for us." Hugh was in his element.

"Enough said. We are our own masters for the next week." William broke into song – a favourite Gaelic tune about forsaken love, with a colourful score that uplifted their hearts as they travelled through the countryside and as the tall mountains ebbed away in the distance, they trundled a long a narrow track of sea-sand to the Point itself. It wasn't a journey for the short sojourn. Cape Point lay beyond Wynberg and Muizenberg, beyond Fish Hoek and Simonstown.

Eventually they arrived at a suitable camping site and knee-haltered the horses once they had rolled in the grass with sheer relief that their work was done. This form of tethering prevented the horses from bolting but afforded them a measure of freedom. Soon the horses were cropping the grass quite happily.

In that week, William relaxed completely for the first time in many months. The two men removed their shirts as they waited on shore for the fish to bite and they soon were tanned a healthy gold of good health with washboard firm chests making their bodies temples for their souls. William's shoulder was healing well but it would leave a scar that would bear testimony to a foolhardy deed. They couldn't swim there as the sea was too rough and the backwash could carry them out beyond the rocks but the smashing waves covered them with spray. The joy of landing galjoen, seabream or steenbras made their efforts worthwhile. They were complete in their isolation.

-oOo-

On the morning of their final day they decided to fish very close to the actual Point where two oceans, the Indian and the Atlantic, mixed in an exchange of warm and cold waters and the sea boiled with plankton and small fish. They had ropes with which to descend from the craggy cliff down to a very small crescent of beach which was only visible at low tide and that day it was spring tide, laying bare the rocks beneath them. They strapped a bag holding their tackle and bait to their backs and slid and scrambled their way down to the white sand. They were hoping to land snoek, barracuda, or larger prey.

After a fruitful morning the tide was coming in fast when a freak wave took them by surprise. William managed to run up the beach but Hugh was caught by the water and the strong rip current pulled him back into deep water. He tumbled like an acrobat and felt his body grind against the ocean floor and then he rose up from the turmoil spluttering as he coughed up water. Dazed he was able to tread water but another wave drew him up and then dashed him downwards. William didn't hesitate, diving into the maelstrom, using their spare rope which he tied to himself while tossing the other end to Hugh who wound it around his chest and then knotted it. William swam strongly back to the last few feet of beach left exposed and pulled Hugh through the bubbling water back to firm land. They hugged and fell down on the sand, their chests heaving and seawater dancing like diamonds on their freckled skin.

There was no time to waste so they bagged their fish and fishing rods and made the slow ascent, rope-climbing upwards to the top of the cliff, stopping on accessible rocks to gather their strength for the next upward manoeuvre. Back at their camp they had to chase off the baboons who were trying to find the food that they had bound up in oilskin bags and tied to the wagon.

"You saved my life out there today," Hugh pulled William to him and kissed him on the cheek and then pushed him away shocked by the love he felt for his friend.

"I did no more than what you would've done if I had been the one in trouble. Think back some decades ago, you saved my life every day at school. Take this as part payment for your role in my growing up more of a man instead of perhaps being scared of my own shadow!" William smiled warmly at his friend and cuffed him on the arm before throwing himself down to prepare a fire and gut the fish which gleamed like silver streaked blades three foot long with the teeth of the predator, sharp and clean, which could efficiently catch sardines in their transient, iridescent shoals.

-o0o-

Cape Town seemed a veritable metropolis when the two men returned to their rooms in St George's Street. Work had accumulated while they were away but William's most pressing engagement was with Governor Napier.

"I've heard nothing but praise for your hard work at the Frontier, Ropert," Napier was affable and pleasant, "I would be grateful if you could brief me about the salient details regarding that part of the Colony."

"The question on nearly everyone's lips was the labour situation and what we were going to do about it," William immediately became earnest, "Vagrancy is a major problem and colonists feel aggrieved that there are no measures to deal with this flouting of their rights by their workers. Thieving and insubordination is rife and some labourers escape to join the Griquas or the Xhosas, offering information to assist the Xhosas in their raids on the settlers' farms. It's therefore not surprising that the farmers want to know what we're going to do about their predicament."

"I would like you to arrange a debate about the labour problems, Ropert. We can't shilly-shally much longer. See if you can get a caucus of members of the Legislative Council together and we'll have it out for once and for all," Napier replied.

The Governor was perturbed as his worst suspicions had been confirmed. He couldn't risk the settlers breaking all ties with the Cape and with England. The Boers and colonists provided the lifeblood of the Colony by producing fresh meat, maize, wheat crops and wool.

"Certainly, Sir, you do realise that our very philosophy is under scrutiny. I fear the labour issues could be a Pandora's Box. We'll hear sentiments that may appear medieval and that the Cape Colony is living in the Dark Ages. It'll be appalling if civilisation here has wound back the clock to those dreadful times in human history." William was deadly serious.

-oOo-

A week later, the men gathered in the Legislative Council Chamber and prepared to seat themselves on either side of a long, gleaming mahogany table. They were all in their dark suits with high collars and bow-ties. Fob watches hung on golden chains. All were clean shaven as that was the fashion of the time. Crystal decanters of fresh water and glasses were at either end of the table.

Governor Napier joined them at the head of the table and gestured for them all to sit down, "Well, Gentlemen, today we'll be starting an extremely important and sensitive debate where we'll be arguing for and against the ethics of this government on issues that are unique to our small world which is so far away from Europe and its ideals. Gentlemen, please begin."

The men attending this session were first and foremost Ebden, in his forties and distinguished in black, silk tie, brightly coloured waistcoat with a narrow face, fashionable sideburns and receding mousy hair and Hamilton Ross with his clean-shaven face, blond hair and fashionable dress also famous for his confidence. Both men were wealthy merchants, John Fairbairn, with his steady gaze, aristocratic good looks with no facial hair bar his fair eyebrows above deep-set eyes stood next to Advocate Cloete who had a ruddy complexion, black bristly eyebrows and a determined mouth and was dressed in legal garb. Then followed Breda, looking as stern as a Calvinist preacher, Hudibras, with a full red beard and a little hair on top with eyes diminutive behind thick glass lenses, William who bore himself erect and serious and Governor Napier, portly and good-humoured who was chairman of the committee.

The Legislative Council, in fact, consisted of six official members and five unofficial members and interestingly, the Boers were unrepresented.

"We all are aware that the Colony is suffering grossly from a labour shortage. This debate is to argue whether we should import labourers from Britain or if you can recommend an alternative source, I would be pleased to hear from you. Hamilton Ross what are your views on the subject?" Napier set the first question to the committee.

Hamilton Ross was a stalwart member of the Cape society and had a hand in any new business venture. He had the ear for anything new burgeoning in the small community. "I'm afraid I believe that English immigration doesn't make economic sense. The wages for an English workforce would be too exorbitant. In fact, I believe the English labourers would more likely be a pest to the Colony and will also do themselves no good."

William got the nod from Napier and he spoke clearly and there was no mistaking his meaning, "The question is, not what sort of labourer my honourable friend would like but what sort of labourer the Dutch Boer as he is generally found, will like. The Boers in general speak favourably of every sort of labour. For instance, if twenty thousand liberated Africans were available, the farmers would be glad to get them".

The argument with Hamilton Ross continued, "If they could get them for nothing!"

"The Boer would rather have the African for nothing than the Englishman for nothing," William countered, "In any case, the Englishman would not work for such wages." William enjoyed a clash of ideas.

It was Ebden's turn at the other end of the long oval mahogany table in the wood-panelled room with its paintings by C.D. Bell and Baines, "It's my opinion that wage levels are already high enough for inducing Englishmen to come and work in the Cape."

"No, I disagree," William was adamant, "that is not correct. I seem to recall that not so long ago you described the African labourers recently arrived as 'savages' and have indulged in some epithets equally unsavoury. The liberated African has no agricultural skill but, on the other hand, how much of the agricultural skill of the English labourer must be useless here for who could attempt to introduce the husbandry of Norfolk into the wilds of Southern Africa? The one has indeed knowledge to acquire but the other has, what is more difficult, knowledge to unlearn."

Hamilton Ross agreed with William, "English immigration doesn't make economic sense as their wages will be too exorbitant. English labourers will end up being a pest to the Colony and do themselves no good." The light from the three sash windows splashed into the room. The expressions on the men's faces were clear to read.

Napier was drawn into the debate, "I believe that the English worker would not adapt well to our South African rural culture when he finds himself away from all his friends and the social intercourse of an English village with no church, no school, no comfortable cottage and garden, no doctor if sick, low wages and a master speaking a language of which he understands nothing. He would certainly be disaffected and probably take to drinking or if safeguarded against that vice up until living in the Cape, he'll find it most difficult to withstand the temptation of drunkenness in a wine growing country. He'll leave his place of work and prefer to reside in towns and villages and therefore the great object of the proposed importation of English labour would be defeated."

Next it was Advocate Cloete's opinion, "Africans are prone to filth and vice whereas our ways are different." He sat back in his chair and his chin was on his chest while he stared at his hands.

Hamilton Ross snorted, "My learned friend has spoken of the immorality and temptations to which Blacks would be exposed in Cape Town, but I maintain that there is not a town in England of its size in which there is less crime and more morality than Cape Town."

Governor Napier, seconded that opinion, "I believe it."

Finally William summed up that people had different capacities for advancement. He added the environmentalist argument that natural skills are shaped by one's environment. He was teetering on the brink of losing his cool control as he wanted to avoid any terms to do with inherent or biological capacity. That would be the ultimate insult to the African people. Nevertheless, he too found himself saying that Africans were a different species to the English species of mankind and could withstand conditions that the English labourer would turn from in disgust or from which they would run away when they couldn't endure the harsh environment.

"I feel that the economics of having African labourers with their keen desire to please as well as their feelings of being given incalculable blessings, far outweigh the disdain of English workers." William added.

Hamilton Ross interjected and offered to ship Prize Free Negroes from St Helena Island off the south-west coast of Africa, at his own cost. He had his own shipping business and wanted to put it to good use. Interestingly, British patrols had often come across slave ships, trading illegally, and had boarded them to free the slaves which were put ashore in Cape Town. Portuguese ships also transported slaves and these were relieved of their human cargo.

John Fairbairn wasn't enthusiastic but concurred with Hamilton Ross, "We regard the introduction of Prize Negroes, from time to time, in moderate numbers as the best practicable mode of enlarging our command of labour."

Advocate Cloete, Ebden, Hudibras and Breda fell into William's camp. They too feared the effects of White racism. Bringing in more Europeans risked creating a feeling of caste in the working class.

His words to the committee were deeply disturbing, "You do realise the foulest and most disgusting of all aristocracies is the wretched aristocracy of skin. White labour is doubtless the best labour where all the mass of labourers are white. But when no human legislation can bring this state of things about, the mixture of Coloured people with Coloured people, may be the most expedient mode of improving your existing labour market for the newcomers cannot possibly look down on those already here, belonging always to the same race and often the same tribe, as they would never dream of regarding their sable brothers as their inferiors."

Hudibras interrupted William, "While I believe that Prize Africans are capable of improvement, they would be decidedly prejudicial to the hewers of wood and drawers of water, who are already in our midst. The Prize Africans would greatly and permanently retard the civilisation, the moral and social improvement of the Coloured races. They would be treated with more contempt and degradation than ever and would sink gradually on the scale of society."

William waved him aside, "Without entering either into physics or metaphysics or investigating the extent of natural capacity, I do not hesitate to say that the African is able to do his work when his employer knows how to set him to his work and that the skill and industry as labourers of the Coloured classes in this Colony exhibit, is as fair a ratio when compared to the skill and industry of their employers, as is usually presented by the classes of master and servant in most other places.

"Talk as we may of stupidity and sloth, I do believe that there is enough in the head and arm of Coloured labourers when the master who is to direct them is found to exert his own faculties and lay his own shoulder to the wheel to draw out the materials of prosperity for them both.

"I'm grievously misled if in his heart of hearts, the genuine Dutch Boer does not look upon English labour with an unfavourable eye. The Boer and English labourers do not speak the same language, their way of working is different, their way of living is different, all their manners and customs are dissimilar. The Boer has some feudal notion of his own importance as a landowner and he does not like to have it intimated by a bare-breeched fellow brought in the other day at the Government's expense that he is looked upon as an absolute ignoramus".

The gathering laughed at William's latter comment but soon the seriousness of the situation returned. A showing of hands proved that the vote had gone William's way. There would be no import of English labour. Was this for the good of the country? He certainly hoped it would be a step in the right direction. Finally it was also agreed that Hill Men from India and Kroomen from Sierra Leone would also be brought to the Colony. All were to serve apprenticeships.

The next point raised was to create a Masters and Servants Ordinance to mollify the Boers and other colonists and to offer them a solution. The employers would have some control over their labourers, with a restraint of movement and disciplinary control. This was across the Colour bar but similarly the labourers would be entitled to protection from ill treatment by their employers. Apprenticeships should be offered and taken up by the Coloured labourers. The basic wage would be fifteen shillings a month plus a wine ration. Oral contracts were binding for one month to one year. Written contracts were required for lengthy contracts. There would be one month's notice with two months' salary for all employees and there would be benefits during sickness. In other words there would be penalties in the form of fines for absence from work without permission from the employer, penalties for theft and broken promises, the rights of both to be protected by a written agreement and notice to be given to free either party from their contracts. Farmers who are found to have inflicted corporal punishment would be liable to fines or worse, and would be brought before a court and could face jail sentences. The Ordinance had a liberalising effect on industrial relations in the colony. Such liberalism was possible because of the Cape's peculiar history, the relative calm and peace, the racial medley and cultural inheritance.

William was saddened by the problems encountered in the Cape. It was a veritable paradise but for the problems of colour. He realised as he mentioned to Hugh later that "The effect of available labour on the economy of the settlement is considerable but it's accelerating the unforeseen transformation of the settlers into a white elite. The differentiation of tasks, skilled and menial, is based on racial lines."

That evening a letter awaited him on the entrance hall dresser and without taking off his jacket, he retired to his study to read it. It was from Fanny and as he read about Fanny's obvious happiness with Amber was blazoned on the page and her delight in the baby made him quell the desire that Amber had been conceived by themselves. He quickly penned a reply:

"My dear Fanny,

Your joy in little Amber is a tonic to my soul. The flame of the brooding loneliness you had been experiencing seems to have been snuffed out by the light of a baby's smile and the music of its cries or unintelligible speech. I am shocked to hear that Delilah was the unlucky victim of the birthing illness and I shall write to John and offer him my condolences. Life grows apace in Cape Town with meetings and court appearances. The mood here is lively and men complete what they set out to accomplish which is rewarding in such a developing colony. I am planning to set in motion marriage plans and with your happiness now coming to the fore, I shall approach the lady with whom I seek to spend the rest of my life. I have been aghast that you can so selflessly agree to such a partnership when you and I have been thwarted by social norms. Surely I should suffer as you have done. But, to have a wife and become a father means I shall lead a more fulfilled life.

I pray you will give me your blessing, Fanny,

Your humble servant,

William."

-o0o-

Feathers flew everywhere in the air as Nerina and Sessy tried to stuff them into pillowcases made out of calico and finally into a large calico slip which Nerina planned she would insert into a decorative cotton cover and sew the pocketing in backstitch thereby creating a Celtic design of her own choice. Her bedroom was soon covered in bits of down. The wooden panelling and beautiful ornamental mirror, plain wooden cross on the wall, the chest of drawers in walnut with bronze handles and its matching fine wardrobe and bed, made a tasteful retreat for the young woman. She always gathered flowers to put on the windowsill.

While sneezing and laughing at the same time she looked in radiant health. At that moment, Leah entered the room with a worried expression on her face although she was the bearer of glad tidings. At last a letter had arrived from William for Nerina. Leah was annoyed with the Attorney General as Nerina had been beside herself with worry and disappointment that he hadn't visited her since his return from the Court Circuit. She had heard from reliable sources that he had taken a week's leave and had left Cape Town for a time to recover his strength before being thrown back into the maelstrom of his life at the Cape. There had been talk that he had an accident on his trip. What the injury was, no one could say. Nor did anyone know that having come within an inch of his life, he had become aware of his own mortality and that his time on earth was not immeasurable…

"My dear Miss Smith, Nerina,

Please accept an apology for my tardiness at writing to you since my return. I've been overwhelmed by events and my affairs. I'm now at liberty to request that you and your parents join me at the Cape Hunt Ball. As you know, I'm not a member of the hunt for ethical reasons but from time to time I ride with the hounds for the exercise and not for the nefarious hunting down of a wild animal. It would be my pleasure to escort you to the Ball on the 6th April 1841.

I look forward to your reply.

Your obedient servant,

William Ropert."

Nerina's spirits rose and a flush appeared on her cheeks. She quickly found her mother who was having her hair intricately arranged by her personal maid, Ruth, Leah's sister. Mother and daughter talked to one another's reflections in the mirror while in front of them the dressing table sparked with cut lead glass and silver backed hairbrushes. Pomade and talcum powder and bottled perfume gave the room her mother's particular scent of which one was immediately aware as her mother swept into a room. Around Liesbet's throat hung a string of large natural pearls which were even more lustrous than her fair skin.

"Mama, we are to go to the Cape Hunt Ball. Isn't that wonderful?! William will escort me and you are invited to join us."

"Well done! The man has not discarded you after all!" Liesbet answered not realising what a cruel thing she had just said, "This calls for a celebration indeed. We'll choose suitable ball-gowns from our wardrobes and plan our behaviour at the Ball as etiquette must be observed and therefore we must study again my little book of advice about how we must behave. We must act with decorum at all times, it's the done thing. Now let me look at you," She pinched Nerina's cheek and prodded her ribcage, "You'll need to put on some weight as you are just flesh and bone. We'll get Leah to prepare egg mixed with sugar beaten up with hot milk for you every day and we should try tortoise soup as it has strong recuperative qualities."

"Heavens no, Mama! I would never have a tortoise killed under any circumstances!" Nerina's eyes were almost too bright as she didn't know whether to laugh or cry.

Later Liesbet joined Nerina in her bedroom and mother and daughter examined the array of garments, some just newly acquired for Nerina's trousseau. A beautiful port wine gown was examined. The satin material was shot with purple and deep red depending how it caught the light and the detail trimmed with cream lace. A slight bustle brought it up to date. Nerina's ivory complexion and lustrous dark hair and dark eyes would set it off admirably.

"We must ask Father to assist us in our dance techniques," said Liesbet, "apparently the quadrille is being replaced by the cotillion and the three step waltz."

"Oh Mama, my heart feels as though it'll burst. This is one of the happiest days of my life." Nerina felt faint. The morning's events had tired her considerably.

-o0o-

William sat in the carriage that was taking him to Seapoint. The horses' dancing hooves clinked on the occasional stone stretch of the dirt road. He had set out well before sunset in order to get to the Smith family in good time to make the trip back to Cape Town in time for the Ball. He was looking handsome although vanity wasn't one of his failings, his hair shone, his eyes and teeth were bright and he was clean-shaven. His hands would not relax and he found that he kept clenching his fists, he was that excited as he had at last made one of the most important decisions in his life. However, he thought soberly he hadn't even discussed the issue with Hugh.

At last, they arrived at Geseende Huis and he took the steps up to the house two at a time. His guests were waiting patiently and after offering him a refreshment, they made their way down to the carriage when William remarked politely on the loveliness of the two women.

"Mr Smith, you are truly blessed to have such beauty to bring pleasure to your eye. I feel truly uplifted to be in the company of these ladies." He smiled charmingly.

"Mr Ropert, I have something for you," Nerina held out her hand and showed him the delicate flower stalk of a Nerine Lily, "I'm named after this flower. Do you mind if I pin it to your jacket?"

William was touched and realised the flowers were a fitting metaphor for Nerina. The florets of the lily were like miniature ballerinas in tutus dancing in a circle.

Nerina decided she would give him the bulbs later to plant in his garden so that he would enjoy their radiance next spring.

On the journey, talking was difficult with the sound of hooves, sea and wind and the four passengers prepared themselves for an enjoyable evening at such an exclusive social event.

The ballroom of the mansion which was the venue was a bright and scintillating expanse of light from many chandeliers reflecting in as many large mirrors. The wooden parquet floor gleamed while the orchestra was tuning up for an evening of entertainment. William ushered them in to the large room and introduced them to his friends and colleagues feeling proud to show Nerina off to Cape society. A tray of sparkling glasses of champagne was presented to his party and everyone enjoyed the bubbles bursting on their tongues and the way the drink loosened their customary inhibitions.

The first dance was a cotillion and William, having practised with Hugh felt he had mastered the steps. For a moment he felt the longing for Fanny as he remembered how she taught him to dance. He invited Nerina to join him on the dance floor and as the music began to direct the dancers, they danced with great aplomb and enjoyment. It was one of many dances and his eyes were always on Nerina. She couldn't escape his gaze and she didn't want to leave his side. Between dances, she stood with a straight back and her long neck held her head with dignity. Her movements in the dances were fluid and she seemed to float on air caught up in William's masterful interpretation of the dance.

Soon it was the last dance of the night and instead of leading her onto the dance floor he danced with her towards the balcony outside. It was their first moment of intimacy without anyone watching them. Down in the garden, William pointed out a phenomenon of nature as darting lights from glow-worms or fireflies were sparks in the pitch-dark. They weren't worms at all but beetles and they glowed to attract a mate.

"It's a remarkable display, don't you think?" William asked her, "If only we humans could do the same. You are glowing tonight, Nerina."

"Am I?" She blushed and turned her head.

"Your glow is wonderful and if you are glowing for me that would be even more wonderful." He said truthfully with a hint of making fun.

"I would be grateful if you would stop teasing me, Mr Ropert."

"I think it's about time that you called me William, don't you think!" He spoke seriously.

The music in the adjoining ballroom faded from their consciousness as William drew her gently into his arms in an embrace. His warmth flooded her soul and her heartbeat was sounding in her ears. His lips touched the top of her head and then he tilted her chin and kissed her passionately on her full lips, coloured and soft as pink rose-petals. Nerina shyly allowed him to taste their sweetness while holding her breath and still trying to maintain control.

As naturally as possible he went down on bended knee, "Nerina, would you do me the honour of becoming my wife?"

Even after all her mother's plans, she hadn't prepared herself for such an event and her emotions were in turmoil. She swallowed hard and tried to keep her head in such a tumultuous rush of relief, love and infatuation, "It would be my honour to say 'yes'. Yes, I'll be most happy to be your wife."

"That's a relief," William laughed and pushed his hand through his hair, "I've been trying to find the courage to propose to you all night. I asked your father for your hand in marriage yesterday at his office and he has given us his blessing. He has kept his promise to keep our agreement secret so that I could surprise you. We must return to the ballroom where I'll announce our betrothal."

William signalled the orchestra for a moment's silence and spoke with joy in his voice and informed the three hundred guests of their forthcoming marriage. Liesbet almost fell into a faint and the whole gathering burst into applause. Nerina had never felt the strong force of such emotions ever before. She was enthralled and felt that such happiness was almost too much for a single mortal to bear.

-o0o-

CHAPTER 12

When William returned home from the ball and the night of personal joy and of celebration, Hugh was already asleep. William would have liked to have shared his news with his friend but he, too, found that he was ready to retire. His thoughts were scattered like a disturbed nest of ants and flashes of Nerina's expressions and snippets of her words kept him awake another hour. When, at last, he finally fell asleep, it was almost dawn and the peaks of the mountains were being gently touched by the saffron rising sun. In the valleys the shadows still lay as dark as night for a while longer.

Hugh was soon up and about and as Saturday and Sunday were Fatima's rest days, he put a pan on the range in which he had laid wood and encouraged the fire to take hold. He found the bacon and eggs in the cool pantry and a loaf that Fatima had left for the weekend. He chuckled to himself. He wasn't that useless in the kitchen.

Soon the bacon aroma wafted through the house and its appetising fragrance broke through to William's sleep-induced torpor. He had probably had too much champagne and gin and tonics the night before. What a night it had been! He sat up in bed as sunlight streaked across the room. Critter, the spaniel, was soon all over him in an effusive display of undying love. William tore himself away and was soon shaving. He gave himself a thorough dousing by plunging his head in the basin of cold water. There was no Fatima there today to bring in a pitcher of warm water. He pulled on his clothes but in a tidy manner, after all one had to appear the gentleman at all times. He grinned, still in a buoyant mood.

When William entered the kitchen, Hugh had laid the kitchen table and presented him with his breakfast, bowing with a flourish, "Your feast awaits you, my esteemed friend," Hugh immediately tucked into the meal. They hardly talked as the matter of satisfying hunger and thirst was uppermost in the two men's minds. At last, they sat back in their chairs and enjoyed the excellent coffee.

"What trouble did you get yourself into last night, William?" Hugh was relaxed and enjoyed being in William's company. His friend was a delight to him and stretched his imagination and kept him informed of all that was happening in the world as a direct result of his contact with the sophisticated Cape society. However, Hugh felt he himself was becoming most knowledgeable about financial matters in which William refused to show much interest until spurred on by him. Sometimes, Hugh felt he was himself too much of an unknown quantity for the people with whom William was accustomed to surround himself. Hugh regretted his own taciturn manner as he had a lot to say about current affairs to William but was hopeless in social discourse considering he lacked William's inherent manners, diplomacy and sensitivity.

"When I tell you what my actions were at the Ball, you must promise not to regale me with your opinions or bad omens".

"This is sounding ominous. Come on, Billy boy, spit it out. You have me sitting here waiting with bated breath." Hugh had an uneasy suspicion that whatever William had done, it was of a magnitude that could tax their very friendship. William was suddenly deadly serious, "I've asked Nerina Smith to marry me!" There, it was out in the open.

"You are fooling me! You bastard, William, I'll have your tongue cut out. You are spinning a yarn just to get my goat. By heck, you are serious. Have you lost your wits, man?" Hugh spluttered as his gulp of coffee went down the wrong way and he had a fit of coughing.

William slapped him on the back till the spasm passed. "You should have let me choke to death," Hugh had caught his breath again, "Did Nerina accept your proposal? By the look of you, you have already answered my question! You do realise, William, that you are old enough to be her father. You are seventeen years her senior. I've heard of older men choosing young brides, but I'm surprised that you are one of them, William. Have you completely lost your mind! I used to admire your common sense but this, this is the most ill-judged thing you have ever done in your life!" Hugh felt as though he had been kicked in the stomach. Such a life-changing decision and not asking his counsel! He was being relegated to a station of casual acquaintance.

William sensed that he had delivered his friend a considerable blow. He was astounded. He knew that Hugh had little time for the Smiths but had no idea that Nerina was so spurned by Hugh.

"What have you got against Nerina? For heaven's sake, Hugh, she is a sensitive, very attractive young woman with a mind of her own."

"A mind of her own! That's rich. We have both found Liesbet Smith very domineering. It's my opinion that Mrs Smith has been behind this from the very start. I used to think their invitations to dinner were a social nicety but that woman has never liked me from the beginning and I can assure you the feeling is mutual! Who do you think writes Nerina's letters to you? Can you hazard a guess? "Mama", of course! Mrs Smith has the character of bagging game unerringly in the matrimonial field."

William shook his head, "You don't know Nerina like I do. All those lessons on Sunday evenings and her conversation do not corroborate what you say. She is intelligent and most pleasing in nature and physical attributes. Any man would be proud to have her on his arm at functions. She'll make an excellent attorney general's wife. I've become very fond of her and there is the question of children and heirs."

Hugh hadn't finished, "You think the John Smith you know, is wealthy and successful? He has kept hidden from friends and business colleagues the true state of his affairs. It's believed that a trader went down in the Atlantic with all his ordered merchandise on board which he was importing to the Cape. It's rumoured that he hadn't had the good sense to arrange insurance for the eventuality of such a disaster and as a result he is in debt, although one wouldn't believe it by the way Mrs Smith spends money.

"Apparently, just lately she has taken Nerina on a spending spree. You may ask why but it's perfectly clear to me that she has been grooming her to be your wife and you never even considered such a set of circumstances. As to Smith himself, I do acquit him of all manoeuvring. That is his wife's trait. You are naïve, William! I may be ill-mannered and inept but you are too inclined to believe in the good in people. You see, that's where we differ!"

William was dumbstruck. He stood up and walked out into the garden to clear his head and the implications of his diatribe with Hugh. Why was Hugh so aggrieved? Was it that he believed that he, William, would somehow turn his back on his life-long friend?

"She'll want you all to herself. What would become of our friendship? I'll no longer have a home with you", Hugh followed him outside. He was desperately hurt and couldn't hide the depth and strength of his feelings.

"Of course, you'll continue to live with Nerina and me. She cannot come between us after all, we are blood brothers. Where the one goes, there goes the other, isn't that what they say." William had never realised that their relationship could be jeopardised by his marriage to Nerina.

"You have no idea, William. You won't only have responsibility for Nerina but you'll have to rescue the whole family and where will that leave you? They'll be parasites on your good nature and your fortune."

"What would you have me do, Hugh? Break off the engagement? Is that what you want? Is this an ultimatum?" William couldn't countenance life without his friend. Their friendship was now being threatened by Hugh refusing to share him with a woman whom William adored, but now that it had come to this dreadful state of affairs, he knew he didn't adore her enough to sacrifice Hugh.

"If you don't break off the engagement, I'll leave the Cape for good and return to Ireland. There would be no reason for me to remain here. I'm here because you wanted me with you. I always said where you go, I'll go too. You have made me what I am, William." Hugh's emotional dependency on William, their love for each other which was a spiritual and emotional symbiosis but wasn't physical, was much stronger than either had fully appreciated, until now.

William felt a huge weight settle on his shoulders. Their friendship was placing an enormous burden on his spirit. Would there ever be a time that he would be free to choose his own desired course in life? Would there be any more women to enter his life and would any one of them be content to share their joined lives with Hugh? William wanted a family. He wanted children and descendants, like any man…any man except Hugh. He took himself into the study and sat down at his desk. He chose a piece of parchment paper and dipped his quill into the inkwell and began to write:

"Dearest Fanny,

I am alone and low in spirit and by writing to the woman I respect and adore above all else, I hope you might restore my faith in my own actions when I receive your reply but with heavy heart I believe you will share my misgivings. Last night I proposed to the woman with whom I have fallen in love and for that I know I have your blessing. Sadly Hugh has informed me that I have made a monstrous blunder by confusing a family's greed for social aggrandizement for an innocent and selfless young woman's love. I am most wretched and know by the time you read this that I shall have rescinded my offer of marriage. Contrary to Hugh's belief, it's my certainty that Nerina will suffer greatly and my heart bleeds for her. Relationships are a riddle and I find myself a callow youth despite my years. Our interaction, Fanny, is as simple as sharing the call of a nightingale or tasting the nectar from a honeysuckle flower or listening to a strain of music. Why is life too complex for us to trust what comes naturally to us and why is it so difficult to discover in others with whom we have to interact, the same elegance and simplicity of our discourse?

Yours truly,

William"

-oOo-

The following two weeks were taken up with many official appointments for William but in any spare moment when he had time to reflect he was haunted by the awful predicament he now faced. He had to tell Nerina as soon as possible that he couldn't marry her. He hadn't seen her since their engagement and was aware that his failure to do so would be causing her anxiety and puzzlement.

At last, on a morning that dawned with foreboding, he knew he couldn't postpone the inevitable any longer. He had been remote with Hugh but couldn't bring back his own spontaneity and light-heartedness which would have eased the situation.

He saddled up his horse which was eager to leave the stable and mounted Knight with a heavy heart. He brought the horse up to a gallop almost immediately and his mind was blank as the images of roads, trees and houses became a blur. He couldn't withhold the tears. What sacrifices had to be made for the sake of his career and for his continued friendship with Hugh!

What he now had to do about Nerina would have dire consequences and he would have to face colleagues and friends and explain himself. However, he decided he would ignore any questions about his personal life. His only explanations would be made to God for whose support he now prayed. Although why God should support him in his actions was debatable. What he was about to do, would be the pinnacle of selfishness, a trait he had never believed he owned. He also came to the conclusion that being cosseted in Dublin in his work environment and home life, had not prepared him well for life in the outside world. He was sadly lacking in some life skills.

Eventually he arrived at "Blessed House" and Leah welcomed him and showed him through to the parlour while she went off to fetch Nerina and her parents.

"The young madam has been waiting for you to call," Leah had no reason to mince her words and her annoyance with him was quite clear, "You have sadly neglected your duties as far as she is concerned. She was so happy and full of plans for the wedding but the last few days…." Her words petered out as she left the room.

Nerina had been in her bedroom trying to read a novel. When Leah brought the news that William was waiting for her downstairs, her spirits rose visibly and the light came back into her eyes, "Oh, Leah, how wonderful. How am I looking? Will I do?"

"Young Madam, you always look fine," Leah was filled with apprehension as William looked nothing like the happy fiancé Nerina was expecting. She wiped a finger over the top of the chest of drawers. It needed dusting.

"Welcome, William," Nerina moved towards him and entered into his personal space of intimacy but he stepped backwards. She had been expecting some show of affection. Furthermore, the suave and usually composed man she thought she knew was now cold and distant. She gestured for him to sit down at the very table they had spent so many hours poring over books when she had taught him so much.

"I've come on necessary business, Nerina. I want you to hear my reasons for what I'm about to say. Please listen carefully," William became flushed with pain and embarrassment, "Nerina, I cannot marry you. I've made a most grievous mistake and thereby I'll now cause you the most terrible pain."

Nerina felt her head swoon but she clung to consciousness. The William she knew would never do something like this. This man was a stranger. Their intimacy was wrecked. She felt her world shatter and found herself looking at him in dumb and uncomprehending appeal.

He saw the dreadful realisation dawn in her usually lustrous, trusting gaze and begged God for the strength to make their discourse as painless as possible.

"I'm far too old to be your husband. I'm old enough to be your father. Already all of society will be remarking on our unsuitability. When you are my age I'll be in my fifties, an old man by comparison. Furthermore, my career demands most of my time and your life would be a lonely one. I'm often required to work well into the night and the Court Circuit will continue as long as I'm chief prosecutor."

She still remained silent but her eyes said everything he would rather he hadn't seen. She was dressed beautifully and sat with her hands folded, unmoving. Her lips didn't quiver. She was frozen like a statue of the Madonna.

"I'll make reparation for my breach of contract. I intend to give your father £2000 to make restitution against the repercussions of my actions."

What he was saying dawned on her. Of course, future suitors would hear that she had been rejected by her fiancé and would wonder what failings she had in her nature or disposition.

Her voice broke as she uttered a few words, "No, William, don't do this to us. I love you more than life itself. Can't you see, you'll be taking away my will to go on living if it means living without you?"

"You must forget me, Nerina. The sort of man who did this to you, isn't worth your love or affection. I just hadn't taken the consequences of my actions into full account."

"And about this, have you taken into account your actions. Have you had the imagination to see what it would do to me?" She showed a flash of her former spirit and he put out a hand to touch her but she pushed it away and looked at her own hand and steadfastly removed his ring from her finger, "Don't pity me, William. Save your pity for someone else. I pray she never experiences this!"

"There never will be anyone else, Nerina. I've sworn to myself that I'll never marry. I intend to keep that promise if it means never having to hurt anyone in the future. You must marry, Nerina, one day. You'll again experience happiness. Have your own family and children. This agony we are both experiencing will pass." William felt his own eyes burn as Nerina ran from the room in tears.

"I never want to see you again!" were her last words to him.

He called after her, "Don't let this change you, Nerina. You must stay the way you were before tonight. I'll always love you!" However, she never heard his last words...

Dejected and emotionally drained, he picked up his riding crop and gloves and silently let himself out and as he closed the door behind him, he realised he would never again be welcome at this home.

-o0o-

When William returned home he was unable to go to his room and sleep. He couldn't turn to Hugh as he had already retired to his room so he poured a whiskey and sat at his desk in the dark, brooding about what he had done and how low and cowardly he had been. Even the dogs avoided him.

If William had seen Nerina that night, he would have been shocked and ashamed as her face was like melting snow and her eyes were dappled with shadows like stones in a running brook. Her mouth trembled like the breast of a captured sparrow and her pillow was wet with tears as she clung to memories of their time together, to try to find out how she had disappointed him, what was it he had found wanting in her, what had she said to offend him. She couldn't be consoled.

She hauled out of her cupboard the big pressing book of dried flowers and turned to the last page. The Nerine flower that she had pinned on William's lapel had fallen from his coat in the carriage on the way home from the engagement party and she had pressed it in her book of flowers. She looked at the desiccated but fragile and perfectly preserved flower with its florets. She would end up as dried out and hidden from view as it was now.

Liesbet made Nerina drink medicinal brandy to ease the pain but she knew that sort of pain would take years not months to be assuaged. She cursed William and now rued the day she had invited him into her home but he had such fine credentials. She had trusted her judgment of him but she had failed to realise that her own failings were partly to blame for the tragedy.

John Smith wasn't a violent man but that night he knew he had the capacity to kill. However, what was done couldn't be undone and perhaps it was better that the deed was done before the marriage than have a situation where Nerina was trapped in a loveless marriage. John sighed. The past few months had been very difficult and he was finding coping with the loss of his shipment and probable loss of his business and now his daughter being spurned in such a manner, very hard to bear. He was also experiencing his own mortality. He had visited a physician recently and the prognosis has not been good. He was to endeavour to eat less and cut down on alcoholic beverages to ease the burden on his heart. When in one's prime one thought one is divine, he mused.

In bed that night, Liesbet and John lay awake for hours before sleep finally came and the events of the day ebbed away. However, Nerina was awake and in her state of chill and shock, she wandered around the house with her candlestick. Shadows danced on the walls and they were almost a form of comfort. They matched the shadows cavorting around in her mind. She sat down at the table where she had sat next to William so many evenings and stared at the flame of the candle watching it weep tears of wax that ran and then congealed. Suddenly she pummelled the table top with her clenched fists and silently shouted, "No, no, this can't be happening!"

She opened the doors to the veranda and the stillness of midnight so high up the mountain was a balm to her soul. There were no clouds and the canopy of the sky and all the stars of the universe were spinning out in space and yet looked stationary. She took a familiar path at the back of the homestead and didn't feel the sharp stones on her bare feet. The candlelight was warm stains in the cold darkness. Suddenly she stumbled and the candle fell onto the ground and almost immediately the *fynbos* or ericaceous scrub caught alight like a match to tinder. Nerina screamed and tried to put out the flames with her hands and feet. She saw a protea bush of which she was extremely fond, burst into flames. "It looks like the burning bush in the Bible," she thought, not feeling the pain in her hands and feet. "I'm going to die," she realised and tried to escape the flames that were almost surrounding her. She ran down the mountain but stumbled in the dark and cracked her head against a rock. Before she lost consciousness she wondered, "Is this what it's like to die?"

-o0o-

Nerina's life had changed dramatically since the event on the mountain. Her father had found her lying unconscious as fire raged around them. Every able-bodied male in the vicinity had fought the fire and successfully put it out. Back home, John Smith and Liesbet were beside themselves with worry for their only child. They seemed to have experienced one set of disasters after another. Nerina lay unconscious for a week and then finally, her spirit returned to her body and she became aware of her surroundings.

"I've been asleep for a long time. I must have knocked myself out. You know I had no intention of setting the mountain on fire. It was a silly accident," she took some water from the glass Liesbet offered her. Leah and Sessy rushed into the room, "Oh Miss, you are back in the land of the living," Leah exclaimed, "I'll immediately prepare an egg drink for you. Come Martha, let's not bother the young Miss any longer," Leah ushered her daughter out of the room.

"William has broken your heart. I'll never forgive him for that," Liesbet was adamant.

"Mama, he had his reasons and I just didn't fit into his life. It's now over and forgotten. I'll manage to live without him however hard it might be." She was too weak to stand and sank back onto the bed. She was amazed that she now felt she could move forward with her life. She would remain single, she was sure of that. Who would want someone who had been jilted so soon after the engagement?

-o0o-

One day a few months later, Nerina was sitting on the veranda one day as she enjoyed looking down at the sea below. To be alive was a wonderful gift. The sea air was refreshing and she soaked up the sunshine. There were pots of ferns, geraniums and gerberas on the porch and they were a delight to the eye. As she tried to piece together the bits of her life, she had an idea she wished she had thought of a long time ago. She would ask her father for William's money and buy a suitable building somewhere in Cape Town and start a school for young women. She would teach and prepare young women to be strong in the world governed by men. Most would probably never work but they would need to be good at languages, music, art and book-keeping in order to run their homes one day. They would need to be able to entertain and to have opinions about current events. She would employ teachers to help her and ask the minister at the Dutch Reformed Church to give the girls a sermon each week.

Six months later, her school opened its doors to the young women who were to become her first pupils. Nerina now had a purpose to her life and she threw herself into her work with great enthusiasm. She warmed to her pupils although there were a few girls who weren't suited to such erudite pursuits and really shouldn't have been at the school at all. She soon learnt how to deal with them and found tasks such as cooking and how to run one's nursery and how to take care of babies, how to sew and mend. It worked and the school was soon running smoothly.

The minister was a man called Pierre du Bois. He was of French Huguenot descent and his family lived in Franschoek across False Bay at the foot of the Hottentot's Holland Mountains. They were wine farmers and their vineyards were strewn over the eastern-facing hills. Pierre's elder brother, Louis, inherited the farm when their father, Charles, died. Pierre who was forty, was unmarried but took care of his elderly mother at his manse in Cape Town. Mrs du Bois was a dignified, elegant woman with an aristocratic air about her. Her eyes which were bright and youthful, never missed anything. When Pierre began to daydream she would snap her fingers and ask what he was thinking. He wouldn't say but laughed and changed the subject.

When Pierre had heard that Nerina had been jilted he failed to understand how anyone could reject a woman of such great beauty and intellect. She enjoyed their discussions about religion and what the topics of his sermons should be about. She had gradually revealed her knowledge on all sorts of subjects and yet she remained a humble and unselfish individual.

Pierre was a tall man of over six foot, with a thin, muscular body. His face was long and narrow and his eyes were quite close together but sparkled with his personality. He had a dark beard which was kept neatly trimmed. His hair was balding in front and hung in wisps, touching his collar.

When he became a minister, he took himself off to the unexplored tropics of Africa to spread the gospel to the Coloured people in the interior. He came across strange rites and the close relationship of people with the dead. He had heard of this form of ancestor worship. The *sangomas* or witch doctors held a powerful sway over their people and exacted awful actions from the innocent supplicants. Killing for magic potions horrified him. Even with such entrenched beliefs, Pierre found that the tribe members came to hear his preaching. They were uncomplicated people and the simplicity of the Bible's teachings appealed to them and many adopted Christ as their God.

The tropics were dark places with strange creatures and insects and of course the dreaded malaria. It wasn't surprising that Pierre caught the disease and became seriously ill. His friends, the tribeswomen, nursed him night and day and eventually the fever abated but the sickness had left him weak and even thinner than before. He had been a missionary for fifteen years. He returned to the Cape to lead a more tranquil life and he longed for a wife with whom he could share his days.

Nerina began going to his church and she would sit in the pew and listen to his heartfelt oratory and realised she respected him. Her thoughts about William had ebbed away as this new acquaintance began to win her affection. She knew that William had been the big love of her life but Pierre would be a constant companion and would have the time for his family.

One day a large chest arrived at the school. It was full of new books that covered many topics. A letter was given to her:

"Dear Nerina,

I believe your school is developing an excellent reputation. Please accept these books as a mark of my respect for you. I'm truly sorry for the way I conducted my relationship with you. Never change – you are perfect in every way.

Yours sincerely,

William. "

It was as though she had been set free as a pigeon so often is so that it can find its way back to its home and at last she could breathe again, no longer suffocated by grief and her mother's fussing. She had the purpose now to continue with her life and realised a new door was beginning to open.

-oOo-

CHAPTER 13

April 1841

Cape Town

It was two years since William and Hugh had arrived at the Cape and there had never been a period of a cessation in William's workload, much of which was self-inflicted. There had been little time for boredom or an undemanding routine. After breaking off his engagement with Nerina, William had thrown himself into his work with even more self-sacrificing commitment. He did see her again but only in church at St George's or a glimpse of her in a busy street. He had heard she had an accident and had been critically ill for many months and wanted to visit her but Hugh advised against it.

Sometimes, in church William and Nerina would catch each other's eye but Nerina would turn pale and she would look hurriedly away. She wore gloves now most of the time and she walked with a limp. Knowing the other person was still suffering, their presence in the same building, was unbearable. Eventually there came a time when she no longer attended Sunday services at St. George's.

He waited to hear of her betrothal to someone else but such news never came. It was some time later that he received a most unexpected invitation to visit her at her school with some urgency and he felt obliged to find out how her school was prospering and he wished to make his admiration for her steadfast commitment to her ideals clear to her.

-o0o-

The carriage bumped along the road to the rhythm of the trotting horse. It was autumn and russet and gold leaves fluttered around in the gardens. The pavements mirrored the blue sky when the clouds parted for moments and the stately homes were a sign of an affluent society. At last, the carriage stopped outside the school gates. Hydrangeas were flowering still and golden marigolds were in sharp contrast in the decorative beds outside the entrance.

William asked his driver to wait as he didn't expect to be very long. It would be too uncomfortable to make small talk with the woman he had hurt so very much a long time ago. He took the steps two at a time with the fitness of a much younger man.

"I'm pleased you could come, William," Nerina smiled and held out her hand.

William lifted it to his lips, "I'll always be indebted to you, Nerina. I gather this matter is of some importance." Her presence was a soothing salve to his conscience. She had blossomed into a noble, deep and resilient woman in her prime.

She led him to the drawing room, "I'm anxious to find a way of sending my gifted students to university. A few have expressed an interest in becoming doctors and others teachers. Your university only accepts young men. Have you ever considered opening your doors to young women? Nerina spoke with her usual careful diction. She was as beautiful as when she was young, William thought to himself. He knew that her inner beauty had kept her looking fresh and unsullied with an air of peace and acceptance in her demeanour.

"I'm a great advocate for women being liberated from the ties that restrict them to, at best, household management. The Cape has a great need for graduates in those fields. I'll try and use my influence with the Board of Governors and immediately let you know what the outcome is." William spoke with the crisp manner of a lawyer.

"I've heard that you are in favour of the emancipation of women so you seemed the right person to approach," She smiled.

"You have set a fine example to women in the pursuit of learning and achieving the extraordinary. I've watched you overcome whatever setbacks have come your way. You're a brave woman, Nerina," He looked contrite, "I am so terribly sorry for my actions regarding our engagement. It was boorish of me."

"You did me a favour, William. I would have always been in your shadow but thank you for your apology." It meant the world to her. The brief letter breaking their engagement had shattered her heart worse than being impaled by an arrow. His apology now set her free of the burden she had been carrying around with her for all those years. Only her closest and dearest had ever seen the hurt and devastation.

"You mentioned in your letter that we should open a school for under-privileged children. That will be one of my priorities for this year. I'll let you know how I get on with finding sponsors for that, too. We must make things happen and not just wait and see!" He would move mountains if he could make Nerina happy.

She offered him tea but he took his leave. It was already more than he could bear. The disease in his conscience had left it bleeding. Outside a storm was brewing....

-oOo-

Hugh and he now had two properties, one in Rygersdal in Rondebosch and a weekend retreat in St James. The two confirmed bachelors enjoyed their home when weekends would set them free from punishing schedules.

On the political front, there had been considerable activity. The labour problem had been partially resolved but unfortunately the fact that there was a differentiation of tasks such as "skilled" or "menial", initiated a premise that tasks were aligned to race. This, too, caused the unexpected transformation of the colonists into a White elite. It hadn't escaped William's notice and often he chewed on the problem into the early hours of the morning.

Hugh had maintained that the KhoiKhoi or Hottentots were "far poorer than the most destitute in England or Ireland" yet they were passed over for the stronger Prize Negroes for choice tasks. William tried to promote self-improvement and self-advancement among men of colour who had broken the law and then jailed. Those who wanted to fight at the Border with the soldiers and farmers, he wanted freed and allowed to go there as free men.

The Colony was once more under attack from the Xhosas on the Eastern Frontier and treaties were put to one side. In recent years, the Xhosas had stolen a quarter of a million head of cattle and sheep and burned four hundred and fifty homesteads. Farmers were killed but the marauding hordes spared the lives of missionaries who lived to tell the tale of the slaughter.

The tensions at the Border had one positive outcome in that it unified the English settlers and the Dutch Boers to fight together against a common enemy. Some Boers, however, left their farms and crossed the Border with their cattle or herds of sheep and "trekked" further eastwards to the Natal Colony which was also under Cape jurisdiction, but too far away to suffer from the same control of the Cape governing body and hopefully far enough away from the Xhosas.

The issues didn't just include the ongoing attacks from across the Frontier but also the fact that the vagrant workforce of 'mixed race' joined the Xhosas. Piet Retief, one of the "trekkers" or pioneers, was known to say in his manifesto, printed in the Graham's Town Journal, "We despair of saving this country from the potential threat posed by the seditious and dishonest behaviour of vagrants who have been allowed to spread over all parts of the country; nor do we see any prospects of peace or contentment for our children in a country in which internal dissension is so rife."

On the other side of the argument, William had learnt that Sandile, chief of the Ngqika tribe, who broke the treaty and his men had been fighting to survive the recurring drought in their region and were faced with aggression on three fronts. Thus confined, it wasn't a surprise that they should look for better grazing for their cattle even if it meant running the gauntlet with the White farmers, the police patrols and commandos. William felt that too little was being done by the colonial authorities to control the situation.

He also had the burning memory of his own father's words in the comparable parallel with Ireland when the British claimed land for themselves in Ireland, "Picture to yourselves the dreadful consequences even of the temporary success of our enemies. Can you think without horror of seeing your native village reduced to ashes, in order to make room for a battlefield more destructive than the flames, the male inhabitants slaughtered in one day of carnage and their distracted families seeking in vain for their mangled remains or weeping in fearful silence over the smoking ruins of the desolated dwellings."

Rev. Ropert never did mince his words. It was a sobering thought. In the Seventeenth Century, there was also the British opinion that the Irish were "Cromwell's Kaffirs – irreclaimable savages not to be trusted or tolerated but to be hunted down like wolves or foxes". The analogy fitted uncomfortably with the problems at the Eastern Frontier, if the colonists crossed the Border to inflict similar punishment on the Xhosas.

As William and Hugh deliberated about the vulnerability of the Frontier, William believed he should form a reserve corps of Englishmen to help patrol the border. He hoped that the vision of a cavalry in the bright red uniform of a British soldier would halt the Xhosa invaders in their tracks. At present, the commandos were unprepossessing and a ragtag bunch of former soldiers, middle-aged farmers, herdsmen and tradesmen. Hugh at first laughed but then agreed that such an insane plan should be put into action.

William soon had an ample number of recruits from notable families at the Cape and training in military matters soon began at the Fort. They became known as the Cape Town Cavalry and William was the Commanding Officer. He ordered scarlet jackets with silver buttons and shining bright silver helmets. "The South African Commercial Advertiser", poked fun at the imposing cavalcade riding through the streets in Cape Town, by referring to them as "The Sparklers". Unbeknown to William, the writer was Roland Craven who enjoyed making fun of his sworn enemy. Roland moved around the Colony as his fancy dictated.

William and the "Sparklers" would not spend years at a time fighting or patrolling but intended to spend a few months at a time in the field. William soon proved that he had the charisma of a popular leader and his "band of brothers" soon respected him as much as he respected them especially after the men had endured weeks of arduous physical training and instruction in the use of firearms and cannon.

He had been particularly fond of a young man, Corporal Flight, who was a blond-haired, blue-eyed, dedicated, young soldier who showed great enthusiasm for whatever was required of him. On one particular sunny day, the soldiers of his cavalry were huddled in the shade of a plane tree cleaning their weapons when Corporal Flight's rifle jammed as a residue of shot was blocking the barrel. He thought he had cleared it and aimed into the air and pulled the trigger to let off one shot and the whole gun exploded next to his ear. He died immediately and was to become the first casualty of the corps.

William was appalled and immediately started to arrange the young man's funeral. It would be a fitting tribute in honour of his courage in joining the army. He would have an army orchestral accompaniment and William would read a valediction and an appropriate member of the Church would officiate in St George's Church. He would be given a six gun salute at his graveside.

At the funeral, William was surprised to meet Corporal Flight's widow, Mrs Flight, as he hadn't realised that the young soldier was married. William was impressed by the young woman's self-control and forbearance at such a tragic time. After the funeral, William promised himself that he would think how best he could help her.

Once more, Hugh was full of admiration for William, "You can't resist an orphaned child, an injured animal, a nestling that has fallen from a nest and now you wish to be the benefactor of this young woman. Just don't fall in love with her, please, William!"

William smiled as he sat at his desk in their wood-panelled study. The light from the lamp showed that he was starting to show his age. The greying hair at his temples, the laughter lines next to his eyes and at each corner of his mouth. Hugh knew he loved this man more than anyone else on earth. They were kindred spirits and their friendship was both comfortable and reassuring. Despite Hugh urging him to be prudent, William wrote a letter instructing his bank to send a sum of five hundred pounds to Mrs Flight immediately.

"Well, the Cavalry and I'll leave for the Frontier next Monday. You'll be there to see me off, Hugh?" He had tried to persuade Hugh to join his company of men but Hugh insisted on remaining behind to do the administration and to manage their financial matters. Both men were amassing a considerable fortune. Hugh had the keen intellect to assess the risk in a venture and to invest money where a good return was guaranteed to be great.

"Don't get heatstroke while you are out in the veldt. You'll need to keep covered up in the strongest sun. I hope hunting for your next meal won't cause you to live off vegetables and bread entirely. You aren't afraid of attack from animals or snakes - spiders even?"

"It's the spirit of adventure that courses through my blood. It's not the amount of food in my belly that drives me onward. It's you who is too fond of his food, not I!" William laughed, sealing his letter. The red wax soon congealed bearing his insignia. The peculiar smell of the wax smoke that was spirally upwards, filled the room. The sun had set and Fatima would soon have the meal ready. Tonight it would be curried sheep's trotters and *zambals*, followed by sago cream.

-oOo-

CHAPTER 14

November 1841

North Eastern Cape

Out of the mirage came the red and silver spectacle of William's Cape Cavalry Reserves. Their horses appeared to walk on water in the shimmering mirror and the sound of their hooves was muffled in the scorching heat. The men were tired after their ten day long journey from Cape Town as they headed for a riverside stronghold to put up camp. The trundle of their ox-wagons and the crack of whips accompanied the hundred subdued men.

The Kei River sparkled with a myriad of suns and as soon as the men leapt from their horses they unsaddled the poor beasts and led them down to the water's edge. Task completed the rest of the cavalry rushed down to the river to drink its sweet water themselves. The brightly coloured uniforms were discarded as they plunged in to wash and cool off. They began to laugh and cavort like children.

William reviewed their situation and was informed by scouts that all was quiet along the Border. They had left King William's Town the day before and were now in British Kaffraria and across the river were the Xhosas. The treaty system with them was continuously being thwarted and the Afrikaners and the English Settlers had asked for urgent assistance as lives were being threatened with each sortie the Xhosas made across from their territory. Greed, hunger and rebellion at the imposed border through land they had always considered theirs fanned the flames of their daring. Each herd of cattle stolen enriched the tribe and their hangers-on of vagrant Coloured men and each sortie fuelled their aggression.

Farmers were alarmed and now gathered at the fort where the Cape Cavalry were encamped, to discuss the problem. It was agreed that horse soldiers would patrol the Border with scouts in groups of five soldiers and five settlers. Farmers would build stacks of sticks, tumbleweed and wood to set alight as and when they realise that a contingent of warriors was approaching their farm. These beacons would alert the cavalry which would then assemble and ride with haste to the threatened farm.

William was fascinated by this new episode of his life. The Supreme Court had to do without his services for the following months. The Governor, Harry Smith, had encouraged him to represent him in the taming of the Eastern Frontier. He wanted William to pacify the Xhosas by force as any negotiation with papers and verse meant little to the Black tribe. When Harry Smith had been governor in the early eighteen thirties before being sent to New Zealand he had won the respect of both the White Settlers and the Blacks across the Border. He had been given the Xhosa name, *Inkosi Inkulu*, great king. But things had deteriorated terribly.

As William sat alone on his horse on the brow of a 'koppie', he could survey the expanse of veldt. It was evening and the air was still. He could hear a plover cry its 'key-wheat-key-wheat-key-key-key' call. The last to settle for the night the swifts still flew in arcs and circles piping short high pitched notes as they swooped on insects rising at sunset. He remembered the swallows that had rested on The Sterling all those years ago. He recalled his hopes and fears of that time and had succeeded in all but not in love. Like a clumsy fool he had damaged his relationship with Nerina. They would have had children and she would have been a dear companion. He was full of regrets.

As he stared, he saw smoke rising in the distance and with light fast fading the fire was a beacon that he feared meant a farm was being attacked. He urged his horse forward and returned to camp, mustering his men. In minutes they were charging towards the glowing light in the dusk.

-o0o-

A young woman tossed dry branches cut from acacia trees onto the flames. She wiped the perspiration from her brow and panted with her exertions. Her children ran out of their house with hoops of glee at the spectacle. She shooed them back inside. Her husband lay on the bed, gasping. He had a broken leg and she had been nursing him and running the farm with only her two herdsmen and a faithful Coloured woman, Elsina, to help with the children and chores. She first saw the warriors sneaking forward in the long grass on their bellies and heard the clink of their spears against stones. Soon they would stand up under the cover of darkness…. She heard the drone of their humming and ran inside to get the musket which she primed and filled with shot. She emptied a bag of bullets for the pistol, too. She was no match for a Xhosa 'impi.' The cattle were in the thorn enclosure and Andries and Kotzer also armed, were trying to make sure they didn't trample down the makeshift corral. The three inch white barbs of the thicket of thorn trees would deter the Xhosas only for a few minutes. The cattle would stampede and escape. She closed the door and jammed a thick beam across it and waited. Outside the windmill squeaked on its tall metal frame as the iron plates rotated and drove the pump for extracting water from an underground well. Then the wind dropped and there was an eerie silence.

Her husband, Johan van Niekerk, struggled to sit up but he collapsed back against the pillows. He was bathed in perspiration and his hair hung in lank tendrils. He was wasting away as his broken leg would not heal and now he couldn't bear the realisation that he was of no use to his family. He struggled to load his hunting rifle. He would shoot his family rather than have them raped and stabbed by marauding Black men. Marika, his wife was only thirty but worked like a man, doing his tasks on the farm. She was suntanned and her long brown hair was always in a loose plait down her back. He had seen her stretch like she used to do when pregnant with one of the children. Now she stretched because she was tired. She had beautiful green eyes with long lashes and her mouth was full but determined. She was full of fervour and brave. They all knelt next to his bed and he read a passage out of the Bible, praying for God to help them…..

The sound of humming changed to a chant and heavy feet stamped the ground. They felt the vibrations inside. The cattle snorted restlessly. Outside, the landscape was lit by starlight and the spears of five hundred men glinted and bristled. In unison, they started to drum their spears against their animal-hide shields. Some lit torches. There were no horses as this impi was made up of foot-soldiers. They were on the move but already William and his Cavalry were covering ground with thudding hooves and the foam spattered horses were being pushed to their limits. The bugle alarm halted the Xhosas and the sixty men from the Cape Cavalry pulled their swords from their scabbards and cheered. Their attack now foiled, the Xhosas retreated and melted into the darkness as quietly as they had arrived. A few cavalrymen jumped off their mounts and took aim into the darkness and fired their rifles. Yells pierced the night as some stragglers were hit.

Marika turned up the light of the oil-lamp and comforted her four children, Fanie, Jakobus, Maryna and Sannie who were still whimpering. Johan levered himself up and hoarsely whispered, "They have gone, Marika. We've been spared. The English came in the nick of time."

Marika unbolted the door and went out into the yard with the oil lamp. William rode up to her and the first thing he saw was the strikingly attractive woman in a trailing cotton skirt and simple blouse and the lamplight threw strange shadows upwards giving her a dramatic appearance. She saw his figure and face light up as he approached and she grabbed the harness of his horse so that he could dismount. "You came just in time! I nearly gave up hoping someone out there had seen my call for help."

"You're alone? You were going to fight off five hundred men on your own?!" William was astonished. She looked at him and found him handsome in his uniform.   His lips were firm and he smiled respectfully with his eyes gentle and compassionate.

"Englishman, I'm here," Johan had dragged himself to the doorway but staggered and would've fallen if it had not been for William's prompt action. He led the sick man back to his bed. He took a quick look at the leg and he was appalled by what he saw. The foot had turned black as the circulation to the foot had been cut off. This man would never walk on it again. Gangrene could kill Johan van Niekerk.

"Find the doctor!" He ordered one of his corporals. The soldiers had all dismounted and had found the reservoir under the windmill and drank thirstily – it had been a gallop of fifteen miles." The horses whinnied and stamped their feet with their sides twitching.

The doctor woken up out of his bed had joined the William's cavalry. He had been prepared for battle-wounds and now opened his medical bag. He felt Johan's forehead. He was burning up. The foot was ugly and the bone in his leg hadn't knit. There was no option but to operate and remove the lower leg and foot. "We have to do this my friend or you will die, you do understand?"

"Do what you have to do, Doctor," Johan was beyond caring. Angus Macintyre gave him a flask of brandy to drink. "Get that down you, you don't want to be conscious for what we have to do to you."

Marika stared at them all, frozen to the spot, her large eyes betraying her alarm as she bit the knuckle of her finger.

"Make us all a cup of coffee, Madam," William took her to one side. "Best to take the children to their room first." The children clung onto her skirt but she picked up the youngest and settled them all in their bed. They were excited and worried but she managed to get them to sleep.

Three hours later, Johan was still unconscious and the new bandages on his stump showed the operation was over and a success. Angus cleaned all his instruments and his hands. He let out a tired sigh as he unfastened his apron which was splattered with blood. He would call on the Van Niekerks in a couple of days to change the bandages and check the wound. He left William alone with Marika and they talked about the troubles and William said, "I would like to suggest you put your husband and the children into the wagon and travel to King William's Town where a doctor can be on hand in case of an emergency. You would all be a lot safer."

"If I leave the farm, who knows what I will find when I return. No, I'll hold out here. The herdsmen will always be with us when they put the cattle in the *kraal* at night. "You don't think I can do it because I'm a woman?!" She was feisty and her face flamed and her eyes flashed. She had such zealous ideals and was as pugnacious as a man.

"Of course, I wasn't meaning to imply…" William dared not laugh.

"To imply what may I ask you?!" She stormed outside. In the yard it was quiet as the soldiers had returned to base camp leaving only a handful to accompany William and the Doctor on their way back to the camp.

"That you - being a woman - can't withstand the Xhosas on your own". He was still smiling.

"What are you smiling at?! I'm not one of your ladies who whimper and faint at the smallest thing." She flounced around.

"Calm down, Mrs van Niekerk," William grasped her arms, "You're right you're not like a townswoman but nevertheless you do need protection."

She calmed down and then broke down sobbing, "I don't want to cry but I can't help it," She sobbed and William allowed her head to rest on his shoulder. He pulled a handkerchief out of his pocket, "There, there. It's just a normal reaction. We'll stay till sunrise and you will need to build a new bonfire tomorrow. Perhaps we can help you with that."

"If that's what you want to do, then it's fine. I'm going back inside to my husband," She sniffed.

"Try and get some sleep," William realised he was exhausted too. He found his horse, unsaddled it and led the animal to the strip of green grass around the small reservoir. He dropped the saddle, threw himself down and used the saddle as a backrest before falling asleep.

-oOo-

Sadly over the next fortnight Johan van Niekerk deteriorated again. This time suffering from pneumonia. Marika tried every Boer remedy she had learnt as a pioneer. She slaughtered a bullock and stripped off the hide and wrapped Johan in the warm bloody skin. She ground up dried sheep faeces and mixed the powder with brandy forcing her husband to swallow the strange concoction. After three nights of a raging fever, however, he drifted off and died, too exhausted to fight any longer. Marika fell asleep with her head on his chest and her arm around his neck, holding onto him hoping to bind him to her so that his spirit wouldn't leave her. The children sat on the bed wondering what was wrong with their parents.

The funeral was a sombre affair with neighbouring farmers and their families attending. Marika had dressed in a black dress with a black bonnet and her children clutched at her skirts with their eyes wide open with the surprise of the pageant.

Marika tossed off her widow's weeds when all the guests had departed and immediately got down to her chores and the running of the farm. William had stayed for a few hours longer and watched over her eventually insisting that she stopped what she was doing to give herself time to mourn. She collapsed into his arms with her head on his chest and he held her tightly until the convulsions of grief passed. Later he gently put her to bed and after making sure all the children were safely tucked up, too, he found his horse and pulled himself into the saddle, urging his spirited mount into a gallop.

Over the next two months, William visited the Van Niekerks' farm regularly. The farmhouse was a small four-roomed building of bricks and an earthen floor where the earth had been mixed with ox-blood and pounded to a shiny surface. The roof was made of corrugated iron sheets and a broad veranda gave shade. Inside it was tidy and genteel, with portraits of parents looking forbidding hanging from picture rails. Wrought iron pots hung above the fire in the hearth and the windows let in cool breezes on the hottest of days. Carpets of an intricate design from Holland were laid over furniture and the walls were painted with white lime. The garden had a patch of green lawn, a willow tree and several fruit trees which were thriving in an otherwise hostile environment. On the fringes of the garden grew cacti, agaves and a trio of eucalyptus trees that could survive drought on the dry plateau. The farmhouse provided shelter and the garden was a small oasis.

He and Marika had the bond of two wanderers converging in that place. Marika looked up to him but sometimes needed to bring him down a peg or two.

"Race you to the koppie over there," She laughed one day.

William pointed to the left of the lonely hillock.

"No over there, man, the *hill!*" She scolded him before leaping on her horse's back with her silky brown hair flowing over her shoulders. She was fast and an excellent horsewoman. Bles, her horse with its white blaze on its nose responded to her heels with zeal and William followed the thundering pair.

On the hillock, they found a cactus heavy with fruit all encased in leathery grey-green skin and clusters of thorns.

Marika took out her knife from its sheath on her belt and hacked off a dozen of the deliciously juicy delicacies. She threw herself down on a flat sand-coloured rock and skilled after years of practice, she quickly skinned her offering and the watery nectar-scented flesh enveloping seeds that felt like bonbons, tasted like nothing he had ever eaten before. Very refreshing and as exotic as dates. Whereas dates were cloyingly sweet like a morsel of meat soaked in honey with cloves, the prickly pear was like gin with its sparkle and thirst-quenching qualities. Equally intoxicated by Marika's beauty, her brown eyes trusting as a doe's and her lips moistened by their feast made him lean forward and kiss her and they began to enjoy the taste and sensations of playing with each other's lips, breathing deeply and fast. A welter of sensations crossed their bodies but decorum made William hold back and he laughed and extricated himself from her embrace. He scratched his beard which had grown since leaving Cape Town and looked sheepish.

"Oh, you English man, what am I going to do with you?" She shouted with frustration and stomped away down the *koppie* with her prize of prickly pears in her hat.

As they cantered over the plain, she led him to an aardvark's burrow but the shy animal was hiding and waiting for night to fall when he would go digging for roots or insects. A contingent of aggressive ostriches watched them, debating whether to give chase or not. She showed him a tortoise she had spotted on their trail and pointed to jackal buzzards wheeling and diving above them. They disturbed a spring hare and it suddenly fell as her shot rang out. "Dinner!" she laughed brandishing her rifle. She was in love with her world and no one could take it away from her, William realised.

"Captain Ropert, would you like to join us in King William's Town this Sunday? It's our Mass. We only get the opportunity a couple of times in the year to take communion, have marriage and christening ceremonies, all on the same day. The next day we'll have a party with singing and dancing with all the other Afrikaner families. It is a wonderful time for us all to catch up on news and to celebrate happenings of the past months," Marika said. She had employed more labourers to help run the farm and so far the Xhosas had stayed away.

William considered how he would fit into the community and then decided to accompany the family, "I'm honoured you want me to join you. Thank you, Mrs van Niekerk, I'd be delighted to escort you all."

-oOo-

At the gathering in King William's Town, William met some of the farmers the Sparklers had helped over the months and he liked his new friends but found himself seeking Marika's company especially. She was in the prime of her life and indeed an earth mother with basic needs and demands. Although he was now in his late forties and should have been serious and dignified, her attention meant a lot to him. He was enjoying being so close to nature with all its rawness and his senses had sharpened making him feel more alive than when he first arrived at the Frontier.

He now knew what made the *voortrekkers* the brave, perhaps arrogant pioneers, they were. Their religion was a strict form of Calvinism which contrasted radically to his liberal Unitarian beliefs. Although perhaps not all were so pious he thought, looking at Marika dancing with her partner. He watched the church service and the ritual of Holy Communion or *Nagmaal*, with the sobriety of an onlooker. Being of a different faith, he wasn't permitted to partake of the bread and wine.

The Afrikaners would rest overnight in their wagons but William found a guest house where he was treated to good English cooking, a soft bed and clean linen for the first time in months. He would soon be returning to Cape Town and would take back with him a wealth of experiences.

The following day the party in the park was underway with people milling around in their best clothes, tables were laden with food of all sorts and fires were lit where several pigs and half an ox were being roasted on a spit. Ladies were making pancakes and others had brought along *koeksisters* - a pastry cooked in boiling syrup – milk tarts and rusks. Strong coffee steamed in pots on the fire. *Bredies* would accompany the cooked meat. In the meantime a dance floor had been made with floor boards and the young men and women danced to the music from harmonicas, concertinas and violins, which were infectiously foot-tappingly good. There were folk-dances to go with the country music.

Marika came up to him, "Captain Ropert, will you dance with me?" She blushed and looked at him demurely. She was a picture in her lovely red dress with its cream lace trimmings and buttoned up to the neck. She wore a bonnet to match. She looked in love.

"It would be an honour, Marika," It was the first time he called her by her Christian name. William looked dashing in his finery but a bit out of place in the festivities. He spun her around the dance floor and she laughed. William felt happier than he had for a long time. Happiness was a state of being that he had never questioned. Of course he was happy.

Later in the evening he stood leaning against a wall smoking a cigar and the tendrils of sweet smoke were white in the black of night. The night creatures were silent in the rain-soaked gardens. The shower had rolled in at the tail end of the celebrations. He thought he heard an owl hoot and then the figure of Marika emerged from the ink-black shadows. "Oh, it's you, Marika" He spoke softly, surprised.

"Yes, Captain Ropert. You seem deep in thought," She joined him and hummed a tune that had been played earlier in the evening.

"I was just contemplating what happiness is. Do you have any ideas on the subject? I look back and see a pleasant state of being so therefore I must have been happy." William was shocked that he had never asked that question before.

"Happiness is completeness. When another person or God makes one whole and that state sets one free to be lifted up to the heavens and be bathed in sunlight. Happiness is being right here with you," She looked at him seriously, "No, don't say anything. Just listen." She was so close, her body almost touched his and she was breathing fast.

"Are you married, William? I can't call you Captain Ropert this evening. I know you're leaving in a day or two but so much has to happen in the next few hours so that I can say farewell to you with a happy heart. I, too, want happiness."

"No, there's no Mrs Ropert. I am just realising tonight that I have been so carried away with my daily routine and the wars won and lost in the boardroom or in court that I believed I needed nothing more. I've been at the Cape nearly ten years and I'm no nearer finding that elusive condition called 'happiness'."

She was like a confidante, this brave and noble creature. Her spirit was alight. She had a soul with the beauty of a bird of paradise, golden and bejewelled. She was an instinctive compass-free companion journeying towards perfection.

"Ask me why I'm standing here with you when my husband is dead and my children are fast asleep in the wagon," She was serious now. The youthful demeanour and fun-loving sprite had vanished and the mature woman stood in her place. "I love you, William. Every time you visited I fell more deeply in love with you. I have chastised myself and have thought that Johan would be turning in his grave if he knew what is in my heart. Have you ever wanted children, an heir who will benefit from all your accomplishments?"

"Of course, what man wouldn't?" William put out the cigar, "I had the chance once but after that failed, I never was much good at finding the right person to marry and then eventually marriage seemed less important. I've very close family ties in Cape Town – it's too complicated to explain, and brothers, back in Ireland. That seemed enough. Working well into the night keeps my mind off such things".

"If I asked you to make love with me so that I can know what it's like to be with the man I've grown to love so dearly and completely, would you be very shocked?" She touched his hand and lifted it to her lips. "I know I cannot leave my family or the farm as the children need me more than ever. But one hour of love will be enough for me. I can then let you go and treasure what we had with a peaceful heart. I know my religion is strict and I may be punished but I'm prepared for that to happen."

William pulled her towards him, feeling his own heart beating fast with a sudden hunger for a consummation of this new relationship that he had never imagined could be possible. He had never had intimate relations with a woman. It hadn't been part of his makeup to seek sexual partners or relationships. His asceticism erased that part of his being.

"Even though you have to leave me I want you to know that if we make love, in my heart I'll still have some part of you with me till I die. I won't hunger for what I can't have but I'll cherish the memories. Am I totally without shame? If we had a future, I would want your baby, William," She raised her face and leant upwards for his kiss.

Momentarily, he hesitated but urged on by male instinct and the passion she had fuelled with her words, he pulled her to him and kissed over and over again. He kept his sense of decorum and behaved considerately with the sensitivity to preserve her dignity and not to cause pain. He could feel her feminine body under his hand and her breasts were softer than the finest white satin and her nipples were sweet as summer berries and perfectly formed.

She kissed him back pulling him on top of her. Their clothes got in the way but it made no difference to their lovemaking. Her skirts hiding her nudity were wrapped around him making him feel he was being embraced by the wings of a swan. He had never reached orgasm with a woman as there never had been a woman before her. The thought he was in his forties and a virgin would never be believed. Nerina would have been his first but when that ended in disaster, he didn't court other possible sexual partners. He tried to put Nerina out of his mind as the waves of intense physical pleasure swept over him. Her warmth surrounded him. Marika kissed his neck as she reached her climax and her gasps made him let go and allow all the pain of the past slip away until he was empty but complete and in step with the great power evolving in the universe, man in time with his Maker.

The wind rose and clouds were changing shape above them and the night sky was blotted out by drops of rain. "I have to go William. The children might be looking for me if they wake up and see me gone. God bless you, my one true love, my William." She kissed him for the last time and tidied her clothes and her hair, breathlessly.

William sat up dazed. What on earth had happened? He was dumbstruck that it had all been so easy. It had been more than he could ever have imagined. He thought with a deep fondness of Marika, the only woman to have succeeded in disarming him and physically cherishing him......He would never forget her. He promised himself that he would always remember her selflessness as a lesson to loving better.

In three days, the Cape Cavalry would begin its long journey back to Cape Town. Sorties against insurgents had been completed. A semblance of good relations between farmers and the Xhosas now existed at the Frontier. A truce had been decided but for how long would the uneasy peace continue?

-o0o-

CHAPTER 15

Spring 1846

Dublin

Fanny cavorted around the nursery with little Amber as they celebrated her 6th birthday. As the exquisitely delightful child laughed with a clear bell-like twittering Fanny prepared her for her birthday party. She had made a striking cream cotton dress out of white cotton pique with its textured weave and had sewn on bands of braided cotton trim and eyelet ruffles. Small satin roses decorated the bodice and the skirt fell to below Amber's knees. The maid, Felicity, had used damp rags to tie up Amber's glorious hair while she slept and now each lock was unwrapped and fell in a soft golden curl around her shoulders.

"Tell me again how many children are coming to your party," Fanny laughed as her dearest charge recited the numbers counting on her fingers.

"Twelve!" Amber sang out the figure, "Will I open my presents straight away?"

"No, it would not be good manners. We'll do that after everyone has gone. We must show the other children the games we can play. You can then invite them to sit down and help themselves to birthday cake and sweetmeats. Be careful not to eat too much as you could make yourself ill! I can imagine one or two of your little friends just might do that."

-oOo-

After the party when everyone had left, Fanny took Amber up to bed. The little girl was yawning and clutching a brand new doll with its wax head, human hair and glass eyes. Its pert little mouth had already been kissed a dozen times and its cotton dress was a replica of Amber's party frock. Fanny had made it, too.

"Thank you, Aunt Fanny – for my new doll. I love her so much. Aunt Fanny you are really my Mother, aren't you?" The little child looked into her eyes unflinchingly.

"No, my Darling. She died when you were a baby but I wish I were your Mother and you were my very own," Fanny became serious.

"I think you are my very own Mother now," Amber imitated Fanny frowning and staring at her aunt doggedly determined not to let the moment pass without the confirmation she sought.

"Yes, we can pretend I'm your very own Mother but it will be our secret," Fanny tucked her up in bed feeling her heart fill up with the warmth of so much love from the sweetest child she had ever met.

"That's good," Amber smiled and within seconds her eyelids fell and her long eyelashes swept down onto her cheeks and she was asleep.

Fanny sat there completely at ease with the world. The past six years had passed so quickly, as she experienced each stage of Amber's development and she and John enjoyed every moment of revelation as the little human being became a little girl with her own personality that was filled with innocence and a love that was so pure. At the beginning, the brother and sister often walked down the street with little Amber in the pram and friends and strangers would stop to admire 'their' child.

They took her on holiday to Cushendall when she was three and they had a glorious holiday with the little girl running into the gentle waves of the sea and playing with a bucket and spade making sand castles. She remembered those days as though they had been etched on her mind with the brightest splashes of aquamarine, azure blue, ochre and green with white titanium cirrus streaking across the sky and white horses leaping in the bay. She was back in that magical world...

"Fanny, come see," Amber had said when she took her forefinger and pulled her towards the rocks where they were laid bare by the spring tide and together they looked into the rock pools and discovered little brown crabs and red sea anemones, purple seaweed and shells full of black hermit crabs. They caught little fish which they emptied into her bucket so that she could watch them darting around in the sea water trying to escape. The little child played tirelessly and eventually as the sun dipped low and a cool breeze arose, John picked up their belongings and Fanny dressed Amber so that they could return to the cottage they had rented. What a sublime day it had been...

During the night, Amber was restless and Fanny could hear her thrashing around on top of her covers so she quickly went over to the sleeping child and found Amber to be feverish and muttering nonsensical words but in addition, she was not responding to Fanny's soothing voice. Fanny noticed that pin pricks of a rash dotted the child's body and she was immediately alarmed and woke up her brother alerting him to Amber's illness. Within an hour he had found the village's one doctor and got him out of bed but the elderly man didn't complain and willingly accompanied John to the cottage. He gave Amber medication to break the fever but when he saw the rash, his demeanour changed and Fanny and John could tell that Amber's condition was extremely critical.

For two days they all sat at Amber's bedside and Fanny bathed the little girl's body with cool, wet face cloths and gradually their prayers were answered and she began to respond to the doctor's treatment.

"She has come through a very serious ordeal. I've seen children with this infection die very quickly and those who survive often lose hands or feet. She is a very lucky little girl," The doctor patted his little patient encouragingly...

Fanny looked at the birthday girl and rejoiced that she was a normal, well-adjusted and intelligent little being. If they had lost her, Fanny felt John's heart would have broken as well as her own and she would have been tortured by all sorts of questions – could she have prevented the illness, did she do enough, was it her fault in any way? She would never have wanted the sun to rise again and she would have questioned whether there was a kind and loving God. She had felt every cell of her body cry out in pain and it made her gasp, so great was her fear and so deep her emotions during those days. She prayed that God would take her instead of Amber. She begged him to punish her not an innocent child, a child so special and good in every way.

She returned to her own bed and lay there for hours thinking of the ways Amber had lit up her life, all the little gestures of a little child, her first footsteps, her doggedness when trying to walk, her quaintness of speech. She could bathe in those golden memories whenever she had time to daydream. She wished Amber was hers but the fact she wasn't, never meant it was a problem. Her one regret was that William had never shared in the most meaningful experiences of her life. How could she explain how she felt about Amber at all in a simple letter when the subject was almost as complex as one's knowledge about God?

-o0o-

Fanny had slept well and she stretched, yawning into the back of her hand, disturbing a sleeping cat which meowed and moved out of the way showing its displeasure and reluctance in its body language. It was her usual time of wakening but as she looked around she was suddenly overcome with raw fear. All she could see was dark night. She felt the covers of the bed and could feel the warmth of the spot where her tabby cat had lain and her feet felt the rug underneath them. But she couldn't see the dark antique furniture, the vase of daffodils, the mirror on the dressing table, the wine-red curtain drapes….. The maid would have taken Amber to get dressed and then given her breakfast.

"Oh my God, God forgive me, I'm blind just like Mother," she whispered to herself in the empty room. She pressed her fingers on her eyes as if checking they were still there and then slowly staggered to the door, feeling her way with her feet suddenly sensitive to the coverings on the floor and her hands felt for the reassurance of a wall.

She walked unsteadily into the hallway and called, "John, are you there?"

She heard the scratching of claw on wood as MacDuff got up from where he had stood guard at her door and trotted up to her. She felt lost and realising she was only dressed in her night-gown, she hugged her arms around her breasts breathing fast.

"MacDuff, I'm blind! Be careful, there's the good dog," She felt the handrail for the stairs and then her heels trod on her nightdress and she fell sliding and tumbling. She landed headfirst but her hands protected her face and the skin was scraped off her fingers. When she tried to move, she felt a stab of red-hot pain in her hip.

MacDuff ran off barking skipping down the stairs with his short legs timing each downward hop confidently and he bothered John until he got up from the breakfast table and led him to where Fanny lay.

"Fanny, what has happened to you?" John cried as he tried to find a way of moving her. Potter, the groom, would be able to help him carry Fanny back upstairs. His mind ticked away in his confusion. What to do for the best?

"John, John, I'm blind – just like Mother. Why, why did it have to happen to me? I treasured my sight. I always knew it was a God-given pleasure so why has he taken his gift back and left me in this night forever?" She couldn't stop sobbing. She berated herself for being so weak. Blind people always seemed as though they had come to terms with their lot but perhaps that was just the face they presented to the sighted. She could hear Amber whimper as the child sensed something was wrong. She smiled and reached out for Amber and somehow by touch in a few attempts felt Amber's little body and hugged her.

"Don't be scared. I'll be fine my little Special One. I promise!" She had relaxed her face into a gentle smile and her body language became more composed. She would try to hide her pain and fear. She couldn't see but in her mind's eye imagined how the little girl had nodded silently but her eyes had grown larger and she had sucked her thumb for comfort.

Dr McAllister arrived a few hours later and was soon examining Fanny on her narrow bed, where she had pulled the bedclothes up neatly to her chin.

"Come on, dear. Let's have a look at you. No need to be afraid," The elderly doctor stared down at her through his spectacles and his moustache twitched as he found where she had been hurt. "Hmmm. You appear to have broken your hip, Fanny. It will take many weeks of bed-rest to allow it to heal"

"What about her sight?" John asked brokenheartedly. His sister was his dearest relative and closest friend.

Dr McAllister flashed a light into Fanny's eyes. The irises however didn't react but remained wide open, "It pains me to have to tell you that you have the same condition your Mother suffered from, Fanny. Very myopic people tend to find their retinas tear and disintegrate, leaving them blind." He tried to break the harsh truth as sympathetically as possible. Poor woman, he remembered her as having many talents which now would be locked away like a carpenter whose tools have been thrown into the deepest river.

"Over the past week I've had flashes of light in both eyes like a curtain suddenly being opened on a sunny morning and sometimes the sense of the curtain falling back and leaving darkness," said Fanny distraught. "This is what that was all about?"

Dr McAllister nodded, "Unfortunately, yes, my dear."

"William, William," She cried when they left her alone, "I'll never be able to see your dear face again. Oh my Love, if eyes are the windows of the soul, our souls won't be able to communicate our feelings to each other, any more. Perhaps your hands, your gentle fingers, my Love, could caress my face or touch my hair. I touch yours every night when I dream. Will you still love me when my letters fail to arrive or if they have been dictated to John?" The pain she felt went deeper than the physical pain from her injuries.

She lay in bed going over all the treasured pictures in her mind opening them like a journal. She would ensure they remained indelible and that they were captured forever. All the rooms in her house, the garden in high summer, the sea at Cushendall, the fairness of little Amber, the faces of all those she loved and above all, William.... She would revisit those images over and over again to ensure they would not fade as her sight had done.

Months later in the Southern Hemisphere autumn of 1846, William was in a reflective mood in his study. He was supposed to be preparing an important speech for the new Governor, Sir Peregrine Maitland about his experiences at the Eastern Frontier with his cavalry. "The Sparklers" had answered the call for troops to muster for the Seventh War with the Xhosa known as the "War of the Axe". As the name suggests war was declared when a relative of Sandile, the Xhosa chief, stole an axe from a shop in Fort Beaufort; the action itself quite mild but it was the last straw after hundreds of thousands of cattle had been rustled across the Keiskamma River in recent times. The Eastern Frontier was a powder keg waiting to erupt with just such a spark. William and his Cape Cavalry were in the field for two months with skirmishes with the Xhosa taking place almost daily. He found the experience exhilarating but also sobering. The Xhosas were being hemmed in between ever narrowing tracts of land.

Now back at "Wolmunster", any peace to describe his experiences was interrupted by some horrifying news he had just received as he opened his mail. His thoughts were now rightly concerned with his family back in Ireland especially with John McBride, his benefactor, and Fanny. John's letter had been a bolt from the blue and he was still trying to digest its contents.

My dear William,

It's with great sadness that I write to you with some disturbing news. Fanny has become blind, like her mother before her. It would seem it's a familial condition. There'll never be a time that her sight could return. As a result, she's in poor spirits and longs for a letter from you. You're like her own son, my boy. To make matters worse, she had a fall down the stairs and has broken her hip. By the time you read this, she should be back on her feet again. If she deteriorates in spirit or health, I will write again. Until then we await your reply."

Yours sincerely,

John

This news on top of everything else sent his world spinning. His stars were not in a favourable aspect, he thought dejectedly. He felt shock and indescribable pain for Fanny. He already missed her own words, the way she would narrate an event or describe a person she had met. Their intimacy was threatened by her blindness. He ruminated for hours and came to a decision. What he would like to do was to send the means to obtain a ship's passage to Cape Town to her, he thought. Perhaps the sea air of the journey and the climate in Africa would be beneficial and he knew just being together would be a salve to her depression.

He had allowed himself to sacrifice her for the advancement of his career like he had sacrificed Nerina for Hugh. Would he again sacrifice Fanny? It was a question he would return to often.

-o0o-

It was time to write to Fanny about her infirmity. The candlelight flickered and long shadows hung silently like shrouds, moving at the whim of the candle's flame. The desk was neat and tidy and all that was on it was a single sheet of paper, the ink well and quill pen.

"My dear Fanny,

I haven't the words to describe to you my sincere empathy with the despair you are experiencing. The idea that your life is now dependent on the kindness of others makes me realise how your spirit must be humiliated as you who would do so much for others and find such reward in your work will never ask for anything or complain.

However, being bereft of sight needn't mean you are bereft of life. The natural world around us provides us with sensations of smell, touch and hearing, so walk with John in the woods and smell the elderflower, touch the bark of a Scots Pine and feel the needles under your feet, listen to the bird song and the rushing wind in the trees when a gale is blowing. Hear the breakers on the beach, feel the foam on your feet and hear the sound of surf.

I've made a decision that may help your situation. I would like to send you the money for a ship's passage to Cape Town. Yes, my Dear, I want you to come and live with Hugh and me. We're fortunate to have a quaint little cottage in St James, some miles out of Cape Town and near the sea. Ideal for weekend sojourns. The weather is sublime and the country is a natural paradise. I could look after you with all the same love and in the same degree that you loved me, if not more, when I needed to be loved.

I'll await the traders arriving at the harbour in the hope that you'll be disembarking sometime in the months to come.

I'll always take care of you and I promise it'll be "in sickness and in health" forever.

William.

He sat back in his chair wearily. Since his arrival in the Cape, he had experienced too many life-changes. If he could make recompense for his poor judgment about Nerina, he would. He sat and contemplated the errors of his ways into the dawn and black rings appeared under his sunken eyes. The lot of the foolhardy was not one to be desired.

-o0o-

Events overtook William's plans and two months later he was surprised to receive a letter from Eliza, his stepmother.

Dear William,

It is with great sadness that I'm writing this letter today. My dear brother, John, took ill ten days ago and is now incapable of speech and movement of the right side of his body. I have moved back to Blackhall Street to look after him. Taking care of him will ease the loneliness of widowhood. Since your Father, Bill, died two years ago I have longed for a mission in life but I never expected that my own brother would need my nursing. I must once again thank you for the annual stipend you have so generously made to me. It has given me my independence.

I am fully aware that you had invited Fanny to visit you in Cape Town three months ago and had forwarded the finance for her sea passage to your bank in Dublin. The bank has now handed over a significant amount to Fanny enabling her to pay the shipping company in Southampton.

I have reviewed the situation and have come to the conclusion that little Amber and Fanny's maid, Felicity, should accompany her. The little girl is dependent on Fanny as any child is reliant on a parent and separating them would be injurious to both parties. Felicity takes care of Amber and Fanny's dress and appearance and assists them in all manner of activities.

My other request is that Frank, being your half-brother and an ardent admirer of your progress in life, has expressed often to me that his dearest wish is to travel to the Cape to learn mercantile law and to be filled with the commercial business acumen regarding imports and exports. He wishes to become a merchant. It would make sound sense that he should accompany Fanny. I have money set aside for such an eventuality.

The money forwarded to Fanny is such that she is able to pay for the extra two sea passages for Amber and Felicity.

I know if John was well, he would concur with my decision.

As there is a ship, "The Empress", setting sail for the Cape in a fortnight, there is no time to await your reply so I trust you'll approve of my actions in this matter. I know you'll take care of Fanny. She is looking forward to being with you which will release her from a state not unlike that of a saint always waiting to hear from God what He desires of her. If it weren't for little Amber, Fanny would hide away in silence with prayers her only discourse. Her blindness has been a terrible disappointment.

I will always remain a grateful friend and stepmother.

Yours sincerely

Eliza.

William was startled by the turn of events and began to plan how he would draw Fanny and Amber into his life and ensure that he would bring happiness and peace to the cherished but undeclared love of his life. He would need to prepare a nursery for little Amber and accommodation for Felicity. Perhaps this turn of events would be his salvation and he will rediscover his grand ideas and ideals, which Fanny had always inspired in him.

-o0o-

It was a bright sunny day when Fanny, Amber and Felicity boarded the trading vessel, The Empress. Fanny's life had been turned upside down by the arrival of William's letter asking her to travel to the Cape and informing her that the money for the ship's passage was guaranteed by his bank in Dublin. She was informed that the ship would be leaving from Southampton and she would need to travel by boat to the port town.

When they arrived, Southampton was bustling with naval people involved in all sorts of occupations, sailors, porters, clerks, chandlers and traders amongst others. Frank was ecstatic and walked ahead of their small group absorbing every detail of their surroundings. The ships were crowding the bay and their masts and ropes were spiders' webs up and down which little humans would climb like miniature arachnids. Bells rang intermittently and foghorns blared out in the middle of the night. If only she could see what she heard! She had spent the night in a boarding house which was pleasant but a little damp and the wallpaper was pockmarked and yellow which she couldn't see but was able to smell and feel. Even so nothing disappointed her now that she was to see her beloved William again. She remembered and amended that thought. She would never be able to "see" him again but she would be able to touch his hand or face…Amber had skipped at her side as they walked into the boarding house and Felicity flitted like a shadow behind them.

Frank had accompanied Fanny, Amber and Felicity from the boat from which they had alighted and eager to explore, he left them to settle into their rooms, promising to make sure that everything was in order for their boarding the "Empress" the next day. Felicity offered to accompany him as she was inquisitive too and infatuated already with his good looks. He was reassured by the ship's captain, Oswald Cousins, that Fanny would be taken care of at all times and this news when he relayed it later, was soothing to Fanny's ears. Felicity was pleasantly surprised by the spacious cabin which awaited Fanny. The porthole would allow fresh air to fill the room. Always fanatical about detail, she watched as supplies of vegetables and other victuals were hauled up the ramp and barrels of clean water were rolled along like skittles. She would narrate all her observations to Fanny when she returned to the boarding house.

The following morning "The Empress" moved away from the dockside and as it left the calm of the port, people on the quayside cheered. Some would never see their loved ones again. Fanny remained in her cabin and awaited the steward's knock to inform her where she was required to be and at what time. It wasn't such an awful experience after all. Outside on the deck, sailors went about their business and above them the sails were being untied and allowed to fall and catch the breeze. Felicity had taken Amber to the deck above to watch England grow steadily further and further away. Their long journey had begun...

-o0o-

The weeks had soon passed since he had written to John about his desire to look after Fanny if she were to travel to the Cape. From time to time, he walked down to the little naval settlement when he saw a newly arrived ship being moored alongside the quay. Today was no different and he stood patiently, dressed smartly in his apparel as he had been in the Court all day. The Mountain was looming up behind him and its granite presence cast a shadow over the town but suddenly the sun appeared in a break in the clouds and the water in the bay sparkled with glittering wavelets. Near the quay, a seal cavorted begging for scraps...

Most of the passengers had disembarked by that time and it was only then that he saw a woman being helped down the gangplank, a child with copper hair in ringlets danced ahead of her and her companion struggled with some of their luggage and a tall good-looking man struggled with the heavier items. The woman was exquisitely dressed in a hunter green velvet jacket trimmed with jet black buttons and flattering her face, a Pierrot collar of black Chantilly lace and a port wine velvet skirt and pert green velvet shoes with neat port wine bows and a Louis heel. Fanny had planned her outfit to the last minute detail.

"Fanny!" The joy in his cry, made the woman look up sightlessly.

"William!" was all she could say feeling herself close to tears, "My Beloved!" was a whisper.

She looked beautiful but now appeared much older than he remembered and the differences in their ages were now more apparent. He thought wryly that when he was a teenager he was too young for her to have feelings for him. It was only in his mid-twenties to mid-thirties that the discrepancy in their ages had not been a problem. Now it would seem that she was too old for him. He would treasure her company and wondered about her health as she had black rings under her eyes and she was extremely pale. She had pinched her lips to make them red and now he touched them gently with his. Her luxurious long brown hair was streaked with silver but attractively arranged with a parting in the middle and in plaits arranged like a coronet. Fanny's expert fingers could have worked their magic even in her sleep.

"I never thought living without you would be such torture!" She laughed happily. He did not know what feature he should focus his attention on as her eyes were dead and her emotions and her intuitive search for feelings in his had vanished. He felt his heart contract with the feeling of loss.

"No more pain and heartache now. I can promise you a carefree life, Fanny. I've a cottage near the sea just a stone's throw from the beach in St James, where I will now take you every weekend. Excuse me for a moment. I just have to hire a carriage. You will see when you arrive that my housekeeper, Fatima, has recommended her niece, Lettie, as a nursemaid for little Amber. Fatima will help Felicity cope with all your needs."

He turned to his half-brother, "Frank, I'm delighted to meet you at last," William wrapped an arm around Frank's shoulders and would have kissed him such was his joy but his half-brother coughed with embarrassment, "William, old chap, you are making me blush. I can't tell you how much I appreciate how you have stepped into the breach and found me a career for me and now that I'm in Africa I can assure you I'll use every effort to succeed in my business dealings with you as my tutor!"

Horses trotted towards them pulling a carriage and drew to a halt when William signalled for them to stop and the coachman jumped down and helped them with the baggage. Frank was dying to ask his brother all manner of questions but he resisted his impulses aware that it was not the time for him to interrupt William's reunion with Fanny.

"This is such fun. Tell me, William, everything I should be seeing. Describe it all to me. I can feel the breeze and hear the far-off cries of seagulls out in the bay. How tall is Table Mountain, is it taller than the mountains in Wales and Scotland?" She was eager to listen to his eloquent commentary as they travelled towards Mowbray.

"I'll have to work in my chambers during the week, Fanny, but you will have my company in the evenings and of course Hugh will continue living with us. I have arranged rooms for Frank in Town. A young bachelor would soon find our company quite pedestrian. I'm taking you to our property called 'Wolmunster' in Mowbray which I share with Hugh. An unlikely pair! There's also the matter of the war at the Frontier. I'll be leading the Cape Cavalry to Kaffraria for spells of six weeks or more from time to time. I'm sure you will enjoy hearing the tales of heroism in action with which I can regale you."

"Tell me what keeps you busy?" She urged.

"As chief prosecutor I'm at everyone's beck and call but I enjoy the legal wrangling of obtaining justice for my clients. But, at this moment, I have to advise the Governor on state law which is fascinating as it's evolving as we speak."

He talked passionately about politics and she remembered he had always done that from old. She had missed their debates as he had valued her opinions and she hoped her viewpoint helped mould him into the thoughtful man she was aware of today. Her spirits soared and tears began to run down her cheeks and she laughed, "Foolish me! I've waited for this moment for so very long."

"So have I, dear Fanny. I'll look after you, my love," He wished he could kiss her like a lover should but the old inhibitions could never be set aside and he knew that sort of familiarity would create many problems especially in describing their relationship to others. His career could not withstand another scandal...

As they entered the gates of Wolmunster, the little girl squealed with delight, "Is this where we're going to live, Aunt Fanny?" She beamed with her pink cheeks like red apples and her hair like spun sugar.

"Yes, dearest Amber, take care getting down there," Fanny put a hand to her face covering her trembling lips.

The spring flowers were blossoming in profusion and the trees in the orchard were adorned with white flowers whose petals flew onto the driveway like snow.

William helped Fanny down and suddenly impulsively he lifted her into his arms and carried her over the threshold of her new home.

Amber laughed and clapped her hands and set about picking petals from the blossom on the trees and she followed the couple inside and as they sat down in the drawing room she sprinkled the white "confetti" over them.

"Amber, we are not married, Sweetest," Fanny chided the innocent child. But, in her heart, she was filled with exaltation. She had always imagined marriage would be just so. Then, however, her face fell as she was forced to admit that their relationship had all the trappings but not the binding of vows nor the sealing of marital relations.

Felicity gathered their portmanteaux and went in search of Fatima. She wanted to give the family the space to be spontaneous. Having a servant looking on would just inhibit the display of affection she had just witnessed

Hugh marched into the drawing room as soon as he returned from the luxurious suite of rooms he and William now owned in Town, "Welcome, dear Fanny," he bowed before her and lifted her white hand to his lips, "You are even more beautiful than I remember. We will make your stay a permanent addition to our way of life. Living at the Cape is very different to living in Ireland. Here we are few in number yet have the entire southern tip of Africa surrounding us, an Eden where there is no evil only that we create and unleash ourselves. Here you'll be queen and we will be your courtiers!" He turned to William, "Isn't Frank meant to be with you?"

"He should be here shortly as he's accompanying the luggage on a wagon. He strikes me as a pleasant man and I feel we shall be bringing the best out of him. I'm looking forward to getting to know him," William was in his element. Family meant everything to him. Distance had barred him from developing close bonds with his brothers and sisters from both his father's marriages. With Frank it would be different.

-o0o-

CHAPTER 16

Christmas 1846

Cape Town

The lamp light flickered in the study casting shadows on the wood-panelled walls. Paintings of African landscapes, some by Thomas Baines, maps and portraits of her parents decorated the room. The huge bookcase was full of books, arranged neatly. A vase of proteas had pride of place on a mahogany chest of drawers in the corner. Her desk was neatly arranged with invoices and receipts, school books and exercise jotters full of the scribbling of her students. Nerina was working till late when she stopped to reflect on personal matters. She was now twenty six years old and still single. Regarded as being a woman full of astute business sense tempered by her selfless commitment to her school and her 'girls', Nerina had little time for the luxuries and joys of life and she ignored the anxiety pangs of being left a spinster. Her joys were seeing the pupils flourish and her career as mentor and leader gave her an unwavering reason for beginning each day with passion and loyalty to her teachers and pupils. She had the further compulsion to work hard as the income from the school helped provide for her and her parents who were getting on in years. She walked over to the window and saw the branches of the trees writhe and sweep against the darkness. Rain pelted against the windows.

There was a knock on the door and when she turned round she was pleased to see Pierre standing there, stooping as he entered the room as he was so tall and the ceiling low. "I thought I told you not to work such long hours, Nerina," He smiled a little exasperated at his work-obsessed friend. "I have brought you a pot of coffee," He laid the silver tray with bone china cups and saucers down on the table. He had also produced slices of bread, a wedge of cheese and butter with two pears on plates and a knife on each.

"I've prepared my sermon for tomorrow. My ministry never ends like your devotion to your students," He poured the coffee and its aroma filled the room.

"What would I do without you?" Nerina pulled a chair up for Pierre, "I was thinking how we are both alone in our cause and set adrift into the world to be tossed about only to weather the storm."

"I have noticed the sadness in your eyes more often than I care to think, Nerina," Pierre took one of her hands and stroked it gently. "These hard-working hands. You weren't made for this sort of life. You should be looked after by a kind and faithful husband."

"Wishing and wanting doesn't make it happen, Pierre," she pulled her hand away gently, "You seem to manage – in fact your work seems to satisfy your needs."

"That's not what I mean. I have needs too. Have you ever considered there could be more between us than just this friendship?" He knew he was reaching a point of no return.

"What are you trying to say?" Their conversation was perplexing her and had she not been so world-weary she would have cut him short.

"Marry me, Nerina," Pierre pulled her to her feet and hugged her to him, like a wounded bird. He was clumsy but meant well. She extricated herself from his embrace, "No, I can't marry you, Pierre. You are dedicated to God. I would just tie you down and get between you and our Lord. I am fine and I don't need to be looked after. I can do that very well myself."

"What about children?" Pierre had dreams of having a family but now at fifty, time was running out for him, too.

"I haven't the time to fit in looking after a family, too. We are both professional people. I enjoy our conversations and you are a dear friend. Let's not spoil that." She smiled gently and touched his cheek.

She loved him deeply but not in the way she loved William....even after all these years.

-o0o-

In 1847 Harry Smith with a company of men including William rode into the area called Kaffraria, the land around King William's Town. Mindful of treaties being drawn up and signed every few years and yet the Frontier was still infiltrated by Xhosa *impis* intent on raiding the White farms, the Governor decided that something drastic had to be done to emblazon on the minds of the Xhosa that it was a case of thus far and no further.

The Xhosa chiefs met Harry Smith at King William's Town and the Governor wore ceremonial dress to impress on the chiefs that he belonged to a noble profession and represented a British elite. Harry Smith who was tall with short black hair, a pleasant face with deep-set eyes and a long nose had endless energy and a capacity for great moral courage and a strong sense of duty. His uniform was black navy with a high buttoned collar up to his chin and he wore gold epaulettes and insignia. William looked dashing in his cherry red jacket of the Sparklers with its high neck, silver collar, epaulettes, sash, cuffs and cumber-band with a sword in its scabbard. His gleaming silver helmet bore a tail of white horse hair.

Sandile was dressed in a maroon robe with a collar of leopard skin cut decoratively in scallops and wore a necklace of lion teeth and a narrow beaded headband. He was accompanied by chiefs of his minion tribes.

Harry Smith stood out in the crowd thronging around them and his voice hushed the onlookers, "If the chiefs expect another treaty to sign and then to flout, they are mistaken. Attorney General and Captain of your company, will you do the honours."

William lit a fuse and everyone watched as the spark snaked into an open field towards a wagon and Harry Smith shouted "Down with the treaties!" and the wagon filled with gunpowder was blown up.

The kings would have made their escape but Harry Smith bellowed, "There go the treaties. Do you hear? No more treaties."

Sandile and his men retreated hastily thinking the mythical great lightning bird was flying over them. Kaffraria was annexed and there was no longer a frontier. In short, White and Xhosa had to live together or keep to their own land. How long would the peace last? William wondered.

With time to spare before returning to Cape Town, William rode out to the Amatolas to visit Marika. The mountains were clothed in forests and silver glittering streams trickled down the tallest that was shaped like a hog's back, an azure pinnacle that had a dusting of snow on its summit and ink-black crevasses etched on its stone face. Her farm was in the plain below the mountains but when he arrived at the farm, it was deserted. An old withered Hottentot man wearing a knitted cap full of holes and a crone toothless but smiling, came out to peer at him.

"Where have they gone? The woman who lived here with her children?" The octogenarian man shook his head and pointed to the Amatolas.

"She went to be with the Boers across the Orange River."

William's heart contracted with a sense of deep loss. The wild untameable Boer woman of Africa had forsaken her farm and forsaken him.

-o0o-

CHAPTER 17

1853

Cape Town

William looked at the personal mail that had accumulated while he was away on the Circuit. He opened letters from Eliza, his stepmother – he still supported her and she continued to nurse John who had never really been aware of his surroundings since his stroke. There were also letters from John Scott in Belfast and from Frank, who married Felicity, Fanny's maid, within a year of arriving at the Cape and who now lived in Natal and had established a reputation as a merchant there. There were letters from close friends that had been with him at the Bar in Dublin. All were concerned for his welfare. Unsolicited they and John Scott were lobbying Westminster to elevate him to the position of Chief Justice. He would rebuff their efforts most vehemently.

The Rev. William Ropert had passed away some years previously which had been a blow to William as he had hoped to return to Ireland for a visit but the War had put pay to that. William was now middle-aged but his good looks were that of a younger, robust man and his lively intelligence as a raconteur had now been whetted by a life full of action and commitment. It was also good to be back in Cape society again.

An hour later John Fairbairn arrived and William pulled out a chair for him at the dining room table and Fatima immediately arrived with steaming soup and fresh bread. Fairbairn accepted a glass of red wine.

"What do you think of the fact that we'll at last have a truly representative Parliament in the near future?" Fairbairn asked, "There is talk that Sir George Grey will be appointed as our new Governor."

He enjoyed exchanging ideas with William. They had become firm friends.

"Yes, I have heard a lot about George Grey," William nodded, "He has been governor of New Zealand so it will make a change to have a civilian governor instead of another soldier-appointed governor. I'm sure it has come to your notice that ideas about how affairs should be run here are a major talking point back in political circles in London. They're becoming anxious to push British imperialism further into the interior but to do so they need the new Government to possess tact and firmness. We mustn't prejudice our relationship with the Afrikaner provinces north of the Orange River. I feel that taking imperialism into their realm will be inviting disaster."

"What excites me is what comes after. I believe our Parliament back in Britain does want to hand over the reins of governing the Cape to us. We will no longer be under imperial control but will have more autonomy and more responsibility. That means we will have to support ourselves financially." Fairbairn was full of enthusiasm. It was about time that events were hurried along.

Fatima interrupted them as she brought in serving bowls of roast potatoes, fresh beans and carrots and roast beef on a platter. The two men helped themselves.

"Yes, I have been asked to draw up a document to lay down the parameters for enfranchising the Colony. We cannot expect men to pay taxes without having a say in how their Colony and communities are run." William stood up and went over to the mahogany bureau and presented a document with notes to Fairbairn. "Read this and tell me what you think. I have studied the American Constitution and have tried to write down our unwritten British Conventions – the nearest we will get to having an American style Constitution."

"Yes, I've studied the American Constitution, a lengthy document defining every nuance and eventuality. There is no doubt what's right and what's wrong. The American Bill of Rights in 1791 encompasses all I hold dear. Freedom of speech, religion, the Press," Fairbairn laughed, knowing he was an irritation to any governor, "peaceful assembly" and the right to jury trials. Now the latter would be another question to debate. Our system at the Cape doesn't favour the American right to a trial by jury."

"I discovered an old document which might amuse you," William went over to a chest of drawers and drew out a battered and faded piece of paper, "Let me read it to you:

'British Colonies and their relationship with the motherland:

Allegiance to the Crown;

Subjects are entitled to all the inherent rights and liberties as if living in the mother country;

No taxes to be imposed on them but with their own consent or by representatives;

Cannot be represented in the Houses of Parliament but able to petition the Sovereign or either of the Houses of Parliament;

It is the right of British subjects in the British Colony to have the full and free enjoyment of their rights and liberties and an intercourse with Great Britain that is mutually affectionate and advantageous.'

Both men laughed at the quaint style of a probably long dead author. Dessert, an apple tart, arrived and Fatima laid down a jug of fresh, thick cream to accompany it.

"I think we should have two houses for our Parliament, an upper house perhaps called the Upper Legislative Council which provides leadership and interprets and enforces laws and the Lower Legislative Council where laws are made." William tucked into his apple pie and finished the wine left in his glass.

"What I want to see, if you don't mind me saying so, is a Bill of Human Rights for the Cape Colony. We should have a written one like in America." Fairbairn was still the idealist, ever striving for equality. "I understand how Britain believes in an unwritten Constitution as it allows the evolution of ideas, conventions and gradually irons out the kinks of prejudice and sweeping xenophobic generalisation. The conventions are always in a state of flux and that is good for debate to fine tune our beliefs. Here, where there's a melting pot of nationalities, creeds, various skin colours and extremes of remuneration and education, perhaps we should carefully accommodate the succinct criteria of voter participation at elections."

"Yes, I agree," replied William, "it would be good to have such a bill passed by Parliament when it comes into being next year. I'm meeting with my fellow Council members in the next couple of days to debate these questions. Our parliamentarians will need to make laws regarding foreign affairs, making treaties, declaring war and maintaining an army. We should be able to coin our own money and establish post offices."

"Do you really think we will be given that sort of autonomy? You make it sound as if we could have all the rights of becoming totally independent from Britain. You always were the dreamer, Ropert," The older man had to reign in William's enthusiasm.

"Well, it seems we will be able to raise money by collecting taxes and we will be able to have some control over foreign commerce. Furthermore, we'll be able to pass our own laws. That is something," William had much to think about.

The two men entered the drawing room and Fairbairn accepted a cigar and William lit the fragrant rolls of Cuban tobacco. Both men enjoyed the pleasure of smoking as they relaxed in comfort in the high-winged back leather chairs. They relaxed with their glasses of port and stared at the roaring fire in the hearth. Fairbairn had another point of interest to discuss with William, "What are your views on voting? That is of major interest to me."

"The way I see it is to follow the British custom. I believe that to qualify for the vote here there should be land-ownership to a value of £25 or an individual's ability to pay a rent of £25 a year, an individual earning £50 per year would also ensure him the right to vote. Furthermore, an individual should be over twenty one and of sound mind and body." William frowned before continuing, "I would dearly love to give women the suffrage but until they achieve equality by investing in or contributing to the economy and society at large or owning property that probably won't happen. If one considers the attitude of other countries towards granting women the right to vote, Sweden and Corsica are the only two who have done just that but it only lasted in both cases for the duration of a period of political liberalism."

"Of course women contribute to the economy but wives and mothers aren't given salaries not to mention recognition. Where would many of us be without the support of our wives? Except, of course, in your case, William!" Fairbairn laughed. William's single status often drew amusement. He picked up the thread of conversation again, "Going unpaid is a poor criterion for withholding the suffrage from them. I can understand withdrawing the vote from men who could be gainfully employed but choose not to work or worse still become criminals. " His words echoed William's support for the rights of women.

"I also feel the vote should be colour-blind," William added thoughtfully, "We would face the darkest times if we restrict the suffrage according to skin colour. 'The right to vote shall not be denied on account of race, colour or previous condition of servitude' – that phrase I have borrowed from the Americans. Therefore freed slaves can vote as long as they meet the above criteria. I am happy for Coloured people to be given the vote as I would rather meet a Hottentot at the hustings rather than in a skirmish alone on a dark night."

Fairbairn laughed imagining such a scene but sobered up as he contemplated all they had discussed. He felt Governor Grey would have an able and very astute attorney general at his side. He and William Ropert had come a long way since their first meeting all those years ago when they had discussed the condition of labourers' slums."

-o0o-

The Cape Advertiser soon ran several columns and an editorial about the new Constitution that the members of Government were drafting. John Fairbairn was like a Jack Russell puppy nipping at William's heels. When more came to light as the debate ran its course, it became known that a liberal sea change had infected the Colony.

However, one man was unhappy and wrote to the Editor, *"As I understand it, the Attorney General known for his soft Whig mentality, believes that his new Constitution is a liberal step towards a general suffrage as long as one is considerably affluent and blessed with a significant position in one's profession or vocation or naturally if one owns property. How liberal is he when women - of course - are still tied in bondage to their husbands' views, facilitated by the Church's stance on a woman's place in a marriage hierarchy? 'Honour and obey'? Would women not just vote in the way of their husbands? An interesting development is that there will be no bar according to colour. Will we not be outvoted by all our black brethren – ah, but how many of them meet the criterion of earning £25 a year or owning their own property? Another aspect the Attorney General has not considered is allowing poor black or poor coloured persons or poor whites to vote. Would that have created mayhem? I believe he's too aware of his own position in Government to risk all in such an action. The card player is hiding his trump card. When will he play it – the card that says there is no class component to this Constitution? For a liberal he should have played that card. I, for one, would have rolled the dice. Roland Craven."*

-oOo-

The marvels and mysteries children bring to one's life made William realise that cold facts of law and dividends from investments were a poor substitute for family life. He pondered on the irony of his situation: he had a wife who wasn't his in matrimony, a child who wasn't his own and a friend who seemed more than a friend while William was always beholden to him.

As he watched Amber on the swing he had erected in the apple orchard when the boughs were heavy with red fruit, and with her delighted cries echoing in his ears, something stirred deep within him. An answer perhaps to his former Descartian questions about life. The addition of women to his household was a golden dawn of poetic possibilities which would gild his life by making actions and thoughts less egocentric and cognitively dull. Already he was setting aside time to spend with both Fanny and Amber and was enriched by their feminine appreciation and remarks, their words more earthy in their sensuality and more winsome in their ethereal excesses. The golden-haired child was as beautiful as the children in paintings by Gainsborough. Her skin was white as milk and her eyes the colour of the blue irises that grew in his garden. He was entranced that such a young creature, a faun, would evolve and each phase would not be like the moon and always show the same face but new images would emerge and these would change him, too.

Fanny sat in the garden and listened to the man who no longer had just himself to answer to and now his repartee with the little girl was instinctive and he allowed Amber the freedom to challenge his old ways and teach him new ones. She wished she could see them and the garden. She was always begging those around her to fill her hearing with sound pictures. She didn't want to be a nuisance.

Amber was settling into life at 'Wolmunster' with the easy acceptance of children to their lot. She had made friends with Abel's son, Imran who was ten. Abel was William's groom and driver and William wanted to tutor the young boy to help him to get on in life. He and Amber played together every week day while Abel was busy with chores. Fanny taught Amber her alphabet and numbers and sang songs or narrated poems from memory whereas William prepared Imran for university in the evenings before Abel retired to his own quarters. Soon Amber would go to school and to give her the best start William had taken Amber to Nerina's school for girls nearby. It was not surprising that Nerina was intrigued to hear that a woman and a child were now living with both him and Hugh. She was very inquisitive and had to bite her tongue before asking for more intimate details. She would never know that Fanny had won William's heart before she was ever born.

Imran became William's protégé and was welcomed into the boy's school in Wynberg. Life would be pleasant in this Cape of Good Hope, Fanny thought, at peace from all her longing and no longer having to have her unwritten thoughts answered in William's letters and the hard endeavour to read his mind in the articulate diction of his replies. The freedom to express herself when alone with him was like rising up from the depths of the ocean when one is drowning and breaking the watery surface gasping for air and at last regaining full consciousness.

That evening Fanny realised she had aged quickly with her body now quite fragile like bone china but she hoped William could see that she still bore traces of her beauty. She sat near the open fire and stroked the tabby cat on her lap. She drew comfort from making the cat purr and daydreamed of the baby she had never had and reflected in silence how blessed she was to have Amber.

When he wasn't busy, William would tell her all about the court proceedings and the cases he was prosecuting and before bedtime he would read to her from novels and they both enjoyed the peaceful end to the day. He would then help her to her bedroom and hug her and kiss her good night and she then got herself ready for bed. She hungered for those moments but realised the passion they had for each other had mutated into a devotion devoid of rash desires...

-oOo-

CHAPTER 18

Wolmunster, Mowbray,

January 1856

Shortly after William had returned to Cape Town after his third and last stint at the Frontier the Xhosa attacks across the border miraculously and suddenly stopped.   There was no rational explanation for this cessation of the sorties and persecution of the White farmers. The farmers and the towns' people celebrated by having festivals and news filtered through to William that a miracle had happened. But, then, William received a strange letter.

Honourable Attorney General,

It is with great pride that I write to you about what has taken place in the Xhosa- held territory.

My story begins with the Xhosa people themselves. It is obvious to an observer that the black tribe with all its branches has been suffering under the increasing numbers of white settlers who have taken land in what is now known as British Kaffraria.

At first, this seemed to be an open invitation for the Xhosa to cross into Kaffraria and steal the farmers' cattle which was probably their way of obtaining compensation of sorts. The number of cattle belonging to the Xhosa was thus on the increase but then along came the lung disease which has infected many which have subsequently died.

The Xhosa have suffered in other ways too. The missionaries are destroying their traditions and customs by converting many to Christianity but the loss of what is truly their essence is creating a society with no stable foundation. The people have now sought to reclaim their ties with the supernatural that had kept them on the straight and narrow before the advent of the White settlers. I have gathered that ancestral worship is a binding and fear- invoking exercise that prevents crimes being committed against their own people and the tribal elders hold sway over the villages upholding values and ancient rites that purify and cleanse and insure fertility and wealth.

That is where my story begins. I have often crossed into Xhosa territory to study their ways in order to see how knowledge about their deepest fears could be used against them. I have witnessed how deeply they revere the long departed or recently departed members of their branch of the tribe and they worship them and believe the messages interpreted by the sangomas, witchdoctors, and more amazingly act upon them unquestioningly, truly believing the instructions come from their ancestors.

There is a river where I sometimes fish in that territory and my black guide and I often camp near a lagoon. It is paradise with headlands of scrubland and beaches of white sand where cattle roam freely watched over by herd boys. I noticed a young slip of a girl who drew water from the river above the tidal lagoon was always alone and bearing designs on her face in white mud. My guide explained to me that she was being taught the spells and magic of the sangomas. Her name is Nongqawuse and she is a pupil of her uncle, a forceful priest-diviner. It came to me in a flash, like Paul's conversion on the way to Damascus, that perhaps I could divine a spell that could act in our favour. I discussed this with my guide and we went down to the river where I dressed in a lion's skin with its mane on my shoulders and porcupine quills in my hair and shells around my neck and he smeared my face, arms and legs with mud and drew patterns with charcoal. My own hair was unruly as it was.

It was just after sunrise when fish eagles were calling and I caught the magic moment of a claw impale a fish as the great bird dipped down to the water. Wagtails searched in the grass for insects, and kingfishers hovered nearby dropping into the river in an endless cycle.

Nongqawuse approached and we hid in the rattling reeds and at a given moment as planned I rose up miming what my Black guide, uttered, as we had rehearsed, "Nongqawuse, do not be afraid. I am the spirit of your ancestor and I bring a message for the tribe. Some of your cattle have lung disease and your elders and sangomas are no longer listened to or obeyed. The White man has eroded your beliefs and you must agree that the spirits are angry. To calm the world of the spirits your uncle, the great sangoma, Mhlakaza, must tell the people to kill all the cattle. Only then will the White man leave you in peace and your lands will not shrink further. It is the desire of the spirits that you must no longer cross over into the White man's lands where temptation and bad behaviour ruin our dignity and pride.

You must now hasten to your uncle and tell him what I have told you. Go in peace, go slowly, my young dove." The young girl burst into tears and left her water-pot at the side of the river and ran off, wiping her eyes.

I can now report that there are no longer attacks from across the border. The cattle have been slaughtered and the tribe is awaiting a better world for the future although for the time being the men are weak from the famine and have lost the will to fight. The girl's uncle, Mhlakaza, promised the people that their dead warriors would return to life and on the 18th February 1857 at the rising of the sun they would welcome them back into the tribe and that they would all be rewarded with living cattle, more than they ever had before arriving from the centre of the sun and above all, the White man would leave them in peace.

You will no doubt have been told of the strange phenomena and that the attacks at the Frontier have stopped. There have been eyewitness accounts of the slaughter of the cattle. I believe we have now seen the last of the Frontier Wars as warriors cannot go to war on empty stomachs.

This letter may be true; but, on the other hand, it could be a means to ruffle your feathers, dear Attorney General. You will never really know the truth and I will watch my poison eat away at your flesh as I pour it drop by drop into your ear.

Yours sincerely or as sincerely as an enemy can be,

Roland Craven.

William took several minutes to digest the contents of the letter and after rereading it several times, he suddenly thumped his desk disturbing the cat on Fanny's lap.

Fanny leant forward startled, "What has happened to make you so angry?" She was frail but still womanly and if it were not for her blindness she would have been startlingly feminine, William thought, for a moment distracted. Some women never lose their allure even in old age.

"There have only been three times that I have been so enraged as to desire to kill someone, slowly and most painfully and each time it has been due to one man," William was seething with fury.

"Is it Roland Craven? What has he done now?" Fanny could tell that the message in the letter had greater significance than a mere attempt to provoke William.

"This man has seen fit to virtually exterminate the Xhosa tribe. They have slaughtered their cattle at the order of a powerful witchdoctor who in turn was deceived by an apparent manifestation to his daughter in the form of a long dead ancestor. The vision was concocted by Roland Craven. The man's devious mind knows no limits. I must find a way to stop him from destroying more lives. Dear knows what he'll be up to next," William was clenching his fists and had the desire to put his hands around Roland's neck and to squeeze the life out of him.

"That is appalling, William. Just think what it will look like if you take this letter to the press or to the Governor. People could always misconstrue it as being an idea sanctioned by the Governor The hatred of both the Black people and the world, would know no bounds," Remarked Fanny astutely.

"You have it in a nutshell. I'm caught between Roland's depravity and the reputation of the Colony. It most probably is Roland's way of getting back at me. He probably wants to sow the seeds of doubt about the mass slaughter of their cattle by the Xhosas themselves. This letter has his mark of lies and Machiavellian manipulation to destroy my ideals. I'll have to deliberate further as I really don't know what to do, Fanny. It can't possibly be true," William looked weary and all of his fifty two years.

"It's still early in the day. Would you like to go for a walk along the beach at Clifton, my dearest Fanny? I need to have some distraction and to have the time to enjoy the blessed peace of walking along the shore, barefoot," He sighed with resignation.

"Oh yes, it's such a warm day and there's no wind. The South-Easter must be having its holiday," Fanny rose and William briefly embraced her, enjoying her scent in her remarkably thick grey hair she had pinned up fetchingly.

An hour later, William tethered their horse and the trap giving the animal a bag of oats to chew. It was late afternoon but still pleasant on the beach with the waves running in rows like lacy frills on a dress and further out at sea the wavelets were foam-flecked and several yachts were enjoying the breeze.

Fanny enjoyed the tactile sensations of wet sand under her feet and the incoming tide washing over them. Conical whelks slid on rubbery protuberances seeking debris to devour and William picked one up and placed it on Fanny's hand.

"Oh it feels cold. Oh dear it has gone back into its shell," She said delighted.

Eventually they sat down above the high tide mark and enjoyed what their senses were telling them. They heard the shrieks of seagulls and terns and the lapping of miniature breakers where waders chased the waves as they rushed back and forth. They didn't speak but enjoyed the moment as though it were their last together.

Fanny lifted her hand to touch William's face and then remarked happily, "Thank you for shaving off your beard, my Dearest. It's all fine and well while you're in the field of battle but it makes you a stranger. Your fine features are a pleasure to touch and I can now re-acquaint myself with your face," Fanny leant her head against William's shoulder and daydreamed.

William was deliberating whether to broach the subject of John McBride's passing. They had received word from Eliza that Amber's father had had a fit and died, after ten years in a comatose state. Fanny had taken it well so he felt it was safe to talk about Amber's future.

"Fanny, risking being presumptuous on the day you have just heard that John has been dead for six months but I feel we need to talk about Amber. If you agree I would like to become her legal guardian and I'll provide for her every need until such time as she marries."

"I have been wrestling with the same issues. You and I are very in tune with each other. My Dearest I am overwhelmed by your kindness and Amber doesn't know what a lucky young woman she is. I know just as I know night follows day that you will always care for her. My mind can rest now," Fanny leant her head against his shoulder and her smile was warm and for an instant her face captured its once youthful beauty. She began to doze while the breeze lifted loose sand and sent it scurrying like a miniature devil wind over the wet beach.

After a while, William stirred and Fanny seemed fast asleep, falling against him as he moved to get up. She looked peaceful with a gentle smile on her face but as he looked at her, it dawned on him to his horror that Fanny had slipped away like a falling feather suddenly lifting upwards to the heavens… the swan of Lir so briefly returned to human form though not that of the young girl onto whom the spell was cast but into an elderly woman with little time left on earth, now tragically ended.

-o0o-

William had managed to drive the horse and trap back to Wolmunster with Fanny cradled in his arms. Tears fell like raindrops wetting his face which was grey with shock and pain. Death came stealthily when they least expected it. Only hours earlier they were discussing the politics of the day and things as banal as the weather.

When the horse's hooves clattered on the driveway, he awoke from the trance of the journey. The groom rushed to calm the horse which was in a lather with foam dripping from its mouth. His gardener, Samuel, was at the side of the trap and William passed Fanny into his outstretched arms. Her body slid down lifelessly. A rush of burnished autumn leaves from the liquid amber tree cart-wheeled around them, clattering in his ears. His senses took in everything tenfold. Samuel carried Fanny up to her room and placed her reverently on top of her bed. Her lips seemed to move and her breast appeared to lift with a breath but it was his imagination. He smoothed her hair where tendrils curled around her ear from which hung a single pearl. She looked peacefully asleep and William threw himself down beside the bed on his knees and blotted out the scene with his hands over his eyes. He cried as only a grown man can cry with sobs dragged from his soul to leave his body in shuddering paroxysms of pain.

Amber now ten, ran into the room and looked at him as he turned his grief-stricken face, "She can't be, no, she can't be dead! First, Father and now Aunt Fanny. I'm cursed. Everyone I have ever loved dies and I am left behind to go on when there seems so little point in carrying on." She threw herself over Fanny's body, pulling her into her arms until William gently removed her clutching fingers from Fanny's dress.

"Come downstairs with me, Amber. I'll give you some brandy to ease the shock," He looked a shadow of himself, diminished by raw grief. In the drawing room he stoked the fire in the grate and flames flickered. He placed a crocheted blanket around Amber's shoulders as she sat transfixed in a wing-backed chair. The red setter dog sat in front of her with his head in her lap and his eyes pouring out his sympathy. William sat morosely in the shadows while the brandy in his glass shone like honeyed gold captured in an icy receptacle. He swirled the liquid and took a mouthful and swallowed. The heat burnt through his frozen soul and he encouraged Amber to drink up. She did so and coughed as the liquid scorched her throat. They both sat in silence listening to the clock ticking waiting for the brandy to do its work, to take away their pain. It was in this state that Hugh found them when he returned. Staggered by the news, he touched William's shoulder firmly and he knew it wasn't time for words, just silence and waiting.

-o0o-

A few days later Fanny was buried in St George's cemetery and William was sombre and reflective remembering their dear companionship that had survived against all odds. She was his mentor and greatest friend and she was all he had wanted in a wife. He battled to keep his emotions in check and turned pale as the coffin was lowered into the grave. Amber pressed close to William with tears running down her cheeks but her sobs were silent. Amber had picked two red roses from the garden which had pricked her fingers and now she gave one to William and indicated he should toss it into the grave to fall on the coffin while she herself pulled the petals off the bloom dropping each petal into the abyss of death like tears of blood. William was not embarrassed as he once might have been. Let the world know of his passionate love for the woman he knew so well. She was gone forever and such desolation that William had never before experienced drove him into a deep depression. Hugh put an arm around William's shoulders and ushered him away with Amber following meekly, while William's bowed head hid his tears…

Much later after their guests had left William called Amber to the study. She had been sitting at the table in the drawing room plaiting a small lock of Fanny's hair. She quickly inserted it into the back of her locket and placed a likeness of her aunt into the locket opposite a miniature of her mother. She was still dressed in the black velvet mourning dress with its white collar of delicate lace. Following her uncle she pulled her shoulders back. It sounded important so she hurriedly sat in the chair next to the desk. William pulled out his chair around to her side and sat opposite the young woman who looked pale and exhausted from the emotional seesaw of the day, "You must be wondering what will happen to you now that your aunt and father have both passed away." His tone was soothing.

"I never knew my father after his stroke. I no longer existed for him as he could no longer recognise me. Aunt Fanny was my mother and father caring for me and bringing me up at her own expense. Who will now fill her role in my life? Aunt Eliza?" She appealed to William, "Please don't send me back to Ireland, Uncle William."

"No, I promised your aunt the same day she died that I would become your guardian and look after your every need until you are married and perhaps thereafter," The light in the oil lamp flickered as the flame fluttered like a ribbon.

Amber leapt up and threw herself down at his knees and placed her head on his lap, "I'll always be grateful to you, Uncle William," she whispered.

"Your aunt brought me a daughter I never had and I'm proud to have you as part of my life. Life without you, dearest Amber, would be exceedingly dull. You've even made Hugh mellow in his attitude towards women." William managed a wry grin.

After everyone had retired to bed, William remained in his study and the lamplight bathed the room in a honey glow. He picked up his pen and dipped it in the ink and began to write:

My Beloved,

With these carefully penned words I hope to reach you as once my letters found their way to your hand and your eyes, even from the long seafaring distance between the Cape and Ireland. I now find myself marooned on an island from which there is no return to a former happier life when you were at my side.

Dear Companion, I, in all conscience, recognise that our relationship should have taken a step farther thus allowing the unconventional to endure in a society critical of the extraordinary. We clipped our wings but you have now flown away swan-like in death and like that creature's consort, I will await death, longing to join you in a purer life, bathed in God's glory.

After all the storms we endured, you came shining through the mists like a never-ending rainbow, reappearing and fading in perpetual motion wherever a promise of beauty was needed, strong, vibrant in all your colours, and you still, even in death, promise joy and fulfilment. Behind your rainbow, I was the second rainbow less colourful, dimmer, fading away to mere drops which had lost their jewels, your shadow over tumbling waters.

Knowing that immortality will return sight to you and you will witness visions of such untold panoramic vistas of heaven and celestial gatherings, and yet you'll be able to see me, a mere mortal on a dark continent, a mere pinprick on your finger to remind you of what we had together. Allow me to anoint your finger with a salve so you feel no pangs of regret. Allow those longings to be only mine.

I will bid you farewell, Dear Heart. Long for me no more. I await the future and all that it promises.

Your beloved servant,

William.

-o0o-

CHAPTER 19

1856

Cape Town

The end of the Frontier wars, not to mention Fanny's death, left a vacuum in William's life. The knowledge of what Roland Craven had done or claimed to have done, still appalled him but he had decided not to tell the Governor what horrific crime had been committed as he had only the word of a felon. The damage to the Colony's reputation would have been immeasurable and repercussions would be felt down the centuries to come.

Shortly after Fanny's death he and fellow lawyers with the incumbent Judge had spent three months travelling with the Circuit Court which meant his grief had been interrupted and now much needed his attention. Would he ever be allowed to mourn the woman who had given him so much?

Left alone in his study at Wolmunster, William looked back over the past seven years. He often read what he had written in his Journals about the trials of living in the veldt under canvass, riding out on sorties from the forts and engaging with the enemy and now he rejoiced in the fact that the experience had been both challenging and rewarding. Those years had been eventful and exhilarating. He had never felt such an explosion of energy as whenever he returned to Cape Town and as usual immediately threw himself back into his work as matters of government needed his attention. Anything to take his mind off the emptiness of 'Wolmunster' without Fanny.

Hugh was relieved to have a semblance of normality return to their household and to their careers. He had embraced William on his return and William had been overcome with emotion. He loved Hugh and now looking at Hugh afresh he could see that he had lost a lot of weight and would have coughing fits from time to time. He was smoking too much. Everything had been sacrificed to maintain peace at the Frontier. Hugh had gone out as he was invited to a night of gambling, drinking and smoking. Maybe his body would suffer with such cruel treatment. But, telling Hugh what to do was a futile exercise.

Amber was the light of his life and reminded him of Fanny whom she resembled in beauty and intelligence if one didn't take into account her luxuriant golden red hair. She had become quite jealous of the time he spent with Hugh or working in his study. He planned on taking her to the playhouse in town to see a Shakespearean drama and the young girl had come alive with enthusiasm and was more like her old self. She had mourned Fanny in the deepest way and for a while, the fire in her had been dampened and they had all felt concern for such a young person feeling so much pain.

William lit a lamp and the wood-panelled walls were sombre. The house was so empty with Fanny dead and Hugh out so much. Amber was spending the weekend at the home of his clerk who was a dear friend. He had a daughter the same age and they both went to Nerina's school.

As Amber grew into a young woman, she flitted around 'Wolmunster' like a 'painted lady' butterfly and she was cheerful and self-confident with all her days beginning with golden dawns and ending with smouldering sunsets, their colours captured in her long auburn hair which made it so distinctive. She skipped instead of walked or ran instead of walking purposefully. At school she blossomed into a clever and conscientious student. She and Imran, William's groom son whom William had supported through his school years and sent to university to study medicine later, were competitive and often had heated discussions in the kitchen about a problem or appreciation of a philosophical thought. She loved her headmistress and Nerina couldn't help being captivated by the charm of Fanny's lissom spirit and budding femininity. She would need to speak to William about his step-niece's future, she thought pensively. If Amber were a boy and if one had a parent as wealthy as William, she would've expected her to go on to higher education. There was also the fact that he was a champion of defending the human rights of women. Perhaps he would listen.

In the meantime, Amber still relied on her memory of Fanny for her inspiration to do well. She smiled at the thought of her Aunt finding out how unconventional she truly was, if she was watching her like a guardian angel. She didn't want to be a spinster like she had been, captured and imprisoned in a solitary life in the rooms of a house like a poor queen bee or confined to a garden, like a canary in a cage. She wanted to be part of the youthful company of young men and women in Cape Town and she was already learning to use her feminine wiles on the young men. Her sexuality came then as a surprise to herself when she finally sat alone in the garden surrounded by the herbaceous borders of African flowers and proteas. She loved Africa, she thought. It pulsated and it was so raw, so fertile, so young. The earth was red with a life-force that made anything germinate; even ideas could sprout from pushing one's toes into its mud. It was for youth not like the decayed ash-grey of European chalk, clay and sandstone which was fine for ancient civilisations and their artefacts. Nothing was wasted in Africa. One took only what one needed and when one died one left no evidence of ever having been there, keeping it new awaiting new infants who will grow into love with it and partake of its fruits and fortunes but always we must let go, Amber thought to herself.

She was a fire sprite and a free spirit and often started heated debates from which she sometimes escaped feeling exasperation and frustration. Why couldn't people see what sense she was talking? Imran would never have entered into the sort of conversations he and Amber had, with other woman but he was patient with the young woman he had seen grow up alongside him and would close the book he was studying while she ranted on and then with a few words he soothed her inflamed spirit with his common sense and wisdom. She wasn't wise, she knew that. But she had ideas, sometimes so many that her head buzzed like a trapped bee against a window pane. Let me out, she thought. I want to do things, important things. That was when she had the idea. Of course, her Uncle William should surely approve and Aunt Fanny if she were alive. She wanted to be a missionary doctor and travel into the parts of Africa where people suffered without medical help during childbirth or treatment for diseases which she could learn to treat. So what if she was a woman. Her uncle spoke of the equality between the sexes, a topic for which he often endured mockery and total rejection by most men. She could prove him right!

-o0o-

Nerina tidied her office and made sure every pile of work waiting to be done was neatly arranged according to urgency. She placed her pen and inkwell in their allotted place and rearranged a bouquet of dried flowers in a pleasing way. She began daydreaming about the past.

Nerina's mother and father had passed away after a virulent influenza epidemic. Sometimes she wouldn't venture out for weeks, lost in her little world, the school. The school won the support of Cape Society so she had achieved part of her aim. She now wanted to open a second school which could be financed by the wealthy merchants but for the children of the less fortunate, for both boys and girls of age eleven upwards. Another aim was to ask William to exert his influence in getting places at the University of the Cape of Good Hope which up to now had been for young men only for her brightest girls including Amber who, she believed, could easily become good lawyers, doctors or teachers.

She knew William would help but it would take a huge amount of courage to approach him. How would he react to seeing her again? Cape Town was a small town so she had often seen him walking with a client or alighting from a carriage. She often wandered into the Botanical Gardens especially in summer and sat watching people go by with loved ones or children. The oak trees and flowers would lift her mood and watching doves strutting about or squirrels cavorting would bring a smile to her lips.

She awoke to the present and sat with her back as straight as a ramrod and tried to keep her hands from fidgeting. She had arranged for William and Amber to meet her that evening to discuss Amber's future.

Her keen hearing alerted her to their arrival and she arose to welcome them into her study. She was dressed more elegantly than she would normally have done and realised she still wanted to possess some allure to catch William's eye. She had selected a purple dress with a high waist line which flattered her figure and a hand-embroidered batiste with Valenciennes lace bands in black and hem trimmed with three rows of black ruffles. She wore her hair in a complicated array of plaits and tendrils with earrings of amethysts. Her hand was steady as she allowed William to bend over it but his kiss didn't touch her skin.

"The weather couldn't be more inclement. I trust you didn't get drenched," She couldn't help talking in platitudes.

"It's lovely to see you again, Nerina," William meant it, too.

His voice with its rich timbre still had a profound effect on her and she smiled and nodded, putting her arm around Amber who was dressed in her full school uniform of a navy dress with petticoats and a sailor collar and a bow of navy ribbon at her neck. Her hair was neatly captured in a long plait.

"We've much to discuss this evening, haven't we, Amber?" Nerina said.

"Yes, Miss Smith," Amber took her seat and sat dutifully upright, "Perhaps you can explain my sincere wish to study further after this year. I know it's unusual for women to have that opportunity but could there be the possibility to go to the University of the Cape in Town?" She looked at her uncle, pleadingly.

William lit a cigar pensively and inhaled the sweet aromatic smoke, "Amber, why do you want to waste your time in cold libraries and lecture halls full of men? It's hardly seemly. You would need a chaperone and all manner of complications can arise."

"You see, Miss Smith. I told you he wouldn't understand. Uncle William, I really want to study medicine," Amber said petulantly.

"It's impossible and I can't believe you have brought me all the way here to listen to such a preposterous suggestion. I've heard of the odd blue stocking who studied literature, philosophy and the classics without ever being acknowledged by having a degree bestowed on them. But, medicine. It's a male orientated profession." William was unamused.

"Imran was accepted. You even provided references about him to the board of governors and you are the chancellor. You should do the same for me. There's always the first time for something. Perhaps I should become the first female doctor in the world? Someone has to break the mould."

"She has the intelligence, William," Nerina smiled gently, "When we were younger, you were allowed to dream and your dream came true. I made mine turn into this school. Can't you allow Amber's prayers to be answered?"

"I'll even cut my hair and wear pants and shoes like a man. I'm that desperate. I'm willing to mix with men as their equal. Who would guess I was a woman?" Amber's youth was clouding her judgment.

"No, Amber, this time you're not getting your own way," William muttered, "It has been my intention to enable you to go to a finishing school somewhere in Europe with a trusted chaperone. It would be more suitable and thereafter you'll no doubt meet a young man and want to get married and have a family of your own. No, it would be folly to nurture such ideas that are flagrantly extraordinary."

"But, what about the sick and the infirm in the dark reaches of this continent. I could help them. Not on my own but with fellow doctors."

"Again, my answer is simply 'no'. The dangers are too many and diseases are rife. Anything from cholera, smallpox, black water fever and malaria. I refuse to allow you to subject yourself to such dangers. The matter is closed. I may just be prepared to talk to the governors about letting you study the Classics and English literature. They would never allow you to graduate, nor would you receive any certification. You can perhaps teach. Miss Smith could perhaps employ you here. But medicine, no." William understood Amber's zeal and feelings of omnipotence. That was the prerogative of the young. Sadly, the reality was she would not survive in the wilderness. He had seen menaces the like of which she couldn't ever imagine. He had taught her to ride with the best, to fish and shoot and more amusingly, to dance but that was the limit of his efforts to make her a man's equal.

Amber sat back dejectedly but she had her uncle's promise of perhaps being permitted to study further at the College. Teaching was second best but still a challenge. Who knows whom she would teach?

The two old friends smiled wryly at one another. Who were they to judge and who were they to alter the course of Amber's life? One day in the future perhaps what she wanted would be possible but she was living now and the facts remained, medicine was out of bounds for a, single, white female immigrant marooned in the 19th Century.

As William and Amber rose to take their leave, Nerina looked at Amber and gestured for her to leave, "Could you please wait outside, Amber. I have matters I need to discuss with your Uncle." Amber dutifully closed the door after her.

William was taken aback and immediately thought Nerina wanted to argue about the question of higher education for young women but he was wrong.

"William, that young woman has a fire burning in her that won't be quenched by offering her crumbs from the table. I've seen that passion before and believe me, it can damage a woman, ruining her for the rest of her life. To have all that talent and intellect and not to be able to use it generously will break her in the end. She really isn't ready for marriage, William. In fact, she would make a bored wife and a disinterested mother while she yearns for her vocation in life."

"I'm at a loss, if what you say is true. Should we just give in to her notions and foster her aspirations in the field of medicine when we know she would never be accepted at the University?" William was still standing and now sat down wearily.

"You could suggest nursing but that can come later," Nerina continued.

"What do you mean by 'later'?" He was finding their conversation disconcerting.

"I've this brilliant idea. Why don't you take Amber with you into the Interior on an expedition which would lead her into wild and dangerous places? As you would be in control no harm could ever come to her. She would be in her element, meeting new African tribes in their own villages and she could assess their needs and consider whether she has the resources both physically and spiritually to accommodate them! She hasn't seemed a very religious person, in fact, quite the opposite so I'm intrigued at the prospect of her becoming a missionary. "

William's demeanour changed and he felt her infectious enthusiasm, "Your evaluation epitomises why men need women in their lives. I would never have dreamt of subjecting Amber to such a trial. But, my God, you are right!" He exclaimed, unaware he had blasphemed.

His imagination took over and he put into words, ideas as they came thick and fast in his mind, "She would have to be fit enough. What about diseases? This is insane. We would have to have a wagon for her and we would need to have provisions and tents,"

"She won't want you to wrap her up like a porcelain doll from China. She is a commendable rider but she couldn't travel on horseback all the time. You could think of her dress. I would recommend Boer women's clothes; they're more comfortable and cooler and a couple of pairs of boots. Definitely hats to protect her delicate skin. The bonnet the Boer women wear shades the face very well. Frills and flounces should remain locked up in her *kist* at Wolmunster."

"I could invite a couple of young men I know to accompany us. One is Edward Wallace, a very accomplished artist and botanist and the other is James Munroe, a geologist. Both are my protégés and they would provide us with company and we would have more protection. I would hire a guide and translator, a driver and a cook, perhaps Lettie could come along to keep Amber company."

They were both excited and William acknowledged, "I have often dreamt of following in David Livingstone's footprints but I'll put it to the vote. I'm sure Amber is wondering what we're discussing. I must take my leave, Nerina and I would like to thank you for a most remarkable conversation."

William re-joined Amber who was agog with curiosity and Nerina led them through the hall to the front doors which opened out into the courtyard where their horse and carriage stood waiting for them in the pouring rain. They went through all the formalities of parting. So much was left unsaid in conversation but when William and Nerina's glances locked, their eyes were full of an expression of some unique emotion, a confirmation that they were still in love. William wondered how he could love and be in love with three women in his given lifetime. 'Wilt thou take …to be thy lawful wife, to have and to hold, in sickness and in health and forsaking all others, keep thyself only unto her, for as long as you both shall live?' He remembered the refrain he had heard so often at weddings.

-o0o-

The next day William retreated to his study, took out his maps of Southern Africa and perused the lettering and geographical ciphers with a magnifying glass. Sunshine fell in a splash over the maps and his bookcases suddenly seemed dark and vacant. What route would suit them best, he wondered peering over his spectacles, their glasses reflecting the light and their gold frames gleamed as his blue eyes darted about. For a man of his age, he was fitter than most. The journey should not be too arduous thus allowing for Amber's comfort. He hadn't discussed his proposal with Hugh and Amber and perhaps it was time to draw them into the planning and preparation for what lay ahead. He knew that it was possible for him to be away for six months researching the facts about the people and their lands hitherto only mentioned in anecdotes by adventurers although Livingstone's account was by far the most useful. In his conversation with the missionary doctor, Livingstone had mentioned lands rich in resources. If he could confirm this there would be ample opportunity to negotiate mining rights.

Feeling prepared to drop this proposition into conversation with Amber and Hugh he left the room in search of them. Both were in the garden, Hugh in the hammock and Amber reading a book in the arbour while Fatima was hanging out washing and above them lost seagulls dipped and soared and behind them the mountains rose with a mauve glow warming them like smouldering embers.

Once he had their full attention they retired to the study, curious and expectant.

"Last night while you were waiting for me, Amber, Miss Smith made a suggestion that was most extraordinary but on reflection sensible and requiring courage and tenacity from us all."

"I knew you were both in collusion sharing some secret tryst," Amber clapped her hands in approval, "Do tell us, what was it? Are you and she going to get married?"

"No, that wasn't the subject of our discussion. You've been reading too many of Miss Austen's books. Miss Smith suggested that you and I should make a journey into the less well-known areas of Southern Africa to give you a taste of what it would be like to live among people who not only don't speak our language but who have different customs and religions." He paused but Amber had already expressed herself with a whoop of surprise.

"What a fantastic idea. Yes, yes, yes, Uncle William, do let's do it!" Amber had at once been transformed into a passionate young woman with a goal within her reach.

"Another of your hair-raising ideas," Hugh sighed, personally not at all excited at the prospect of spending all those months alone at *Wolmunster*. He didn't feel inclined to accompany them as it would be gruelling and his health wouldn't stand up to the stresses and besides it would take him away from the Stock Market, "I take it I can hold the fort here until you return?" He gave William an intense look which conveyed his chagrin.

"Now all that's left to us is to make the decision of which route we should take," He pointed to the map and with his finger traced a journey leaving from Cape Town by sea to Durban and the trails to the interior of Natal, "We could put into port at Durban and visit Frank and Felicity. Frank is now trading in the export of sugar as the farmers' first crop of sugar cane has resulted in a plentiful supply of the commodity. Mpande, chief of the Zulus, welcomes visitors into his kingdom if they mean no harm. He hasn't Dingane's fighting spirit. We could visit the villages or kraals and become acquainted with their culture and then travel by sea northwards to the Portuguese colony of Mozambique," William noticed that Hugh was inclining his head to see better yet remaining a disdainful distance from them with his hands clasped behind his back.

"Mozambique would interest you as Arabs traded there since the 5th Century A.D. and exchanged beads, glass and ceramics for gold mined by the Karanga people and of course, they were wanting to purchase slaves. The Karangas believe in a god called Mwari so if you want to save their souls, Amber, they would need a lot of convincing. The Portuguese colonised the country in the Fifteen Century."

"What other routes do you suggest?" Amber noticed another route travelling from Port Elizabeth to King William's Town up towards the Amatolas skirting the kingdom of the Ba Sotho, along the Orange River on the border of the Orange Free State, a Boer republic, up to Kuruman," Her finger stopped there when William explained how Livingstone had lived in Kuruman before his later journeys to cross southern Africa from the Atlantic Ocean to the Indian Ocean. Livingstone had confided in him that he had a dream which was to find the source of the Nile.

"Trespassing through the two Boer republics could cause too much political strife. We are not popular with our Dutch-speaking neighbours who are lording it over us as it was the first time we have ever withdrawn from a Trekboer territory and we are also at loggerheads with those British settlers left stranded there as they believe we've betrayed them. Just recently our Government granted independence to the Boers, which is why they would rather chase us off their land than tolerate our interference with the black people they have subdued into submission even if we wish to save their souls."

Amber's finger returned to Kuruman, "This route is intriguing as it goes into the land of the Bushmen, then the kingdom of the Bechuana people. Uncle William, the route you have marked out goes north-westwards following the Limpopo River into the land of the Ndebele. Isn't there a chief called Mzilikaze?"

"Yes, he and Mpande's brother, Dingane of the Zulus, fought doggedly for decades and with his warriors he also overran the chiefdoms of smaller clans until the Boers pushed him over the Limpopo River. Yes, this route would lead us into Mzilikaze's territory." William was delighted that Amber was so enthusiastic.

"Missionaries and doctors do get killed if they go where they're not wanted," Hugh tried to put a dampener on their high spirits, "In the centre of Africa the cannibals would boil you for their dinner!"

"Oh shush, Hugh," Amber shook his arm petulantly.

"We won't decide immediately. I intend to invite two further potential members of our expedition to come to dinner on Sunday and we will all discuss the topic then and put it to the vote." William smiled aware of the air of mystery he was spinning into his yarn.

-o0o-

The winter at the Cape Peninsula with its mist and drizzle was like sucking lemons, a painful experience yet deliciously pleasurable. Edward Wallace was hiking along the south-western range of mountains behind Table Mountain, the Twelve Apostles, and the insipid sun splashed down on his blond hair which was sun-bleached like dry, ripe corn. He was six foot tall with a lean, healthy physique and he spoke with a refined accent placing him squarely in the educated middle class emerging in Britain. Thanks to William Ropert he had studied at London University and learnt much of what he knew from spells working at Kew Gardens in south-west London with its enormous glass greenhouses where the ecology and physiology of plants from distant corners of the world were studied. He also spent time at Oxford where there was another excellent collection of *flora*. To further add to his knowledge he had travelled to Holland where he had spent months outside Amsterdam in glass houses examining specimens as well as learning the art of propagation and the skills used in looking after specimen plants. It was there he came across the name of the famous botanist, Linnaeus, who lived in the Eighteenth Century and his studies of plants as described in his *Bibliotheca Botanica*, *Genera Plantarum* and *Flora Lapponicae* persuaded Edward to give

Page | 215

vent to his own passion to become renowned for his contribution to botany.

He had chosen to study everything he could about a little known plant, the Disa orchid. It now amused Edward that only recently he had learnt that the great Linnaeus had spent two years at the Cape collecting plant species to name, keep alive and to take back to the Netherlands. Linnaeus had no doubt been sent to the Cape by his patron, George Clifford of the Dutch East India Company which had a strangle-hold on commodities coming out of the Cape. Plants were considered highly valuable as they were totally unique and had never been seen before in Europe. Edward had the feeling he was being followed by Linnaeus' spirit and the great man was breathing his ancient essence over him to commune with his youthful thoughts and aspirations.

Like any enthusiast, Edward intended to discover as many orchids as he could find in the Cape Colony and his search had begun on the Cape Peninsula. He had his notepad in a pocket and a pen to jot down where he had found any new species and paper bags wherein he could keep specimens for painting later with minute accuracy or sometimes he would just sketch a picturesque scene as he was developing a reputation as an artist. He would then return the next day with his oils and canvass and work out in the fresh air. His two passions clashed inside him. Was he a scientist or an artist?

In the pocket of his cotton jacket was the carefully folded invitation from William Ropert inviting him to dinner the following day. He sat down on a rock which had been disfigured with lichen and the sea far below rolled shore-wards like blue treacle, lazy and unctuous. His hand had shaken with excitement and he experienced the feeling that this all was familiar and that he was about to embark on a journey that could change his life. He had been there in that identical situation in some previous life - the epitome of the young man about to make his way away from the clan across glaciers, deserts, seas into unknown territories from which he could possibly never return. That knife-edge anticipation whetted his appetite as he waited to hear what his patron had in mind.

-o0o-

The American clipper, "Harvey", sailed into Cape Town harbour and on the deck, James Munroe surveyed the scene in front of him and noticed that the South Easter had poured cloud like sea foam down the face of the great Behemoth edifice, a creature not a mountain crouching over the graceful town with its Dutch, Malay and Georgian architecture. He was well built and five foot nine inches tall with black hair which he wore slicked back from his face and his deep-set brown eyes were bright under his high forehead and his skin was tanned to a polished gleam. His long nose had been broken in a fray in a mining town but somehow added to his looks. This was his country, he thought and remembered how his boyhood excursions around the Peninsula had given him rich pickings as he searched for various rock types and identified the geological periods of their origin. He was a man obsessed by his profession and his pick-axe and trowel were always to hand.

He couldn't wait to see his siblings and his parents. His tour of North America had had a profound effect on moulding him into an adventurer and prospector. It had all been thanks to his patron, William Ropert who had suggested that he followed the gold trail in California after the metal had been discovered in Sutter's Mill in 1848 and to learn as much as he could about precious metals and minerals and how to discover gold seams in the Earth's crust or pipes of crystals and the Queen of all, diamonds. William Ropert believed that southern Africa was a rich, untouched country that would offer up treasures the like of which the world had never seen. The fact that he had been away for two years and still wanted to return to explore Africa and keep his promise in that regard to his benefactor showed his strong commitment to the deal that had been made. He found he was not exhausted from his travels but instead full of optimism and energy that needed to be unleashed.

At his parents' home and after the initial demonstration of affection, the family crowded around him and no doubt thought how much he had changed. He left a boy and returned a man. He, in turn, looked at his family with a new perspective. They were homely, gentle folk so different from the die-hard prospectors with whom he had to work and from whom he had learnt so much. His sisters were so innocent and acquiescent, pure as love doves whereas the women he mingled with in America were flagrantly enticing like tropical flowers to humming birds when they conversed with men and showed off in the bars or brothels.

"There is a letter for you that just came this morning," His mother said going through her correspondence. Funny that it should arrive the very day you returned to us," She was endearing, loving but astute and he had never lied to her.

He recognised the seal immediately and tore the red wax and unfolded the paper, "It's from William Ropert. I wrote to him giving him details of my return some time before I left America. I had expected to be back two weeks ago but the ship's mast broke in a storm and we limped into port at Rio de Janeiro for repairs. He probably thought I had been back for some time. I'll reply immediately and accept this invitation to dinner on Sunday. I've so much to tell him I can't wait for the day to come soon enough."

His mother put an arm around him and smiled, "It's so good to have you home again. I prayed every night that God would keep you safe and bring you back to us unharmed and He has done that so all I need to do now is to thank Him every night for the rest of my life for blessing our family and keeping it whole." The candlelight made her eyes shimmer as tears sparkled and fell and her rosebud mouth often puckered by worry trembled. His father was ageing and felt like a sick bird when James had hugged him. He felt he could crush him if his embrace were any stronger. He never thought he would feel pity but he did knowing his father had never experienced the excitement and lust for life that he had enjoyed. James felt a sense of uneasiness. He realised he had been away too long. To make up for his absence, he handed a leather pouch to his father, "Father, open it. It's something I want you to have, something from my travels."

His father tipped the contents into his hand and everyone gasped when they saw the small ingots of solid gold. "Thank you, my son," his father whispered, his voice squeezed by a spasm in his throat, "With this the family can live comfortably for years. You have removed all my concerns in one miraculous moment. God bless you, James. I won't be as hard on you from now on. Forgive an old man from doubting you."

"Of course I forgive you. Being accredited as being your son is all I ever wanted." James smiled a little thinly. The memory of being the black sheep of the family was emblazoned in permanent Indian ink on his soul.

-o0o-

Sunday was the day of rest but in *Wolmunster*, it began with Fatima and Lettie opening all the windows of the house to allow the perfumed breeze to waft in from the garden. Beds were made and downstairs Fatima began setting the long, gleaming stinkwood table. Upstairs, washing in a hand-basin with a jug of warm water, Amber allowed the water to run down her arms and the soapiness was washed away. She splashed her face with the water and sucked in the wetness. She brushed her teeth with a soft stick from the peach tree which as she looked at the scene of the back garden she could see was heavy with blossom and beetles were bumbling along to find an early rosebud to devour. A bokmakerie bird with its yellow and mauve colours was calling and the dogs were playing tug o' war with an old cloth.

She began to dress and Lettie laced and tugged at her corset drawing in her waist and turning her into a wasp-like creature and she lifted her arms to receive the organza dress and it slipped over her head and for a moment she felt trapped but the dress was soon buttoned and the three layered style was most attractive and the pattern of navy blue flecks on a white background was elegant and perhaps made her look old for her age or, looked at another way, too feminine for the rigors she wished to endure on the trip. Her hair was arranged in tendrils around her face and a chignon spilt more curls which draped one shoulder.

The doorbell sounded and she heard her uncle go to the front door and open it. She could hear him welcoming one of their guests with tones of fond affection. She forced herself to descend the stairs like a princess with her heart beating wildly. Who were these two young men? Would they like her and accept her as an equal? She doubted it and was ready for battle, her spirit already inflamed by all the mystery. She bit her lower lip and her eyes danced with devilment.

The second guest arrived as she was being introduced to James Munroe and he passed her hand to Edward Wallace who raised it to his lips. The two men were nothing like what she had expected. They were younger and madly attractive, perhaps a little in love with themselves, she thought.

Edward was a baby and she wondered if he shaved yet. His face had soft down on it and his cheeks were red, perhaps now with embarrassment. James on the other hand had met her stare with his own fearless gaze and for a moment she thought she saw a second of amusement and worldliness. He might want her in the biblical sense but for very unbiblical activities. She arched her long neck and raised her chin while inwardly enjoying her mischievousness.

The conversation was refined and witty and she chimed like a clear bell whereas their voices were sonorous.

Unexpectedly, the doorbell rang for the third time. To her surprise Imran, William's groom, Abel's son, entered and William led him to James and Edward making the necessary introductions.

"What is Imran doing here, Lettie?" Amber whispered as Lettie circulated among them with a tray of champagne.

"Your Uncle invited him to join you to talk about the trip, Miss,"

Lettie smiled enjoying Amber's shock and tell-tale annoyance. She was a bit jealous of Imran as he was allowed to study medicine but her talents as 'the cook's daughter' were squandered and she was the one left behind in no man's land.

Imran found refuge in Amber's chatter and thought how attractive she looked. He was of Malay descent about five foot eleven inches tall, lean with a well-chiselled face, large limpid brown eyes, a short, flat nose with wide nostrils, flared now because he was nervous, and erotic lips, full and inviting, now pursed and unsmiling. She wondered how it would feel to have his lips on hers. Blushing, she turned away to look for her uncle just as he invited them all to join him in the dining room.

Fatima's delicious fish soup, followed by racks of lamb with rosemary and garlic, roast potatoes, cabbage and baby marrows outshone her previous menus which always excelled. Their meal was soon drawn to a close with stewed fruit compote with apricots, peaches and plums served with her velvety custard.

"At last we can begin and I can tell you why I've invited you all here today. The topic of discussion is a proposed trip into the Interior and I want you four youngsters to accompany me," William smiled knowing he had set the cat amongst the pigeons, so to say.

"But, Amber is a woman. You surely aren't inviting her to join us?" Imran looked shocked.

"It's because of Amber that this trip will be undertaken. You may have already discovered she's a young lady with firm attitudes about life and helping others," William paused, "I must be completely honest with you I do have selfish reasons of my own for you three in particular to join us," He pointed to the three men individually, singling them out."

"Why should I want you to accompany us, James?" He looked the younger man in the eye and knew he had been tried and not found wanting.

"It's about my interest in the geology of the country inland and you want to put my knowledge to the test. Isn't it that you want me to discover minerals before others do? Copper and silver have already been found in the south-western Cape. There is a veritable mountain of copper north of here."

"Good answer. Yes, I want you to join us and your contribution will be valued and as an individual you can both teach the rest of us about your speciality and on the other hand perhaps you would benefit from others in the group. Who knows? Edward, you're next. Same question."

"You've always been interested in protecting the *flora* and *fauna* of the country. There's the danger that whole genera and species could be wiped out if the export of the plants continues at the present rate. I am personally on a crusade to discover all the orchids in the country. I chose orchids because of their complexity and distribution in various different ecosystems. I'm particularly interested in the Disa orchid but I'm interested in finding as many new plants as possible in order to make a record of them and their habitat." Edward looked at his companions using his hands to describe his passion.

"You've forgotten one of the reasons I've asked you to join this expedition. It's for your painting. I want you to go out there and paint landscapes, flowers, you name it and I'll support you", William said gruffly.

"An artist! How wonderful!" Amber clapped her hands together with delight. Edward was a shy, solitary character and blushed helplessly looking for a way of escaping from their scrutiny.

"Good lad," James patted him on the back, "I admire any man who can make an image with such poor materials. If I've a paintbrush in my hand I end up making a very sorry mess indeed!" James laughed and tried to rescue his new friend from his discomfort.

"Imran?" William waited for his first protégé's contribution.

"I've just qualified as a doctor," Imran rose to his feet, "Presumably you'll be requiring my medical knowledge and skills not just for ourselves but perhaps for others we may come across who are in need of our help. You can definitely count me in!" Imran spoke confidently and his teeth flashed in a quick smile. Amber looked at him with respect and squeezed his hand as he sat down. She knew she sometimes teased him unfairly.

"And you, Amber, why do you want to come on this expedition? Take your time," William said encouragingly. The three men looked astounded. How could this chit of a girl fit in with their plans?

"I would like to object on the grounds that the veldt is no place for a woman. I have seen what living rough does to women in America," James interrupted passionately.

Amber stood up and lifted her chin and her back was ramrod straight like a soldier's, "I know what you're all thinking," She began looking at each of the young men, "Why on earth would I want to venture into unexplored country? Well, I'm aware of all the risks and great carnivores, spiders and snakes do frighten me, but that's life. There are many frightening situations and events one has to experience and I'm not afraid of those so perhaps the rest will be easy. I want to meet indigenous tribes and learn about their beliefs and would like to see if they could believe in our God and of course I want to treat the sick and dying. I would love to help women give birth less painfully and learn about local African remedies. Imran, you'll be my teacher!" She sat down with her heart beating like a captured bird in her chest. Imran reached out and held her hand.

"Come through to my study and we'll look at the options we might have," William looked at his gold watch suspended on its fob attached to his waistcoat, "I'm sure this won't take very long if you are all in agreement. I'll explain the advantages and disadvantages of each journey that is marked on the maps."

After an hour of mulling over the southern third of the continent "My preference is to go to Kuruman and then explore the north-west beyond the Limpopo. But, instead of leaving from Port Elizabeth we could perhaps travel to the Orange River taking a route up the west Atlantic coast and then across the semi desert as I've heard of untold wealth of precious and semi-precious stones. I could also prospect for minerals in that area," James was the first to air his opinion.

"The terrain is very inhospitable with scrubland and very little water when the rivers dry up. It might be unsuitable for Amber," William had to remind them that there was a woman in their midst.

"No, don't discount anything just because of me. I'm prepared to endure the same hardship as you. I don't want to go on an expedition that is just a walk in a park," Amber rebuked him.

"I would be happy with the route leaving from Port Elizabeth. If it's not the general consensus James and I could take a detour and ride out to the west at the confluence of the Vaal and Orange River and re-join you in Kuruman after a few weeks. I'd like to record what plants can survive in such a dry region," Edward had liked James from the start and it would be an adventure.

Imran studied the map and realised that once they crossed into the northern territories they would be in malaria country but whatever route they finally chose, there could be several diseases to which they would be exposed. He would have to be a stickler about hygiene. "The trip to Durban and visiting the land of the Zulus and marching on to Mozambique is my choice as Natal is fast developing into a profitable part of the Colony and I'd like to see that for myself," He said with some passion.

William sat and ruminated for what seemed like hours but then he leant forward and with his pen pointed to the mighty river, "We'll travel from Cape Town to the Orange River and then trek to Kuruman and make our plans as we encounter obstacles. We'll leave towards the end of winter so we have a few months left to acquire our equipment and food. I'll purchase a large wagon with a team of oxen and we will become Trekboers for the duration of the journey. Also, we'll need strong mounts for each of us."

"Thank you for including me in your team, Mr Ropert, I'll make sure you aren't disappointed in me," Imran stood up and prepared to leave.

The other two had so many ideas coming thick and fast in their imagination that their chatter with one another was proving useful and it was no doubt facilitated by the fact that they liked each other and felt they could work together.

Amber fell silent and realised the men had all the advantages. If truth be told, she was a little daunted but then looked at the calibre of the men and decided she would be well protected.

In the following weeks golden dawns couldn't come quickly enough for her as she whiled away the time, imagining all number of delights and dangers.

-o0o-

As James and Edward walked to the stables behind *Wolmunster*, James suddenly broke the silence as their footfalls crunched on the gravel, "What do you think of the idea of taking a mere chit of a girl on such an expedition?"

"It is extraordinary considering her age and sheltered upbringing. Her skin will burn and her hands will have blisters. She'll be saddle-sore after a day on horseback. If she were my sister I would admonish her to reconsider her decision," Edward put a foot in the stirrup and heaved himself onto his horse, a black stallion. The horse was impatient.

"Perhaps we will be examined as potential suitor material. I'll wager a bet that she'll accept my affection above yours by the end of the trip," James laughed jumping into his saddle smartly.

"If it's a wager you want, you can count me in. She would find you rude and unsympathetic. I'll woo her with charm and my sunny good nature!" Edward laughed digging his spurs gently into his horse's side. The competition had begun. He wondered if he should have made another wager on whether Amber would actually join them on the journey. It would take a very brave girl of her age not to be put off by tales of savagery and inhospitable landscapes.

-o0o-

CHAPTER 20

Cape Town

Table Mountain was his host for the day and Edward festooned with rope and armed with a sharp pickaxe balanced precariously on a ledge with a dripping overhang. The town below was miniaturised and in the bay the anchored ships dozed like ducks with their heads under their wings. The young man scoured the new territory he was covering. His great desire to find rare orchids had not abated and he worked his way across the towering ridges. He had no idea where in the Cape he should search for his prize for indeed it would be the pinnacle of his life. He never for one moment believed as he set out for this last climb before the journey into the Interior that today would render up anything special but he foraged for specimens of fern while enjoying the heady heights of the mountain.

On his way down the rope slipped for an instant and he plummeted down before clamping on the flying thread for that was how inept it felt, a thread of silk on which his life depended. He let out a sigh of relief as his feet found a protruding rock. Below him was a cavity like a grotto which was glistening with water from a small rivulet seeping into it and at the back was a plant almost primeval in its uniqueness, so rare to be other worldly, a Disa orchid with its carmine holy Trinity of main sepals, one hooded altogether three inches in diameter, supported by a single bract from behind and the inviting flagrant invitation of two male anthers confined in a bowl of small petals was like a delicate creature that could envelope a finger. The sticky pistil protected by the broad white rostellum displayed some feminine allure too. He let out a whoop of joy and just stared at the botanical jewel before carefully reaching down, with his face pressed against the rock on which he was lying, and feeling with his hand for the small plant with its pair of ruby blooms. Touching it he carefully removed the *disa uniflora* from its lair and lifted into the sunshine dew dripping from its leaves. He would now have something unique to show to the Royal Botanical Society on his next visit. Perhaps this would be a new variety of the Disa and would be named after him! The experts would be able to tell. He wished Bergius and Linnaeus' son were alive. They were the first to add the disa to their lists.

He would have to wait for an opportunity to sail back to England until he returned from the expedition. The students at the university would be ordered on pain of death to care for the specimen until such a time.

-o0o-

The next day Amber received one of the disa's perfect blooms in a small glass casket lined with wet cotton wool, with a note from Edward,

"This beauty dims in the blazing light of your countenance. Paint it or press it to immortalise it. I look forward to the day our expedition begins and I shall see you again. The time is nearly at hand. Your humble servant, Edward."

-o0o-

The dawn broke over the Hottentots-Holland Mountains bathing the Cape Flats and the eastern faces of the peninsular peaks in a golden glow and the sunlight broke through the chink in the curtains of Amber's bedroom. Motes of dust danced a silent ballet around the room. She put an arm over her eyes and sighed languorously stretching her body and then sat up, muddled by sleep. Suddenly she remembered which day it was. A cry of anticipation escaped and she rushed to the wash stand and poured the water into her basin for a thorough wash. She had been waiting two months and now there would be no cancellation, no breaking her promise to her uncle.

William had been up for hours and now was having his breakfast with Hugh. "It really stirs my soul to action when I embark on these expeditions either to war or for exploration. Taking Amber is a decided risk and I'm aware I cannot really treat her in the same way as the men no matter how vehemently she insists that I do. I do worry about bands of outlaws, former servants and ne'er do wells who roam the interior looking for travellers to loot and women to despoil.

"I think you are quite mad embarking on this adventure at your age but you know my feelings about that. We're not as fit and keen witted as once we were. I hark back to those times with fondness and no regrets. But, I worry about you, you old devil!" Hugh coughed on a crumb of toast. At least that was what William thought.

"Shall I slap your back," William rose to help his friend.

"No, I'll be fine," Hugh spluttered. He was concerned about the coughing fits but didn't want to alarm William. He hoped that he would have recovered by the time William returned.

"I'll miss your charming countenance every morning when I wake up in my tent," William teased.

"I hope you choke on your coffee in that case," Hugh laughed. Their camaraderie was still as strong as ever.

William had arranged to meet Edward and James in Green Market Square in town where the wagon and team of oxen were to be delivered into his hands by the wagon maker, Du Plessis. William was keen to emulate *Trekboers* and their lives as they were constantly moving from one place to another. Their provisions would be provided then too. It was time to leave. Amber was downstairs and had her *kist* of clothes and possessions ready. William retired to his study and returned with a leather-bound book, "Amber, I would like you to have this." He handed the book to her.

"Oh, thank you, Uncle William," She replied turning the pages.

"It's a journal for you to keep. You should write down in it everything you experience and here is a set of watercolours and brushes in case you would like to illustrate your entries. I have bought you a writing slope in walnut wood in which you can keep your journal. It has a lock and a key so you can be sure your thoughts will remain private. Your Aunt Fanny urged me to keep a journal each year. She kept a running journal, too, and when you are older, her journals will be given to you as you will learn through her example about life and relationships. A plethora of emotions and thoughts can be experienced when reading the entries. I know."

He had wept when he came across the very poignant accounts Fanny had made about their innocent love "affair" and her words had haunted him.

Amber noticed tears filling William's eyes, which blinking rapidly he tried to hide from her. "I'm delighted to have this. I will write in it each day. It can be a record of our time in the wilderness," She smiled charmingly.

The carriage was ready and William waited for Amber to get in first and then Lettie who would be accompanying them and who had shrieked with delight to be invited along. Her wish had been granted! William clasped Hugh around the shoulder and mumbled "If anything happens that affects my position with the Governor, let me know. He has allowed me to have this sabbatical but something might happen that would make it obligatory for me to return. Look after yourself, Hugh."

"On your way!" Hugh laughed, setting him free to roam and explore, activities about which William was so passionate. He would play the Stock Market and continue to make money for himself and his friend.

-o0o-

Cape Town was busy with market stalls brimming with food of all descriptions, hardware and crockery. People were milling around, laughing and talking, shouting to anyone a few yards away. Flowers in buckets adorned the square, dogs sniffed the ground for titbits and seagulls wheeled overhead in the sky like torn strips of printed paper. Anything and everything could be bought or sold. Their carriage drew up alongside a large, handsome jawbone wagon with its hooped white canvass hood, a trailer cart and the ten oxen that would pull them stood stoically with the driver occasionally flicking the whip over their heads. The store had already delivered fold-up furniture and bedding, crockery and pots and pans, tents, and all the food, some of which was dried, like oats, flour, beans, rice etc., and fresh potatoes, onions, carrots, eggs, cured meats etc. The wagon and trailer were loaded and held a huge amount so much so that there was still room to spare. Then there were the spares for the wagon itself as it would be unheard of to make such a journey and not have something happen to the wagon. Essential for their survival were of course their guns, picks and knives.

James and Edward walked up to William and shook hands. Their mounts followed on timidly behind them.

"Good to see you chaps," William smiled, "It's a pleasant day for us to make a start. The weather has been kind to us. " He was saddling his own horse, a beige stallion with a reddish brown mane, while the animal twitched and stepped about in one place.

"Has Miss McBride stayed at home," James asked cynically. He didn't see Amber march up to them nor did he recognise her until she spoke, "Miss McBride is right here!" Amber stood up right next to her own horse - a white mare with dappled grey spots. The young girl squared her shoulders.

Both young men gasped as Amber was no longer the society debutante but a strong-willed pioneer girl wearing a *Trekboer* woman's plain grey dress with its white lace collar, boots and a white *kappie* or bonnet with a broad frill falling from the back of the headdress onto the shoulders to protect the neck from the heat of the sun and the brim of the bonnet was deep so that her face would always be shaded. Her eyes twinkled as she rotated to show off her frock which without cumbersome petticoats, whale bone corset and bustle made her laugh, "I feel so liberated I could jump for joy!" Her long auburn hair was no longer in ringlets but tamed into a large plait that fell down her back.

Edward laughed to himself and was pleased he hadn't made a wager that she would not join the expedition. For a moment he remembered the other bet. "It is a delight to see that you will be joining us," He bowed, politely, "I am pleased you were surprised and grateful to be given the *disa* bloom." Amber had sent a note that thanked him for his unique gift.

"You must tell me all about it when we have time which I'm sure there will be many such moments over the next few months," She curtsied.

"Miss McBride," James acknowledged her with a curt nod, "It will be a significant trial for you and I am wondering about the wisdom of your joining us. Many a man would think twice before entering the wilds of Africa. You won't find any grace and favours on this trip."

Amber's anger smouldered, "I am well aware of what I'm letting myself in for. Nothing you can say will sway me from taking part on this expedition, Mr Munroe."

"Has anyone seen Imran?" William tied a heavy reel of rope to the side of the wagon. They were all set and if Imran failed to turn up he would be left behind. But, as he spoke Imran arrived, his chestnut horse clattering over the cobbles. He sharply drew up the young gelding and leapt down to shake hands with William. He had a rosewood box of medicines, one of those with many drawers and lead crystal bottles with silver tops, a medical bag containing larger items among his medical instruments and a camphor chest with his personal belongings all in the wagon that drew up beside them a few minutes later.

"Time to go," William swung himself onto his stallion. Amber followed suit and her long boots hid her calves as she sat astride her horse and she modestly draped her riding cape, the only piece of clothing from her normal wardrobe, over her legs to hide any sight of a petticoat. The two young men pressed their own horses, both chestnuts with black markings, forward and she tagged along behind them.

Lettie wearing a printed yellow dress with white butterflies and a straw hat with a very wide brim sat on the wagon seat next to Hendrik, an ageing Hottentot, who would drive the oxen and wagon and he had brought with him a young boy called Lucky who would look after the cattle and the boy's dog, Spitz. Koos, a teenage boy was to be the *voorloper* or forward walker to lead the oxen throughout their journey. Hendrik with his grizzled hair and moustache and thin beard with his black cloth hat adorned with an ostrich feather pulled through his blue hat band at just the right angle was a keen tracker and he knew the Western and Northern Cape like the back of his hand. He would know where there were waterholes and springs in an otherwise dry landscape. He sniffed some snuff, pursed his thin lips, narrowed his eyes then cracked the whip and the oxen started to move forward.

-o0o-

The mountains lying beyond the Cape Flats began to loom up on them as they galloped, stopping now and again to rest and take refreshments and the distance between them and Cape Town and Table Mountain grew larger with each passing second. The young men left the main route and with Amber just behind them they made detours of sometimes five miles into new parts of the plain. They passed groups of ostriches and quaggas, the plains' zebra, lifted their heads before resuming their meal of long stems of grass. The horses seemed eager to reach their destination and the fields of fresh pasture that awaited them while the team of oxen pulled the wagon with resilient strength and would catch up with them much later. The young people waited for William to draw up alongside them to point out where they would pitch camp for the night. Amber was panting with the exertion but the way she and her mount flew across the sandy plain made her seem experienced with unflagging energy.

At last in the valley between two mountain ranges William pulled his horse up and the beast snorted and stamped with sweat glistening on its flanks and foam flecking its mouth as its tongue played with the offensive bit. The others caught up with him and jumped off their mounts and stretched, exhaling and inhaling slowly to calm their breathing. A shallow river ran alongside the bottom of the mountains where it had carved out its bed of off-white boulders and pebbles with banks of verdant grass and tall Eucalyptus trees introduced by the early Dutch settlers and imported from Australia. Pine trees clothed the mountain slopes. The water trickled quickly past and they led the horses to the river to slake their thirst. Amber knelt down and cupped her hands and drank in the sweet liquid, then removing her bonnet she splashed her face to cool it down.

"So do you think you can keep up this pace for months on end?" James looked up at her while he removed his boots and waded into the water. Amber unsaddled her horse and led it to a grassy area, flanked by bulrushes and knee-haltered the animal which immediately began grazing. She took some time before answering him.

"I'm a lot fitter than you give me credit for," Amber replied spiritedly.

She sank gratefully down on the cool river bank, "I'm ravenous! How long will we have to wait for the wagon to arrive?"

"Here, have a stick of this," James tossed a dried piece of *biltong*, the dried meat the Boers cured, to her. "It'll keep you going." James was quite impressed with her riding. She showed no saddle soreness and it appeared she was ready for more adventure.

"Thanks," She reluctantly had to admit that James wasn't completely obnoxious. Grudgingly she found herself even beginning to like him.

William sat down beside Amber and withdrew the map from his satchel, "We have made good headway today. We'll camp here for the next few days as James and Edward have plenty of opportunity to explore the area for their own ends. I don't want to rush this trip but to take a leisurely pace. After a few days we will make our way through the mountain pass at the Kloof." He turned his head to look at James and Edward, "There are a few hours of daylight left so if you want to reconnoitre further, please go ahead. I know you both want to excavate or forage for unusual minerals or plants. Imran, you can help me clear the site for our tents."

After the young men knee-haltered their horses, they set off on foot to see what they could find. Edward looked about with both a scientist and an artist's eye and decided he wanted to paint the scene of the encampment as soon as light permitted the next morning. He was in high spirits and searched among the *Ericas* to see if there were any unusual heathers amongst them. Silver-leafed trees shone metallically and below them proteas were in their winter garb.

Back at the river, Amber was staring at the nearest mountain with its head of broken cliff, rock upon rock making its features and then the fall to its soft mannish breasts of ericaceous vegetation to the jagged cliffs forming splayed hands clutching its stomach of soft foothills. Would Edward paint it? She decided she wanted to immortalise it and intended to sketch their camp beneath it.

Amber turned to William who was sitting on a rock and with a telescope was sweeping the area for any dangerous animals and for that matter, humans who could harm them. But, the area was tranquil and the evening shadows drifted into larger puddles of purple splashes beneath white limbed trees whose loose bark hung like decaying rattan. "I'll go and see what firewood I can find. As soon as Hendrik and Lettie and little Lucky arrive with Koos and the oxen we can put a coffee pot on the fire and get dinner prepared."

"Allow me a minute or two and I'll be able to accompany you, Amber. We don't know what's out there," William liked her high-spirited nature.

"No, I'll not stray too far from here. Don't look at me through the eyes of a parent. See me as an equal, Uncle William," She laughed and left him helpless in the face of such self-confidence.

She soon had an armful of kindling but had suddenly felt the hairs on the back of her neck lift and she sensed that she was being watched. A twig snapped and something bounded away. She looked over her shoulder and saw nothing. Something slithered over her foot, which made her gasp with shock and she turned and almost ran back to the camp quite out of breath. With combating the fear, came a sense of accomplishment. She let out a sigh of relief.

The wagon had arrived and Hendrik, Koos and Lucky were 'outspanning' the oxen and herding them towards the luscious grass and to the river to slake their thirst. The dog, Spitz, barked happily. Lettie ran to Amber and shared the load of wood and gasped. "I have never felt so excited in all my life," she confided to her friend.

When Edward and James returned, they set about erecting the tents, one for Amber and Lettie, another for themselves and one for William and Imran. Hendrik, Koos and Lucky each had a *kaross* of animal pelts and would sleep near the wagon. The goats were tied to a post and allowed to graze. William and Hendrik lent a hand and Hendrik laughed, "You are living like my people live. The one thing people are wrong about us is that we are not Hottentots but we name ourselves Khoikhoi – *men of men.*"

"I have heard that your people are nomads and that you travel from place to place for grazing and live off the wild plants and roots that the women find."

"We don't have canvass for our homes but make them by using fresh saplings which we weave into a dome shape and then we place mats that the women have woven over the cage of bent sticks. They are very good at keeping out the rain and they are much cheaper. We can move out of an area in hours!" Hendrik inhaled the smoke from his clay pipe which was firmly in the grip of his jaws as he lent upwards to pull at the roof of the tent.

Suddenly they all became aware of a horseman approaching from the south, and a man wearing a black broad-brimmed felt hat and black shirt and pants and heavy spurs entered their camp. The stranger whose face was in deep shadow drew up and nodded to them before urging his horse to cross the river and to continue on its way. Amber thought the man could have been more communicative and she allowed her imagination to create possible scenarios as to who he could be, a husband searching for the wife who had run away with his best friend; a bank robber or even a sea captain on his way home after being at sea for months and months. The men seemed unaffected by the dark interloper.

William's table had been assembled and as though he were on a military campaign he sat at the fold-up table gathering his thoughts before writing them down in his new journal which was to record the beginning of his memoirs. He had such a wealth of experiences that thoughts fell like a waterfall obliterating the green pool of clear thought. Soon darkness fell and torches were lit. The fire danced like dervishes in a trance and soon they all retired to bed, wishing each other a good night.

Bird song rang out in the valley at dawn and another noise awoke the sleeping travellers. Pots banging together and other utensils thrown about had everyone running outside. Baboons had invaded the camp and Hendrik could be heard shouting at them and making menacing movements with his gun he shooed them out of the area. One large baboon cavorted straight against the girls' tent and the image of its body looked so menacing that they both screamed. In a matter of seconds, their uninvited guests had vanished, barking in deep guttural coughs until the sound faded in the distance. The men stood sheepish in their long johns and the girls had blankets tied under their chins but the look of delight on Amber's face made Lettie forget her fear.

"Come, we must get washed and dressed," Amber pulled at her hair which was in mad disarray. Lettie was ready first and she took a large jug down to the river to fill it with water so that they could both wash. She was awestruck by the magnificence of the mountains and the silver and white rushing river. Outside his tent, Imran was praying, kneeling with bowed head touching the earth facing Mecca and then straightening up on his haunches; he was at one with his God.

After breakfast, Edward hitched a canvass ready and primed, to his back and carried an easel to a vantage point and immediately set to work. The smell of linseed oil and turpentine was pungent and overwhelmed the perfume of leaf, flower and earth. Pigments were mixed and the correct colours emerged on his palette and he daubed and the water became an iridescence of blues and pinks in the calm pools and the white created by broken water rushing by. Trees of olive green and purple and trunks of ochre and the grass thin lines of the smallest paint brush appeared. The mountain was burnt sienna against the azure sky with petrol green forests fading to silver protea bushes.

Amber joined William at the table in the shade and opened her journal. She began to draw the scene in front of her of the neat little camp with its tents and smouldering fire and the tall trees and undergrowth. She even attempted to draw a baboon.

William was discussing religion with Imran. "I have always been fascinated by the Muslim religion. With so many faiths in the world we all seem to worship the one God."

Imran's limpid brown eyes widened and his eyelids fluttered momentarily, "I'm perhaps not so open minded as you are, Sir. My uncle Hadji leads us in prayers and for us there is only our heavenly father, blessed is his name, to pray to for everlasting life." He thought warmly of his uncle with his silver hair bound in a turban of linen and his white billowing tunic with its ample sleeves over which a tunic of orange depicted his holiness. His dark, lined face, hooked nose and his clipped beard were purely Malay.

"I want you to read the Quran to me on this trip as I would like to learn more about your religion. I must admit I know very little," William wanted to embrace the serious young doctor like a father would hug his son.

"I will recite the Quran verse by verse to you in Arabic and then translate into English. In translating I must maintain the holiness of the meaning of the words. As Muslim boys, we learn verses off pat", Imran was genuinely pleased that William was so interested in his religion.

Hendrik was walking past when he heard what William was saying, "Do you understand the KhoiKhoi religion, Master?"

"No, only a bit but I would like it if the three of us could talk about our religions together and by doing that we will understand each other more implicitly," the enlightened Irishman was practising his Unitarian religion and its liberalism brought faiths together rather than divided them.

Amber lifted the lid of her wooden writing slope and opened the ink bottle and after stroking the maroon feather of her pen and watching the hooks of each strand knit back together again she then dipped into the blackness and put her thoughts down in her journal in exquisite copperplate writing.

"Yesterday was a life changing wealth of experiences and I cannot hope to describe the sense of freedom, the anticipation of the raw forcefulness of nature and the dome of the sky that at night disappears allowing the stars to prick through its immense expanse. Riding my horse was a form of flight that made my heart soar above the thuds of hooves. The wild animals that I must notate herein were plentiful, from the ostriches running alongside us in their confusion to the

wheeling birds of prey in the air above us. How I wish I could tell Aunt Fanny my news. Perhaps she is looking down on us and can share in our adventure. Camping is like a children's game, erecting temporary shelters, eating in the open which whets one's appetite and bathing to refresh our bodies.

Drawing is a pastime I'm beginning to enjoy although I'm a poor amateur but if my strokes and colours can remind me of this place, then I'm satisfied. In a few days we will strike camp and traverse the cutting through the mountains and discover what lies on the other side. I am almost loath to leave this idyll."

-oOo-

They struck camp the morning of their seventh day and swiftly loaded the wagon and Hendrik, Koos and Lucky in-spanned the oxen which bayed their irritation. Edward's painting was finished and hung on the outside of the wagon to dry. He hoped it would escape undamaged by the dust of the journey. They left the site so that it seemed untouched by any visitor, given back to nature. Although they had partaken of its wealth of beauty, yet that beauty was undiminished.

The Kloof rose up before them and the granite tops of the mountains were in shade and looked almost gruesome in their forbidding heights. Two waterfalls fell vertically down the frown lines of a monolithic face. A battle between the Goliaths and the little 'Davids' had begun. The way grew more treacherous and the oxen groaned and this time the riders kept at the side of the wagon to help pull the load over the stony track ever upwards.

By three in the afternoon, the worst was over and they all rested in the mellow lee of the mountain range. The lee side was quite different. Drier, it looked as though the earth had erupted like a giant fingerprint with so many fissures and rock cracked row upon row of sandstone and quartzite as James explained. Hendrik and William felled two heavy boughs from a tree and tied them to the wagon allowing the wagon chassis to rest on the wood and then removed the back wheels which made going downhill so much safer and easier for the oxen. Much like the sledges North American Indians were accustomed to use to pull behind a horse ideal for transporting the injured or frail, James explained. The wagon was so heavily loaded the force of gravity could cause it to break up if this method wasn't used.

Down below was another river and an emerald valley where vines crossed and crisscrossed on metal wire and they were just beginning to give birth to diminutive buds of leaves. The small town, Paarl, meaning pearl, lay in the distance and they would be making their way there to spend the next few days. The town lay like a gem in a lush valley which was like the flesh of an oyster and was surrounded by crusty granite mountains, the oyster shell. They would reach it by sunset, in time to set up their camp. They would struggle to find a suitable site as it was *Nagmaal* and farmers and their families would be arriving for the act of communion. Amber was excited by the prospect of meeting Boer families. She could speak the language fluently as Miss Smith insisted that all her pupils should learn the language which so many of the colonists spoke.

That evening, in the light of many fires, the air grew damp and heavy and the smell of smoke was pungent. Voices travelled across the valley. Cattle herds had to be corralled and Koos and Lucky arranged boughs brought down in storms in a circle and the oxen were soon grazing on grass inside. They filled a trough with water for them to drink.

That night Amber was too tired to write in her journal and she and Lettie fell promptly asleep.

-o0o-

The following day the little town was a hive of activity with people buying and selling food and wares and once they had had their breakfast and tidied up, Amber and Lettie walked into the town to mingle and to buy some essentials. They were given stares by some who were intrigued by the two girls of different race walking hand in hand.

In the evening after *Nagmaal*, there was great celebration for couples who had just been married, or families where there had been christenings and confirmations so Amber begged to be allowed to experience the jollity and dancing.

Lettie stayed behind to do the chores in the camp so Edward and James escorted Amber but soon went in search of some good wine. A young Boer man just older than Amber engaged her in conversation and Amber enjoyed their repartee and she noticed her new friend thought she was a Boer girl. They danced to songs of love and flirtation. The liveliest of all was "Jan Pierewiet". They were having so much fun that Amber never realised how late into the night the festivities were lasting.

"So here you are," a sardonic voice behind her made her jump as James placed a firm hand on her shoulder, "Time to go, Amber. Say goodnight to your friend here, like a good girl."

The young Boer called Martinus staggered backwards with shock at the realisation that she was English. He smiled sheepishly and wished them a good night. Amber wanted to run after him to arrange to meet again but James was intractable. They met up with Edward who was slightly the worse for wear, not surprising, considering the amount of good Cape wine he had drunk. James had got him tipsy deliberately in order to make fun of him the next day when he would most certainly have a hangover.

The night was sweet as they walked or danced which Amber was doing when suddenly the scream of a child shattered the wall of blackness and they ran towards the sound. A child had fallen whilst carrying an oil lamp. Flames were beaten down by throwing a blanket over the girl, who could not have been more than seven. "I'll fetch Imran," Amber shouted above the clamour.

Reaching their camp out of breath and gasping, Amber ran to Imran and explained what had happened in the nearby town. Imran quickly gathered up his medical bag and rosewood box and followed the young girl who led him to the injured child. Imran was quickly shouting out orders, he needed clean sheets to be soaked in cold water to cool the girl's burnt torso, to remove as much heat from the wounds, water to wet her lips and above all for everyone to remain calm. A Boer woman brought him a pat of butter but he turned it aside muttering "Do you want to fry the poor child!"

Some Boer men looked on suspiciously, "You say this man is a doctor from Cape Town but, he is Malay.   Malays are builders and carpenters."

"I am a builder who repairs broken bodies," Imran stood his ground. Edward and James were reticent but Amber's temper flared and she spoke with a tone of steel, "You have no one better to heal your daughter. My uncle is in the camp under the willow trees and as attorney general you possibly might believe that he can vouch for the doctor here."

When they returned to camp, William was not pleased with Amber, James and Edward but he praised Imran for going to the aid of the little girl. He ordered them all to bed while he sat up at the table writing by lamplight until the early hours of the morning. Moths of various species crowded docilely on the canvas which had become a beacon where the lamplight beckoned. The evening was balmy and insects and frogs made up the mesmerising cacophony of night sounds just above one's consciousness. Occasionally he heard a cry of a goat or the rumbling complaint of a tired ox.

He folded the letter he had been writing before placing it in his writing slope. He could recite his own words by heart.

"My dearest Beloved,

I am so alone although I surround myself with people; I am so empty although I eat plenty; I laugh but my soul weeps; I sing but have forgotten the tunes of melodies I once loved; I read words but they are mere ciphers; I write reams of words but not enough meaning can describe my thoughts and feelings. Now I am destitute although comfortably off. In my abject poverty of spirit I have only you whom I can turn to for finding meaning in my life. You could sum up a situation so astutely; you could mould an idea into a work of art; you could recreate me into your ideal and beloved attorney general. Am I not your creation? You have left your parrot without a perch, a general's marble bust without a plinth; an author without a story. My life should be a storybook but when I open its pages they are blank since you left me. The artist within me fails to paint my landscapes of battles fought and won; I'd fall on my sword and admit defeat but your belief in me enables me to stand upright and strong, discovering each new day the songs in my heart that you put there. I will endure everything until death releases me to be lifted upwards into your heavenly company. When will I sing my swansong, My Fanny, my swan?

Your devoted soulmate.

-o0o-

The following day William dressed more formally and rode into town with his spirited stallion eagerly chomping at the bit. He had arranged to meet the mayor and the *heemraden* to hear for himself, how matters stood in the interior of the province. He had also invited bankers, farmers and shop owners to attend the meeting so that they could voice their own opinions about current affairs.

He was welcomed into the gathering by the intense and rigid *predikant* or minister of the Dutch Reformed Church who led them all in prayer before proceedings could begin. William was at ease in this role. He knew what was expected of him, "I am particularly interested to hear whether your labour matters are now resolved. Have the new laws concerning farmers and labourers provided you with greater reliability and mutual respect?" He looked every bit the statesman.

"Attorney General," a tall bearded farmer of some social repute stood up, "I must first thank you for your intervention regarding these matters. Vagrancy is now a rare occurrence and the stability that offers enables us to be more profitable – to have pickers when the grapes need harvesting and pruners in the autumn - it stands to reason we will increase our yield."

"Attorney General, the fact that we can now take a worker to court if he or she fails to turn up for work or if they steal, means that workers now behave more responsibly," Another younger man agreed.

"Have you had fewer complaints from workers of bullying or suffering worse treatment by their employers?" William looked around the hall.

From right at the back a gnarled and bent elderly farm worker raised a hand, "We hear it still goes on but less of my people are being hurt."

At his side and perhaps his son, another worker spoke loudly in order to be heard above the grumble of disagreement by the white landowners, "I would ask the Attorney General why we cannot vote if we don't earn more than £25 a year or own property of that amount. Will we workers never have a say in the way politicians rule over us?'"

"The buck doesn't stop with the politicians but with your relationship with your employer. You should negotiate terms of contract whereby your salary increases as your responsibility grows. It's that quality of responsibility that is looked for in earning the right to vote. With just working and not advancing you will not be of any use as a voter. You have nothing to lose."

A rumble of agreement filled the room and William continued, "I'm a Unitarian and my ideal is that each employer here today should nurture his workforce, make sure each family's lot improves with time, educate the children so that they one day can be landowners instead of unskilled workers. Skilled workers should be rewarded well. I urge you to treat your workers with humanity and maintain at all times their dignity." The few workers present began to clap and cheer.

"It's not much to ask," William turned to the mayor before joining in the applause, "Thank you all for coming here today!"

He quickly left the hall with a last wave but not before he had seen a tall man dressed all in black wearing what he thought was an American Stetson. The man slipped away in amongst the crowd before William could catch up with him. The way he just disappeared convinced William that the man didn't want to be discovered. William's wildest speculation was that it could have been Roland Craven or one of his henchmen or some enemy perhaps that he had made as a politician and there were enough of those.

-o0o-

Two weeks later the day dawned and the sky behind the mountains was a saffron blush leaving the valley clothed in indigo and a spectrum of greys and pinks. Hendrik was up and about stoking the fire to make coffee and checking on his cattle which nosed up to him in the makeshift kraal of interwoven branches. Koos was still asleep nearby so Hendrik prodded his ribs with his knobkerrie. Little Lucky skirted in amongst the herd nuzzled by some and butted by others, his dog, Spitz, prodding and nipping the large animals. The boy's large brown eyes sparkled in the half light. Everyone had been involved in packing up after William returned from the last of his meetings and lunch the day before so the only work now to do was taking down the tents. Lettie made porridge and dried rusk biscuits were dunked in the sweet coffee. She had made sure all her iron pots and the "potjie" a small cauldron on three metal feet that sat in the coals, so useful for "potjie kos" or stews, were gleaming and her boxes of foodstuffs had been replenished and hauled up into the wagon. Earlier she and Amber had walked into Paarl to fill up a small urn with still-warm milk at the dairy. It would augment the milk the goats produced.

As the small train of wagon, cattle and horses including Hendrik's donkey which he had just purchased left Paarl, Amber was yet again excited. Each phase of the trip was a new adventure.

"Our destination is Wellington or maybe further," William shouted above the noise of wheels moving over stones and potholes.

"This is my people's country", Hendrik's arms embraced the landscape around them. "Our ancestors' spirits live in these hills".

"What makes your people different to all others?" William drew nearer to the wagon, his interest as ever keen and his desire to learn still that of a much younger man.

Hendrik scratched his ear, "At the dawn of our nation we lived somewhere far in the north of Africa and gradually moved south to avoid treacherous tribes who would enslave us. We were then hunters and our women gathered food from the bush; but over time we picked up lost cattle that had wandered off from those tribes and gradually bred those to increase our herds and at last we had a means of bartering and our wealth grew. We also picked up fat-tailed sheep and we bred those too," Hendrik paused sending the whip singing above the heads of the oxen, "The spirit of the hunter is still alive in me today and there's nothing better than to follow a spoor that will lead me to my prey. I know all the signs of what the animal does, eating grass here, rubbing its horns against a bush, prints in the mud of a stream," He enjoyed daydreaming about the days when he had been satisfied with just living off the land and fending for himself; but he was ambitious and had made his way to Cape Town.

"You must relate your tales about your ancestors to me when we have time in the camp. Are those ancestors your gods? You must tell me the sort of things they can help you with or the sort of things they tell you to do." William nodded to Hendrik before galloping away to keep up with his charges.

They approached Wellington a few days later as the light began to fade and set up camp on a nearby farm with the owner, Karel's permission. The farmhouse was thatched with low eaves and the whitewashed walls had faded to cream and mud caked on the bottom of each wall. Pots of bright red pelargoniums dotted the front entrance. Cattle grazed on the lush grass near a small river and large trees sheltered the beauty spot. Smoke curled above the chimney drifting off into the evening sky.

Every one set about making camp and the farmer's wife, Elsabet, invited Lettie and Amber into her kitchen which was comforting as there was warm bread straight out of the oven cooling on a rack. The kitchen was tidy with an earthen floor spotlessly clean. In one corner lay a pile of wood ready for adding to the fire which was in a clay oven built into the wall. Pots were bubbling away on an iron grid and above the fire were shelves with a mantel clock ticking next to a tin of flour and two woven baskets contained eggs and fresh vegetables. Elsabet was quite petite with a friendly feminine oval face and her hair was pinned up under a cap. Her nimble fingers never stopped working, drying dishes as she talked, eager to hear any gossip. The lot of a farmer's wife was a lonely one, Amber thought as she told Elsabet what functions were on in Cape Town, balls, weddings and the like. The Boer woman encouraged Lettie to use the kitchen for preparing that evening's meal and the girls had soon filled the room with their produce and Lettie drew up a stool and began shelling peas at the stinkwood table which was scored with marks knives had made over the years.

Amber went in search of James and Edward who were bringing a sheen to their horses' hides with round brushes. She found a brush and began to groom her mare with gusto and her cheeks flushed with the exercise. The saddle would have to be cleaned and oiled, too.

-o0o-

Since Karel had mentioned that there was a pan of slightly briny water that hundreds of thousands of birds frequented just north of Wellington, first thing the next morning Amber, James and Edward set off to find what would surely make a unique spectacle. William remained behind, wishing to talk to Karel about political matters.

With her mount cantering politely behind the two men, Amber squeezed her knees against the docile mare's sides and she immediately accelerated into a gallop and Amber could feel her hair escaping from her cap and her eyes had tears swimming in them and then dropping onto her cheeks. It was all so exhilarating... but, suddenly she felt the mare's hindquarters lift upwards and she could feel herself being propelled through the air and landing embarrassingly on her bottom. The two men were at first concerned and then amused but before they could snort out a laugh, Edward pointed to a Cape Cobra with its head fully erected and its hood extended just feet away from Amber.

"Freeze, Amber, don't move a muscle!" Edward put a finger to his lips. With her mare watching a few yards away Amber wanted to run to her and mount her but Edward's instinct was correct. How long would this impasse between human and serpent last? Out of the corner of her eye she could see it sway as though to a tune an old Berber in North Africa would blow on his flute.

"I'm going to take a pot shot at it," James removed his pistol and pointed it at the snake's head.

"Don't you dare," Edward glanced at his companion, "We aren't at a fair and this isn't just target practice.

"I'm an ace shot. I could blow its head off in a second," James scowled. However, aware of the inactivity around him the mesmerising reptile relaxed and slowly eased itself back onto the ground and it slithered off, its steely eyes behind their translucent scales filled with deadly cunning.

Once it was a safe distance away Edward and James dismounted and immediately congratulated each other for solving the problem, making Amber burst out laughing. She got up and dusted herself down and removed a devil thorn and a couple of paper thorns from her hands, "Ouch! Well I wasn't expecting such excitement this morning and oh yes, Edward, thanks for saving my life. As for you, James, remind me never to have to rely on you, to solve a sticky problem. Can you imagine if the worst had happened how you would have felt? Taking me back to camp to die? Even Imran couldn't have saved me!" She took the hand up that Edward offered and mounted her horse giving her a reassuring slap that sent the mare thundering away from the danger zone.

The Drakenstein Mountains formed a chain of mauve peaks to the south and tall cumulus clouds towered like citadels of the gods above them. They approached the pan of water which was as wide as a lake but quite shallow and where sequins of sunlight sparkled. Suddenly with geometric precision the birds rose into the sky in a pink haze that dipped and turned like a shoal of fish, light changing their colours with each movement, their bodies a ball of feathers between their long necks and stretched out legs. Their pink and black wings carried them upwards into the deep blue sky. The poetry of their motion was reflected on the mirror of water below them.

Amber gasped at the sheer beauty of the flamingo flight and they waited for the colourful display to end as the birds sank back down to wade in the mud again, their feet stirring the mud while their beaks sifted minute organisms from the plankton stew, the beady yellow eyes of the flamingos stared warily at the humans. Other waders ran in and out of the water's edge with their backwards and forwards motion appearing quite like a ballet and Egyptian geese waddled about on dry land on strong bandy legs. A cloud of finches suddenly appeared and settled in the trees and the birds covered the branches like new singing shivering leaves. White ibises like prophets almost walked on water there.

Both Edward and Amber had packed a sketchpad with pencils and water colours and they each found a vantage point to draw the lively and noisy scene. Edward added notes so that once they were back at camp and if they had sufficient time for him to complete an oil painting, he would set to the task immediately, light permitting. He had another trophy to take back with him. It was a *leucospermum* plant, one he had never seen before, nor had any knowledge that it existed. He had found it on a hillock where had they stopped to rest their horses. The plant was growing in amongst sharp rocks and stones far away from the habitat of other *leucospermums*. In addition its salmon pink pincushions of flowers were relatively inconspicuous unlike some of its relatives. He would painstakingly draw it in exact detail that would inform fellow botanists of its novelty. From time to time Edward left his vantage point to check on Amber's attempts at sketching. Each time he put his arm around her shoulders and felt the warmth of the sun on her skin.

"You've captured the shape of the flamingo with its head feeding in the water at its feet. Perhaps you can draw one dozing with its head under its wing. The composite rendering of the birds in flight needs refining." He was proud to share his knowledge with her.

"What colours would you use for the flamingos? Carmine and white?" Amber continued working anxious that her work wasn't completely a failure.

"You should try rose madder and white for the birds and raw sienna for the edge of the lake. You can make the lake reflect sunlight by having pinpoints of white and yellow.

On one occasion he held her hand making the movements necessary to capture an image of a flamingo attempting to take off from the water and both of them immediately withdrew their hands as an intense feeling of a pulsating energy was melting them together like solder on iron. It was the first time that Amber had ever felt physical attraction for someone. She looked into his blue eyes and for a moment they connected with one another with the Damascas moment surrounding them with sensations and confused thoughts. She blushed, so this was what falling in love felt like, she thought to herself. Her heart beat faster, her eyes sparkled and every sense was accentuated. She hoped that magic would continue as she was curious to discover or experience where it all could lead. Her lips parted as she longed for Edward to show such intimacy once more.

For the first time, Edward had surprised Amber. His relative youth set him apart from James and she felt she could listen to his voice for hours especially when he was describing plants with their phylums or *phyla* as he would say, genusses or geni, species etc. It was upper class and public school diction and she often longed for an accent such as his although her musical Irish accent had moderated since living at the Cape.

James, on the other hand, had come from English working class roots, his parents having emigrated from England and had now fallen on hard times and his accent was indefinable, attractive but it did not melt her knees. At least, she fought against any such admission. She silently laughed at her musings and continued experimenting with setting down on paper the birdlife scene before her irrevocably in coloured pigment and she leant backwards, screwing up her eyes. Yes, she was pleased with the result. However, for the first time she wished she was wearing a fashionable dress of white muslin embroidered with sprigs of heather, a few bouffant petticoats and on her head she would have worn a straw bonnet with flowers and a mauve ribbon and on her feet, dainty mauve shoes. She sighed and then dabbed the final touches, her signature and the date.

-oOo-

James left them in order to do some reconnoitring of his own. There were rocks on the first of the chain of shark-tooth Drakenstein Mountains, a mountain fortress worthy of a fire-breathing dragon that they had passed the day before with its bronze cliffs and soft padded foothills that he wanted to inspect and take a bore-sample. His horse tiptoed upwards delicately finding footholds in the flinty, sharp shale and from that vantage point the plain below seemed to stretch for miles, covered with Karoo succulents and herbs and the occasional tree. He intended to keep a look out for a buck or guinea fowl or two to take back to camp for the pot. Flamingo would definitely not do!

He had given some thought to Amber and mused how she had changed herself from being a gilded butterfly to a dusty moth. He still intended to woo her by a devilish game of taunting her and being disinterested and bordering on being cruel, his cynical remarks would entrap her. Women fell in love with men who treated them badly. His thoughts turned to his sisters and for their sake as well as his he desperately needed to find a seam of rock bearing copper or iron or even gold. There was apparently a mountain of copper which they would pass on their expedition and it was already being mined. It proved there were minerals buried underneath their feet somewhere. His fortune depended on a positive claim and he prayed he would discover gold. He had seen how the precious metal had turned normal, sane and sensible men into crazed, fanatical lizards, clawing and digging in the mud of a "find".

He tethered his horse and climbed up the gradient examining bits of quartz and sandstone. A mouse darted over his foot before it disappeared down a hole. Hundreds of ants were on the march and he carefully avoided those before reaching a cave that appeared empty; but, suddenly he heard a snarl and some creature was approaching him with what was clearly malicious intent. Yelps from the young in the pack made James realise he had inadvertently stumbled on a nursery of pups and the animal that was after him was a guardian or whatever the animal equivalent would be.

He turned and hurried back down the mountain and leapt onto his horse and the strong stallion slipped and slid its way downwards with the jaws of a female Cape hunting dog snapping at its heels. This species was a ferocious fighter with the unusual cream and brown markings on its fur and its large round ears were facing forward, alert to any sound. One kick of a hoof sent the wild animal flying. It was hurt but its bark had attracted the rest of the pack and soon James had to flee as fast as his horse could carry him. As the baying of the wild dogs grew closer a shot rang out and the leading animal fell mortally wounded. James swivelled in his saddle and saw a lone horseman, all in black. The man lifted his rifle in the air signalling to James that it was he who had shot the wild dog. James waved his hat but seeing the stranger unnerved him. Who was this man? It served to remind him that being out in the wild of Africa had its dangers. What would lie in store for him next?

-o0o-

William relaxed under the canopy of the main tent and read a letter that had been kept for him in Wellington, sent there by Hugh who knew the route the small caravan of explorers would take. William had taken himself off to the small town and called at the post office. His heart lifted when he found in amongst the mail sent on to him was one letter from Hugh.

"My dear William,

How very much I regret not accompanying you on your sojourn in realms where one is not at the mercy of numerous sorties on one's pre-planned and ordinary life. The empty places at supper remind me of what joy you impart when you relate the events of your day with such wit and novelty. I sadly lack the ability to amuse myself in any comparable fashion. Amber's good behaviour at table and as yet limited conversation will no doubt be embellished after her experience of the raw wilderness of adventure and physical challenges.

You'll be interested to hear that there are now plans to build a railway to the interior of the Cape. A train would have been more comfortable than your wagon. Buildings for the development of another commercial area are being erected like mushrooms popping up out of leaf mould and it is rewarding to watch such growth in the town. The contractors are ahead of time and the work has been well executed. The labourers have shone in the best colours of their profession.

Cape Town is suffering from the wretched South Easter. That wind might be known to some as the good doctor but it sets off my chest in fits of coughing. Contrary to the way that must sound, I am in good health.

Your esteemed friend, Miss Nerina, came by the office today to inquire about your progress. It probably behoves you to write to her?

The horse races have had their first meeting and I have been following an excellent gelding called Golden Grail and he is in fine form. I laid a bet of five pounds, a princely sum and the race was run over three miles with a lively field of horseflesh coming down the strait. At the very last minute Golden Grail is given his head and he crosses the finishing post one and a half lengths ahead of the next horse. I made myself a small fortune but the excitement could be the death of me. To feel the rush of pleasure and success revives a faltering spirit of a man in his fifties.

A word of warning: there are restless rumblings being emitted from Graham's Town and among those farmers and businessmen from Algoa Bay stock. I believe you can expect a battle to uphold your power in Cape Town stretching as far as the north-east.

I have not anything further of interest to write about but would endeavour to inquire if you could reply to this letter with one of your own.

Your affectionate friend,

Hugh"

William sighed and admitted to himself that he missed Hugh's company very much indeed having surrounded himself with young adults who needed shepherding and nurturing in the ways of nature and the wider world. He wondered whether it would have been better to have sent Amber back to Ireland from whence she could have gone to school in Europe to learn the cultures and history so much older and rich in deeds. He had often dreamt of making the dream into a reality but never managed to carry it out. How very different that experience would have been. The Italian lakes and Florence, the art and literature of Rome, Vienna and the Swiss Alps, Paris and Barcelona would have been invaluable gifts that would have given her sophistication and a mind that is capable of redefining the world around it. Her plan to become a doctor and to heal the sick was still of concern to him. He could imagine her becoming a missionary and travelling through darkest Africa strengthened by her vision whilst ignoring the fundamental needs and desires for which her body would hunger but not be fulfilled. Her fate lay in his hands.

His thoughts returned to Hugh and he began thinking of his reply to his friend's missive. The eastern frontier had always been like a precocious child. If matters deteriorated he would have to return to Cape Town to decide how to deal with the problem. He asked Hugh to keep an eye on matters and to keep him informed.

-o0o-

When William awoke the following morning, Imran wasn't in the tent and yawning William remembered that he had arranged to spend some time with Imran to hear him chant a section of the Quran. Sunrise was when the holiness of the message was most profound and that was said to be the best time to read the Quran. After a few minutes William lifted the tent flap and peered outside before setting off to find the young man. The camp was still with the fire grey and dusty and the birdsong was late, which was an unusual occurrence.

William wandered down to the river past Karel's house which was silent and locked. The light was still dusky and the only colour was a mixture of olive green and grey washes and the water of the river was an inky slow serpent flowing away in its usual bed with muffled gurgling. A man rose up from where he had been kneeling dressed in a white silk robe, black fez and sandals. He gestured opening his arms wide, "I felt I should dress as the Muslim I am for Allah's sake. I wish to believe that I can be an *imam* or teacher of the Book today."

"I believe it is right to honour your Lord whom I wish to honour too as I learn about Him," Moved, William hugged the young man and patted his back. The town dandy was nowhere to be seen.

"Mr Ropert, I took time yesterday to translate the verses I will narrate to you today. It was a difficult task as I should not embellish the Word or weaken its message. The exercise was a holy one. I am also not skilled in writing English in verse format," He gestured to William to remove his boots and he removed his sandals. He then asked William to sit with crossed legs on the bank of the river. "We will first pray according to the Holy Book,

> *"In the name of God, the mercy-giving, the Merciful, praise be to God, Lord of the Universe*

The Mercy-giving, the Merciful!

Ruler on the Day of Repayment!

You do we worship and you do we call upon for help.

Guide us along the Straight Road

The road of those whom You have favoured

With whom you are not angry

Nor who are lost!"

William said amen and Imran felt he had to explain how the Book had been in existence for fourteen centuries and it was matchless and inimitable, it had essential *"ijaz"*.

"The Book says that you will be able to understand its sacredness even if you are a non-believer," Imran's large brown eyes were indelible and their whites flashed as he looked upwards, "We recite the holy Book on solemn occasions for comfort, morality and guidance. It's every Muslim's duty to read the Quran and understand it. It's also said that any divine Message should be related in the recipient's own language," The young Muslim turned his palms upwards.

"Those are the words of a wise man, Imran, and I appreciate the time you have spent preparing passages to narrate to me. I hope I'll be worthy of your efforts," He smiled gently, feeling closer to the young man than he had ever done all the years he had known him and watched him grow up from a young boy.

"The Quranic message is easy to learn as it is divided up into a hundred and fourteen chapters so that chapters can be read in sittings or read straight through. That is why I have only translated a few passages for you. It will take months of my work and your endeavour for you to really understand everything," Imran picked up his translation, "You will see there are a lot of sacred symbols which help a believer to look at the universe in a different way and they also set out a lifestyle which tells us how things are and how they should be. The contradictions in life is explained in pairs like father, mother; heaven, hell; hell and Hades (*Johannam* and *Jahim*); Heaven and Earth; night and day; heat and cold; *halal* and *Haram* i.e. the permitted and the forbidden.

"For today I've chosen two sections which you may want to ponder over:

> *"The blind and the sighted are not equal*
>
> *Nor are the darkness and light*
>
> *Nor a shady nook and a heatwave*
>
> *The living and the dead are not alike*
>
> *God lets anyone He wishes listen*
>
> *While you will not make those in their graves hear"*

(Originator 35.19-22)

"When you consider being conscious and compare that state with the Unseen you can perhaps grasp the opposing principles for knowledge as well," Imran explained, "Bodily pain is the opposite of physical pleasures forming another pair of opposites linked to Heaven and Hell in our minds. So good and evil form a strong pair throughout God's creation. Both come ultimately from God but they are not equal in power. We need to change evil into good since both states come from God. You see God may have allowed evil to be present in the World but that doesn't mean that he ordered its existence," Imran hoped he was conveying the true meaning of the Word.

"As a believer of God that isn't far off what I believe as a Christian," William nodded enjoying the experience of being the pupil. The day grew brighter and at last the birds began to sing, the night finally relinquishing its hold on the day.

> *"I will end with Abraham and Ishmael's prayer,*
>
> *'Lord accept this from us!*
>
> *Indeed you are the Alert, the Aware!*

Our Lord leave us peacefully committed to you

And make our offspring into a nation

Which is at peace with you

Show us our ceremonies and turn us forwards;

You are so relenting, the Merciful!

Our Lord, send a messenger in among them

From among themselves who will recite

Your verses to them and teach them

The Book and Wisdom!

He will purify them for You are the Powerful, the Wise."

"We are in tune with each other, Imran when listening to your recital," William felt a warmth spread inside his heart which had been cold since Fanny's death.

"It is strange to take on the role of messenger," the young man straightened up quoting another passage from Abraham "*We have not sent any messenger unless he was to explain to them in his folks' own tongue.*" I trust I have explained the message well?"

"Yes, of course, Imran. I look forward to our next lesson. You're succeeding in making me look at the Old Testament through a Muslim's eyes. I am looking forward to hearing the Prophet's own words as well. Well done," William put an arm around his protégé's shoulders.

For a moment Imran was quiet and then quoted in Arabic, "*Waallathina kafaru amalulum kasarab biqiat.*"

The musicality of the sentence made William stop in his tracks, "What does that saying mean?"

Proudly, Imran translated, "Those who disbelieve will find their deeds are like a mirage on a desert". That is from the Quran, Light 24-39."

Was that a veiled threat, William wondered as he took his leave from the natural shrine which had now been consecrated. He had much to contemplate. He would look forward to further daybreak lessons and prayers.

-oOo-

Another evening in the wilderness presented itself with a richly textured sunset and with everyone in the camp occupied with various tasks, William opened his writing slope and sat down to compose a letter to Hugh.

"My dear Hugh,

Many happy felicitations to you and my gratitude for your most welcome letter cannot be expressed deeply enough. I'm relieved Cape Town is managing to do without my services. It serves to remind me that no one individual is indispensable and it behoves me to remain aware of any thoughts of higher office. It is not my intention to rise above my current station as the work would be less and the office more pretentious with the ambient air more rarefied.

I'm delighted the railway line is growing at such a pace as it will benefit trade considerably. The sooner the infrastructure to connect all outlying regions to Cape Town the better, as it will stabilise the province.

News about the Eastern Frontier is troubling. I insist that you discover who the instigators of the revolutionary element in politics there are and look into the whereabouts of Roland Craven, as ever a thorn in my flesh. There has been a lone horseman who has been keeping his distance yet invading our activities. It is not clear if he is a benevolent stranger or if he has some intention to harm us.

I am hoping to lead the expedition onward toward Namaqualand and our next stop will be Ropertdal where we've been invited to a dinner and pleasure activities with the mayor and owner of the small town, Karl Uys. You may remember the famous trial settling a dispute between the two brothers. Tulbagh will be a town with a post office where you could address your reply to await collection. We'll travel at a leisurely pace over the coming weeks.

I hope your health is improving, my good friend. I look forward to your next letter.

Yours sincerely,

William."

"Uncle William, may I share your table and lamplight with you to write in my Journal?" Amber interrupted his train of thought. She had washed her long auburn hair and it hung in curls like an aura seen in icons. Her fair skin was glowing, her eyes were as bright as stars and her lips quivered into a smile. It had become a nightly event which both of them enjoyed.

"Tonight I will address my thoughts to you, Aunt Fanny", she began to write, *"I am totally bereft bearing the loss of your company all alone and longing for the way in which together we always dispatched my problems so sensibly.*

I'm in a muddle with the crushing load of thoughts and feelings. I'm having the time of my life which I know will never be repeated but the wonderful freedom makes me feel vulnerable. I am having a plethora of emotions about Edward and James. I have never felt so overwhelmed with joy the one minute and then despair the next. Sometimes I miss my lovely dresses and my hair being curled and plaited into such intricate ways but perhaps in society in Cape Town one needs to stand out and show off to men and ladies alike. There young women can be vicious when the competition is too strong. Here I have only Lettie as competition but we are both equal in dress and position. Oh how she deserves clothes like the ones I have at home. I do want to attract Edward's attention but I don't know what to do when I have his eyes gazing into mine or when his hand accidentally brushes mine. There should be more to follow but it remains clouded in secrecy.

Aunt Fanny, how does someone of my age interact with an older man? James is so attractive but in a dangerous way. I don't think he would respect my youth and innocence, for innocent is what I surely am; in fact I think he would ravish me. I'll make sure I'm never alone with him. If in any doubt I will try to imagine what you would do in a given situation.

I hope you can see the picture I painted today at the lake. It was a heavenly spectacle as I am sure God will have such beauty spots in heaven. What a queer creature a flamingo is; totally unique and from elsewhere in the universe most surely. But, now I must end as it is pitch-dark outside and Uncle William and I are the only ones awake, bathed in lamplight and listening to the insects.

Farewell, with all my love, as always."

William walked with her to the tent she shared with Lettie before returning to his writing. He had sealed the letter to Hugh but now he found it an urgent necessity to write to Nerina about the pitfalls of parenthood.

"My dear Nerina,

I find myself lacking in the qualities of a good parent. In fact the latter is a mystery to this middle-aged bachelor. Dreaming of fatherhood has long ago faded away and in fact would have died within me if it weren't for Miss McBride leaving me with a young girl to bring up as my own. Perhaps she knew I would have no other opportunity to shape a child's life and provide for her every need. I have a few young men as protégés but being in loco parentis is only occasional and usually I seem to have a reasonable imagination for their needs and education. But, a young girl like Amber is totally out of my sphere of learning and experience,

She is basking in her new-found freedom. One can see her shaking off the stuffiness of Cape society and I despair when she runs around barefoot or allows her bonnet to slip down her back. She is lively with more energy than a sheep dog and the inquisitiveness and playfulness of a kitten. It won't surprise you no doubt that she has rearranged our lives. Wash day is Monday and we're all required to wash our soiled clothes and bed linen and we have rotas for collecting firewood and keeping the fire alight. Fortunately, she doesn't expect us to share the cooking but she helps Lettie with peeling and chopping. She certainly has shaken up the young men into useful activities. They're the crux of my problem.

Hugh warned me about taking a young woman on a journey that has been oriented towards males rather than females. How do I explain to her what to expect from young men especially in the light of her vulnerable female gender. You can imagine my difficulty. Perhaps you could enlighten me sensibly on the matter. No doubt, I should never completely trust my protégés and should chaperone her more closely. She craves to be set free but that could be a most rash action and reeling in the bright ribbons of her joie de vivre will be painful for both of us. Today, she narrowly escaped being crippled by a fall off her horse and bitten by a cobra which really drives home to me that I have taken liberties with her very life in order to allow her greater freedom. Perhaps I should have asked Fatima to accompany us instead of Lettie considering Lettie is only a few years older than Amber. Fatima would no doubt have kept proper control over the men and kept Amber under her supervision.

I urge you to reply to me swiftly and to send your letter to the post office at Tulbagh where I hope we will find ourselves in three to four weeks' time.

Your respectful friend,

William"

-o0o-

A fortnight later William's ox-wagon and riders entered the Breede River valley and the magnificence of the Obiqua and Witzenberg Mountains on either side of the river impressed the newly experienced young travellers. The indigo and mauve Witzenberg Mountains which at a height of over six thousand feet were capped with snow after a cold snap, something quite rare in the Cape. The vines formed rows upon rows of bright green budding foliage softening the wizened well-pruned vineyard stock. Fortunately the late frost hadn't reached the valley. The horses hooves rang out on the main street and the wagon trundled along behind the tired oxen. The town's architecture was Cape Dutch for the most part and houses with their ornate gables and surrounding low whitewashed walls with tiled front courtyards were impeccably well kept. William pointed out the Oude Kerk, the first Dutch Reformed church built at the Cape. Its simple lines were classical and understated.

"I would dearly love to paint the buildings. The way the town has been planned is aesthetically very pleasing," Edward was almost jumping out of his saddle with his enthusiasm. The artist in him was always searching for something to claim as his own and by painting a canvass he felt he owned the subject. A state of religious creation. To mould a figurine in clay honours the subject the figurine depicts but its beauty belongs to the person doing the moulding.

"What are we going to do while we're here," Amber piped up, quieter than usual but they were all tired and dishevelled.

"I've a surprise for you," William smiled at them all, "We'll stay at the inn and I'll order a fine meal with the best wines of the Cape and we'll sleep in comfort tonight and for the next few days. There'll be hot water for bathing in each room and your laundry will be done for you."

"That's so wonderful, Uncle William! After camping, I'll never complain about a bad night's sleep again. What absolute luxury to have a feather mattress and warm blankets." Amber had never dreamed of such a treat.

The "Al Onse Gesellen" Inn had a graduated step gable design more in keeping with Amsterdam and the many paned sash windows were tastefully framed with green shutters which were accentuated against the whitewashed walls. Earthenware pots of young pink pelargoniums dotted the courtyards whiled the pergolas on either side of the building were laden with the stems of gnarled old vines and pomegranate red coloured bougainvillaea with wedding white and claret bejewelled rambling roses.

Before dinner, Edward with his blond blaze of hair and suntanned face looked debonair in the trousers and jacket he had packed for just such an occasion as he knew William had always been an epicurean and enjoyed the finer things in life and such an occasion would be inevitable. Leaning against a pillar in the courtyard, James lit his pipe and his dark good looks gave nothing away of the military manoeuvre he was planning. He inhaled the aromatic richness of the burning tobacco, filled his lungs and exhaled through his nostrils. The men had all shaven and Imran gave instructions to the cook about how his food should be prepared and finally, the two young women joined them all in the dining room.

Amber wore a black Boer woman's dress with lace around her neck and shoulders and a belt with a buckle that was adorned with pearls.

Lettie had brushed Amber's long hair and had pinned it up into a plaited coronet. Lettie was dressed in red and to embellish her simple cotton frock had picked a rose bloom growing in the arbour outside the inn and pinned it in her hair. Koos and Lucky were with the wagon and also had the full responsibility of looking after the oxen which had been herded into a field adjoining the Inn. Hendrik had found a friend from his past and had invited him to have supper with them. William had given instructions that they should have a tasty meal sent to them albeit not inside the inn but where they were stationed.

At the inn the conversation grew louder as everyone except for Imran enjoyed the wine. They all agreed that the rack of lamb and fresh potatoes, carrots and spinach were delicious and not only was the dessert, an apple dumpling pudding and custard, a sweet delight but it finally satisfied their hungry appetites.

Afterwards, Amber went out into the arbour and leaned against the white-washed pillar and noticed it was a full moon, "I could get used to living like this again," she thought out loud.

"I thought the brave pioneer woman was all an act", James appeared out of the shadows and walked over to her. Without warning he pinned her against the wall in the darkest part of the outdoor garden.

"No, James, don't be stupid", Amber tried to push him away but his mouth covered hers and she found it was futile to beat him with her fists. She was a fluttering butterfly with its thorax pierced by the collector's pin. After her inept attempts to escape, she succumbed to the pleasure he was giving her…she never thought about the pleasure he had been intending to obtain for himself. Nor had she the vocabulary to give voice to his ulterior motives. This kiss had been stolen, would he have to steal the rest of his booty?

Neither of them had seen Edward enter the garden to smoke a cigar. He realised that James was with someone. Not wanting to invade their privacy he retreated back into the inn. He was troubled as the possibilities as to who it was that was with James were not that many.

James was instigating a Machiavellian plot between the three of them, of which he wanted no part.

Amber skipped up the stairs holding her dress up to her calves for safety sake and burst into the room she shared with Lettie, "I've so much to tell you, Lettie," She embraced the surprised Lettie and danced with her around the room, "Guess what? James actually kissed me in the arbour. It was the most spellbinding moment of my life. I couldn't breathe for the time his lips were on mine and nearly fainted with my heartbeats throbbing in my chest."

"That man is not trustworthy, Amber. No, listen to me. He's been around and even travelled the world. He's no angel and if he is not an angel he must be a devil. You mustn't put your trust in him. Passion is not love. It's daring and forbidden which makes it so exciting. Think what you would do if you were at home at Wolmunster when Miss Fanny was alive. You would have been shocked and would have felt violated." Lettie wasn't going to mince her words.

"Don't spoil it for me, Lettie. Let me dream. Perhaps tomorrow I'll have more sense and regret my stolen kiss but for tonight I'll remember the warmth of a man's embrace, the fresh smell of his skin, the smooth shaven cheek, his demanding lips," She touched her own lips and grew quiet. What if she had made a terrible mistake?

-o0o-

While William was entertaining his party and everyone was enjoying their evening together, in another part of Tulbagh, a man dressed in black found lodging for the night. He was weary having been in the saddle since leaving Cape Town stopping only for snatched sleep, water and dried food. He had a chiselled face with a jutting jaw and deep set blue eyes and his lips were thin and tight. He was getting closer to achieving his goal. How would he know when the time was right for making his next move?

-o0o-

After a fortnight in the comfortable inn with daily forays climbing mountains and walking along the river, being entertained at night by the townsfolk, they packed reluctantly as the weather was closing in and the next part of the journey would most likely be affected by storms; but, progress they must was William's intention. The women Amber met arranged afternoon tea the previous day and presented her with an exquisite royal blue evening bag embroidered with gold roses and fleur de lis. She promised them she would keep in touch by letter. Along the roads and in towns they were making lifelong acquaintances.

"You won't probably know of the village we are heading for," William told them at breakfast, hesitating for a moment to drink some of the aromatic coffee, "It isn't on the map as yet but no doubt will be added to newer editions when the cartographers update their records. Our destination is Ropertdal which has been named after me and I'll explain why I have been given this honour on our journey. Naturally it was related to a famous court case which made the national press and when we return to Cape Town I can show you the newspaper clippings as they make interesting reading."

The memory of those weeks in the Supreme Court in Cape Town was unblemished by time. It was a landmark case that had caught the imagination of the press and the town alike…

One sunny morning with light shafts penetrating the gloom of their rooms where shelves of files or briefs tied in pink ribbon grew dusty Hugh brought an angry young Boer man through to his office and introduced him as Martinus Wessels. He was a good-looking man, very muscular and tall with brown hair and a deep suntan and he crowded William's room with his sheer physique. It was only when he looked into the man's eyes that William realised he was very angry and full of unabashed hatred.

"Please go ahead and explain why you are here," William drew up a chair for Martinus and resumed his place behind his fine stinkwood desk which was impeccably arranged with a fine lamp with a green shade and brass base and pen and ink stand in silver.

"It's a long story but this time my father has gone too far. In life he made us sweat for the farm from daybreak to sunset. We own one of the largest vineyards in the Cape and produce a high quality white wine which has been well received by wine connoisseurs here and in Europe. It is a good export product for the colony. Anyhow, one day a few years ago my father introduces us to a young coloured man called Khalil Wagiet and informs us that he has experience as a winemaker and would work in our establishment. We were naturally put out by the fact that he wasn't one of us. You understand what I mean but I give the man his due, he knew his art. It came to our attention later that my father had sent him to a thriving wine farm at Franschoek to be trained in the art of wine making. I'm the eldest of five brothers and four sisters. As a family and a business we need the proceeds of the farm to provide for us all and for further developing the farm. Our father was good to his staff and some time ago he built a small village for our workers on a part of the farm that lay fallow. He brought a teacher from Cape Town and her mother and gave them a small house. He also built a small shop which he ran with one of his faithful servants, Ishmael. The village took up a third of our land but he insisted that he was giving back to the people what God had given him." Overcome with emotion Martinus coughed.

William poured water into a glass and handed it to him, "I can see this is a very emotive issue, Mr Wessels."

"You have no idea what I am going through. It's hard to explain just how much my father has betrayed us. After a short illness Father died a month ago and he had left his last will and testament to be read out by me. I had never seen the document before. My mother, sisters and brothers sat in the drawing room of the farmhouse with all our ancestors looking down on us. How they must have felt looking down on us from heaven. At the last minute Koos, Duppie, my father's servants and Khalil Wagiet, a wine maker on the farm entered the room. After they were seated, I began to read the Will that the solicitor handed to me," Martinus took out the offending article from his bag, "I'll read you what it says."

"The said Albertus Wessels hereinafter named the Deceased has given the prokureurs Ettienne Loubser en Seun instructions to carry out the probate on his estate. The Deceased has left instructions that he wishes to be buried in the family graveyard on the farm "Groenendal". The Deceased has nominated his eldest son, Martinus Wessels as the executor of his estate. He will read the Will on the day of the Deceased's funeral with all the family gathered together. The Deceased has requested the presence of his trusted manservant and his groom as well as his viticulturist, Khalil Wagiet."

Martinus turned to William "Everyone in the room began to whisper and looked around them noticing that the three employees had entered the room at a signal from the solicitor present. I remember clearing my throat like it has done now and then I continued."

"I confirm that this is my Last Will and Testament and that any other preceding testaments be declared null and void. Signed by me Albertus Wessels at "Groenendal" on the 6th September 1855.

I bequeath to my trusted servant, Koos Meintjies, the sum of fifty pounds for his lifelong loyalty in assisting me in many ways and a further five pounds per year until he dies.

I bequeath to my groom, Duppie Du Plessis, the sum of thirty pounds plus two pounds per year to continue to look after my horses till they are all dead.

I bequeath the farmhouse and all its contents with an annuity of one hundred pounds to my loving and hardworking wife, Elmarie.

I bequeath to my sons, Dirk, Albertus, Fanie, Kobus, Frikkie and Pikkie each an annuity of twenty pounds.

I bequeath to my daughters, Susanna, Matilda, Kristina and Marguerita a dowry of thirty pounds each.

I bequeath to my eldest son, Martinus, two thirds of the vineyards as drawn on the map of the farm attached hereto and the wine cellars.

I bequeath the village, the wine making laboratory and one third of the vineyards to Khalil Wagiet, my viticulturist, with the proviso that he cares for the welfare of the villagers and prevents that land being appropriated for cultivation.

It is my wish that Martinus and Khalil should run the farm together."

Martinus remembered how he had felt his anger rise within himself suffusing his face with blood. It couldn't be true. To share his beloved "Groenendal" with a coloured employee? His father had lost his mind when he wrote out his will, surely that was the case? He was filled with questions that would never be answered. When Duppie, Koos and Khalil shuffled out of the room, he had heard himself shout "Get out of here! Go on, out, out I say! And you, Khalil, get off this farm immediately. I refuse to honour my father's wishes and I intend to talk to my lawyer."

"You will perhaps now understand my situation, Mr Ropert. I have heard all about your reputation and I want you to fight against this will on my behalf on the premise that my father was not in sane mind when he wrote these instructions," Martinus folded the offensive document before handing it over to William.

"I'm afraid to say that I cannot act on your behalf in this matter as I have already received instructions from Khalil Wagiet to act as his defence attorney against the court case with which you have threatened him. He has also told me that you have said you intended to demolish the village and run the villagers off the farm and that you would withhold the third of the vineyards that is rightfully his," William returned the will to Martinus.

"He is not my father's son – I am! I'll fight him in every way I can but I am not obeying the instructions of an elderly man in his dotage. It's a matter of blood. I am of his blood not Khalil. That will be my claim."

The young people at table with him had listened intently to William's account of the day he met Martinus.

"Don't stop there, Uncle William. What happened next? Do tell us!" Amber begged.

"We will never reach Ropertdal if I sit here sharing anecdotes with you all day. I'll give you the next instalment tomorrow night after we pitch camp."

"The fact that we are visiting Ropertdal gives the ending away," James laughed amicably.

"Shhh you!" Amber playfully punched his arm, "Don't spoil the story".

-o0o-

Khalil Wagiet was a good-looking young man with short black hair, large brown eyes and of medium build. He left the drawing room in the old farmhouse feeling elated on the one hand and shocked on the other. His mentor had not forgotten him and his position at the vineyard was protected as well as that of his mother, Saheera, the teacher at the farm school. Saheera had originally been brought to "Groenendal" by Albertus Wessels before Khalil was born to help his wife with all the children. Her very elderly mother had accompanied Saheera. However she had been taught to read and therefore wanted to share her knowledge with the children of the farm workers.

Khalil had not been aware that Albertus Wessels had been structuring his tuition to give Khalil the foundation for studying viticulture. When he was sent to "Welgelegen" he learnt the tools and skills every winemaker needs. How to test the grapes in order to ascertain when they should be picked; to choose vines that were suitable for the type of soil; and to test wine fermenting in barrels in order to know when the wine should be bottled. He returned to "Groenendal" after two years and immediately set to work doing the job he loved above all else.

Albertus was a tall, distinguished looking man with silver in his hair, moustache and beard but Khalil only ever saw kindness and good humour in his benefactor's sharp blue eyes. He knew Albertus had built the village and had brought his mother there to teach the children of the farmworkers in a school that had only one large classroom where Saheera taught all the different age groups miraculously at the same time.

It was only recently that he had wondered who his father was. Saheera always changed the subject with a blunt retort that his father was dead. She was a charming sophisticated Muslim woman and she looked forward to Albertus' visits with her mother ever present. Khalil never saw any tell-tale sign that she loved Albertus but it was only following the reading of the will that he suspected that he was his benefactor's son.

"Why did you never tell me that I am his son?" Khalil pushed his mother aside when he arrived back at their cottage and sat down with his head between his hands, "I could have shared so much with him."

"Like I shared with him? One night soon after I arrived at "Groenendal" I was preparing my lessons for the following day when Albertus knocked on my door. I let him in and we talked for hours. He always said he could think when he was with me. He found he was shut out of his home when he was there. Everyone was so demanding of him but with me he could just let out his pain and anger. Yes, he was an angry man as his sons with the exception of Martinus were a disappointment when they failed to work hard at their studies at the school in Wynberg. He loved his wife and daughters but found conversation with them limiting. He always said the topics of conversation were recipes, hair styles and clothes. He was a highly intelligent man. You can be proud of him." Sameera wrung her hands, her fingers miming her words, "One night – I remember there was a huge storm - he didn't go home and we slept together. My mother slept deeply and never knew what had transpired. We had shared so much for so long that we couldn't hold back our love that just wanted to pour over the edge like a waterfall of emotions. I held him tightly. I wanted to keep him with me forever and to that end I succeeded as part of him always remains with me from the moment when you were conceived."

-o0o-

The travelling party were one day away from Ropertdal and had out-spanned under trees. By now they were adept at putting up tents only to strike camp the very next day. The young people huddled together for warmth around the fire that night listening to the cracking and hissing of the burning logs. William joined the small party and sat down with them.

"You promised you would finish your story about the trial," Amber cajoled William, "Do tell us what happened after you agreed to defend Khalil's case."

William picked up the threads of his tale and a born storyteller he had them hanging on his every word:

After his meeting with Khalil he had packed and called for his horse to be prepared for a journey and any previous arrangements with clients were to be postponed. Together William and Khalil began the long journey to "Groenendal" as it was necessary for William to meet potential witnesses who could strengthen their case whereby Khalil could claim his rightful inheritance.

A storm bubbled up on the last few miles of their journey and bedraggled and wet they led their horses to the stables in the village. The farm and vineyards were a watery impression through the diaphanous sheets of rain. The Hottentot men and women peered through open doors to welcome their champion home. Greetings were shouted to drown out the rolling thunder and sousing rain. Khalil led William to the cottage where Sameera and he lived. It was an attractive abode with a thatch roof and picture windows with a multitude of panes and flowers of all descriptions were a damp riot in the small garden. Khalil's dog was barking from within and a moment later Sameera let them in, quickly finding towels with which they could dry themselves. Stripping off in front of Sameera was as matter of fact as a child being urged to remove wet clothes in case of catching a cold.

William looked at the woman fussing over them. He had rarely seen such composure and her oval cream-coffee tinged face with her slightly slanted brown eyes and arched eyebrows, even nose and full inviting lips were astonishingly attractive. Her dark hair was hidden behind a white hijab and her flowing dark blue cotton dress was almost identical to the apparel of the Virgin Mary William had seen in artistic interpretations.

"Welcome to our home, Mr Ropert. I am delighted you can help Khalil with the situation that has developed here at "Groenendal". I'm all agog to hear how we may now proceed. Its general knowledge that Mr Martinus believes Khalil hasn't a claim."

"I'll start my inquiries tomorrow but from what Khalil has told me I do believe I may have the strategy with which we can defeat Martinus Wessels.

William said in between mouthfuls of chicken broth and freshly baked bread.

"I'll begin by interviewing you privately," He turned to Khalil, "You don't mind, do you?" Khalil shook his head in answer.

The following morning dawned dry and bright and dewdrops trembled on every grass stalk reflecting sunbeams. William prepared to write his notes at the kitchen table.

Sameera sat opposite him composed and vigilant. Encouraged to tell William her life story, she began to speak. Soon her soliloquy ended with giving birth to Khalil.

"You do realise that I need to ask a very personal question, who is or was Khalil's father? You were a young Muslim woman all alone in this village where there were no other Muslims. That was no doubt a blessing as in your own community you could have been stoned to death for adultery."

Tears sparkled in Sameera's eyes, "Albertus Wessels was Khalil's father and only he and I were privy to that secret. Even Khalil was taken aback when I told him who his father was, on the day the will was read."

"Have you any proof of that fact?" William looked into her eyes intensely almost like a surgeon about to operate on a patient.

Sameera went over to a bureau and withdrew a document from between the leaves of a book, "I think this is what you're looking for."

"Excellent!" William exclaimed, "Wessels believes Khalil is illegitimate but this birth certificate makes it quite clear that Albertus is his father."

"Albertus himself registered his birth with the authorities. I have never dared give him the Wessel's surname, that is, until now."

"Tell me more about your relationship. It would seem that the intimacy you shared with Albertus was fleeting." William looked at her in sympathy.

"When Khalil became a little boy we stopped our love affair if you can call it that. He could have inadvertently blurted it out that Albertus was his father."

William sat back after blotting his notes. He wiped his quill pen and closed the ink bottle, "No one can argue that Khalil is a bastard and that his father could be one of many. Martinus Wessels is probably intending a two pronged attack. One that his father was incompetent and secondly that Khalil is not a blood relative. He would never dream that his father, a man with an impeccable reputation could have had an affair let alone that it happened on his farm so close to home."

-o0o-

Later that day, William visited the workers as they dug up weeds between the rows of vines. The smell of the earth was like damp mushrooms and the chlorophyll in each cell of the vine was virginal and young. One by one, they confirmed one fact and that was that Albertus had been an employer with deep humanity.

The next phase of William's attack was to question Elmarie Wessels and he wondered how she would react when he knocked on the farmhouse door. According to the farm workers, Martinus was away which was of help and his siblings only paid him a passing glance as they were preoccupied with what they were doing. William hit his boot with a riding crop while he waited for someone to come to the door.

The door swung open and Elmarie Wessels appeared before him. She was a dumpling of a woman, soft and wholesome with bright blue eyes, auburn hair that was now going grey and a pert little mouth which was usually turned up at the corners in mirth or surprise.

"May I ask you a few questions about your staff on the farm? I am doing research in the area," William explained. He didn't know what direction his line of questioning would take but often if one allows a talkative person to have free reign important facts usually emerge.

"I do want to convey my condolences to you. I believe your husband died recently?" William began, politely.

As he expected, Elmarie couldn't bite her tongue but related in minute detail all the developments that led to the discovery of Albertus' body in the bath where she believed he had a heart attack. Next she prattled on about the doctor's visit. At this point, William leant forward, "Was your husband's mind clear in those last few weeks?"

"Of course, Albertus was a sharp one. I can tell you he kept me on my toes. He would always say that I was a gossip and should have more to keep me occupied than discussing the neighbours, the minister and weddings and funerals. No, he had a fine mind with an above average memory! Now I must tell you all who came to the funeral and what they wore. We had a wonderful wake!"

His next question had to be obliquely addressed, "Would you say he was the sort of man who would like the ladies?" William coughed with embarrassment.

"Oh no, Mr Ropert, Albertus was a God-fearing man. You should have heard how he would drill into our children passages from the Bible about a woman's virtue and a gentleman's honourable leadership. He castigated the erring woman in the Scriptures." Elmarie for a moment looked serious and penitent.

"Why do you think your husband gave Khalil Wagiet a third of the farm, the village and the laboratory?" William prodded her with the forensic skill of a barrister.

"Why? He had trained Khalil so well that he's essential to the production of wine on the farm. Martinus is the business man. He gets involved in book-keeping, exports – things like that; but, Khalil has the tricks to achieve great wine. His ability to taste wine and to know what grape it's from, what part of the farm it's from, is absolutely the sign of a genius. Albertus used to say to me that the two of them would fit together like a hand in a glove. They would always need each other." Elmarie was astute enough to become aware of what William was after. But he had what he came for, if he could get Elmarie to swear under oath that these facts were true.

"Mrs Wessels, may I call on you to swear to that in court? With you as witness, Khalil will win the case." William said matter of factly.

"I'm afraid not, Mr Ropert. Martinus would never forgive me. He has already asked one of his brothers, the workers' foreman and an uncle to testify to the fact that Albertus was senile," She hesitated for a moment and then continued, "The people you can count on are our doctor and minister. They are both honourable professional men who will tell the truth.

Surprised that she was being so accommodating, William thanked her and set out on horseback to find the Rev. Malherbe and Dr. Steyn who lived on farms in the vicinity from where they tended to their human flock. After a day in the saddle, William got what he wanted and both men agreed to testify to Albertus' sanity. With their help and if Sameera would present the birth certificate and verify its contents in court, he could win the case. What other line of attack beyond the obvious two issues that Martinus would put forward could the eldest Wessels consider? William didn't believe there was any.

-oOo-

There was rain in the air and William sat back and looked at Amber, Edward, James, and Imran who were huddled together for warmth, and

Hendrik who could barely keep his eyes open, had the sleeping boy, Lucky, on his lap. "Which one of you can finish the story?" William asked. It would be interesting to listen to their take on what could have followed.

The four young people each adopted a role, Amber was Sameera and the prosecuting attorney named Konradie for sake of the game, Edward was Khalil, Fanie, the brother, James was Martinus and Imran was the workers' foreman and Duppie, the foreman. William was the judge. Lettie had gone to bed after clearing up once dinner was over.

It was all played to perfection. Sameera loved her son so much that she revealed her private life in court and as promised she produced the birth certificate; the doctor and minister confirmed under oath that Albertus was not incompetent at the time of writing the will. Martinus' attack would disappear in a puff of smoke when his witnesses lied under oath and there was mentioned that they had received bribes from Martinus. He would be obliged to face the fact that Khalil would be staying on at "Groenendal".

"The Judge stated that Albertus Wessels had ensured that "Groenendal" would be run by his two sons in close co-operation and furthermore he believed that the farmer was an astute judge of character and convinced that the two young men would put their differences to one side and acknowledge each other as brothers and co-owners of the farm. This would guarantee that the vineyards and the village would be preserved for generations to come. "Shortly thereafter Khalil informed me that they had named the small hamlet after me." William grinned happily.

"What a capital story. That was so much fun, Uncle William. How wonderful to hear all about the different people we'll meet tomorrow." Amber yawned stretching her arms out wide.

"Do you believe Martinus will welcome us?" James asked enjoying the irony of the case.

"I believe so. We parted in good spirits after the trial. I don't think Martinus was as ruthless an opponent as he may have expected. Anyway, I'm turning in for the night. We must strike camp early tomorrow. Good night! I will turn you into advocates yet!"

-oOo-

When they arrived at "Groenendal", William and his party were cheered and the workers led them to a pleasant vacant piece of land in the village where they out-spanned the oxen and pitched camp. Khalil found William and the two men embraced. William held Khalil by the shoulders at arm's length, "It's good to see you and to be back in this delightful countryside. How is your mother?"

Khalil laughed, "She is well and less shy. In fact, her story has made her famous in the district. Instead of shame, she now carries herself with pride and the Hottentot women feel she is now one of them."

A horse and rider approached William and he recognised Martinus who leapt off his mount and shook William's hand, "No hard feelings, Attorney General?"

"No hard feelings, Martinus," William smiled affably.

"We have slaughtered two sheep and a pig and will roast them each on a spit for a party tonight in your honour," the blond giant laughed.

The festivities began at sunset and the Wessels family intermingled with guests from neighbouring farms and the farmworkers joined in the jollity by providing the music. The musicians played the fiddle, reed flute and drums and of all people, Hendrik produced a concertina and happily found his place with them in the barn. Soon people were dancing a jig, clapping hands and laughing out loud. It wasn't long before the players struck up the music for the Boers' favourite dances and women lifted their skirts slightly in curtsies and the men bowed to them followed by energetic routines. Lettie joined the village women who were the waitresses and together they handed round wine in copious quantities. The meat sizzled as the spit turned above red-hot coals and food such as *mieliepap*, the porridgy maize accompaniment to the meat, tomato *bredie* and potatoes baked in the coals until their skins turned black, whetted their appetites. One of the neighbouring farmers, Gerrie Marais waylaid Martinus and introduced him to a tall man with silver hair down to his shoulders, a long nose and chin and eyes so light the irises looked white inside a circumference of blue and thin lips.

"Martinus, please let me introduce you to Stan," Gerrie shook Martinus' hand vigorously. The tall stranger put out a hand in friendship. "Stan came to the farm yesterday looking for a place to stay for a few days. I brought him along as I knew you wouldn't mind. I thought it would be a pity if he was left behind while we all came to the celebration."

"You did the right thing. Where do you come from and where are you travelling to?" Martinus was curious.

"I've a travelling man. It was always my intention to visit the Cape. Right now I'm heading north to the Kalahari Desert. I believe the desert people are most interesting," Stan never blinked and Martinus seemed satisfied with his answer albeit his replies didn't completely answer his question.

"Ah yes, the Bushmen. I see you haven't a glass in your hand," Martinus gestured to Gerrie and Stan to follow him, "Annatjie, give these two gentlemen some wine. That's a good girl."

Stan's keen gaze swept across the throng of people, eating, drinking and dancing. Suddenly, he saw what he had come for and his eyes never left their quarry. He was as deadly a snake in the grass as one would ever find.

Khalil and William sat on the damp lawn and savoured the cool Riesling wine.

"You should consider taking the young people to Namaqualand when you leave. The rains have been so the landscape will be a carpet of yellow, orange, red and mauve daisies. It is breathtakingly beautiful. You've mentioned one of your fellow travellers is an artist. He could find nowhere more beautiful!" William nodded and decided he would digest that morsel of information the following day.

The festivities carried on into the night and Amber found new friends and was soon dancing with them while James and Edward propped up the bar becoming pleasantly inebriated. Imran wandered through the melee like a prophet among the heathen. It was well after midnight when people dispersed sleepily like in a pageant within a play; they had played their roles to the end.

-o0o-

CHAPTER 21

William and his young dependants had by now been travelling for two months. Their progress was slow but sure and they had traversed impressive rocky mountains, crossed silver-glinting rivers with days on end of sunshine and deep blue skies. However, now the rains had arrived and their progress on the muddy road was beset by pitfalls with wagon wheels becoming stuck in the quicksand and oxen complaining and straining to move their load forwards.

Before leaving "Ropertdal" William had held a meeting with the young people and it was decided that they should take a detour to Namaqualand. After two days on the road they were now entering a flat landscape virtually treeless and peppered with boulders and hills jutting out of the earth like ships overturned and plunging down into the depths. Grasses were grey, brown or red and straw-coloured stubble and small tough prickly bushes with yellow flowers were all nondescript until the sun emerged from the torn clouds and the scene changed before their very eyes as the host of daisies unfurled their petals in a sweep to the very horizon. It was a Persian carpet of immense beauty.

"Consider the lilies of the field how they grow; they toil not nor do they spin and yet I say unto you that even Solomon in all his glory was not arrayed like one of these!" William quoting from the Bible, shouted the words so that they rang out over the vast expanse.

"What a transformation," James felt like Moses when confronted by manna from heaven in those long years in the desert.

"Now that's something worth painting Edward," William sat back into his saddle as they stood on the ridge with a whole new world stretching out before them. The horses gingerly picked their way down to the plain while William and Hendrik looked for a site suitable for their camp. Hendrik believed there was a spring between two headlands of rock and the small group of travellers headed in that direction as water was an essential criterion for their wellbeing. "Tell me, Hendrik, what do you feel when you see the scene before us?"

Hendrik rubbed his sparse beard, "Well, flowers always alert us to the food they will produce and that is pleasurable but these flowers aren't going to produce food for us so we pass them by; but what is important is that they are a sign of the fertility of the earth left there for us from our ancestors."

Imran rode out ahead of the others enjoying the spectacle that reminded him of sayings in the Quran and his heart felt as though it would burst with joy. *"It is He who sends down water from the sky. Thus we bring forth plants of every type with it; we produce green vegetation from it. We produce grain from it piled tightly packed on one another and from the date palm, clusters close at hand produced from its pollen, as well as the orchards full of grapes, olives and pomegranates which are so similar yet dissimilar. Look at their fruit as he causes it to grow and ripen."*

At last they dismounted where indeed there was a stream with sufficient water for the animals and humans alike. It was good that there would be a continuous supply whilst there were low rain-bearing clouds. Lucky and Koos freed the poor oxen of their load and allowed them to graze. The horses were unsaddled and they too found the grasses worthy of eating.

Their encampment was soon complete and they felt its many "rooms" were familiar and homely. The fire was soon snapping and crackling and grey smoke rose upwards and as soon as the fire settled into emitting a searing heat a kettle was hung on an iron tripod over the flames for coffee. James, the provider, disappeared for a while only to reappear with a young springbok which he and Hendrik skinned and disembowelled. They would enjoy venison for dinner.

"While I was out hunting, I encountered seagulls flying overhead. Are we near the sea?" James inquired intrigued by his discovery.

William unfolded a map and tried to find their location, "I believe we're in the middle of nowhere."

Hendrik overheard and grunted, "Let me see that paper, map, whatever you call it," He bent over the table to make sense of the ciphers and then straightened up, "We are there. These are the only two headlands so close to one another and we're camped next to the smaller of the two. You were asking how far we are from the sea," Hendrik turned to James, "I would say it's a day's ride away. This evening we should smell salt in the air when the night mist rolls in over the land."

"I would like to travel to the sea to see what wrecks could be rotting away on the beaches," James drank the last mouthful of coffee before spitting out the dregs, "I've had a fascination for shipwrecks since I was a child and I've heard there are rich pickings along the west coast of the Cape."

"You might discover there are others such as you on those beaches. They're called the "*strandlopers*". I believe the term in English is beachcombers. They're dangerous men. You would need to take your gun and rifle. Best be prepared," Hendrik enjoyed adding spice to his story.

Amber, Edward and Lettie returned from a short climb to the top of the hill of boulders, "We're not alone out here," Amber announced excitedly, "Someone is camping about half a mile away. We saw the smoke of his fire. It's strange to think we have to share this paradise with a stranger."

Taking out his telescope William quickly climbed the hillock and focussed the lens on the plume of smoke. He could make out the form of a man and a black horse. There was something oddly familiar about the man and he decided he would keep an eye on their fellow traveller.

-o0o-

The moonlit night had been chilly and it was a relief to wake up at dawn to sit around the fire that Hendrik had kept alive while the others slept. James was busily saddling his horse and Lettie packed some cold meat and fruit for him and filled his canteen with water. Fearing marauding vagrants, he strapped his pistol in its holster to his midriff and the shotgun hung on his back between his shoulders.

"We'll expect you back in two days' time. I'm concerned that you'll also be facing the danger of desert lions besides the human flotsam and jetsam. Take care," William slapped the rump of the lively chestnut gelding. Horse and rider soon disappeared into the distance without a trace.

Imran was about to pray and asked William, "Would you like to pray with me on the boulder on top of the hill. He was dressed in his white robe and fez.

"I will first wash my hands, face and feet," William nodded. He knew the Muslims strong sense of cleanliness and its ritual.

On the rocky knoll William felt the religious significance of Christ in the desert as he knelt down to pray. After a while, Imran sat back on his haunches and invited William to sit cross-legged with him, "I have translated more of the Quran for you.

"Everyone has some course he steers by, so complete in good deeds. Wherever you may be God will bring you all together; God is capable of everything. No matter where you may set out from, turn your face towards the Hallowed Mosque. It means the truth from your Lord; nor will God overlook whatever you are doing, no matter where you set out from, turn your face towards the Hallowed Mosque; wherever you may be, turn your faces towards it so that people will not have any argument with you except for those among them who do wrong. Do not dread them but dread Me; so that I may complete my favour towards you and so that you may be guided; just as We have sent a messenger to you from among yourselves to recite my signs to you and to cleanse you and teach you the Book and wisdom and to teach you

what you did not know. Remember Me, I shall remember you. Thank me and do not act ungrateful with me". Imran went on to discuss the passage with William explaining the significance of the Hallowed Mosque in Mecca in Arabia and then prayed:

> *"Our Lord do not take us to task*
>
> *If we have forgotten or slipped up!*
>
> *Our Lord do not lay any obligation on us*
>
> *Such as You placed on those before us.*
>
> *Our Lord do not overburden us*
>
> *With more than we can bear!*
>
> *Pardon us, forgive us and show us mercy!*
>
> *You are our Protector*
>
> *So support us against disbelieving people!"*

Like Imran, William wanted to say the Lord's Prayer out loud while he looked across the plain marvelling at the way the sun illuminated each shrub, each rocky crevasse, turning the stream into a golden snake, melting the mist minute by minute; but he remained mute. Instead he sang the Twenty Third Psalm and Imran found himself singing along quietly with him. After all it was sung to the God of the Old Testament.

-o0o-

The light was dying and there was no sunset on the horizon but the great gunmetal grey ocean was rolling landwards with heavy swells and tumbling breakers. Sea birds were flying towards the land, their day on the wing at an end. James was exhausted as he set about unsaddling his horse that was quivering and sweating, foam flecking its muzzle. He led it to a safe place for the night and it tore at the sparse grass which was already wet with dew. Walking along the high-tide mark, he gathered driftwood and built himself a rudimentary lean-to against a rock and made a fire. He was excited about the adventure that lay ahead and imagined what he could find; he wanted to find buried treasure just like in tales he had heard while sailing on ships to and from America.

The following morning dawned bright with sunshine and most of the clouds left over from the day before were sailing away across the plains. Amber and Lettie cooked breakfast with Lettie turning soda bread on the cast iron griddle. The Irish recipe worked well for the conditions wherein they found themselves. The chickens still produced eggs which was a wonder considering the amount of travelling they had been through and the goats were producing enough milk for cooking and drinking. Miraculously they had been spared from marauding carnivores whilst in their pen.

Edward had perched his easel at the top of the hill of boulders which gave him a panoramic view of the plain and the sky. After breakfast, he set to work immediately with Amber at his side, watching and learning. Some cloud was moving in from the northwest and the sky appeared with white and black paint quickly mixed with a tinge of green creating the low cloud and white calcium carbonate paint became a lively dance of low mist clearing and cirrus clouds streaking across the heavens like the stripes on a zebra's flank. Amber knew this subject was well out of her range of experience. As he worked, hills of rocky outcrops appeared, some dark malachite green mixed with cerulean blue where they were in shadow and others lit as though from the light from heavenly spotlights with Naples yellow mixed with calcium carbonate white for the highlights depicted the sunshine on the rocks. The canvass was a theatre and nature was the artist. Edward quickly executed thin washes of undercoats of cadmium yellow, alizarine red and verdigris green for the plain on top of which he would pick out the yellow, orange, white and purple flowers by overlaying lighter or darker mixes once they were dry. His brushstrokes were lively and his palette rich in a variety of pigments.

Bored from watching paint dry literally Amber walked into the field of daisies of every hue and sat down amongst the blooms. Picking one daisy after another she began to tie them together to form a daisy chain which when completed she placed on her head like a crown and she found herself remembering her childhood with Fanny. Edward had been watching her and he suddenly leapt into action removing a sheet of paper suitable for watercolours and filling a glass with water he rushed over to Amber.

"Don't move," He sat a few feet away and sketched the scene before him and then in minute detail filled in the colours of her hair and skin, dress and Namaqualand daisies. It was pure romance and the subtlety of his interpretation resulted in a picture of haunting wistfulness. One day when he returned to Cape Town he would paint it in oils on a life-size canvas.

Amber re-joined her uncle where he sat at the table still deep in contemplation with his pen poised to write only for it to dry out as his thoughts remained tethered, forbidding expression. He felt he had achieved so little in his lifetime and this journey was a voyage into his inner being where God reposed only occasionally. He had so many questions and few answers from his Maker. His niece opened her writing slope and removed her pen and ink and began writing in her journal. She was missing James with his devil-may-care attitude and handsome features. Would he ever kiss her again? At the party at *"Ropertdal"* he virtually ignored her or was he self-conscious as he was inexperienced in Boer folk dances? After all he was very proud.

Twenty miles away James was having his meat and bread and he had found a stream trickling to the sand dunes and winding its way into the sea. He had a small packet of coffee some of which he emptied into his canteen and heated it over his fire. He had also discovered a colony of seals and their barking and rumbling could be heard from some distance away. Penguins had marched past him to spend the day fishing in the ocean and he smiled at their toddling gait. Before prospecting for precious minerals or stones he led his horse to the stream and the animal drank the sweet water in long swallows. Remembering Hendrik's warnings, he wore his pistol and slung his rifle over his shoulder. Soon he was searching rock pools for his booty after all he had been told that the western coast was rich in gems.

At last after several hours of searching on the rocks left bare by the low tide, he found iridescent glass nuggets no bigger than a peppercorn and with excitement he began overturning stones and small rocks where crabs scuttled away and sea anemones sucked in their tentacles. If he was right he could be rich by the end of the day. He found large rose quartz, amethyst and agate semi-precious stones with all their beauty but these were not the prize he was seeking, but he placed those in another leather pouch as well.

He returned to his lean-to and found the sieve amongst his belongings and began sifting the dry, powdery and white, sea sand above the high tide mark. He was a man driven by his own greed and he worked on the dunes for another two days barely taking time to eat or drink. He was uncomfortably aware that William would be searching for him if he didn't return in the next forty eight hours which was all the time left to him. He was like a man possessed in that striving until suddenly a clear sparkling irregular iridescent crystal lay in the sieve. It was almost five carat he thought to himself and hurriedly took out his magnifying lens to examine its quality. He threw his hat up into the air with joy. In all his wildest dreams he had never believed he would find something so exquisite and so valuable. After his whoop of joy he continued sieving the sweet salty white-talc sand and by the afternoon had found four smaller gems but he wanted one that would be more valuable still. A few hours later another stone appeared in his sieve and it was the largest of such stones that he had ever seen before. Its value was beyond his imagination.

There was a sudden explosive crack from a shotgun and the sand rose up in an arc and James with no time to think, threw himself down on the sand trying to judge from which direction he was being fired at. He fired a shot from his shotgun and then lay down again. Another shot nearly hit him and he sat up in a crouching position and fired again but this time, the shooter succeeded and James collapsed in agony. He had been shot in the shoulder and his left arm hung uselessly while blood trickled down his body from the wound.

"Throw away your guns! Now! Or I swear I'll finish you off for good!" a well-spoken and familiar accent triggered a faint memory in his mind so he tossed his weapons over the top of the dune. He could hear someone pick them up and remove the bullets from them in two sharp clicks. Out the corner of his tear-filled eye he saw a man dressed all in black and wearing a Stetson. Of course, an American, James thought and he sought wildly for a clearer rendition from his mind's portrait gallery.

"You don't know me but by God I know all about you! I've been on your tail since I arrived in Cape Town. It didn't take me long to find out who you were and what you were doing. I didn't have much to go on but your fondness of wine and telling your stories of California and the Gold Rush at the Waterside Inn rang a bell in one landlord's ear." The man smiled grimly and played with his revolver.

"When I said I didn't know you it was the truth. I haven't the foggiest clue. By all means enlighten me!" James held his injured arm while the white hot heat of the wound burned into him.

"You married my niece, Francesca. Her father took you in and in all your depravity you married a young woman for money and not for love. No sooner you were married than you stole from my brother, no doubt your passage back to the Cape. But, that wasn't enough so you took his pouch of gold nuggets, his fortune. Do you know what it does to a young mother to lose her husband and find herself scandalised in social circles? Do you know what it does to a man to be robbed of his life's work? No you wouldn't have a clue!"

James hung his head, "I did what I had to do for my family back home," He tried to explain.

"Grant me some intelligence! I swore to my brother who is now a broken man that I would find you and seek recompense and today I believe you may have something that I want. Hand over your pouch. By the way, allow me to introduce myself. I'm Stanley Baxter. Like you I'm a traveller and time does not matter to me. You'll find I'm a very patient man."

"You have been stalking me since we began our expedition. We wondered who you were," James mumbled as he gave the leather pouch to Stan.

"What beauties! You'll not be seeing these again. They will be a down payment on what you owe Arthur and Francesca. Make no mistake I will squeeze you dry."

"They're all I've got!" James squirmed.

"Well, you'll have to think of ways to repay my brother. Start sifting - I'm sure you'll find more of these priceless stones. I'll work out what you owe and I'll keep a book tracking all our transactions. I expect you to pay interest on the amount of gold you stole. I will follow your every move even if I lie low some of the time. That's a promise." Stanley threw James' pistol and shotgun at him and walked away from him across the dunes to where his black stallion was waiting. He swung himself into the saddle and put on his Stetson so that it shaded his steely grey eyes, turned his horse sharply round and galloped away.

Faint and weakened by loss of blood, James pulled himself up and staggering forward he picked up his guns placing the pistol into its holster and holding the rifle in his good hand. He remembered the sieve and managed to hold it under his arm as he returned to the lean-to. He realised the sooner he left the area the sooner he would get to the camp where Imran could treat the wound. A jackal had already found his scent and was warily walking in a wide circle around him and it wouldn't be long before hyenas would arrive. Above him a Cape vulture drifted on a high thermal with the outer feathers of its wings splayed but its magnificence was not awe-inspiring but rather sent a chill through his veins. After whistling for his horse and dragging the saddle and reins to the animal, he battled to push the saddle over its back with only one good hand but eventually he was able to fasten the buckles and push the bridle over the horse's head. He gathered up his bed roll and the rest of his belongings and fastened them to his saddle before leaning over the animal's back and kicking his right leg over to the other side. His breath was uneven and sweat poured into his eyes. Each movement he made was agony and almost unconscious he nudged his mount forwards and started the long journey back to his friends. There was no sign of Stan and his black stallion nor that they had ever been there. It was so surreal that he decided he would not reveal the complete truth about who had shot him and why. He had to admit he wasn't feeling very proud of himself.

It was a moonlit night and shadows crossed the plain when clouds passed over the face of the moon. James was aware of the sounds of numerous wild animals and the laughter of hyenas but no carnivore paid them any attention knowing the horse would outrun it by miles. From time to time, he stopped to drink the water in his canteen and splashed some over his face then continued on his way. The hours passed and he checked his compass from time to time. It was just before dawn that he entered the camp waking Hendrik, Koos and Lucky and soon everyone was awake and fussing over him. He virtually toppled into William's outstretched arms.

"Didn't I warn you that there were such dangerous men out there," Hendrik took hold of his horse's bridle while William helped James to a seat next to the fire. He was shivering with cold and yet his body was on fire.

Imran was soon rummaging through his medicines and cleaning the wound while William put a cold wet compress on his forehead. The two young women looked on with wide eyes holding their shawls around them. Edward's hair was up on end from sleeping and he couldn't stop yawning. Hendrik put a kettle on the fire coals. Something warm and sweet would be good for the boy, he thought empathetically and with a dash of something stronger, as an afterthought.

"You're lucky to be alive," Imran poured more brandy into the mug of sweet coffee, "the bullet is lodged next to your collar bone which has been fractured. I need to remove the bullet to prevent blood poisoning. There are already signs of sepsis. This must have happened twelve, fourteen hours ago, if I am right?"

James nodded and swallowed the fiery liquid. Once he showed signs of inebriation, Imran began digging in the wound with forceps. James' cry was a loud outburst of anger and pain. Now he knew how soldiers on a battlefield must feel. He couldn't control his breathing which was fast and furious.

Soon it was all over and the offending bullet lay in Imran's hand. Mercifully James fell into a drunken sleep and was carried to his tent with his upper torso bandaged and bare. Amber had felt compelled to be at his side but William shook his head. Her heart was beating like the wings of a dove against a window pane. Was this love? She wondered.

William dressed and as dawn was breaking climbed to the top of the boulders with his telescope and scanned the area in a wide sweep. Their fellow traveller had obviously moved on without them. Beachcombers, James had said. If so, wouldn't they have killed him, stolen his watch, rings and guns and his horse, William pondered.

Amber felt her heart contract whenever she visited James in his tent and learning from Imran she would remove his bandages and wash the wound and carefully placed clean cotton on the bruises and torn flesh and strapped his arm firmly to help the collar bone to heal. For once, James resisted tormenting her and lay back on his pillows with much to think about. He had done wrong and betrayed his parents' values not to mention William's trust and good faith. He had every intention of visiting the beach again on some other trip and in the meantime he would remain silent about his most precious discovery.

-o0o-

A week later when the time had come to move on, a bed was made up for James in the wagon with Lettie keeping a watchful eye over their patient. Their small pageant of an Irish attorney general, a Muslim doctor, a geologist, a painter and botanist, a Khoikhoi and two women, a voorloper and a boy reminded William of Chaucer's Canterbury Tales by the way they all entertained one another on their many excursions over new terrains. As they journeyed onward to Okiep he was teaching Hendrik some of the Irish folk songs which the seasoned traveller and musician soon learnt and adapted the ditties to his concertina and had them all singing along.

> *My Nellie was a lass of great beauty and happily did sing*
>
> *Of her lover and her future all wound up in a ring*
>
> *For all her laughter and hair the colour of ripe corn*
>
> *She smiled and sang with music in her heart and feet*
>
> *And yet in her life was sadness and in her heart grief*
>
> *Her beloved a young Irish lad boarded a ship one night*
>
> *Leaving her so forlorn and out of his sight*
>
> *To make his fortune and build a home in America's town.*
>
> *Oh how he missed his Irish colleen*
>
> *And all the fairies of the Emerald Isle*

The shamrock green no luck did bring

And how he drank and wasted his shilling

In the bars and streets of new New York

And he would awake and lament his bride, our Nellie

Who was waiting in old Dublin town forsaken and unhappy

And with the passing of the years, her love not won

Our Nellie began to sing and dance again her love for the taking

On table tops she danced with laughter her hair coming undone

She met a young Englishman whose love for her he uttered

'Marry me,' he said and 'yes,' she did reply loving not faking

And he prepared their wedding of priest and wine

And they prayed and danced till early blackbirds sang

So no longer his bride would grieve and wait no more

For that Irish lad of old Long Ago.

The singing stopped as they approached Springbok, the town near the copper mine at Okiep. With forays out over the plain, Edward had searched for new specimens of *gazanias* and *osteospermums*, both looking much like large daisies but of a different genus and he believed he had found an *osteospermum whirligig* where each petal was twisted in the middle so that half of the petal was back to front with the back of the petal another shade, which he hoped he was the first to discover. He also kept an eye open for the rare osteospermum Amber followed him on horseback and stopped to pick five different coloured *gazanias* to paint when they set up camp that afternoon. They were such colourful flowers almost gaudy in all shades of yellow and orange petals with black bands like ethnic African material. Their green-silver foliage was designed for days of perpetual sunshine. Edward told her that they were called the 'treasure flower'. She would write all these facts in her journal. Like the *osteospermums, gazanias* closed their petals at night and on grey cloudy days. Edward told her that some acacia trees' leaves closed at night, too. She never knew that. It made those plants and trees animal-like and one could imagine the boughs bending down and snatching one upwards leaving one writhing in their grasp. Edward let out a cry of victory when he discovered the rare white *gazania.* Having the compulsion to collect seeds that he could grow in the conservatory at Kew to introduce the Western world to Africa's gems he conscientiously collected the seeds of both.

"The name of the *osteospermum* means 'bone seed'" he told Amber "and both these families belong to the Asteracea family of daisies. The daisies in Namaqualand belonged to the Calendula family and Dimorphotheca species and they are not perennial but arise from seed with the spring showers. They had flowers of two different sexes instead of each flower being asexual."

Amber found her face flush but asked, "How you remember all those Latin and Greek names is a constant marvel to me."

She held onto Edward's arm as they walked back to their horses. He felt so strong and warm. He looked down at the young woman's face aglow from riding over the veldt and he felt a strong desire to kiss her but mustering all the will power in the world he resisted the temptation. Under no circumstances did he want an innocent relationship be spoiled. After all, she was the same age as his youngest sister.

-o0o-

The small town of Springbok was virtually the size of its main street but as their ox wagon and cart, riders and oxen carried on down the street, people rushed to their windows and doors to welcome them to their town. William decided they would camp near a small river. As they journeyed further north, rivers and streams were few and far between. They out-spanned the oxen and erected the tents and started a fire. They worked like a well-oiled machine and soon they were free to lend their time to other pursuits.

William wasted no time at all in going to the post office and was delighted to collect three letters, one from Nerina for himself and one from Nerina for Amber. There was one from Hugh as well. He had given the two young women money with which to buy provisions and a few luxuries such as *koeksisters*, the twisted plait of dough boiled in syrup and delicious; and biltong. They all returned in high spirits and William sang another favourite folk song teaching Amber and Lettie the words as they walked along. That afternoon William realised the following day would be a busy one as he prepared his speech for his meeting with the farmers and businessmen during the next week and he intended to take James to the Okiep copper mine to meet the manager and miners the next week. He believed James would be able to ride his horse as the wound was healing and the bone was knitting well.

Under the acacia trees stood the main tent and William looked every bit the British colonial, Panama hat, new in town, included. His light-coloured cotton pants and jacket were more comfortable than the current style of dress for around Cape Town. His array of maps were strewn in front of him as he planned their route to Kuruman, the most hazardous and longest stretch of journey they had yet to make. Water was always essential and he would find those farms that had boreholes from which they could obtain water for the animals and themselves. He had read articles about water in the Karoo and the general consensus was that there was subterranean water in abundance and Boer farmers and the Khoikhoi and San people learnt where there was water from the behaviour of swallows and other animals that are drawn to such sites. There were certain plant species that indicate a source of underground water supplies and Hendrik had mentioned the signs to which he had become accustomed on his various trips northwards. For instance he said he could smell water a mile away. Edward was immediately interested and both Hendrik and he agreed they would search for such plants on their journey together.

William folded up his maps and found he now had time to read Hugh's letter which was short and succinct.

"My dear William

It was with great pleasure that I read your letter although brief it opened up the world you are now experiencing, so much more different to the one you left behind. Cape Town grows apace and the new inventions coming out of Britain and America make me consider preparing for new lighting for the Town and suburbs and the use of paraffin for heating and cooking. New matches are being manufactured which when swiped over a rough surface ignite. Wood exports as a result are growing for that purpose above and beyond for furniture, the railways and building. The call for copper is being received from England and I have taken out shares for us both in the Cape Copper Mine Limited. I envy the ease with which you find yourself in the company of men of the farming and mining communities and that they in turn listen to your plans and put forward their ideas.

On a more personal note, John Scott has written to you informing you that he is at present lobbying the British government to promote you to becoming the Chief Justice here at the Cape. Your brothers are intent on having some authorship in your career but I am aware that your own ambitions are less demanding than those of your family back in Ireland.

My health since you so kindly inquired, is middling but I must accept that I am not as robust as when we first arrived at the Cape. I must go for more walks but without you to accompany me I am sadly lacking in the self-discipline that you enjoy or endure at your own cost and subsequent good health.

You mentioned Russell Craven and I've made inquiries about his whereabouts. I've been told that he is in Graham's Town and that he has a regular column in the Graham's Town Gazette, fuelling the flames of a settler revolt against the authority Cape Town holds over the Eastern Frontier. Politics are as perplexing as they are entertaining.

I believe your next objective is reaching Kuruman. I trust you will have a pleasant tour across the upper Karoo. You should find a letter from me awaiting you there.

Your sincere friend, with felicitations,

Hugh

William sat back and ruminated, admitting to himself how much he was missing Hugh. When he was alone he would imagine what conversation he would've shared with his friend if he had accompanied him on the trip. He sighed and picked up the letter from Nerina and broke the seal. He had been looking forward to receiving sound feminine advice if not a scolding from the headmistress.

My dear William

I was pleasantly surprised to receive your letter from Tulbagh. You must be seeing sights that many of us would ordinarily only see in a lifetime.

Your concerns about Amber amused me and I was less than shocked by your revelations. Giving Amber her head to break out against convention you will no doubt live to regret, I'm afraid. However, for a young girl to experience such freedom shall not diminish her personality and inner being but only make her strength of character stronger. I do agree that Fatima would have kept Amber on her toes and insisted on deportment, how to sit with a straight back, not to show too much ankle and to speak when spoken to. I will write to Amber with more advice about how to behave when living in such proximity with the opposite sex. I trust my advice will come in the nick of time. We don't want her to fall in love with one of your protégés and to behave with them inappropriately. If her aunt had been alive she would no doubt have filled the role of adviser.

I'm looking forward to your return which I believe will not be for some time as you intend to spend some months in Kuruman. Your stories and anecdotes will brighten up an otherwise humdrum world. I do insist that you persevere with your memoirs. All the time in the world can often be suddenly ended and then it will be too late. **Carpe Diem!**

With sincere regards,

Neurone

In her tent with her candle flame flickering and creating shadows of witches and dragons, Amber curled up and read Nerina's letter. It was strange to receive a letter from her headmistress but she realised that Nerina was not merely her headmistress but rather a close friend of her Uncle William.

My dear Amber,

You are no doubt wondering why I am writing to you. It is of a sensitive nature and I request your understanding and participation. I believe from your uncle that you have thrown caution to the wind and have been behaving as a blithe spirit on your journey. That isn't a problem in itself but it is worth mentioning the unmentionable. You're no longer a child so as they say childish things should be put away. As you forget your sense of dress it is for me to inform you that your hair undone and bare feet with your calves and ankles bare give the incorrect signals to a young man. He will dream of what lies above those bare legs and if you have undone your buttons at your neck he will imagine what lies beneath your dress. In all accounts you must discipline yourself and become a young lady again to protect your honour. One never knows what a young man will do if he is so enamoured with your body before ever getting to know the young woman of decorum that he will woo with months of subtle communication driving him onward to learn your mind and heart. The question that he must ask must be out of deepest respect for all you are complete in heart, soul and body. You will be the epitome of innocence, the mother of his children.

For now, you must dress with dignity and wear your boots, tie up your hair and wear your bonnet. Forget about passionate kisses snatched in the dark. Romance such as is written in modern novels shouldn't encourage you to become a femme fatale or a penniless heroine a lost man falls in love with. Real life is more constrained, dignified and your self-worth is determined by your self-restraint in every sphere of your life.

Beware of men who would take advantage of your innocence. Don't touch them or allow them to touch you. One thing can lead to another and you may not be in control of your situation. We do not want you to become a fallen woman.

I invite you to reply to me as my friend rather than pupil. You must have many questions that I have not covered in this letter.

With my fond affection,

Nerina Smith.

Amber's heart began to beat uncomfortably. Miss Smith could read her mind, it would seem. She felt resentful at first especially about how she should dress. It was about self-discipline but that put such a cloud over her life. To feel her hair, feet and body hidden and thereby her feelings subdued too. It would be purgatory to return to the norms of Victorian life. Not to touch Edward or kiss James would painful, at the same time Miss Smith would not have advised her otherwise if it weren't with good reason. Oh how was she going to change? She thought of Imran and his self-discipline, reading the Quran and praying three times a day. Could she muster the strength to become a woman of high principles and of faith? She would watch and learn from him. He had never used innuendo with her nor had he looked at her with desire. She knew he was pure. She came to the conclusion that she would have to put aside her coquettishness and lock her chastity safely in the locket of her heart where it will be surrounded with gold, pearls, ribbons and a small Bible until such time her true love would unlock the casket and set free her innocence.

-o0o-

After prayers with Imran, William joined James for a quick breakfast of eggs and soda bread and steaming hot coffee before they mounted their horses and rode out of the camp eager to explore the district so rich in copper ore. The countryside was stony and plants few and far between and the heat of the sun baking the landscape made them sweat yet it was only ten in the morning.

They soon realised they were near the mine when they heard explosions and puffs of white smoke appeared near a formation of hills not quite as tall as mountains, followed by copper coloured dust clouds like the devastation wrought by exploding canons in a battlefield. The sky was a clear blue china bowl and the sun a furnace in its centre.

As they drew nearer, they could see the different levels where the ore had been blasted out of a man-made crater in which small human beings were clambering about like ants. The mountain or rather as it turned out to be, a large hill had been eaten away and the destruction was a shock to William who wondered if one day there would be no trace that it had ever stood there. Mules pulled wagonloads of blasted ore out of the mine. It was hard labour for both man and beast. It was taken from there to the crushers.

They were met by the Manager of the mine and he shook their hands and invited them into his office. At the door stood a rock of about eight feet in height and six feet in circumference and stroking it he remarked, "This is solid rock of the copper mineral of chalcopyrite. You will notice the green colour. In all my life I have never seen a rock of this size with such a concentration of copper."

James felt the rock with its roughness and cool temperature, "I had heard of the mountain of copper when I was in Cape Town but never truly believed the rumour. What should one look out for when searching for copper seams?"

"From your studies, you'll realise that copper is found in alluvial deposits of granitic and basaltic rock and when one drills downwards the pipe of the strata of minerals makes it very easy to identify as you'll have seen with my rock. As we have depleted the hill, we now need to follow the seam below ground level so we have built a Cornish shaft and also a pump house to provide air to the underground tunnels."

James had more questions for the Manager, "How does one remove the copper from the ore. I presume you don't do that here"

"No, we don't. The chalcopyrite and malachite can treated with hydrometallurgical processes and the copper oxide can be leached with sulphuric acid. It's then roasted. Chalcocyte is smelted more easily than the first two using gravity separation circuits and flotation cells. Pyrite, sphalerite and galena minerals are by-products."

"Wait a minute," William threw up his arms, "This is a layman you're talking to!"

"If you wish, James could spend a few days with me and I can teach him all I know," the Manager suggested.

William concurred, "Yes, of course."

"As you don't smelt or use sulphuric acid processes here, where does the crushed copper ore go to for treatment?" James was in his element and William delighted in the young man's passion.

"Does it get sent abroad, say to Great Britain or other places where there are plants for such extraction? As a businessman and a politician I can see the merits of processing the copper somewhere in the Cape and we can benefit in a greater way. There's talk of new uses for copper but these are in the developmental stages," William spoke earnestly. This subject he could debate with ease.

"You are right; it is sent overseas to Britain. The railway line delivers the ore in wagon loads pulled along the rails by mules to the small fishing harbour at Port Nolloth on the Atlantic Ocean," The Manager replied. William nodded as he had heard talk about the port.

The Manager, Michael Hargreaves, continued, "You may ask why we use mules? Well, we couldn't use steam locomotives because of the water shortage in these parts."

William and James left the mine feeling it had been a day well spent and enjoyed the gallop back to the campsite. The others soon joined them to hear all their news.

-o0o-

It had been a day since receiving Miss Smith's letter and Amber had digested her Headmistress' advice. She knew she had been behaving in a nonconventional way but having experienced such freedom it would be difficult to adhere to the caveats and suggestions put forward to her. However, she knew her Uncle William had received a letter from Miss Smith the same day and there was little doubt what the letter was about. He would be stricter.

She was sitting at the table with her writing slope in front of her and her journal open. She wrote and read her entries almost daily and she was creating an adventure tale of such fervour in nature's marvels and explanations and finding herself now more educated in the architecture of Western Cape homes and towns with their folklore and characters. Her favourite pastime was to talk to people. It seemed she had a natural penchant for conversation and the making of friendships.

She had laced up her boots with steadfast determination and plaited her untameable auburn hair in a long plait and the street urchin was transformed into a young woman of sixteen, from a good family and having such good references a caring young husband of equal charm could not find fault with her and would surely find her marriageable.

"Oh hush my heart. How would James and Edward react to the return of the docile, reserved, pious (heaven forbid!) virginal young woman that they first met at "Wolmunster"? How do I enjoy being as dedicated to caring for others as a nun for after all that is the destiny I have chosen. It certainly would be the crown of thorns that prick the scalp but it would have such honour and holiness. I should have gone to a nunnery as curtailing myself to the parochial nature of duties and tending to wounds and agues is no doubt all I would be able to attain. Becoming a doctor was a mere dream belonging to another Earth, another Universe, another time perhaps when women are given the right to vote and own property both of which Uncle William intended to strive towards. Alas it will not happen in my lifetime. Not to flirt and to miss the excitement a glance could create, or the warmth a hand in his hand causes longing to spread throughout my being and the rapturous kiss, a fruit more pleasurable to taste, the sweetness and breathlessness so divine. I could weep and perhaps now only religious fervour can replace such ecstasy which they do say wanes when girls become women and women become unwomanly with age. But religious fervour and feeling can continue throughout my lifetime and if there is a man who will share those with me I shall have the best of this world and the next. Will I be blessed with children? It would seem they would

*be the fruits of such labour and be sweet and rejuvenate me when I
run with them on the lawn or play blind man's bluff or hide and
seek. They shall be my treasures. Tomorrow I will join Uncle
William and Imran for prayers to teach me self-discipline because
by God I am so lacking. To sit straight up even in repose is purgatory
but getting up at dawn is worse and because of that I must lay myself
down prone with my arms outstretched and my face touching the
ground to teach me who God is and where I come in the natural
order of things."*

William had asked her to reply to Miss Smith's letter and reluctantly
she took out a fresh page of paper from her book of note-lets and
started to write.

"Dear Miss Smith,

*Thank you for your letter which made the reader more humble and
bearing feelings of regret concerning her behaviour. I drank in the
advice you gave me like a dry plant being revived after a shower of
rain. I have been privileged to take part in this expedition and I owe
it to my uncle to put his mind at ease. There will be no more
misdemeanours as I value my self-respect and my uncle's good
opinion of me. I have been imbibing the fresh wind in the evening
and the glow in the east at dawn and in between sunrise and sunset,
a plethora of stimulating essences of living outdoors which make my
senses drunk with happiness. You need not fear that I will become a
fallen woman as I am fearful of the advances of men far more
experienced in relationships than I am. They shall not touch me nor
kiss me unless I believe it is with pure thoughts and not raging lust.*

*"Already I feel I have left girlhood behind and I believe I am fast
becoming a young woman after all I have had many situations to
manage from housekeeping and cooking in the camp to learning
about nature and the wilderness with its dangers. I have even helped*

Imran when he was called upon to treat a patient who had been scalded and when James was shot. It reinforced in me the desire to perform healing practices on those afflicted in some way or other.

"Once again, my sincere gratitude for all your concern and for sharing 'woman to woman' wisdom with me.

Your ever thankful pupil,

Amber"

-oOo-

The following morning was as fragrant as honeysuckle or jasmine. One could drink the dew like sweet honey where it hung trembling on grasses and herbs.

Imran sat down and then bowed till his head touched the ground. William knelt and prayed out loud:

"Lord, we who are gathered here together pray for your blessing as it was you who said where two or more are gathered in your name you would be present. We bow our heads in contrition and in adoration of you, our Holy Father, our Lord God's Son and the Holy Spirit. Inspire us on this new day to honour you in our work and toil and during the time that we are free to meditate, bring us your peace and we pray to you for those whom we love in this world and the next, may they be blessed with the warmth of your love. O Holy Father bless our recreational activities so that they honour you. Amen."

The sun rose in a triumphal procession of golden clouds and phalanxes of shadowy warriors marched beneath them and the glow spread to the four points of the compass and finally the sun, the emperor appeared resplendent in the fire and the heat of his sphere was hotter than any kiln or furnace on earth. Imran read from his Quran,

"SAY "If you have been loving God then follow me, God will then love you and forgive you your offences. God is Forgiving, Merciful!""

"SAY "Obey God and the Messenger" Yet if they should turn away God does not love disbelievers. God selected Adam and Noah, Abraham's and Imran's house over [everyone] in the universe. Some of their offspring are descended from others. God is Alert, Aware.

"Thus a woman of Imran said 'My Lord, I have freely consecrated whatever is in my womb to You. Accept it from me, You are Alert, Aware.' When she gave birth she said, 'My Lord, I have given birth to a daughter.' (God was quite Aware of what she had given birth to for a male is not like a female.) 'I have named her Mary and ask you to protect her and her offspring from Satan the outcast. Her Lord accepted her in a handsome manner and caused her to grow like a lovely plant and told Zachariah to take care of her.

"Every time Zachariah entered the shrine [to] seek her he found she had already been supplied with food. He said, 'Mary how can this be meant for you?!' She said: 'It comes from God for God provides for anyone He wishes without any reckoning.' With that Zachariah appealed to his Lord, he said: 'My Lord grant me goodly offspring from your presence for you are the Hearer of Appeals.'

"The angels called him while he was standing praying in the shrine, 'God gives you news of John who will confirm word from God masterful yet circumspect, and a prophet [chosen] from among honourable people.'

"He said: 'My Lord, how can I have a boy? Old age has overtaken me while my wife is barren.' He said: 'Even so does God do anything He wishes.' He said, 'My Lord grant me a sign.'

"He said 'Your sign is that you will not speak to people for three days except through gestures, Mention your Lord often and glorify Him in the evening and the early morning hours.'

"So the angels said: 'Mary, God has selected you and purified you. He has selected you over [all] the women in the Universe. Mary, devote yourself to your Lord: fall down on your knees and bow alongside those who so bow down.'

"Thus the angels said: 'Mary, God announces word to you about someone whose name will be Christ Jesus, the son of Mary [who] is well regarded in this world and the Hereafter and one of those drawn near to [God]. He will speak to people while still an infant and as an adult will be an honourable person'.

"She said: 'My Lord, how can I have a child while no human being has ever touched me?'

"He said: 'That is how God creates anything He wishes. Whenever He decides upon some matter He merely tells it "Be!" and it is. He will teach him the Book and wisdom plus the Torah and the Gospel as a messenger to the children of Israel: 'I have brought you a sign from your Lord. I shall create something in the shape of a bird for you out of clay and blow into it so it will become a [real] bird with God's permission. I shall cure those who have been blind from birth and lepers and revive the dead with God's permission.'"

At this point, William wanted to contradict Imran and offer his church's conviction that Jesus is the son of God, not merely a messenger and he wished he could persuade the young Muslim that the God of the Christian Church was borne by Mary and together God, Jesus and the Holy Spirit were one God. He stood aside metaphysically to his inculcated faith and listened to Imran who was continuing his recital. Jesus as the messenger continued his promises…

"I shall announce to you what you may eat and what you should store up in your houses. That will serve as a sign for you if you are believers, confirming what I have already [learned] from the Torah. I shall permit you some of the things which have been forbidden you. I have brought you a sign from your Lord, so heed God and obey me! 'God is both my Lord and your Lord so serve Him. This is a straight road!'

"When Jesus sensed disbelief among them, he said, 'Who will be my supporters in the cause of God?'

"The disciples said, 'We are God's supporters! We believe in God; take note that we are Muslims. Our Lord we believe in what you have sent down and [thus] have followed the Messenger, so enrol us among the Witnesses.' They plotted while God plotted; however, God is the best Plotter!

"So God said, 'Jesus, I shall gather you up and lift you towards Me and purify you from those who disbelieve and place those who follow you ahead of those who disbelieve until Resurrection Day. Then to me will be your return and I shall decide among you [all] concerning anything you have been disagreeing about. As for those who disbelieve I shall punish them severely in this world and the Hereafter. They will have no supporters.' As for those who believe and perform honourable deeds, He will repay them their earnings. God doesn't love wrongdoers.

The sun had risen higher in the sky and the shadows shortened. They could hear an ox lowing and a horse whinnying. The rooster in the coup crowed. "The passage is a complex one, Imran. It shows aptly where our religions take different forks in the road. We could debate the rights and wrongs but inevitably we would perhaps offend one another."

"I would genuinely enjoy arguing about our two beliefs. Perhaps our faiths can find a meeting point of different cultures." Imran had wanted to stoke up the smouldering coals of bias that both he and William nurtured in their breasts.

William had concentrated hard absorbing the long, laborious convoluted text and hoping to understand it, "Christianity doesn't dictate or order us but there is encouragement nor do we have to plead for mercy, Christ says we are already forgiven. Of course one should not go on sinning because of that."

William winced at his own conclusions but he added, "Yes, we must actually confront each other about such issues and that could affect our friendship but perhaps we could trigger a change of heart in each other and be able to live with one another in harmony."

The young Muslim man smiled and his eyes had tears in them. He put a hand on William's shoulder and the two men embraced and then laughed however incongruous that was.

Later that day William took out his writing slope and began writing to Nerina.

"My dear Nerina,

"Your letter was received with much gratitude and the fact that you could rescue this fallible father figure and help him steer his 'would be' daughter along safer paths, drives home to me how much Amber must miss a mother figure. With her usual quiet determination she has not let me read your letter to her and she has informed me that the womanly wisdom that was shared in the letter should remain between the women concerned. I can confirm that she has returned to her former reserved if not pert ways and does not flirt with James and Edward but endeavours to elevate their banal behaviour from

masculine bravado and egocentricity further towards responsibility and altruism. I fear I have not been successful in persuading her to relinquish her passion for a lifetime dedicated to nursing and healing the sick. Africa would devour her body and spirit if only she could have the insight to see and understand that.

"If there's a letter from you awaiting me in Kuruman, I'll be a happy man. I trust that you are well and that life is being kind to you.

With kind regards,

William"

After closing the letter and affixing the hot red sealing wax and leaving the imprint of his signet ring, he took out another leaf of paper and thoughtfully composed a letter to Hugh.

"My dear Hugh,

"Your reply to my letter was waiting for me when we arrived in Springbok for which I was most thankful. Your news brings you nearer and the distance becomes a mere measurement of imagination. First of all let me convey to you just how much I am concerned about your health, my dear friend. Your lifestyle is such that you do not treat your body kindly. Don't forget your body is your earthly temple.

"About other matters of mutual interest, I was most grateful to hear about the recent developments that have occurred since I've been away from Cape Town. Cut off from that world has given me an insight that distance is the key and the lock can be opened only when there is truly need to do so but on the whole I keep the lock firmly closed. I am devoting leisure time to writing and evaluating life and the world around us here in Africa.

"May I ask you to reply to John Scott and to entreat him not to seek favours for me back in Britain? I no longer suffer from a desire to obtain accolades and positions of honourable high office. I wish to be among people who share goodwill and works to the greater good of ordinary people.

"As you can imagine, I will have many anecdotes about this journey to share with you when we return. I can assure you there have been moments of high drama and times of sheer indulgence in the allure of Africa and its people. I look forward to sharing your companionship once more when I return. Perhaps you would be so kind to send your next letter to Kuruman.

Affectionately,

William"

-oOo-

Stan, the American, after sending a small but very expensive and undisclosed parcel off to his brother in California had found the temptation of discovering more diamonds on that beach in Namaqualand too hard to withstand so in Tulbagh he bought various items he would need for his prospecting, a spade, a sieve and a jeweller's magnifying glass so that he would check for impurities in the crystals and a small pair of scales. He had his bedroll, canteen, frying pan and oilskin mackintosh in the event the rain would roll in from the Atlantic. He eventually arrived at the very spot where he had wounded James and immediately set to work building a rough shelter as James had done. He worked with his teeth biting a cigar and his face screwed up against the elements, each wrinkle or freckle outlined on his skin. In the matter of an hour, he was working at the dunes digging and sieving with a fanatical urgency, his hands grasping the sieve tightly and shaking it round about until that action became magnified a hundred fold.

On his third day he wandered further north to try another site and within an hour he found a lustrous scintillating diamond formed as a square crystal, fashioned by molten temperatures in the earth's crust millions of years ago. He was elated and threw his Stetson up into the air and took out his pistol and fired a shot through the crown of the hat. He weighed the diamond and calculated its size and value and then safely put it into a pouch. Had he and James been very lucky or were there hundreds of thousands of gems all along the coast?

He had to go fishing for food for his supper and was sitting on a rock holding on to his line with a hook at the end. The minutes passed and then suddenly there was a nibble at the morsel of bait and he pulled the line sharply catching the fish with the hook and he reeled in the line until it delivered his catch into his palm and he put his hand over the thrashing *galjoen* and carefully removed the hook and hit it behind the head to kill it. After all, he was a humane fellow.

The fish was baking on the hot coals and Stan's stomach was rumbling as he sipped his bitter coffee. He looked weather-beaten with salt encrusted on his breeches. His gaze swept over the rocks and to his surprise he noticed that he had visitors. Three vagrants approached him riding mules. He took no notice of them until they were a matter of feet away from him. "Good evening," he said somewhat unamused by the interlopers.

"Good evening," the refrain was taken up by his visitors, "We've come to take your money, watch, rings, anything you have. And, of course, your horse over in the field. Give them to us and we'll leave you alone."

Stan knew he was in mortal danger and reached for his gun but the leader shot him through the head and he fell over without a nerve twitching. The three 'beachcombers' quickly filled their pockets. One of them found the leather pouch with the diamond but he threw it into the sea, "What does he want with that piece of glass?" He sniffed noisily, "We've had a very good catch here, brothers." He fondled the gold pocket watch and then they ate Stan's grilled fish and smacked their lips with satisfaction.

-o0o-

CHAPTER 22

The vast, flat Kalahari semi desert stretched out to the north of them and its saffron and yellow ochre sands made any vegetation stand out in relief in colours like dried bamboo or dried olive leaves and their shadows fell in royal blue splashes with pink highlights. Edward the painter as ever made mental notes of the scene in front of them. They had managed to strike camp early and prepared to become yet again a caravan moving through the desert.

"Where is the grey goat?" Lettie ran out from behind the cart which carried the cage wherein they kept the goats at night. The fawn and white nanny goat was there but the black and grey one was missing.

"Is there any way in which it could have broken out during the night? Has a wild animal broken into the cage?" James rushed to the cart but whoever had taken the animal must have been human. Perhaps a local worker had stolen into the camp that night and had claimed the animal for himself?

Hendrik had been away on his donkey during the night and now ambled into camp with the donkey bearing his weight with great stoicism. He noticed the pandemonium as Edward and James leapt onto their horses to search for the missing goat.

"No, stop you two! I can explain," Hendrik pleaded with his face creased up in painful repentance. "It was me who took the goat. You see that lonely tree, the only tree for ten miles; well, you'll find the goat there. I killed it," He felt his throat close up with anxiety.

"Why on earth did you do that?" William demanded slowly comprehending what might have happened.

"Yes, why Hendrik?" Amber echoed, saddened by the goat's demise.

"It was very important to pray to the ancestors for a safe journey to Kuruman as there are many dangers on the way with the problem of water and grazing and the terrible heat. I had to wet the earth with the goat's blood and to eat the liver myself. I prayed you would understand." The old Khoikhoi tracker, holding his battered hat in his hands, stood to attention expecting the worst.

"I am disappointed that you didn't see fit to ask me if you could sacrifice an animal. I could have made arrangements to purchase a sheep. However, it's done and perhaps all of us should pray that the next few weeks pass quickly without any harm befalling any of us. We should now begin our journey and face the days that come with impunity." William looked at his companions and saw the four courageous young people including Koos, the child, Lucky and the ageing Hendrik and was impressed with their eagerness to start their next adventure. He silently got onto his stallion and waited for Amber, Edward and James to mount their horses. Amber had returned to being the Amber of old, neatly turned out with her hair plaited and wearing her boots and she now stood next to her mare, waiting for Edward or James to give her a hand up.

"Where are your manners," She spoke softly when the men were about to dig their heels into the flanks of their horses.

Feeling embarrassed that he hadn't offered a hand Edward slid off his horse and provided his two hands for her to put a booted foot into before throwing her weight over the mare's back to reach the stirrups, "What's got into you? You usually manage on your own. You've reverted to being the Cape Town debutante. Grow up, Amber. You were fun to be with when you didn't put on these airs and graces."

"You never took me seriously though. I don't want to be treated like a younger sister. You have to admit you took me for granted," Amber replied.

The oxen had been inspanned and with Lettie and Lucky and his dog on the wagon seat next to him, Hendrik whistled to Koos to walk forward with the leading pair of oxen. He flicked his whip over their heads and the sturdy animals set out on their longest journey yet.

Having entered the northern part of the Upper Karoo the time between setting camp and striking camp grew shorter as they tried to cover as much distance as they could at night and to spend the least amount of daytime on the move. Hendrik taught James and Edward to follow the spoor of animals and how to find water in dry river beds, digging deeply to create a natural well where the water table which was near the surface would fill the hole and provide enough water for all even the oxen which were able to endure thirst longer than the horses or humans. He took Amber and Lettie off to find bitter melons and roots that were thirst-quenching and nourishing and sometimes they met the nomad San people who sold ostrich eggs filled with water or fresh ostrich eggs for cooking. They often had pelts and ivory to trade for pieces of iron or beads.

"You know, the San people are my cousins. We grew bigger than them because we had more food when we separated many, many years ago when my people moved to the southern Cape and the San who once roamed the beaches in the southern Cape east of Cape Town, living off fish and shellfish drifted here and to the north. Once upon a time we Khoisan people were spread as far as the Drakensberg. We learnt to farm with cattle and sheep and grew taller from the good food and although we moved from place to place to find grazing for our animals, we weren't moving from place to place daily. Just like the Trekboers."

They were all fond of the small bands of San people, the hunter gatherers, with their petite frames and big bellies and bottoms. Their scant dress, thongs, necklaces of beads and teeth of animals were all they wore but they had well cured hides in the form of *karosses* in which they wrapped themselves at night. Each of the men had a quiver strung over a shoulder and a bow which when an animal was in sight they quickly armed with arrows dipped in a poisonous substance from the larvae of a certain type of beetle and shot these off at the animal in close proximity. The arrows were small and fell off easily leaving the poison to do its work and they would track the spoor of their prey with great accuracy. Finally the wounded animal would fall and lie dying and then it was an easy matter to put it out of its suffering. The wound was the only area carrying any poison so the flesh was safe to eat.

William always tried to hold a conversation with the "Bushmen" and Hendrik acted as interpreter. On one such day William squatted down onto the ground with the elders while the younger men went hunting. The high cheekbones and hollow cheeks showed they had not an ounce of fat on their bodies and the old women had faces with many lines carved into their skin and their breasts were just desiccated flaps of skin. The young women carried babies on their hips and shyly smiled at him. Their bright eyes were inquisitive and the men were amused that a white man should hunker down with them.

"Ask them if they live off the land and see what they say," William asked Hendrik on one such occasion. Hendrik translated their reply which was punctuated with clicks that their tongues make against the palate and soft palates of their mouths.

"The land is our home without the boundaries that the white people make between farms or houses. We are free spirits that fly over the land leaving no mark that we were ever there. Our three gods of the land and air and water rule over us and protect us from evil supernatural beings. Those who have died and who were good will always provide for us and we pray to the animals that we track to hand themselves over to us in spirit so that we can strike them down. The gods created animals for the good of the earth and our nation. Our rock paintings depict our prayers and the cave painter draws the animal which will become our quarry when we go out to hunt."

"So they pray to their gods like we do?" William asked.

Hendrik translated and their reply was, *"We have medicine men who communicate with the gods or supernatural beings by using substances that make them go into a trance and they seem drunk, twisting their bodies out of shape while dancing with their eyes rolling around in their head and in this state they give messages to the gods and deliver back to us messages from the gods.*"

William nodded and acknowledged his comprehension to the elderly leader. They bowed at one another in mutual respect. At this moment, six young San men ran up to them, their expressions on their faces showed fear and deep anxiety. They pointed to a large cloud of smoke.

The leader spoke to Hendrik, "My warriors say that a Trekboer's camp was attacked by a band of evil Griquas on horseback and the man and his wife were firing muskets at their attackers but there were too many for my men to overcome although they sent arrows into the crowd, which reached their targets. After setting fire to the ox wagon, the band of Griquas quickly rounded up the oxen and the Boer's sheep. They don't know if anyone is left alive."

William called James and Edward and when they heard what had happened, they armed themselves and the three of them mounted their horses and galloped towards the drifting pillar of smoke. When they arrived, the camp was in disarray and the farmer and his wife lay dead where they had fallen and the bodies of their KhoiKhoi retainers lay closely. The fire was still blazing when they heard muffled screams coming from the *wakis*, the wagon seat in the ox-wagon and beating back the flames, James quickly forced open the lock on the lid which must have fallen down accidentally and pulled a young boy of six to safety.

"What is your name, lad?" William held out his hand and the little boy put his hand into William's.

Two tracks of tears marked his face and he rubbed his nose, "Andries, meinheer."

"Can you tell me, Andries, if you have any uncles or a grandfathers to whom we can take you?"

"No, I don't know of anyone. It's always been just Papa and Mama and me. I want my Mama," He sobbed and threw himself down on his dead mother's body. His grief was overwhelming. William, Edward and James began digging shallow graves which they would cover with big stones to keep hyenas or jackals from finding the bodies. William recited a psalm at the burial and spoke respectfully about the women and men who had died that day and the little boy stood silently at his side only crying out when the last stone was laid on the four mounds. It was a miracle that he had survived. William thought with a heavy heart that he should keep the boy unless someone who knew him could be found. In the meantime he would not leave the wagon train for any length of time in the event the Griqua robbers should return and attack them.

-o0o-

Later while planning their route for the final push to reach Kuruman, William on his horse stood frozen on the edge of a plateau and surveyed the plain below and it truly appeared to resemble a lava spill from a volcano that had solidified but kept the hot tones of the liquid magma and small boulders pock-marked the ground in every direction. The following day it rained and immediately tufts of grass appeared through the grains of sand and bushes sprouted green or grey leaves. The wet skies were less harsh and no longer a magnifying glass through which the sun's rays fell, melting stone and rock with heat waves and mirages, playing with one's sight.

Winding its way through the harsh landscape was the mighty Orange River with its white sandbanks and reeds with their inhabitants of *hammerkop*, Red Bishops and yellow weaver birds fluttering and moving about making the tall plumed grasses shiver as they busied themselves hunting for insects or foraging for seeds. The black widowbird rose and fell as it beat its small wings desperately seeking to move forwards with the weight of its long tail. The longer the tail, the more successful it would be at winning a mate.

There was a low bridge over a shallow part of the river and their crossing was timely as there had been rain in the mountains where the river had its source so far away in Moshweshwe's kingdom but the wave of new water from inland summer storms hadn't made the river swell yet. William was relieved when the last of the oxen set foot on the white sand. There were also dangers such as crocodiles in the vicinity so he urged Hendrik to move the oxen forward more quickly. He thought of the small Boer republic, the Orange Free State which was in its embryonic stage, where the Orange River formed a boundary between it and the Cape. The young Boer Republic to the north rubbed shoulders with the Orange Free State. He would have enjoyed speaking to the Boers but he wouldn't have been welcomed with open arms. These were hard bitten, bitter men who had given up their farms to escape from the clutches of the English.

James had been out hunting for the pot and he rode towards them with an impala already disembowelled slung in front of him on the horse. Lettie and Hendrik pulled the dead animal off the horse's back and took it to the back of the wagon. They would skin it and put it on a spit to roast when they set up camp that evening. While he was galloping through the veldt James was still of the notion that he was being followed by Stan. The hairs on the back of his neck would stand on end and he would look round only to find he was alone. After shooting the impala, he took his time cantering back to the others and it was then that he discovered the baby meerkat abandoned by its clan perhaps because it had dozed off in some hole. It looked strong but it was cold from hunger and some goat's milk would go down a treat. He put it in his shirt and it became quiet as his warmth was comforting. Once back with his fellow travellers James pulled the little animal out of his shirt like a conjuror lifts a rabbit out of a hat, and gave it to Amber.

"I know how much you've missed the dead goat. This little chap needs your maternal skills," The rough diamond of a man was eager to give Amber something of real value to her.

"Oh, isn't he a darling," Amber held the little creature with its inquisitive brown eyes and long nose and slender catlike body with a tail used for balancing when it stands up on its hind-legs. It was protesting at being manhandled but her eyes examined him like a mother would her child. I'll see if he will take some milk from my finger," She looked up at James, seeing him in a new light, "Thank you, James, I really do mean that. He is a darling. I just hope we can save him. She didn't complain that he was flea-ridden but intended to give him a bath immediately and wash him with carbolic soap and she made a collar for him and tied a rope to it, which would stop him from wandering off as he would surely die if he escaped. He was nimble enough to keep up with her or to snuggle into a sling when she was riding her mare. Little Andries played with the little animal for hours and that lifted his mind from the horrors he had witnessed.

James was still finding various minerals on the journey and his chest was filled with rock core samples among them one containing quartz, feldspar, garnet, marble, magnetite; another of graphite and pyrite; and another mix of sillimantite, quartz, garnet and Gunerite. There was a fold of a strange mineral weaving through the ore. Could it be zinc? He was sure there was some significance of these minerals but would need the expertise of a more experienced geologist to define what precious metal could exist in an area bearing those rock zones. He was still excited by his work. While drilling bores into the earth's surface or chipping away at the surface of rocky outcrops, his mind was less inclined to dwell on his personal failings.

Edward's collection of seeds and plants that he was accustomed to dry in a press had grown and he spent many a morning drawing from live specimens capturing their form accurately and then painting in the colours with delicate watercolour tints. Amber admired his skill and from time to time sat with him and produced her own drawings which she treasured. A lady was required to draw and paint and she wanted to excel at everything she did. She missed her harpsichord and dancing but would sing songs while she helped Lettie with her chores.

Mischief, the meerkat, soon regarded her as his mother and there was no need of a lead as he followed her wherever she went.

The days passed in a predictable and almost boring way after all they had been on the move for three months and they were all becoming restless wanting the journey to end. William encouraged their flagging spirits and gave them projects to do for instance entertaining their companions with recitals of poems or to take part in general knowledge quizzes to fill their time in the camp. In this part of the country, nature seemed to have ebbed away leaving only a few examples of wildlife, most of which came out mainly at night.

One morning in December, William rode out ahead of the others with his spirits rising and he laughed out loud with the joy of having his instinct rewarded. Kuruman lay waiting in the baking sunlight, only hours away. He galloped back to the group accompanying the wagon and gave them the news.

"I can't believe we have almost reached our destination. I couldn't have borne the monotony much longer!" Amber felt her spirits soar, "Will we be able to stay in a proper house with rooms and proper beds?" She cajoled her Uncle.

"Even I have had enough of rough living, my dear Amber. Yes, I have arranged for us to live in the house that was built for David Livingstone while he lived in Kuruman. It will certainly be more comfortable. Imran will even have rooms in which to set up his clinic and you may consider helping him with his patients, if this is what you want to do with your life." William was delighted with their enthusiasm.

"Oh, Amber, I'll have a proper kitchen again. I can't tell you what a pleasure that will be," Lettie grinned widely unable to contain her joy. She raised her hands and covered her face, shy at giving vent to her feelings, too.

"I can't wait to get there," Amber turned to the young men, "Let's ride out ahead of the wagon. I wonder what it'll be like," She pressed her mare's sides eagerly and cantered away with William taken unawares.

"Hooray! Here we come, Kuruman, ready or not," James shouted waving his hat in the air and galloped away leaving Edward and Imran standing but they too laughed and followed hot on his heels.

-o0o-

Kuruman lay in a natural oasis and James, Edward, Amber and Imran cantered eagerly into the small town with its lush vegetation which owed its luxuriance to the natural spring called *Gasegonyane* or Little Calabash as William had explained on their trip. He had to give them something to encourage them to believe their journey would end somewhere where the barren, hot and waterless semi desert would be conquered. They found the river at the fountain head and jumped off their horses. Amber led her mare to the crystal clear water and the steaming animal drank deeply while her withers trembled and twitched. Amber wished she had a little calabash or a tortoise shell to fill and drink from like the San people but she knelt down and cupped her hand, drinking in the sweet water after which she bathed her face and sprinkled water down her neck. She untied her boots and paddled at the water's edge. Her self-control had its limits, after all, she thought wryly. The men threw themselves on the mat of green grass, still panting from their ride. They laughed and joked and then Edward rushed towards Amber and splashed her and she, too, burst into laughter.

The town was small. Mainly a high street with houses and shops. The church stood in the town's centre and the Dutch form of architecture was discernible in the neat homes with their many paned windows under dark thatched roofs. The abundance of trees provided pools of shade and a cacophony of birdsong confirmed the prolific animal life.

They hoped they would be invited to a Boer farm to go hunting and to meet the farmers' sons and daughters.

They were soon back in their saddles and ambled through the town looking for the house and clinic that William had arranged as their abode for the months to come. They waited patiently for the wagon to arrive, aware that they were being stared at through the lacy curtains that were moved aside and then dropped revealing their new neighbours' inquisitiveness.

At last, Koos led the oxen and the wagons into the town and Hendrik waved his blue hat with its ostrich plume with relief that they had crossed dangerous country and escaped unscathed. Lettie stretched and yawned languorously and Lucky jumped up and down with excitement. William had Andries with him on his horse and the little boy squealed delightedly.

Wild-fig trees formed green curtains in some of the gardens, their gyrating thick branches hanging downwards like pythons. Other gardens had fruit trees which were heavily laden with delicious peaches, apricots and plums. William found the house he was looking for and tethered his horse to the picket fence lifting Andries down from the saddle. He lifted the doorknocker and tapped the door three times. A homely and bosomy middle-aged woman with her hair neatly tied up with an ornate clasp and dressed in a beige crinoline skirt and shawl opened the door, "It's Mr Ropert, isn't it?" She smiled with a dimple appearing on a flushed cheek, "We've been expecting you and my, what an entourage you have," She remarked looking at each of her new visitors.

"You'll no doubt be wanting the keys to the house we have prepared for you. It was built for David Livingston and our daughter, Mary, after they were married and before the wanderlust spirited them away from here. I have prepared your beds with fresh linen and towels and the stove is packed with wood ready to be lit. By chance I have two loaves of bread in the oven so I will bring one over to you later."

William thanked her and began to explain about the boy, Andries who never left his side as far as was possible. His blond hair shone in the sunlight like a halo and his blue eyes showed a sadness that devoured any sense of playfulness or proper communication.

Mrs Moffat knelt down to look the little boy in the eye, "I have a little bedroom for you which is full of toys. Would you like me to take you there? After that you can have a bath and I'll wash your clothes for you. I have new clothes that could fit you."

Andries replied in the kitchen Dutch dialect and he nuzzled into the folds of her ample skirt.

"I will announce what has happened to his family in church. We have a very mixed congregation of all faiths. Perhaps someone might know his parents. You will love our little church, not so small now in comparison to the mud and thatch one we used to have. We're immensely proud to have a stone church with wonderful wooden beams which came all the way from the south coast." She smiled warmly at William.

"I'll look forward to worshipping with you there. I'm hoping to meet Mr Moffat as I have much to discuss with him." William could see there was no sign of the missionary.

"He has been living with the Matabele the past few months but I'm expecting him home any day now. He has immense energy and he never tires at spreading the Gospel to our heathen folk," Mary Moffat was full of zealous spirit like her husband, William silently noticed.

"I'll keep the boy here with me as I feel he needs stability and a mother figure to whom he can turn. Looking after a child after such a long time will be a pleasure for me!"

"You'll be relieving me of a duty I'm perhaps not best able to perform," William bowed and after a few more exchanges between them he left Mary and returned to the group at the ox-wagon. They soon moved off down a tree lined dusty street to find the mud house with a thatch roof that had been prepared for them. Imran was the most filled with anticipation as this was where he would spend the next few years of his life, administering to the sick and dying. Amber, too, was looking forward to a more homely existence in the small hamlet and she was eager to help Imran. Little children ran alongside the wagon, squealing and laughing.

-o0o-

The oxen were outspanned and Hendrik, Koos and Lucky herded them towards a green field where the exhausted and dehydrated animals could drink from the river and enjoy the good pastureland. The others dismounted and lifted their saddles off their horses and unstrapped the bridles with their offending bits and led their horses to the same field. The only tents being erected were for Hendrik and his two helpers.

Before they had even begun to unpack the wagon, a young San hunter ran nimbly into the yard and in broken English and mime imparted the request that a doctor was needed urgently. Imran quickly found his medicine bag and wooden chest of instruments and called to Amber to follow him. Knowledge of his healing powers had spread among the San people even before he had arrived.

"I'll accompany you if you wish," William offered but Imran and Amber waived aside his offer of help.

They didn't have too far to run and soon found themselves inside a gathering of San people whose insistent chatter created a cacophony of clicks and foreign staccato words. The site was well brushed earth that was as hard as cement and dotted around were small dwellings that could be dismantled in less than an hour. Imran was led to a small hovel of sticks arranged to form a type of tepee only big enough for two people and there a young San women was in the early stages of childbirth but with insistent gesticulation it became clear that she was convinced that something was wrong with the labour. With great sensitivity Imran gathered that the baby was lying in a breach position in the womb. In the melee the young woman didn't even offer up a groan.

"Usher everyone away," Imran asked Amber beseechingly, his large brown eyes full of concern for the woman and his handsome good looks were striking impressing the "bushmen" and women who admired his clothes and box of instruments each peering over another's shoulder to see better what was going on.

Amber knelt near to Imran and watched as he tried to manipulate the baby with well-practised techniques of externally shifting the baby's position between contractions. They seemed to have been there for hours when he sat back on his haunches and spoke to Amber, "The baby has turned. This young woman should now have less difficulty in giving birth but we should assist her all we can with the delivery as she is exhausted."

"Of course, you managed to help her so well. It really is a gift – medicine, I mean. I'm so pleased you are allowing me to stay right up to the birth. I have no idea what it will entail. One hears such horror stories. This won't end tragically? I do hope she and the baby survive." Amber's thoughts were darting about like glittering goldfish feeding in a deep green pond.

"One gains experience with each confinement. No two births are ever the same. The length of time, the degree of pain and the final outcome are all unpredictable," The tall Muslim relaxed as they waited.

The hours passed and the diminutive young woman began to show signs of distress.

"She's in so much pain and so exhausted, we're going to need to help this baby into the world. Pass the large forceps to me," He frowned concentrating deeply so as not to create more pain for his patient. The metal instruments with their ladle-like scoops fitted which was halfway through crowning and with each contraction, he pulled gently until the baby finally slithered out into Amber's waiting hands. Both silent and relieved, they smiled at the young woman who they now were told was called Tiny in her own tongue. An older wizened woman held out an animal skin that had been kneaded and pulled into almost the same softness as a towel and she scooped up the baby from Amber's arms. Everyone peered at the baby and the little boy was shown to each member of the clan with such pride and love.

"This is why I wanted to become a doctor, Imran," Amber sighed contentedly, "There can be no better feeling in the world than that of helping to save someone's life."

"You were a great asset to me today, Amber. I think your presence and the assurance you were giving to Tiny were almost as beneficial to her as my using instruments to assist the birth. It's all relative. Look, Tiny has fallen fast asleep and her mother will take care of her from now on. Come, it is time to go home," Imran smiled widely at the thought that he was now "home".

Amber, too, felt the significance of the word, "home" but home still meant "*Wolmunster*" in Mowbray even if she was not wanting to admit it. She couldn't deny that she did feel homesick and a longing to feel Fanny's arms around her brought tears to her eyes.

-o0o-

The village atmosphere of neighbours leaning out of windows and talking about the latest news in the region and of wagon wheels clattering over stones and roosters and chickens darting in and out of gardens was both bucolic and a tonic to the soul. Red geraniums and rose trees were jewels and vegetable patches of each residence the iron and grit of the hamlet. Fresh produce was sold at market and Lettie filled her baskets with a good variety of greens, carrots, onions and sweetcorn and the new potatoes still bearing the ground they grew in would taste nutty with an indefinable earthiness. Mischief, the meerkat, was soon well known to the community as he would often stand guard on the wall of the veranda of the clinic and he spent as much time with Amber as was sensible in the light of the nature of her work.

While in the clinic with Imran, Amber was learning all the rudiments of medicine, cleaning wounds, applying dressings and bandages, using splints and keeping patients clean and comfortable and he encouraged her to act independently but also to assist him whenever he needed her. Imran now seldom wore western dress but would appear in pristine white robes or *shalwar kameez* looking like a prophet. He took pride in his profession and thanked Allah daily for showering him with such gifts.

James and Edward occupied themselves in gleaning information about the area. James obtained more ore samples which he believed contained manganese ore, the silvery grey hard metal that was also inclined to be brittle and could oxidise easily. He had grown a beard while in the desert and it put years onto him. His hair had grown over his collar and his blue eyes often stared into those of his companions, like those of a fish eagle, undaunted, supremely confident. He had put aside the feelings of uneasiness that had dogged him for months. Stan hadn't crossed the desert of that he was sure.

Edward spent hours drawing and painting in watercolour the new plants he had discovered on the journey. In the desert one particular discovery was of an alien tree or plant; it was difficult to tell if it was animal or plant as it had flailing leafy limbs like a green octopus turned upside down. He left the large specimen where it grew as it was king in its realm surviving drought, incessant heat by day and freezing cold by night. Drawing it couldn't do it justice but he persevered as he wanted to exhibit the drawing at Kew in order to discover if it was known to other botanists. He also sketched animals he had seen in the desert; the sidewinder snakes, mice, lizards and scorpions. He also drew the antics of Mischief in various poses. As he worked, he realised he missed the companionship of Amber as she had followed him around learning from him firstly as a less mature scribbler but she was changing, too, becoming a fine artist herself when she had time for her hobbies. She seemed obsessed with medicine and caring for others and that had become her focus. He felt something stirring in his veins, too, and realised he wanted more adventure. He began reading books left in the house by David Livingstone. A notebook contained the description of the immense waterfalls north of the Limpopo, the Victoria Falls which Livingstone had discovered. Edward couldn't hide his excitement. To capture such a natural wonder of the world in oils would be a challenge he would readily accept.

He went in search of James and divulged what was on his mind, "I've discovered accounts of David Livingstone about the land to the north. I have a craving to travel again. Would you consider joining me? We still have two months before returning to Cape Town and I feel there's more to offer in the kingdom of the Matabele tribe and the northerly Bechuana."

"You have the same drive that spurs me onward to new challenges," James felt relieved that he wouldn't have to leave Kuruman alone, "I'm sure Mr Ropert will support us."

"I've a notebook here that describes the smelting of gold by an African tribe," Edward showed James.

"Excellent!" James couldn't hide the excitement coursing through him like a hot firestorm, "That is what could lead me to gold deposits. William Ropert and I both believe this part of Africa could be rich in precious metals and my exploration has been disappointing thus far. To change my fortune will cheer me up considerably. We must make sure we are the first Europeans to stumble upon such rich pickings. The Boers will be making similar efforts to enrich their coffers' so we must beat them to such a discovery."

Both young men found more notebooks and poured over them with renewed interest. That night at dinner they described their findings to William who sat bolt upright in his chair and gave them his full attention, "Excellent! You both have my blessing provided you return by February. You are aware of the tropical diseases that are prevalent the further north you go?"

They nodded and James and Edward discussed the logistics for such a trip. William suggested they should use the jawbone wagon and a team of oxen accustomed to walking through deep sand with a new driver and his assistants. Hendrik, Koos and Lucky would remain behind in Kuruman to prepare for their return to the Eastern Cape with William's entourage where at Algoa Bay they would board a ship to return to Cape Town. They would trek through the Orange River Boer Republic into Moshweshwe's kingdom down to the coastal road alongside the Indian Ocean on the South East Coast of Southern Africa. He had no desire to return via the way they had come mainly as the route would be shorter and the geography of the countryside would be more amenable.

After hearing the men's deliberations Fanny felt once again the frustration of being a woman. They never considered her accompanying them on this new adventure. It was expected that she would remain behind with Imran and Lettie while they awaited the return of Edward and James. She realised she had formed close attachment to each of them and if she were to be asked with whom she was in love, she would not be able to give an answer. Surely she could not be in love with both young men? The evening after they set out on their journey, Fanny tearfully sat down at her writing slope and began to write to Miss Smith.

Dear Miss Smith,

Thank you for your last letter which arrived shortly after we set up home here in Kuruman. We're living in the house built for David Livingstone, the explorer. As you advised I am Imran's very shadow and the work I am doing is of benefit to patients and I'm learning much about medicine. However, as time passes, I'm aware that a woman on her own couldn't practise as a doctor. The joy I am experiencing perhaps indicates that I could become a nurse or missionary but bearing in mind that I have the parallel wish to marry and have children, the practicality thereof is questionable. I admire your single-minded determination to succeed in a man's world but it has robbed you of having your own family. I wish I had your qualities and forbearance.

You are aware of the two young men accompanying us on this expedition are both very eligible and I must admit to you as one woman to another that I have fond affection for both Edward and James. Surely one cannot fall in love with two men equally? Whom do I choose, the young man with upper class privileges and a kind, brotherly disposition who flushes when he looks at me; or the man of the world who has risen up from humble beginnings and who has kissed me with a passion that makes my heart stop beating as it's all of a flutter? Or thirdly that I love neither romantically and that someone still remains undiscovered somewhere in my future? The two men concerned have left this very day to travel northwards in the footsteps of David Livingstone to continue their exploration but on the proviso that they return two months hence. I am no doubt already missing them like a dog which frets when it is left behind when its master has business abroad.

I would discuss this matter with my mother or aunt if they were they alive. But, with no one to advise me I must again turn to you for your wise counsel. It's imperative that you advise me before the young men in question return from the north. I must not act just on my whims but rather on your rational judgment.

It's sad to realise that I'm no nearer to deciding my fate and perhaps there is no decision that can be taken just on the success of this expedition. I have learnt how to survive in the wilderness, to read the stars and to rise at daybreak to find the strength to persevere with the goal akin to finding the Holy Grail or just to become a young woman who is perhaps more farsighted and confident than she would have otherwise been if still attending school to read

Shakespeare or to learn how to cook and sew. What does my future hold?

Your devoted student,

Amber

-oOo-

William sat on the sunlit garden deep in thought and feeling the chagrin of not achieving as yet the completion of his memoirs. His years in Ireland as a youth and scholar followed by student and barrister were sweet memories and lately he longed for that same joie de vivre that had buoyed him up and sent him on an ocean current of adventure. He had steeled himself on putting aside his love of seeking new experiences and began concentrating on the fascinating people he had had the pleasure of meeting. His depth of knowledge about current affairs and his affinity with men of state provided many pages that any gentleman would find satisfying and illuminating especially when he delivered the coup de grace which would see off a scoundrel or elevate someone less well known to a position of renown on his recommendation. How he wished he was a Boswell or Samuel Pepys. His prose was less ostentatious but with its conciseness came clarity. His journals, thanks to Fanny, offered a wealth of detail according to date, time of entry and where he had recorded the actual speech made by an individual, he verified its correctness by offering other witnesses' corroborations in subtexts. His world had been blessed with a wealth of ideas, philosophy, oratory, staged theatricals, music and poetic indulgences. Out in the wilderness he had no proximity to libraries or newspapers but his accurate memory was such that he could remember who the subject was, where he was, what he had said, what he or she was wearing and his subject's effect on bystanders or newspaper editors. He believed in being brief rather than longwinded and as a result provided a tale with plot, passion, alacrity, climax and denouement.

Sitting under a locust bean tree with its mottled shadows falling in out of focus pools   like the markings on a leopard hide and engrossed in his writing he didn't see a man approach him. The individual was stooped and elderly with luxuriant grey hair and a long woolly beard.

"William, dear fellow, it is so good to meet you at last," Robert Moffat held out a gnarled hand and his face was compelling with his direct stare and kindly expression.

"I'm honoured to make your acquaintance, Sir," William rose and shook Moffat's hand vigorously, "When did you get back?"

"Yesterday, and not a moment too soon. My wife was spitting like a Scottish wild cat that I had left her for such a long sojourn amongst the Matabele people," Moffat could see that he was going to enjoy William Ropert's company.

"I've heard that the chief of the Matabele is Moselikatse. Hasn't he instigated genocide against lesser tribes?" William invited Moffat to take the seat opposite him.

"That may well be why he is searching for forgiveness from a greater being. He had heard rumours about me and my God and sent for me so that I could introduce him to a powerful being who looks kindly on human folk especially those with so much spilt blood on their hands," Robert Moffat chuckled.

"You must be quite a linguist to be able to talk to the indigenous tribes in their own languages. I have as yet not acquired knowledge of any one African language but I have mastered a few phrases the San allow to trip off their lips and from their palate," William smiled, "I would dearly love to learn their language. It's surely one of the oldest languages on the earth. I believe it is poetic and expressive."

"That will be my pleasure, William," Moffat replied, "It hasn't been easy to learn comprehensively the local languages and dialects but one day after a crowd of would be worshippers once again left my Sunday sermon under the acacia trees sheepishly shaking their heads that they knew not what I was preaching, Mary saw my frustration and helplessness by suggesting that anyone would turn away if they didn't hear the Bible message in their own tongue. She had made a pivotal observation when I couldn't see the wood for the trees."

"Yes, I heard you had translated the Bible into Setswana, a feat so great that no one had attempted it before you!" William respected the septuagenarian's fiery spirit.

"I started off with a spelling book and then progressed to a catechism and had those printed in London so after six months we had the rudiments of expressing God's love for all of us and how well we ought to worship him. I followed those with a translation of the Book of St Luke and eventually the whole of the New Testament. I decided why bother to send my manuscripts to England so I visited Cape Town and bought my own printing press and after transporting it all those miles to Kuruman, I couldn't wait to see the pages roll off the machine. You'll find when so isolated one becomes a master of many trades, preacher, doctor, printer, blacksmith, carpenter and bricklayer. The young doctor you have brought with you will be welcomed with open arms. I will be relieved that the new born, ill and dying will be cared for with the right medicines and correct surgery. I begged God to run the sangomas, their medicine men out of the villages. You have been in our little church? I will be struck down by a bolt of lightning for my hubris. Before it was completed Mary wrote to the London Missionary Society and requested a communion chalice set to be sent immediately and when it arrived it was used for our very first communion. The timing couldn't have been better! We had nine hundred men and women attend the opening ceremony and two hundred and fifty newly converted Christians were able to take communion."

William was feeling fond affection for the older man. He had read comments before the trip that Moffat had made to a journalist when it was reported that he had said that the people in his congregation "were thoroughly sensual and could rob, lie and murder without any compunctions of conscience as long as success attended their efforts". William had imagined that the preacher would be paternalistic and lacking a deep understanding of African culture. Was that the case and if so, should he, William open Moffat's eyes to the cultural maturity and dignity of the people to whom he preached and that he should not denigrate the traditions that were as important to them as ours were to us? He remembered more of the newspaper article, where Moffat was quoted as saying, "They turn a deaf ear to the voice of love and scorn the doctrines of salvation, but affairs in general assume far more hopeful aspect. They have in several instances relinquished the barbarous system of commandoes for stealing cattle. They have also dispensed with a rainmaker this season."

Lettie made a little curtsey when she approached the two men with a glistening jug of water and two glass tumblers on a wooden butler's tray covered with a tray cloth. A lacy doily covered the top of the jug to prevent thirsty flies and midges drowning in the liquid. As it was ants were streaming into the kitchen through the crack beneath the stable door to carry off bits of sugar she had spilt earlier in the day.

Robert remembered the little waif William had rescued when he was left behind by the murderous band of robbers, "The boy you saved from imminent death is coming along nicely. He managed two sentences today. I'm sure when the shock wears off, we'll discover if he has any family who can take him in. These commandoes of lawless renegades torment us all so completely that I don't hold much hope that the roads through the desert will ever be without incident and tragedy. I was able to convert Jager Afrikaner, a notorious Griqua who terrorised travellers in Namaqualand. Having committed many murders, Jager waylaid me on one of my many journeys and begged me to teach him and convert him to 'Jesus' religion'. I was in fear of my life but in the kitchen Dutch dialect I led him up the path of righteousness. It was deeply moving."

"Hearing what you have just said makes me realise how important religion is to all the people in southern Africa. It's a moot point whether we should convert them to our Anglicised Christian religion or to respect their religions. Who are we to say we know best? However, if a heathen comes to one and requests salvation what a joy that must be," William's liberalism was unveiled and Robert Moffat retreated into himself and sat for a few moments with his chin on his chest as he considered William's comments.

"Tell me more about how you felt after translating the whole Bible? It must have required superhuman strength?" William changed the subject adeptly.

"I felt it to be an awful thing to translate the Book of God. When I had time to realise that my work of so many years was complete, a feeling came over me as if I would die; my heart beat like the strokes of a hammer. My emotions found vent by falling on my knees and thanking God for his grace and goodness for giving me the strength to accomplish my task." Moffat spoke softly and so convincingly that William allowed the silence of companionship to bind the two of them in friendship.

After a few minutes the two men resumed their conversation and William thought he should introduce his charges to the older man. He ushered Robert into the house and the three young people who were in the kitchen stopped what they were doing and stood up. "I must introduce you to my protégés, all three of them, Amber, my ward, James, a geologist and gold prospector and Edward, a botanist and very fine artist. You will see his paintings are hung in the sitting room."

"I will most certainly have a look at them. To be able to paint must give the artist a feeling for what God felt when he created the world out of nothing. A blank canvass touched by paint to reveal a moment in time in a scene existing somewhere on earth, such a wonderful gift." Robert Moffat spoke encouragingly. Edward flushed and bowed his head.

Moffat turned to James, "I hear that you have all been reading my son in law's notebooks and you wish to explore the territories north of here. James, being a prospector, I have information for you which might inspire you even further. As you know I've just spent a sojourn with Moselikatse and while there I noticed the great warrior chief wore a necklace of pure gold and there was evidence of iron smelting as the arrowheads of his warriors were metal. You will no doubt want to find the source of the gold. I will write a letter to the great chief introducing you to him. He's illiterate but one of his generals can read.

"I'm very grateful, Sir, and must admit I'm most excited by your news. Edward and I are eager to start our journey as soon as possible." James' dark eyes were sparkling with tears which he wiped away as he laughed.

"And this young woman must be Amber", the pastor held her hand, "You have the unenviable position of having the courage of a lioness but you have to become a gentle lamb. I can understand your frustration about your gender. One day there'll come a time that women can do all the things a man can do. I'm most certain of that. Be patient, little dove!"

Later as Moffat walked home, the little town settled back into its sunlit, dreamy peace, content that its master had safely returned.

-o0o-

January 1857

Cape Town

The sea was crashing against the rocks far down below as Nerina sat at her writing bureau in the chintzy bedroom of her parents' home, now hers. She wore a summer outfit of loose, flowing, printed floral georgette and her hair, with streaks of grey and brushed a hundred times, flowed down her back. The sound of the crashing surf became muted as she concentrated on her task.

"Dear William,

I'm most grateful for your last letter which brought me up to date with your life in Kuruman. I'm delighted to hear that you have found a true friend in Robert Moffat. He sounds interesting and humane.

I can only imagine the peaceful hamlet town with cockerels on the roof at dawn and chickens and geese meandering through its few streets. Bottled ginger beer and preserved peaches with cream sound delicious

You must be missing the two young men. Have you had word from them about the progress of their travels in the northern territories?

I also received a missive from Amber which was most moving but deeply personal and I must admit, she appears to see me as a mother figure or at least someone to whom she can discuss matters concerning the female heart.

I'm delighted to learn that you have written copious accounts of your life and described the people you've met with anecdotal detail that only a period of time in the wilderness would afford you the opportunity to tackle such a task!

I have been blessed by a glorious summer and have taken part in parish matters at church and running my school. My ongoing dedication to my pupils keeps me so occupied that I have little time for my own thoughts and often planned activities to the theatre or on outings into the Cape countryside have had to be cancelled but that is quite my preferred option. My pupils are my children and doesn't a mother give all of herself to her young charges? You are in the very same position, are you not, my dear friend? Isn't it ironic that neither of us has married and we don't carry on our family line?

The news at the Cape is unexciting so rest assured you have not missed any intrigues or disasters or great celebrations. Your name does appear sometimes in the newspapers and the Town knows of your sabbatical and its purpose and writers appear to be supportive.

I believe this will be my last letter to Kuruman as you will soon be leaving to begin your journey back to Cape Town. You will be warmly welcomed home. Perhaps you, too, are looking forward to a sense of normality in your life. A messiah cannot spend the rest of his days in the desert. There is work a plenty awaiting you here.

Wishing you God's protection on your homeward journey.

With kind thoughts and looking forward to meeting with you when you return,

Nerina.

Nerina smiled and her eyes lit up. She had so often prepared for his homecoming when she heard of his expeditions to the Frontier to command his mounted corps. She had always followed his movements in the newspaper columns but this time there would be more. She felt it as surely as blood flowed through her veins.

She took out another sheet of paper and a giggle trilled in her throat. Amber, dear Amber. What would she tell the dear young woman?

My dear Amber,

I was delighted to receive your letter. You will find it a relief to hear that what you are feeling is as predictable as nature can make it. My dear girl, you are not in love if you need to ask me for advice. You've become fond of Edward and James much as though they were your brothers. Of course you love them. Your uncle would never have chosen them for the expedition if he had found them uncouth and unpleasing. He was thinking of his own pleasure as well as yours, I am sure.

I do not believe you have experienced the intensity of romantic true love that exists between two lovers. The racing of your heart, the dryness of your mouth, the butterflies in your stomach and oh, the sheer heavenly bliss when his hand touches yours. The humdrum world only exists in fact it becomes a place of shadows when he is not in your presence instead he invites you to a heaven with all its perfection which makes every leaf golden and every birdsong, music of such rapture and like all the saints in God's presence he is the bravest, most compassionate human ever to have loved and you feel immortalised when he tells you that he loves you. Your spirit soars and your senses are intensified beyond imagination. You become truly alive!

I believe you will soon begin the long journey back to Cape Town. Allow your questions to stop and enjoy the last few weeks of having brothers around you. I'm sure you will also miss Imran as I believe he will remain behind. You have said little about your aspirations to become a doctor. I do believe the best you can hope for is to be an assistant of a doctor, capable of what he does but not given the recognition, the cachet. It is our cross to bear. You may wish to offer your time to the poor, to teach them, to feed them, to dress them. There is no better reward than selfless service.

I look forward to your return and you can reveal all you have learnt. I pray that I did the right thing to sow the germ of an idea into your uncle's mind. You both grasped the nettle in no uncertain manner and I believe you will return older and wiser and richer for the benefit of such experiences.

I bid you farewell till we meet sometime soon again.

Yours with affection,

Nerina Smith

-o0o-

CHAPTER 23

The small party of travellers had left Kuruman a week ago and the oxen under their yokes moaned when pressed to walk faster. They were hugging the Limpopo River along tracks that were almost as old as mankind itself. The sands of the desert had been replaced by a rich, red clay where grasses were in clumps and acacia, mimosa, umbrella trees were dwarfed by baobab trees the bark of which looked alive like the skin of a hippo or like grey clay which while it was so wet, it dripped in places. The short branches adorned the head of the woody column like a Medusa's headdress. They stopped from time to time for Edward to paint a scene as the landscapes were evocative of a different planet. Large boulders on apexes of hills were giants in the plains. When they finally crossed the Limpopo the vegetation changed to become denser bushland.

James' keen eye scoured the ground and outcrops of seams of strata were clear signs of geological upheavals but the presence of precious minerals and metals so far eluded him.

Edward still had a fascination for the changing vegetation and samples of unknown seed pods, and flowers to press were always quickly pounced upon. His interest in the indigenous people spurred him on to paint portraits or scenes of village life. The Tswana people were friendly and hospitable, now accustomed to westerners much due to a steady trickle of missionaries making their journeys through their land.

The day came for them to cross the Limpopo into Matabele country and immediately the wilderness became untamed like a writhing snake or an enraged elephant bull while and around them were buck and their followers of lion, hyenas, foxes and carrion birds like the marabou stork with its red pouch under its chin. Birds screeched out musical notes that sounded strange and unrecognisable. Glossy black starlings with yellow, beady eyes would perch in the branches of trees like iridescent carvings of black opals.

Having set up camp near a small river, James and Edward were preparing their evening meal of venison and vegetables purchased from a village when they heard the thuds of many feet getting louder and louder and cries and ululating preceded the Matabele impi surrounding them. The noise sent shivers down the young men's backs and the hairs on the back of their necks stood on end. The faces of the men were close enough to see the inflamed excitement and rolling eyeballs fixed on them with ferocity. Koos, their driver, bravely went to meet their uninvited dinner guests and while the warriors were jumping up and down, he ascertained from the leader that the white men were to go with them. There was no doubt that there would be no negotiation. They were allowed to strike camp and prepare the wagon and animals and throwing themselves into the saddle, James and Edward urged their horses forward and followed the general pressed on all sides by young Matabele whose fitness and endurance were never in doubt.

It wasn't long before they entered Moselikatse's encampment with its earth and thatch huts which had no windows surrounded by a stockade and into an adjoining kraal cattle were brought at night. James and Edward hid their fear well as they had learnt that the African whoever he may be, admired fearlessness so they walked like Capetonian dandies and their air of importance made the villages whisper among themselves and the young maidens tittered like sparrows as they passed by. Moselikatse sat on a carved wooden chair regal in his finery of leopard skin, feathered hair dress and robe of fine wool. Gold bracelets shone on his muscular arms and gold rings adorned his fingers. He was no longer a young man, in fact, far beyond his prime being in his late fifties.

"I have a letter for you from Dr Moffat, your Excellency," James walked forward and gave the piece of folded paper bearing Moffat's seal, "I believe your Excellency can read."

"Of course I understand English. The good Doctor teaches me more each time we meet. How is his health at present?" The Matabele King began to read the document.

"He is well and urged us to visit you as he said there was much you could teach us," Edward bowed his head in deference.

"What is it you want to know?" Moselikatse looked unblinking into Edward's eyes.

"I'm a botanist and I am looking for any unusual plants that may grow in your Kingdom," Edward said, stuttering a little, "And, if it pleases you, I would like to paint you and your people here," He waved his hand to encompass the surroundings.

"And you, The White man with the Dark Eyes, what is it you want?"

"I'm seeking to find gold and silver even iron and coal. I wish to become rich for the sake of my family," James' brow furrowed with earnestness.

"Yes, I saw your face when you looked at my gold bracelets," Moselikatse smiled knowingly, "Every young man seeks his fortune. For you it will be necessary to seek gold with my cousin's son, Umdabuli. He makes this jewellery for me but where and how he produces it, is a secret he's allowed to keep for himself. It is only the honourable who deserve such a status and to be allowed to bear secrets from the King."

"I am truly grateful, Your Excellency," James smiled, thinking you sly old dog, nothing escapes your attention.

"Umdabuli, come forward and meet this man. Dr Moffat has written confirming these men don't wish us any harm. They will be in your care and you can arrange for them to set up their camp, outside the kraal. If they have need for anything you are to provide that to them."

"Great Father, I thank you," Umdabuli spoke in his native tongue, bowed his head respectfully and led the two Englishmen out of the kraal.

"Dr Moffat believes I am his best pupil. He praised me for how quickly I picked up the English language," Umdabuli smiled, his brilliant white teeth and the whites of his eyes sparkling in his dark face. "I have much to teach you, White Man with the Dark Eyes."

"Please, my name is James. Call me by my name," James also smiled begrudgingly. "I gather you are skilled in making things out of gold?"

"I learnt the skills from my father. It has been handed down from father to son for many years. I plan to smelt gold in my forge tomorrow. You can come and see how it's done, but," Umdabuli looked serious and full of wonder, "It is a mystical experience. Our Creator-God, only lets me have the power over the metal. It means I must be without blemish. I must be pure tomorrow so I will sleep alone outside the kraal and pray. I cannot lie with my wife on such a night."

"I think you have a deep responsibility, Umdabuli," James was careful not to show any signs of scepticism and admonished himself for his godless ways.

"Tomorrow, I will fetch you at your camp," Umdabuli looked mischievous, "I'll work my magic and you will see a miracle!"

-o0o-

At dawn Umdabuli set to work making a clay mould in which to pour liquid gold – this was his favourite part of the whole process and then he set the coal furnace alight so that it could reach the required temperature using the bellows to make the ruby red coals turn orange with a white heat. He arrived at the camp as Edward and James were finishing breakfast.

"Good morning Sirs, I have prepared the furnace and we can begin your first glimpse of jewellery making

James leapt up, wiping his mouth with his serviette and swallowed the last mouthful of toast. His alacrity amused Edward who followed his companion with slightly less enthusiasm.

"Do you smelt other metals in your forge, Umdabuli?" James struggled to keep us with the lithe figure of the Matabele man who was possibly his age. They entered the hallowed place set aside for Umdabuli's work. It was strictly off limits for the other warriors or the women in the King's village. The earth was baked hard and Umdabuli had swept the ground around his workplace and forge with a handful of tough elephant grass stalks.

"Yes, I smelt iron, copper and nickel to make alloys and with the iron I beat out the blades of assegai spears and arrow-heads for my fellow warriors and also make cooking pots for the women. I'm often a busy man but I can only use my skills when the ancestral spirits look kindly upon me!" Umdabuli was reverent and humble.

"How did you learn to speak English so well, Umdabuli?" Edward asked out of curiosity.

"There have always been a steady stream of missionaries passing through and of course, Dr Moffat, has spent many hours with a few of us to teach us English and we teach him Ndebele. We have pictures and he writes down the meaning and tells us what the English word is and then we give him the corresponding word in our language. Then we progressed towards learning adjectives, adverbs and verbs. Then spellings: Dr Moffat gave us each a printed book of spellings. Mine is nearly worn out as I use it a lot. I find such a pleasure in learning. Your language is a complicated one but one of my desires is to learn to read and write, myself," Umdabuli flashed a wide smile showing perfect white teeth.

"The fire looks white hot. Do you want me to work the bellows for you?" James asked, his curiosity unquenchable.

"You would assist me greatly, Sir," Umdabuli set out his tools and the two visitors sat on tree stumps, looking on with interest, their faces glowing red from the heat.

At last the moment to which James was looking forward. Umdabuli set a few small ingots into an iron spade the size of a couple of inches long and he carefully inserted two nuggets of gold into it and uncovering the top coals he laid the spade on top of the white glowing coals beneath. James had set to the task of injecting air into the coals to provide oxygen for such a white heat to last.

At last the gold had melted and Umdabuli poured the liquid gold into the mould. The two visitors gasped at the ingenuity of the process that had been known to man over five thousand years before Christ. The dense metal soon cooled and was carefully removed. The golden face of a leopard sprung out at them and they were filled with awe.

"This is an absolute wonder. How many men have looked into the world of the priest who is adept at fire making and melting gold for jewellery," James was euphoric. "Please tell me where you found the nuggets," He asked breathlessly.

"It is a long way south eastwards from here perhaps taking a few days in your wagon," Umdabuli was a wise man and he could see desire in the eyes of the foreigner, a desire to own and display. He could tell them such tales, "I have heard that a gold digger found a nugget of the weight of five pounds six ounces in between two rocks in a fast moving stream. This has been told to me by other furnace makers. Everyone keeps the secret so that the special site is not plundered. You will have to swear to me that this knowledge is meant just for yourselves."

James would have sworn on the Bible had Umdabuli so desired and Edward however would keep his own counsel.

"Will you take us there?" James felt his throat contract with anxious anticipation.

"If you give me five pounds of your money I will most certainly lead you there," The young Matabele was enjoying the attention of the strangers. He would look for more nuggets himself; therefore it would be a great opportunity.

"When can you take us there?" James asked, hoping the answer would be "tomorrow".

It was.

-oOo-

Kuruman

1st February 1857

The clinic adjoining David Livingstone's house was busier than usual when a young Tswana girl of ten was brought to Imran. He could see immediately that her illness was extraordinary. She was having great difficulty breathing and he could see that a membrane had grown in her throat, covering her tonsils and part of her windpipe. If only they had medicines to help the young child. He could try to make an incision in her throat and insert a tube helping her to breathe but usually in such cases the patient dies from other complications but creating an airway was a step in the right direction. He had marvelled at the operation when he was a student and admired the ancient Egyptians for being the first to consider such a device. However, he was soon serious again knowing that the dreaded disease diphtheria had come into his rooms.

"We must isolate the child," he barked at Amber "and we must boil her clothes and at all costs, we must avoid inhaling her breath. Oh yes, and keep washing your hands with soap after touching her," He had to bring down the child's temperature which was far too high and

Amber set to work mopping the body of the child with cold water. Her patient she discovered was called Nyoko. The heat was burning her up, Amber thought to herself. This was something more sinister than the usual stomach flux or winter fevers. This was serious like cholera or measles. Imran's usual patient and studied approach had evaporated. She realised he was not telling her the complete truth. Whatever it was, he was keeping to himself.

Nyoko's throat began to swell and her breathing became more laboured. Her mother looked at Amber with anxious stares, willing herself to understand what the white girl was doing. Surely her child should be kept warm to burn up the fever. Her wide open eyes searched Amber's face for some signal to say her daughter was going to recover. Amber smiled at the mother gently while she scurried back and forth. Suddenly, Nyoko made gurgling sounds and mesmerised by the child's plight, Amber tore herself away to run to find Imran. She burst into his room and saw him lancing a boil on a man's back, "Hurry! The young girl is battling to breathe!"

Imran took his instruments with him realising he had to cut the tissue that was invading her throat away from the trachea so immediately took out and washed the scalpel before operating. The child was already unconscious so he asked Amber to hold the child's mouth open and he cut an opening at the top of the windpipe and immediately the girl started to breathe better. For how long? Imran questioned himself. Her throat was so swollen that the trachea would be shut off. The result? The child would die!

Amber remained at Nyoka's bedside into the night with the young girl's mother who was also unable to sleep. In the morning the girl's condition worsened and unable to offer any hope, Imran included Nyoka in his dawn prayers.

At eight thirty that morning Nyoka died as her windpipe was totally compromised by the membranes. Nyoka's mother began to wail and wanted to embrace her child. "No, you must not touch her; she could infect you!" Amber's brow was furrowed with concern and the woman hearing a tone in Amber's voice that never had been there before, removed herself from the body and stepped back, "Could other children get this?" She asked with her deep pain making her slump against the wall.

"The doctor says that could happen. It is a dreadful disease if it can kill in such a cruel way," Amber walked over to a basin and jug and promptly began washing her own hands and her arms, showing the woman how she must take care to do the same.

-o0o-

North Eastern Transvaal

January 1857

Moselikatse's kingdom was fast disappearing as the wagon and cattle began the journey to the rivers that contained the alluvial gold. James and Edward explored the countryside around them while the ponderous wagon and its load took routes more accommodating to the traffic of wagons on tracks made by Boer trekkers. Umdabuli travelled with Koos as he and his fellow Matabele possessed no horses, occasionally a mule but they didn't horse-ride. He gave eloquent descriptions of what they could hope to find.

They soon found a large canyon where the deep river wound through the gorges it had fashioned over many millions of years. Down in the canyon the bushveld had been replaced by sub-tropical forests and Edward wasn't going to forego such an opportunity to search for unusual plants and he and James found an ancient path down to the bottom of the canyon. James was struck that it was a green canyon as most canyons are desolate and bare of any form of life. There were three mountains which were cone shaped each with another cone placed on top and a stockade of sandstone rocks divided the two.

"Like our huts," Umdabuli said to them later when they told their tale. The horses slid down the steep path and soon they were enclosed by forest where animal cries haunted the lush green world. Edward was in his element as he saw rare trees and cycads, yellowwood, white stink wood, Cape chestnut and mountain cedars. He sketched while on horseback and planned on painting what he had seen once back in their camp. Both men used telescopes to identify what animal had made a call and often were able to see the otherwise invisible animal life around them. They sat frozen and just watched and enjoyed the antics of samango monkeys, vervet monkeys and they could hear woodpeckers while loeries and sunbirds fluttered through the canopy like sparkling jewels. When they reached the bottom of the forest, they saw hippos and crocodiles and above them vultures hung in the air letting the thermals take them higher. They identified falcons, kestrels and sparrow hawks by their outlines in the blue dome of the heavens. Having brought with them fishing lines they placed pressed cooked maize meal into the shape of a juicy insect and cast their lines into the deep water. After a few hours, James caught a large fish which they cooked over hot coals. James intended hunting one of the many antelope in the forest. A bushbuck would provide food for the next day or two for them back in their encampment. They watched as a fish eagle dropped like a stone with claws outstretched to catch the fish sunning itself in the warm green shallows. This was truly paradise. But, they had yet to reach the rivers that bore diamonds along their stony beds.

In the cool evenings Umdabuli told them tales that were buried deep in his culture and they began to learn about Monamatapa and the Queen of Sheba who was reputed to have built her palace somewhere in the north. He told them of Ophir and Sofala from where gold, silver, precious stones, monkeys, peacocks and sandalwood were sent to King Solomon every three years. James, his head swooning from such stories, imagined himself on the threshold of becoming a wealthy man.

A few days later, James and Edward made their last journey to the canyon and their exploration took them to where the river was at its most shallow but not before they saw the weeping face of a waterfall where the water had left mineral deposits on the rocks transforming them into bearing the features of a man. A few hours away they came across a gully of potholes in which dark water swirled carving the sandstone into bowls the size of a giant's bath.

The countryside reverted to grasslands interspersed with evergreen forests and on the plain, wildebeest were seen to darken the area in their tens of thousands. There were numerous zebra herds and buck of various types in droves. The ubiquitous impala grazed in utter contentment. Eventually they reached the creek through which a shallow stream flowed quite jauntily.

"This is the spot where I found gold. There are also two other small rivers where I've been lucky. But, we can first try here, may our gods guide us!" Umdabuli stood in the water and lifted his arms to the heavens.

The quicksilver rivulet covered their feet as they began their search by overturning stones and small rocks along the way. When they had been searching for hours, James fetched his pan, sieve and spade from the wagon. He dug up material from the river bed and placed it in the pan and began swirling the water in the rushing water and stone material was washed away leaving pebbles and sand. He examined the stones excitedly hearing the pulse of his heart in his ears. A small nugget the size of his little finger's nail lay at the bottom of the pan. It wasn't iron pyrite but yellow gold. The rest of the pebbles he discarded and swirled the water through the mud at the bottom of the pan until all the sand was washed away leaving sparkling grains of gold dust.

"Umdabuli, Edward! I've struck gold!" James was crying and laughing at the same time and soon his two companions began laughing, too. Fortunately James had brought a further couple of iron dishes of different sizes so soon all three of them began to dig and pan for the most expensive metal on earth.

By the end of the week, they had each found nuggets the size of marbles and enough gold grains to fill half of a leather pouch.

"I can't believe my luck!" Edward laughed when he found one of the nuggets. "Who needs to work?"

"What do you think we are doing?!" James laughed bent over the rushing rivulet, "I'm prepared to do this for years if it will make me rich!"

Umdabuli moved them on to two further rivers and again the trawl was spectacular and to crown it all, James found a nugget wedged between two large rocks that hadn't moved for thousands of years when they had been carried downstream by some cataclysmic geological event.

"Edward, Umdabuli, look at this blighter. It's our biggest so far. I reckon the nugget is twelve ounces in weight. I'm serious about this becoming my life's work. That will entail a permanent camp and contraptions facilitating sieving and dividing with a sluice of water where not even the smallest golden grain would escape."

"You know this land all belongs to the Zulu king, Mpande. You would have to buy the mining rights from him. He has given me permission to hunt for treasures. He doesn't know I'm a Matabele. My life would be worth nothing if he finds out. If you have tobacco and whiskey, you could offer those as payment." Umdabuli smiled heady with their success!

James had sufficient luxury items hidden away amongst his possessions to negotiate with Mpande. He had heard that black chieftains could be seduced by "forty boxes of cheap cigars".

They arrived at Mpande's village via an easy route which was kinder to the oxen. It was grassland and it hadn't rained yet that summer and the ground was cracked as the sun beat down on man and beast quite mercilessly. All of a sudden they were travelling through the remains of a village. The ash circles showed where the huts had once stood and a deathly hush fell upon them all. No birds sang there.

"We destroyed the Sotho tribe who lived here." Umdabuli spoke in hushed tones expecting the spirits of the place to descend on him like a flock of vultures, "We killed all the men but took the women and children away with us."

"I've heard of Moselikatse's wars of extermination. He must be strong and merciless and yet when we met him he was friendly and a good host," James felt uneasy.

"You aren't a threat to him like the Boers or Shaka or the Sotho. We pushed the Sotho out of the Transvaal," Umdabuli whispered.

"But, in the end the Boers and Zulus chased you all across the Limpopo where you have now settled," James said wickedly, his tone making Umdabuli laugh with his hand covering his mouth.

Mpande agreed to an audience with James and Edward present and Umdabuli presented Mpande the ring he had made with the impression of a leopard's face. The King gasped and quickly tried on his new trinket holding the piece of jewellery up to the sunlight to see it gleam and when the matter of the mining rights for the gold digging was discussed, the King asked what the two white men would be prepared to offer him and when James mentioned forty boxes of cigars and whiskey, Mpande laughed and held out his hand to shake hands on the deal. James had pro forma documents drawn up before setting out of the expedition so all that was required was Mpande's mark.

James wanted to begin work on his dig immediately but Edward wished to reach the Victoria Falls to see one of the wonders of the world for himself. David Livingstone's notebook burnt a hole in his pocket. Painting such a spectacle could set him apart as an artist. Perhaps he would yet be hung at the Royal Academy of Arts in London. He would take his new paintings with him when he next visited Kew.

"We have an arrangement to complete this trip together and you owe it to William Ropert to at least see him before you begin your own little gold rush," Edward was determined that James kept his end of the bargain.

"If you won't tell William Ropert about the dig, I'll accompany you to the waterfalls. I'll continue prospecting for other sites where gold or diamonds can be found on his behalf. Ropert deserves that from me!" James replied.

-o0o-

Kuruman

February 1857

A glossy starling paraded around the yard stealing titbits from the chickens and fruit lay fermenting under the overladen fruit trees. Insects buzzed noisily and beetles foraged in the fruit like miniature prospectors. It was already eight a.m. and the household was awake.

Amber lay in bed believing she was being very lazy and Imran would scold her. She was feeling cold and her muscles ached but she washed and dressed herself neatly then sat on the edge of her bed puzzled by how weak she was feeling.

The clinic was abnormally busy with parents bringing healthy children to be examined and to be diagnosed with or without diphtheria. Imran tried to impress on the parents of his patients to keep the infected children isolated at home to prevent the disease spreading. His time was taken up with making frequent journeys to visit his young patients. He was working long hours and it was taking a toll on his health. Amber worried about them all and found solace in writing in her journal. When she harboured the idea of becoming a doctor secretly in her heart, she had never expected herself to dread going to outlying regions with Imran to give treatment to all the ill children.

Their patients with diphtheria nearly always died and seeing death at such proximity was beginning to affect her mind.

She rose from her bed and feeling suddenly lightheaded she fell down in a faint. When she regained consciousness she was in bed and Imran was bent over her examining her eyes, ears, throat and her neck.

"I feel so cold. Can you see how I'm shivering," She appealed to Imran, dreading to hear the diagnosis of her illness, "It's just influenza. I've had a sore throat for weeks but I'm sure I'll get over it in a day or two. Maybe Lettie can take my place at the clinic." The look in her shining green eyes locked with his gaze which was full of concern. It wasn't diphtheria but when Imran felt the nodes on her knuckles and knees which were hot with inflammation and adding to that Amber's fever and symptoms of a weak heart as he listened to the powerful organ with his wooden stethoscope made him suspect rheumatic fever.

"Can you bear it if I tell you the truth?" Imran opened a window to let plenty of fresh air into the small room.

"I have it, haven't I?" She wanted to feel sorry for herself but strangely she was looking down on herself quite dispassionately.

"No. It's not diphtheria but rheumatic fever but you're not alone. I'll be with you throughout the course of the illness. It can be life threatening so you must listen to your body. I've seen patients with this when I was a student and most have recovered and I'll do everything in my power, in Allah's power to heal you. You must rest in bed and fight this illness from within yourself. If you give up you could die. Your heart will need all the help it can get," He soaked her facecloth in the basin of cool water and placed it on her forehead to cool her raging fever. She felt herself drifting in and out of consciousness, sometimes aware that her uncle was in the room mopping her brow and talking to her quietly trying to reassure her. Imran treated her with tinctures of willow bark and leaves for the fever and laudanum to help her sleep.

Night fell suddenly as it does in Africa. There is no twilight just blackness and her room was dark and she writhed around, trying to breathe, trying to rest her heart. This was a battle she had to fight all on her own. There was no let up. What joy it would be if she could sleep and wake up to be able to breathe properly without feeling each breath is an immense battle and that it would be a normal day. How wonderful to wake up free of the pain in her swollen joints which was often excruciating. She wasn't alone though. The meerkat, Mischief lay next to her on the bed.

They all took turns to stay with Amber and William was distraught. He had never foreseen the likelihood that she – any of them - would become seriously ill. His bravado in leading the young people into the wilderness perhaps had been folly in retrospect. He sat in the dark and contemplated their fate and what remained of Amber's future.

-o0o-

It was five days since they left Umdabuli at a crossroads which made them take opposite routes. Umdabuli was used to travelling on his own and would reach Moshweshwe's kingdom without too much hardship. James won over by Edward accompanied him across the Limpopo and into the land of the Tswana people. Their oxen proved to be strong and hardy creatures as they crossed the semi desert conditions. Robert Moffat had drawn a map and had mentioned Zyangabywe, a village where they would find friendly 'natives'. James immediately went prospecting and Edward set off to find what little vegetation there was in the dry countryside. The young geologist struck it lucky finding evidence of copper and copper-nickel and nickel. He remembered Okiep and realised mining was possible but smelting not so due to the lack of water with the countryside receiving little in the way of rainfall. After regarding their visit to Zyangabywe as a success, Edward and James were back in the saddle for another long trek. Eventually, they encountered the part of the trip that Livingston had cursed. The Linvati Swamp and Savuti Marsh which once had been a vast inland lake but now had shrivelled into two bowls where mosquitoes and tsetse fly thrived. Livingstone's textbook revealed how great a threat those two pests were to humans and animals alike.

The marshes were teaming with life with hyena, wild dogs and zebras. This was where Quelea finches flew in their millions creating waves of flocks veering in patterns across the sky and filling one's ears with their calls that sounded like one song that grew stronger and drifted away and then rose again to a crescendo.

Their horses were overwhelmed by the wet tracks and their fine legs became inflamed. It wasn't long before Edward's beautiful chestnut gelding began to totter and drop his head in misery. Umdabuli had warned them of the dismal swamp and had pointed out that the tsetse fly in the subtropical lands made horses disease-ridden which is why the African tribes relied on Shank's pony. Only the Sotho in their mountainous kingdom of Moshweshwe are renowned horsemen with their ponies which were healthy and energetic in the cooler climate. The nagana and rinderpest diseases were rife north of the Tropic of Capricorn. In a few days, the chestnut was so ill that Edward was forced to end its misery with a shot to its head. He hid his tears and cursed the land they were traversing. He had no option but to join Koos on the wagon-kist and to journey at the steady pace of the oxen which seemed to endure all but never complained at all. James, now, would be the only pathfinder.

At last they reached the Zambezi River and followed it to the great spectacle of the waterfall where tons of water from the Zambezi ran over the hundreds of yards long edge of a canyon carved by the mighty ongoing cerulean blue and cobalt green wet flood that fell hundreds of feet to the bottom of the gorge with the sound of rumbling thunder that never stopped and disappeared in froth and ferment in the cauldron. At the edge of the waterfall water condensed on their lips, skin and hair and trees dripped incessantly. Silver droplets refracting in the mist created two rainbows and Edward rejoiced. It had all been worth the pain and heartache of reaching his destination. He would paint to his heart's content.

-o0o-

CHAPTER 24

March 1857

Kuruman

It was sunny outside in the courtyard when William carried Amber out to her chair under the wild fig tree with its convoluted grey trunk and branches heavily laden with leaves. He fetched her writing slope and he and Amber began to write at the table. William had an air of despair about him and Amber was still an invalid and convalescing. She was thin and as pale as alabaster and her legs could barely support her. Imran had told William that he was optimistic that the young woman would recover but whether there would be permanent damage to her heart only time would tell. The courtyard was quiet. The clinic was closed and there was an air of expectation and waiting seemed the only option. Mischief with his morning of standing guard at an end, came running towards them and leapt onto Amber's lap, curling up and resting his head on her arm.

With every sunrise, William hoped that day would bring all those who were missing from their expedition back to Kuruman. In his heart there was the fear that James and Edward had come to some sort of harm. The feeling of misgiving was hard to bear. He now understood the anxieties of parenthood and the necessity to encourage the child to explore his environment and to learn from its experiences and not to blame oneself if the child gets hurt in the process. Life was full of brushes with death or coming to harm. Life was uncertain.

The hours passed but William wrote sporadically, his memoirs almost completed. He was in the process of summing up his entire life in a succinct last chapter. The wit was still there but an air of defeat appeared in each paragraph. Fanny would have urged him to pull himself together and to acknowledge his part in the process of bringing wealth and commerce to the Cape with his usual unassuming humility. Singing his own praises was anathema to him. Praise in any form had been regarded as being too soft on a child. That was the generation of the past. He would never boast or make a child's head swim with feelings of superiority and self-indulgent pride but he would give 'credit where credit was due'. His protégés would support that argument. He had wanted to give them a chance in life much in the way John McMahon and Fanny had endeavoured to show him his potential and how to develop it into skills. It was up to him to learn everything there was to know about law amongst many other areas of interest. Some people called him 'wise' but he refuted that. Wisdom was a word that signified an air of self-importance where everyone hung on his every word and every phrase was plucked from his mouth and examined. He was no Aristotle or Plato.

The barking of the dogs in the street hardly registered on William and Amber's quiet deliberation towards their work but the cacophony grew louder and doves flew up into the trees and windows opened and then shut again and front doors were ajar for the occupants to see what the melee was all about. Then out of the cloud of dust, a wagon drawn by oxen appeared and William's heart lifted. They were home. James and Edward had returned and not a moment too soon. He needed their help desperately.

He walked briskly to the wagon and waved his hat at James who was on horseback. There was no sign of Edward and his heart fell. He could see a dirty bandage around James' arm. There had been trouble after all. His misgivings had been well founded.

"Welcome home, James! How good it is to see you!" His voice was hammering in his head, "Where is Edward? Has he been delayed?"

James looked at his mentor and knew he would have to break the news carefully, "We've made a bed for him in the wagon. He's very ill, Mr Ropert. We were faced with marauding animals, uninhabitable lands not fit for humans and the sickness. Edward's horse was bitten by tsetse fly and went downhill so fast that we had to shoot it. But the cesspool of the tropics also infected Edward with fevers and severe headaches." James leapt off his horse and shook William's hand and then turned to Amber as she struggled to walk towards them using two walking sticks. He caught her in an embrace as she pitched forwards, her legs too weak to walk further. She wrapped her arms around his neck and smelt his sweat which wasn't acrid but sweet, his unshaven cheek soft not rough as she had suspected. She whispered in his ear. "I missed you so very much. Life was quite dull without you"

"I missed you, too," James had lost his bravado and spoke from his heart at last.

"Oh, how wonderful you are home!" Amber wanted to clap her hands but hesitated, "But, what has happened to you both?" Her eyes were dark circles in her pale, beautiful face.

James took in her appearance with a sweep of his gaze, "I could ask you the same," He laughed weakly, "Let's get Edward washed and changed into clean clothes and put him into bed. I'll then give you and your uncle all our news." He gave her to William who picked her up and held her as she watched the events unfolding.

James stepped onto the wagon and with Koos' help he assisted his friend up out of his sickbed. William was shocked at the young man's state.

Edward lifted his head as they half carried him inside, "Amber, you must not concern yourself. This is some daft tropical disease. Nothing that Imran cannot fix." The pain inflicted by the glare of the sudden exposure to sunlight made his face screw up, showing his discomfort.

James caught the glance that travelled between William and Amber,

"There's something you aren't telling me." His voice cracked as he realised getting back wasn't going to be an end of his fears.

"Yes, yes," William said reassuringly, "There will be time once we have taken care of Edward."

Amber assessed James' condition and she could see the wound that he had bound with a strip torn from a shirt was weeping and she would need to clean the wound and insisted he should firstly bath. Both men reeked of sweat and dirty clothing. How she wished Lettie were there to give them a good scrub. She still had no strength to tackle such matters.

Sometime later Amber was sitting at Edward's bedside and slowly checked his symptoms but from her experience she believed he was suffering from the disease they called 'bad air' malaise. Imran's medicine chest had bark and leaves from the cinchona tree that grew in South America producing quinine that would alleviate his pain and stop the disease progressing any further.

"Did anyone ever tell you that you're an angel?" Edward smiled at her, no longer regarding her in a brotherly way. His flush of embarrassment was conveniently concealed by the flaming red cheeks of his fever.

Amber laughed, "You won't be saying that when you swallow this mixture. Just think of how much better you will feel in a few days!"

She coerced James to come to the clinic and she looked at his inflamed arm, "What animal is responsible for this?" She asked out of interest.

"An old lion at death's door. It was a lone male and starving. The sight of our healthy fat oxen was too much to bear for him. I shot the creature and when I tried to move the injured ox, he regained consciousness and came for me. Luckily I had my hunter's knife with me and it must have pierced his heart but not before he did this to me!" He still felt a shiver go down his spine as he recounted the moment when he stared death in the eye.

"I want to put maggots into the wound to clean it and I'll give you willow bark and laudanum for the pain and infection," Amber was efficient. Imran would be proud of me if only he were here, she praised herself silently.

In the afternoon Mrs Moffat visited and invited them to dinner. She was loyal to the Attorney General and his wards. She was longing to hear the stories of the young men's adventures. She had always had misgivings upon hearing her son in law's adventures as he insisted their Mary should travel with him to the ends of the Earth, facing dear knows what terrible dangers. It was best not to know the details of such misguided bravery.

After she left and they had all retired to the drawing room, James couldn't contain his curiosity any longer, "What has happened to Imran, Lettie and Lucky?"

"They have been taken," William found talking about that fateful day difficult and his heart contracted painfully.

"What do you mean 'taken'?" James was getting irritated by his mentor's reluctance to describe what had happened.

"They were kidnapped. Two weeks ago. We are still reeling from the shock of it all. It came out of the blue. Three hooded horsemen, we believe Boers or the renegade Griqua robbers, galloped into town one night with an extra horse and two of them rushed into the clinic where Imran was sleeping and threatened him with a pistol and bound his hands and forced him onto the back of the spare horse tying his feet to the stirrups. I was in a meeting with Dr Moffat and the men of his congregation discussing the lack of rain this summer and it was only when the interlopers shot into the air that we knew people were in danger. Little did I believe it would be Imran, Lettie and Lucky. We all rushed outside and some of the men had pistols but were reluctant to hit our small group of friends. I shouted at the leader whose face was hidden in the shadow of his hood, "You can't take them. They are free individuals. No one has the right to bodily remove them. They aren't slaves or have you not heard that slavery was abolished years ago.""

'You would swear you believe that these poor servants have souls like us. They are no better than animals. I need animals like them to push the plough, wash my floors and herd my cattle. They were here for the taking. As simple as that, old man.'

"I swore at him that I would find them and free them but the man just laughed, 'You would do that, old man. You don't know what you're dealing with here. This is not the Cape of Good Hope. We come from the Orange Free State of the Boers. What we decide, no man will dare challenge unless he is one of us.'"

William reminded his audience that the Free State was little more than a day's ride away. The Boers' first state over which they have claimed sovereignty, lying between the Vaal River and the Orange River, the latter being the boundary between them and the Cape. Their hatred of the British had grown more bitter as they revelled in their own strength and autonomy. There was even talk of the Transvaal area has been claimed by another set of Boers and that there was animosity between the two new states."

"'I'm the Attorney General of the Cape," He continued his tale. 'Think about to whom you're talking!' I shouted at him in anger."

"The Boer replied, 'Do you really think I care! You could be Queen Victoria and it would mean nothing to me. You stole from us. You forced us to leave the Cape. We've no time for people like you. Goodbye, Mr Attorney General. You'll never see these three again. I can assure you of that.'

"They had bound Lettie and Lucky too and forced them onto the horses behind two of the men. I could hear Lettie trying to scream but she was gagged and her eyes were wide open in terror. I could do nothing to save them but we all stood watching them ride out of town. The other men just shuffled around disgruntled but forming a posse to go after the kidnappers was dismissed. They had seen it all before. Servants would be taken or people in Khoikhoi or San encampments were forced to suffer such losses as though having no free will. People should not have their freedom removed from them by lawless thugs.

'Do you know those men?' I asked my companions.

'No they're not from around here." They replied.

'But, Imran is Malay and a qualified doctor. Are they going to make him plough their fields, a man of his calibre, worth more than a whole contingent of Boers? I object and I'm going to find them and bring them home.' I said and the others immediately offered to assist when I decide what to do." William was flushed with restrained rage. The memory of the raid was still emblazoned on his mind.

James stood up and turned and leant on the table, "What plans have you made so far? I take it you are waiting for something to happen before setting out to find Imran, Lettie and Lucky?"

"Hendrik came up with a smart plan. He's visiting all the farms on the border or just across in the Free State on the pretext that he's looking for work. He'll then check who the workers are before moving on if Imran and Lettie are not among them. He left on his mule immediately and we are awaiting his return."

The baked earthen floor of the hut was uncomfortable and Imran, Lettie and the little herd boy, Lucky, lay together in each other's arms. Imran waited for the child to fall asleep before talking softly to Lettie.

"We have been here fourteen days now and we must seriously think of a way of escaping. If only we could let Mr Ropert know where we are. I'm sure he would rescue us. He may already be on his way to save us. We must pray that some word of where we are, might reach him," Imran's body was in spasm and he moved to find some form of comfort.

"Your wounds need treatment, Imran. Those men are sons of the devil. Why else would they lash you with the sjambok whip? You aren't a ploughman so how can you do what they expect of you? They are working you too hard. Look at your hands. We must cover your palms with cloths. I will rip off a length of material from my petticoat" Lettie found Imran's hand and kissed his wounds gently. She raised her hand and found the outline of his face in the dark and wanted to touch his lips and to kiss him. They had been thrown together by fate and she had found herself falling in love with the gentle doctor. Imran touched her face and found tears trickling down her cheeks.

"They haven't laid a hand on you?" Imran stroked her cheek.

"They threaten me but I keep my mouth shut and work so very hard that sometimes I feel my back is breaking. When I stop for a rest they torment me about my looks. They say things like they wonder how I'd be if they took me to bed. That they would shame me. I feel so much fear and each day is pitch black like this hut although in the dark, they cannot see us, cannot reach us," Lettie felt the warmth of his body next to her.

"Tell them you can cook. It could possibly save you from such physical hardship," Imran whispered.

"And you? What can we do about your back-breaking days at the plough and preparing the land for winter crops?" Lettie felt he was caught in a trap like a rabbit, one more move could result in his death. Any rebellion would be impossible. The sjambok could flay his skin even further and one day he would not get up again. They were trying to break his spirit.

Their clothes were dirty and there was only a little water to drink or with which to wash. Their food was just mieliepap, the maize-meal porridge.

"I thank Allah that you are with me, Lettie. It's for you and the little one that I carry on and bite my tongue. I live for the hope that one day the brothers will feel Allah's anger and that He will punish them in more ways than I can." Imran's large brown eyes filled with tears and he put his arm down to act as a pillow for Lettie.

-o0o-

He had been travelling for two weeks, Hendrik thought miserably, and yet he hadn't found out where Imran and the others were being kept. He, his patient mule and Spitz, Lucky's dog, had covered fifty miles, with each journey fanning out in a radius around Kuruman. Servants and farm workers he met just shook their heads and he had no option but to leave empty handed.

The day before, a herd boy who shared some food with him mentioned that in his travels there were no worse men than the Joubert family. Under the thorn tree, with a herd of cattle grazing nearby, Hendrik stared up at the blue sky and thought how wonderful life was, if one was free, that is. The herd boy gave him instructions on how to reach the Joubert brothers' farm, of which he took a mental note and then set off on his next journey. He bobbed up and down on the dun-coloured mule with its gentle eyes uncomplaining and its ears cocked while Hendrik smoked his pipe. He was one of the fortunate ones. A free spirit with a thirst for roaming.

Two days later, he watched all the activities on the farm "Wilgestroom" and immediately recognised Imran in the field where the heatwaves made his white garment shimmer. He fell and nearly lost the reins and the plough veered off track. Hendrik heard the crack of a whip and could imagine the anger and frustration within Imran. If he were Imran he would have grabbed the end of the whip and wrestled it from its owner and given him some of his own medicine! But it wasn't he who was in trouble. If it were he would have had a few minutes of venting his rage on an evil man but then he would certainly have been killed. It was Imran who had to stay alive. Hendrik had seen it for himself. These men were notorious which was why they had to kidnap their workers.

Spitz, Lucky's mongrel dog, began to whine and sniff the air but Hendrik moved away to a thicket of mimosa trees and dismounting allowed the mule to graze and put a rope around Spitz's neck and tied him to a tree trunk. The dog could be an asset or could possibly wreck all his plans.

-o0o-

It was full moon which was an advantage on the one hand, enabling him to navigate his way to the farm and a disadvantage on the other, as he could easily be spotted skulking along the path and into the servants' quarters. The animal and insect sounds were music escaping to the heavens that night and he had tied a strip of cloth around Spitz's muzzle to prevent him from barking. Once inside the grounds Spitz led him straight to a round hut with a thatch roof. He saw the lock in the door as it shone in the moonlight and the chains were thick and unyielding. Spitz began to scratch at the door and his plaintive whine made Lucky arise out of his sleep and pull at Imran's sleeve to wake him up, "It's Spitz outside! We're going to be saved!"

"Quiet," Imran touched his lips, "Who is out there?"

"Hendrik," The old man laughed softly. He had succeeded at last and barely in time, "I'm a happy man to have found you. I've been on the road looking for you so long my bottom feels it's made of leather!"

"Can you let us out?" Lettie whispered through the gap in the doorway.

"I haven't the right equipment, my lovely young Lettie but I will now return to Kuruman and we will gather a group of men from the village and neighbouring farms and come after these louts who are holding you here against your will," Hendrik spoke softly. Spitz scratched impatiently at the door.

"Do it quickly, Hendrik. I don't know how long I can take this torture," Imran implored his friend. Things must be bad for Imran to descend to begging for help, Hendrik thought.

"Of course, my friend. We'll come for you the moment I get back. Mr Ropert wanted to come with me on my search but he would have been too conspicuous and it would have alerted the Jouberts to our presence and they would have moved you elsewhere. My friend, hold out I beg of you. Release has been slow in coming but just two more days, that's all I ask of you," Hendrik replied. Suddenly he thought he heard someone behind him and he melted into the darkness out of the moonlight with the dog which was eager to be with Lucky and had to be coaxed along.

"Two more days, Lettie. Just two more days of this hell. Help me get through this trial," Imran hugged the young woman and she put her arms around him, "Not long now, Imran," She whispered in the dank gloom.

-oOo-

The house was quiet and Edward was recovering well. James was relieved that their trip north had not ended in disaster. He hadn't joined the expedition to experience the passing away of a friend. He remained very self-contained and was outwardly completely relaxed in the others' company. After Amber's emotional outburst and his own response, neither party knew how to move their relationship onto another footing.

William was waiting for Hendrik to return and often leaned on the gate of the picket fence and stared down the road, hoping to see the elderly man sitting on his mule with his legs stuck out at an angle which was so endearing. He ruminated on the outcome of their expedition and was loath to define it as being an unmitigated disaster. Amber was recovering slowly but the pains in her joints might never go away and what would happen to her if she should become pregnant and had to face childbirth. Would she survive such a rigorous test?

At last William saw the familiar figure of Hendrik ambling down the street on the mule towards him. William threw his hat in the air and shouted to the others the news for which they had all been waiting.

Hendrik grinned as he saw the gathering at the gates of the clinic and he whistled in reply to the shouts that welcomed him home. He would play his mouth organ and then they would have a real party. Spitz, Lucky's dog, wagged its tail and allowed James to pat him and make so much fuss that it embarrassed the canine member of their rag tag community.

When Hendrik gave them the good news that Imran, Lettie and Lucky were alive, everyone cheered again and he was bundled into the kitchen and given a hot meal and a dram of whiskey. "You should have seen us, Spitz and me in the enemy camp and when Spitz began to whine I knew we were on the right track..." His storytelling had them all hanging on his every word.

"I promised them we would come for them in two days and now a day has passed which means we must leave tomorrow to launch an attack on the Jouberts and rescue them," Hendrik was most insistent that they should work out a plan of action and to get as many men in the small town to join them to form a hunting party and it wouldn't be animals that they'd be after but the vermin Jouberts.

William had made some staunch new friends in Kuruman and they all were men of God and would never let a neighbour suffer on his own and now when a solution to the problem meant going shoulder to shoulder for the sake of others, they soon rallied round. Dr Livingstone's house was bustling with fathers of the village and eventually everyone dispersed to enjoy a good night's sleep before setting out at daybreak.

William and James were up and dressed before the first cockerel had crowed and they packed food, water and Imran's medicine bag in case anyone was injured. The horses were saddled and guns checked with metallic clicks reverberating in the courtyard. One by one their numbers increased until fifteen men were all set and ready to leave. Amber held Spitz as the poor animal would never keep up with the posse. As the village fell silent, another rider on a golden palomino with its white mane and tail streaming in the air, galloped down the road in their wake.

Amber returned to the house and found Edward in the kitchen and although weak and shaking, he looked well on the road to recovery. He saw Amber's concerned frown and fixed gaze and knew she was thinking of her uncle and James. It seemed the bet he had with James had been settled and he was not the one fortunate enough to have won her heart even though he, Edward, had lost his to her. Hendrik sat bleary-eyed near the hearth as he had celebrated his return too well. Fortunately he had been lucid enough in the morning to give William his sketched map for getting to *Wilgestroom*. His memory was still sharp for his age, he thought to himself.

-o0o-

It was mid-afternoon when the contingent of men flew across the savannah plain on their horses. The animals nostrils were flared, their muzzles foam-flecked and their ears flattened against their heads. William was filled with a sense of foreboding. The operation should be a simple one: retrieve a couple of human beings from the enemy. He wanted the day to go according to plan. By their sheer number, his men would intimidate the Jouberts into handing over Imran, Lettie and little Lucky. But, if the Jouberts were as nasty as their reputation they could initiate a full scale shoot out.

Imran was in the sandy field using the oxen to pull the plough that cut a deep wound into the ground. Underneath the earth was dark and sweet and would produce well. He heard the pounding of horses' hooves and noticed that his tormentor had left him alone while he went indoors to arm himself. He rallied his brothers and they left the rundown farmhouse and one of them held Lettie close to him with his arm around her neck. They would not just hand over their captives. That wasn't the way things were done at *Wilgestroom*. Imran unyoked the oxen and went in search of Lucky who was in a field where the cattle were grazing. He had to do something to get the eldest Joubert to let go of Lettie.

Imran and Lucky were about to disappear when they heard a horse in hot pursuit of them and the youngest Joubert, Karel, nearly mowed them down. With his musket trained on Imran's head he barked his order, "Get back to the farmhouse. No one is going to escape today. Graves may be filled instead but you are going nowhere!"

They all filed into the farmhouse which had stained brown wallpaper and bare wooden floorboards and with their two bull mastiff dogs, the brothers bolted the doors and waited. It wasn't long before the fifteen riders galloped into the dirty courtyard of the farm. The whole place was deadly silent and at the house the curtains were closed but William noticed a drape move slightly and he saw the muzzle of a shotgun trained on him. "All of you dismount or you'll have your heads blasted off. Find cover and work your way into the farmhouse. I have gunpowder in a small keg which we can set in place at the back door and detonate it." William and Christopher, a new friend, dodged the bullets that traced their path with singing thuds while James aimed at the windows. Glass shards fell tinkling down onto the veranda and he knocked out the glass and pushed himself through the window. No one was there. The men must be in another room, he let out a sigh of relief. His gun was hot in his hands and he crossed the drawing room and the floorboards creaked. He burst through the doorway just as William detonated the dynamite. He could hear men's voices raised in the kitchen and flinging the door open he saw the three Jouberts lying on the floor and in amongst them Imran lay unconscious with a weal across his forehead where he had been struck by the butt of a gun. Lettie squirmed from underneath one of the brothers and little Lucky opened the broom cupboard where he had been hiding. The two vicious dogs were stunned but they leapt forward towards him and with two quick shots, James had eliminated them from the attack. The other men of the posse dragged the barely conscious Jouberts out into the courtyard. It had been a pity that they were still alive. Now they would have to be taken back to Kuruman and placed in jail and would have to face a judge.

James led his horse to a trough of water as everyone prepared for their return journey home. The Jouberts' wagon and draught horse were prepared for transporting the Jouberts, Lucky and Lettie. Imran would take control of the cart. He had regained consciousness and tended to the wounds they had all sustained. Fortunately, their wounds were mainly superficial. His own head was painful and he hoped there was no haemorrhaging between the linings of the brain. His sight was disturbed but he was sure it would settle down.

Inside the barn in the dusty shadows where reins and bridles hung and old plough discs and plough lay dormant like Death in the Apocalypse, a golden horse moved forwards with its rider and James looked up in utter amazement. It couldn't be him, surely not but his eyes weren't deceiving him.

"Yes, it is I, you insidious little runt. What have you done with Stan? He wrote me that he had found you and sent over a small handful of diamonds. There isn't a better brother in the whole world and he has disappeared off the face of the earth. He told me he would avenge the theft of my gold and obtain reparation for Francesca's failing health. For the final time, where is he?" John Baxter had travelled across the Atlantic for this very moment.

"I have no idea, Mr Baxter. We met at the coast and he came to get what I owed you. He took what he had come for and rode away, leaving me with a gunshot hole in my shoulder. I believe he left me there to die." James' eyes filled with tears of anxiety and he blinked them away. He had always regretted his foolhardy act then and most certainly now. How he had ever imagined he would get away with no repercussions.

"I tell you what, son," John Baxter burst out laughing at the thought he had once called him "son", "You owe me much more. The life of my brother, the sickness that has befallen Francesca,"

"I'll give you all I have," James tossed the pouch he had been safeguarding towards John and the older man caught it neatly in one hand, "Ah, gold, I see. You appear to expect me to grant you clemency by paying for your freedom, for your life with this. It isn't going to happen, son. Now how about you get out of here as fast as your horse can carry you and don't look back."

"I'll go nowhere. There's only one way we're going to sort out our differences and that is with our guns," James leapt forward and pulled the trigger of his pistol. But, the older man was quicker and his bullet hit the young man's chest and James fell, bleeding profusely.

William and the other men had heard the shots and rushed to the barn. John Baxter's palomino reared up and brushed past them, "He never was your bright, clever protégé, Mr Ropert. He was a very silly boy with a strong sense of moral ineptitude which you should have discovered a long time ago. Don't follow me! I'm returning to America immediately, my purpose for being here is now completed. I am sure you will understand that I don't care that much if he lives or dies," John pulled the reins and kicked his heel into the sides of the magnificent horse and they galloped down the sand road leaving a cloud of red dust in their track.

Imran and William ran to the crumpled form of James. He was conscious and looked up at William with pain etched on his face and a plea for forgiveness in his screwed up blue eyes. William thought perhaps inappropriately what a handsome lad he was.

"Forgive me, Mr Ropert," his voice was a thin tremor and blood began to froth in his mouth.

Imran looked at William and shook his head. He held James' hand and in seconds it was all over. The young adventurer and ladies' man had passed away. William felt a deep sadness overwhelm him and although never having had any children, he knew it was the sadness that any parent feels upon losing a child.

-o0o-

The house was silent and Amber tiptoed into Edward's room only to find he wasn't there, not asleep as she had thought. She found him on the veranda where long shadows now streaked over the pot plants and the red earth floor. He was peering through William's telescope at the road that disappeared like a ribbon over the horizon. He couldn't wait to hear about the outcome of the rescue operations,

"I regret not being out there with your uncle and James. It's just that I don't think I would've managed the journey on horseback. I can imagine the scene with such a large group of men – Boers and Englishmen - riding into the Jouberts' farm. The excitement must have been overwhelming. Perhaps there was a shootout and men injured or even killed." Edward smarted from the consequences of the fever that had left him feeling ineffectual as a man.

Amber sensed his loss of confidence when she stood next to him and put an arm around him in companionship, "They'll return victors with their spoils of war and their captives bound and humiliated." She sounded like her uncle and Edward grinned.

As they watched waiting for night to descend, a dust cloud puffed up behind travellers approaching them. The sinking orange sun was growing larger and then fell behind the horizon. The men came in one by one on horses that were near exhaustion. They were silent but doffed their hats to Amber and Edward.

At last, William appeared leading the giant draught horse that pulled the wagon that had James' horse in tow. She saw Imran on the wagon cracking the whip over the large horse's head to manoeuvre the vehicle into the courtyard. He was wearing a dirty *thobe*. He had obviously not been able to wash his robes, she thought as she hobbled towards him as he dismounted.

Amber pitched forward losing her walking sticks and he caught her as she threw her arms around him with joy, "Oh, Imran, I'm so happy to see you!"

Not accustomed to displays of emotion, Imran patted Amber's back and smiled showing a flash of his teeth in the last of the evening light, "And I am relieved to be here. The past fortnight has been hell on earth. Allah has now heard my prayers and my captors are in turn captured and they will pay for their crimes. An eye for an eye…"

"And Lettie and Lucky are in the wagon?" Amber peered at the small group of travellers arriving last.

"Yes, but I have to give you bad news, Amber. It's James…" Imran's tone was deadly serious and she turned to him with her questions flying off her lips

"He's been hurt? That's why you have had his horse in tow? How bad are his injuries?" The dreadful thoughts of James' condition filled her with fear.

As the wagon entered the courtyard, William's horse tiptoed into the flare of the torches that had been lit every evening since the posse had left the town. William's face revealed his despair and pain, "Amber, you must prepare yourself…"

But, Amber had staggered to the wagon and she saw the three notorious Boers tied up with rope, Lettie and Lucky and to the back in the darkness lay a body covered from head to toe with a blanket. He was dead. Her James had been killed, murdered. She began shouting, "You scoundrels! What have you done to him? I could kill you all. If I were a man I would shoot you in cold blood as you have done to him!" Her swearing was forgiven given the circumstances.

"You mustn't see him like this," Imran took her in his arms, "Let me prepare him for you. Lettie and Lucky have been through so very much. Please attend to them. We must make sure that these men are under lock and key and then we will be back in no time at all."

Later, after Lettie and Lucky had had their baths and had dressed in clean clothes with a good meal inside them, William called Amber to see James' body where it lay on the dining room table. He looked surprisingly peaceful and there were no obvious signs of injury as Imran had dressed him in his best clothes. If James had been a Muslim and a good man he would have prayed for him. Instead his lips barely moved as he thought of the words he would've used "May Allah hold you in his palm and raise you up to his golden palace and forgive you any wrongs you have committed during your earthly life." Imran stood to one side as the young woman swayed on her feet about to faint. Imran gathered her up and allowed her to look at James.

"Oh, Imran, Uncle William, make the pain go away. Why is there so much pain in our lives?" She cried with her voice betraying her misery. She couldn't be brave, not now and perhaps never again.

Their adventures had tried the young explorers in many ways and most were such that they strengthened character and forged courage and self-confidence, or so he had thought at the beginning of their expedition. Now William found he had two invalids recuperating and three other charges freed from enslavement but worst of all, he had lost the life of one of them. Africa was a dangerous place and he had sailed forth with such high hopes and enthusiasm. Perhaps he was being punished for his sincere if foolhardy optimism. It was time to go home.

"Now that we are all gathered here together, I want to impress on you all how I have admired each one of you during the past long months out in the wilderness. I believe with time you will look back at these experiences with fond affection and you will remember James in your thoughts and you may wonder why such a young life was cut short. But, it is now time to return to Cape Town."

There was a silence as they gathered their thoughts and there was no jubilation but rather a sadness that their time of exploration of the country and of their own inner worlds was over.

Imran stood up and motioned to Lettie to join him, "Mr Ropert, as we agreed at the start of the expedition, I will obviously not be returning to the Cape but will carry on the practice here where I can help poor sick people who will trust my skills and medicines. But, what you do not know is that I have asked Lettie to stay behind to look after running the clinic with me. We have grown very close over the past months and our experiences since the kidnapping have consolidated those feelings. To have someone with me who understands me and my goals matters so much to me.!"

"Of course, I will arrange for Fatima to visit you, Lettie." William's optimism was resurfacing and the atmosphere in the parlour was no longer smothered by death. Lettie laughed like a golden chiming clock. If all went well, perhaps her mother would bring an imam with her. Time would tell if there would be a wedding.

They were going home, Amber smiled and clapped her hands. Edward looked ever so much like a young dandy as he poured them all a flute of champagne that had travelled with them all those hundreds of miles.

"Let me propose a toast to a safe journey for us, good health for Amber and a time of dedication and duty for Imran and Lettie." He was serious for a moment and then joined in the laughter.

Outside Spitz, Lucky's dog, had found his master and the two of them were asleep next to Hendrik and Koos in their karosses under the stars. The little meerkat was curled up and asleep on Amber's bed.

-o0o-

CHAPTER 25

Autumn 1858

Cape Town

It was a gunmetal grey day with gold, yellow and russet leaves falling from the trees and the stone buildings and the churches' spires almost touched the low cloud.

William reflected how Sunday morning at St George's Church had been an uplifting experience. He enjoyed singing and was lucky to have what his friends described as a 'melodious voice', 'a tenor of some distinction and pleasant to listen to' as they sang the hymns. Hugh didn't sing out but mumbled a semblance of a tune.

Suddenly after the hymn of *O God our Help in Ages Past*, Hugh began coughing to the extent that William hurried him out of the church leaving the congregation wondering what was wrong.

Nerina had returned to St George's after Pierre, the religious instructor of her school, had escaped from a conventional life to win souls in central Africa after she had turned down his proposal of marriage. She had missed the English style of worship. Now she grasped her skirts and made her way past the men and women in her pew and followed the two men. William was helping Hugh into the waiting phaeton carriage when she emerged into the sunlight, "Can I help, William?" Nerina gasped as she ran up to them, "I have some experience of looking after ill people."

The helplessness on William's face eased as he looked at Nerina. This was the first sign of their close affection for more than twenty years. It had taken Hugh's illness to rouse both of them into regarding each other as friends. She wanted him to use her as a friend for both their sakes.

After hesitating, William gave in, "Come with us. We must help him breathe," William knew Hugh's illness was progressing. He had seen the congestion and blood on Hugh's handkerchiefs. They had consulted doctors but all had shaken their heads in the knowledge that there was nothing they could do about the lung disease that was destroying Hugh.

When they arrived at *Wolmunster*, the coachman helped William support Hugh into the house and Nerina followed gracefully yet purposefully. She had a still air about her which instilled in people confidence and an intimacy of shared kindness. Amber rushed to assist and welcomed her former headmistress.

William undressed Hugh and put him into a nightshirt while Nerina examined the kitchen cupboards for camomile, honey and lemon to make a hot soothing drink for her patient. She took a basin to his room and poured boiling water into it and sat Hugh up to inhale the menthol vapour with a towel enclosing the steam around his head.

"I don't need any help from a woman," Hugh growled between spasms. Concerned for Hugh and fearing his death, Amber sat on the floor leant on William and put her head on his lap.

"Don't be a cad, Hugh. We need a woman's common-sense right now. I don't exactly have the skill of nursing the sick whereas Nerina does." William was alarmed and wondered, was this to be the beginning of the end? He knew his friend was extremely ill. He felt his heart contract with the pain of watching such suffering especially if there would be no recovery, just more agony and even worse.

Eventually, the coughing eased and Hugh slumped down into an exhausted sleep. William prepared himself for a long vigil and Nerina, having given William clear instructions, took her leave from them and the coachman and his team of horses drove her back to Cape Town. She said she would return in the morning. She couldn't very well stay the night, people would talk. Tomorrow, Fatima and Amber would assist her in looking after Hugh. She was aware that Hugh had only days left to live. He was dying and knew it. She would make him as comfortable as possible and prepare William for his friend's imminent death. She was deeply concerned as the two men had been like brothers virtually all their lives. What would William do without his best friend?

William wiped Hugh's brow with a cool cloth which he rinsed in an enamel basin, the water dripping into the bowl as he wrung the facecloth out, and as Hugh's eyelids fluttered he saw how Hugh had aged. His black curly hair had thinned and his flashing brown eyes were now sunken in the folds of his face. His eyebrows had thickened and his mouth was no longer a tight serious line. His lips had slackened like the muscles under his skin on his cheeks and jawline. William felt a sense of regret that age had crept upon them without warning and now this illness was going to take Hugh away from him. He couldn't imagine life without him.

William had been aware of Fatima's hands making the bed and pulling up clean white sheets. Pillowcases were changed and Hugh's head would sink into them and he would attempt a smile. Nerina's hands would hold spoonfuls of soup or porridge up to his lips. The women's hands fluttered and administered while William sat in the dark holding Hugh's hand. He succeeded in shaving the sick man and the intimacy of the act brought tears to his eyes. He was attentive and loving although endearments were never uttered.

Hugh suddenly struggled to sit up, "Could you call Reverend John, now! I would like to take my last communion. I need my God right now. Help me, William," Hugh knew he was slipping away from them and his hands pulled on William's shirt. His voice was rasping and breathing took all his strength even to utter those few words. Amber's hands flew to her face and she rushed out of the room.

The Reverend John McKay arrived in the dead of night and he was shown through to the bedroom, shadows creeping along the dimly lit hall. The women left the priest and William alone with Hugh. The simple ceremony of taking bread and wine was followed by the taking away of sin and preparation for life hereafter was administered.

Hugh sat up and held his arms up for an embrace from William, "I have loved you wholly and deeply all my life and I dedicated my life to you. You have provided me with the pure love of friendship and yet all the time I wanted a profane love and for that I now ask forgiveness. I've wanted to show you love and more love," He sank back into the pillows, his confession at an end. Reverend John excused himself and left the two men alone.

"Oh my God, Hugh – you loved me as a lover and never told me? We have hugged and thrown our arms around each other more times than I can remember. How hard that must have been. Surely you should have walked away from me when you knew I couldn't love you in that way."

"It's a sin to love in that way, my beloved William. You were the most generous and affectionate friend. To lose you meant death of all that I am; that is why I stayed. To watch, to join in, to suffer, to enjoy, to love life with you meant everything to me. To love you and just to be with you was all that mattered to me." He fell into a coughing fit and each breath was a hoarse gasp.

"I'm fading fast." He whispered and held out a hand for William to clasp and at last Hugh slowly fell asleep. It was to be a coma and not sleep and his breathing changed into a horrible, rhythmic death rattle. Each breath was the body holding on to life. The spirit was departing but nature clung on and the horror intensified as William waited for the next gasp, and the next and the next.

Suddenly, it was over. Hugh had breathed his last and his body was at peace. All pain washed away, the person he was, the love he gave all ebbed away and gradually his body grew cold. William sat with him till morning and then he washed Hugh's body with the gentleness of a lover. He shaved his sunken cheeks and combed his hair and laid him out for the coroner. The body was no longer Hugh although it had his features. William knelt beside the bed and grief overwhelmed him.

The next morning Amber found William still kneeling beside his friend and she gently eased him up onto the chair. She found a blanket and wrapped it around him and let him sleep. Tearfully she closed the door and left them alone together.

-oOo-

1858

Cape Town

Hugh's funeral took place in St George's Church and a small number of close friends and colleagues attended. Nerina was dressed in black with a lace veil and behind it her face was pale and her eyes expressive although what emotion was there was only known to her. Her demeanour was quiet and from time to time she bit her lip.

William was now free but would he realise he had been kept a prisoner for so long, she wondered. Her heart still pounded in her breast when she stood beside him. She would look up at him and had to keep her adoration to herself for the sake of decorum. She caught Amber glancing at her from time to time and realised the young woman knew her secret and that she was her ally.

William read his eulogy with his love for Hugh plain for all to see. He wasn't one for fluffing his lines but now he battled with his emotions, stuttering and pausing as he tried to get a grip on himself. "Our friendship meant everything to Hugh and to me. Hugh offered brotherhood and companionship over all the years.

"I knew him through our deepest conflicts and in our warmest affections. We travelled the seas to this new country and helped each other define our roles in this society.

"After a busy day we entertained each other with our stories of life's idiosyncrasies. He was an astute listener and taught me many things about myself that I had not understood. It wasn't always good news to me but he helped shape me into the man that stands before you now. I would only be half a man without Hugh's influence and patience with me. You would all consider me rather proud but I hasten to add, there is a trembling being beneath the surface and Hugh was always able to placate the fear in me. Only he saw the truth of who I am.

"I wish to send him this valediction. God speed, my dearest friend, you are surely the kindest man and the best of friends either in Heaven or here on Earth. May you now shine brightly in Heaven. My life and soul are now in darkness."

William found words were not enough to convey his deepest emotions, "Thank you for your life-long friendship, Hugh. Goodbye, my dear friend," William left the lectern and walked slowly back to his pew. His head was bowed and his eyes downcast, his shoulders raised and his hands were balled into fists, such was the tight rein he kept on his emotions.

Nerina read all the signs and her heart went out to him. His grief would know no measure and she would never know that the confessions of a dying man now weighed heavily on William's shoulders. He had taken his cue and bestowed on Hugh the highest praise but even that did not come near filling the deepest cavern of his soul that Hugh had vacated. He was inconsolable.

The wake was held at *Wolmunster* and people who knew Hugh from commerce and trading circles attended. Everyone was sombre and William tried to lighten the mood by giving an account of Hugh's life and his anecdotes about his friend's career and the adventures he and

Hugh had pursued, reminded his guests of the deep bond between the two men.

The tone of the party improved with William's skill as a raconteur and a measure of jollity made the wake a very Irish affair. Nerina was there, too, and William took her gloved hand in his and lifted it to his lips. His eyes bored into hers, "Thank you, Nerina, for all you did for him at the end," His gratitude was heartfelt.

"I know he had little time for me but I think I understood your relationship with each other. He didn't want to share you with anyone else. If it hadn't been me, it would have been another woman and he wouldn't have approved of her either. I'm pleased I could help you, William. At such times, a woman does have her uses." Her eyes hadn't left his and the moment was timeless. In that infinite moment of time, they were united in love and respect for each other.

They both spoke at once but Nerina gave William his cue, "I would like us to begin again, Nerina," William didn't want her to feel he was speaking in haste so added, "I've watched you from afar and have never stopped loving you. Ending our relationship was one of the greatest mistakes of my life."

"Don't you know that I've done the same? I've followed your career and have applauded so much all that you've done for people at the Cape. You are the man I most respect in the world. If you had married me back then, neither of us would have advanced as far as we have done. I've my school and you've been offered the office of chief justice and your name has been mentioned for having a knighthood bestowed on you."

"I've declined both honours, Nerina. I'm not in the business of looking for accolades." William had never let anyone so close to him besides Hugh. He felt it strange to rediscover Nerina in the twilight of his years, at a time he was most in need of comfort and love.

"No, I'm aware of that and it's what has impressed me most about you. You cling to being a gentle man with the greatest humility especially for someone who has achieved so much," Nerina said smiling and her former beauty flitted across her face, now lined with life's etchings, reminding him of the young Nerina. This woman with her agile and creative mind and dedication need never be beholden to him but rather it was an honour to be in her company and to court her at this late stage of their lives. It would take the right time for him to consider asking her to marry him. It was a thought for the future. He wanted her to be in no doubt of his affection and he would wait for the appropriate time.

Nerina remembered their earlier relationship that had filled her with weeping smiles and laughing tears. Now their relationship could fill each other with loving laughter and gentle smiling love. Warm companionship during their mature years would ease their journey towards the end of their lives.

She looked at his hands as he gesticulated while speaking to his guests. She couldn't take her eyes off his dear face that was remarkably youthful despite his age. His lips were quick to smile and never twisted in bitterness or dislike. His mind was full of ideas and his conversation spirited and people continued to be drawn towards him just as when he was young. There was hope for the future, for their future together. It was written. It was part of their destinies.

-o0o-

CHAPTER 26

November 1860

Cape Town

Spring in the Cape was a gentle explosion of blossoms, young green shoots and leaves and bulbs of tulips imported from Holland, ranunculi, anemones and lilies were splashes of bright colours in the Botanical Gardens. William and Nerina took a walk down the long avenue. She was dressed in an elegant ensemble of lace and pink and white seersucker and she held her parasol aloft. They made a striking picture. The gentleman and the elegant woman were often seen walking along together.

"I have some news for you, Nerina," William dared to speak his mind, "I want to return to Ireland. With Hugh gone now two years and with Amber harking back to her childhood in Dublin, I've suddenly realised that my only remaining family are there and I haven't seen them for nearly twenty one years. Many have already died. I'm also feeling my age and a break from the court circuit and government affairs would do me good. Now, my dear Nerina, you don't expect me to leave you behind which means I must make an honest woman of you." He smiled and patted her hand tucked into the crook of his arm.

"I gather that is your way of asking me to marry you, is it?!" Nerina smiled and held onto his arm more tightly, "This is where I swoon and you need to hold smelling salts to my nose! Of course, I will marry you, my dearest William. I've waited a lifetime to get this far. Well, I'm very excited at the prospect of visiting England and Ireland. To venture away from these shores, has long been a fervent wish of mine. When do you intend to put all these plans into action?" Nerina thought of the thousand and one things she would need to do. She would need to find a headmistress for her school, for one. "How long would we be away?" She asked excitedly.

"A year to begin with and if we find it to our liking, we could stay permanently. I long for Ireland despite the fact that I love this beautiful Cape. I always regarded this as my home but just lately I have had a hunger for County Antrim and Dublin's bustling streets. There are many old friends I would like to look up. Many of them are responsible for my being here. I guess many of them have departed this life."

"I have heard that you have again been offered a knighthood for your service to the Crown" said Nerina. Nothing was kept private in the town. Tongues did wag at a sniff of a story to gossip over.

"I'm amazed how these facts about my business get bandied around!" William retorted irritably. "Yes, it was offered to me but I turned it down. I would hate to lord it over others that I'm some "Sir" something or other. You may as well know that I have accepted a lesser title of Companion of the Order of St Michael and St George. I'm not altogether modest." He smiled at her fondly.

Nerina was delighted to see his generosity of spirit had not gone unnoticed but she understood how he would be embarrassed that it had become publicised. She had always admired his humanitarian spirit. He had belonged to the Humane Society and the Agricultural Society and he had been responsible for the widows of the soldiers from the Cape who fought in the Crimean War receiving pensions from the government. He had also arranged for a relief fund for the Great Famine in Ireland. Another fund paid for the new university to be built in Cape Town and it was also his brainchild. He paid £500 a year towards it and became its Chancellor.

If anyone was in need, William would step in and solve his or her problems. For instance, he helped the widow of a dear friend return to England. He treated her with the same kindness as he would have shown his own wife. He had also supported his stepmother and brought his brother Francis to the Cape. He gave him £2000 to help him set up a business exporting sugar. No one knew how very wealthy William had become. Hugh had left him all his worldly goods which were substantial and Hugh had named in his bequest, William "to whom I owe it that I possess anything to bequeath".

In the months that followed the expedition Amber was courted by Edward and they were as close as brother and sister with all their shared experiences making their relationship deep and rewarding. Edward nevertheless still had the compulsion to travel wherever his interest in botany led him and he spent months in England presenting papers he had written on his discoveries to other botanists. His paintings became well known and much sought after and he would hold an exhibition once a year. When he proposed, Amber was at first elated and then, having a sound head on her shoulders, she declined as she felt they would for most of the time be leading separate lives.

After they had been back in Cape Town for a few months, Amber discussed her future with Nerina and explained that the fire inside that drove her nearly to her death was finally quenched and she now wished to become a teacher. "I feel I have so much to offer young girls. Perhaps I can instil an independence and thoughtfulness that will help them during their married lives."

"Don't you want to marry?" Nerina asked remembering the passionate young woman who had sought her advice about relationships with men.

"I'll come to that bridge when the right man comes into my life. I'm sure I'll recognise him immediately. I know it will be love at first sight. I loved James and love Edward but I now know it is the love between siblings. They were the brothers I never had," Amber admitted with an adult wisdom.

She was older than her peers in experience not years and Nerina agreed, "I'm relieved you don't want to become a missionary. I want you to lead a rich and rewarding life in a safe environment. In a hundred years we may find that women will be allowed into the hallowed halls of universities and win the right to become doctors. Sadly, you were born ahead of your time," Nerina breathed a sigh of relief. She couldn't tell the young woman that travel would be too demanding on her health.

-o0o-

The marriage ceremony was a modest affair in St George's. Only close friends attended and Amber, now twenty, was her only bridesmaid. Nerina wore a silver-pearl satin gown with a necklace of freshwater silver-coloured pearls and attached to her waist a satin train that glided behind her as she joined William at the altar. Her hat had the elegance of understatement. He wore his Captain's uniform and looked distinguished and proud of the woman he loved. Nerina cried during the exchanging of vows. For many years she had never in her wildest dreams imagined this could happen to her. Soon they had all departed for *Wolmunster* to celebrate a Wedding Breakfast there.

The wedding reception was in full swing when Fatima indicated to William that she needed him. He was flushed with the good food and wine and wiped his lips before leaving the table. "Isn't this a happy occasion! What is it, Fatima?"

"There is someone here to see you, Master William", her eyes were big with anticipation. William followed her into the drawing room and saw a young man standing with his back to him and as he turned around, William gasped. It was like looking at himself in his late teens or early twenties. His visitor had light blue eyes, blond hair and a fair complexion. His lips and his hands with their long artistic fingers were the same as his own.

The visitor held out his hand, "I'm Willem Van Niekerk. My mother, Marika, sent me to visit you. She said you would know who I am and would help me. I'm looking for suitable work and perhaps a career.

Unlike my brothers I'm not interested in farming." His smile was charming and William tried to regain his composure. It was surely not possible but the proof was in the face of his visitor.

"Yes, of course. Your mother warned me a long time ago to expect you," William's words tripped off his tongue hiding his surprise, "Welcome to Cape Town. You must join our wedding party. What an opportune moment to arrive. You can enjoy this special occasion with us. But, first your news. How is your mother?"

William's thoughts were racing and a happiness he had never experienced before engulfed him like a warm wave of accomplishment, the ultimate pinnacle of his life. He had a son! The youngster must never know as it could bring dishonour to his mother, Marika. He would have to find some way of telling Nerina, one day...

"My mother is well and carries on against all odds. My brothers and sisters are in good health."

"You speak English very fluently," William looked at him, studying him and seeing his potential. He seemed intelligent and brave.

"My mother was a good teacher," Willem replied earnestly, wanting to please.

"Let me introduce you to my wife and my friends," William led him into the dining room. He wanted to tell his closest and dearest but this joy he had to keep to himself. Life had never prepared him for this miracle....

"Everyone, meet my new protégé, Willem van Niekerk", William said proudly. Amber stared at the young man and saw something familiar in his face as though she had known him all her life. She hadn't grasped the fact that he looked like William. Even if she had she was allowed to think of him in a romantic way as she was no blood relative of William. She beckoned him to sit next to her and when their hands touched, she felt a bolt of lightning had passed from him to her. She was in awe of his good looks.

Later, that night in bed, Nerina curled up next to William, "You never told me you had a new protégé. You must tell me all about him. Will he remain here in Cape Town while we are away or will he accompany us to Ireland?"

"I would like him to come with us to Ireland. It would give me no greater pleasure than if I can arrange for him to be educated at university there or in England. I can tell he has the makings of a scholar and then maybe a lawyer, priest or doctor. You don't mind any of this, my darling Nerina?" He looked down at her face below his as she rested her head on his chest.

"Of course not, he will be like a son," She smiled gently. She had not escaped noticing the same good looks she had fallen in love with all those years ago. Like father, like son. She wasn't upset or jealous. It was all just meant to be. One day William would talk about the boy's mother. She had William now and that was all that mattered...

-o0o-

The sun was just rising and William left the bed he had shared with Nerina, on the first night of their wedding nuptials. She turned over in her sleep and he saw that she looked relaxed and at peace. He walked through the house that still bore the signs of the celebration. Proteas in large copper vases looked like a strange natural phenomenon of bird within a flower.

He sat down at his desk and began to write:

"My dear Marika,

I am bereft of words that would help me describe my joy of knowing I have a son and my gratitude that you have given me the ultimate gift a woman can give a man is heartfelt beyond description. I am most impressed with the signs of your nurturing care in Willem's development from infancy to adulthood. I see myself in him but his personality is more like yours. He radiates energy and interest and my guests yesterday were soon enjoying his company including my ward, Amber who is of the same age. I will help Willem to reach goals in whatever direction he wishes to take. I am intending to return to Ireland imminently and will ask Willem if he would like to accompany me. He would learn much by travelling through Europe and returning to enter university in Dublin. It would be my pleasure to show him the world and his place therein.

Marika, I do not want to take him away from you and I will insist that he returns to begin his career and I will set him up as well as I possibly can. He will be free to visit and be with you as anything else I'm sure would bring abject misery to your spirit. Well done, my Boer friend and thank you for the love we shared in those fleeting moments that we knew one another. I fervently ask God to watch over you and also to give me the inspiration to know how best I can direct Willem.

With my fond affection,

William"

A few weeks after their wedding and the arrival of Willem, they were all packing to get ready for their trip to the mother country. William was excited and sorted out his worldly goods, what to take and what to leave behind. Nerina and Amber fussed over their clothes and had winter gowns made to cope with the grey English and Irish weather. The sheer delight of seeing places they had only read of in literature and history books now filled them with anticipation. Willem, too, had appropriate clothing made and he had written to his mother and told her what had transpired since meeting William. For the young man, nothing could now surprise him and he took the change in his fortunes in his stride, learning as he went. He had not told his mother about

Amber. That should still be their secret. The hours spent in each other's company were precious and their love was like a breath from God above.

The day of their departure dawned and Cape Town lay quiet in the awakening hours and no one was about. Their carriage and wagon clattered through the streets and the horses hooves rang out in the silence. The air was fresh and salty. The "*Camperdown*" a Union Line steamship that had also the benefit of sails lay in the harbour. It was able to take a hundred passengers and of course all the mail.

After settling into their cabins, William took Nerina up to the top deck and they admired the views of Cape Town. He told her about his outward-bound sea journey to Cape Town and how excited he and Hugh had been. "Looking back over the last twenty four years makes me reflect on how young perhaps not in years but rather in experience we both were. That seems a lifetime ago. I had always intended to return to Ireland after a few years but those turned into decades. How young Cape Town was then. It was just a small town without a proper harbour and it had dirt roads. It has grown into a beautiful city with macadamised streets, gas street lighting and many new buildings for the Government and commerce."

"Your interest in the development of the city can now be seen everywhere, William. You are one of the fathers of Cape Town. Do you know they talk of you as being its 'greatest citizen and only orator'? Nerina was so proud of him and she held onto his arm tightly as they stood at the ship's rail. Down below some friends had gathered to see them off. The small crowd of well-wishers waved to them and amid cheers and smiles sent them on their way. Amber and Willem waved back excitedly and he drew her to him and she felt the warmth of his hand on her side. William and Nerina waved, too, and looked deep into each other's eyes. They were leaving so much behind them but they would have their memories to keep them warm on a cold Irish night in front of the fire!

The *Camperdown* sailed out of the harbour and Amber and Willem joined them at the ship's rail. Amber was now an exquisite, fine porcelain, enchanting woman, and Willem, a dapper, courageous young man and they had all their lives ahead of them. However, in the back of her mind the knowledge of having a weak heart always haunted Amber.

For William life was now complete. He would spend his old age in comfort and with the people he loved most in the whole world…

-o0o-

EPILOGUE

Autumn – 1860

It was the first evening on board ship and William, Nerina, Amber and Willem were invited to sit at the Captain's table for dinner. The dining room was elegant and lamp-light brightened everyone's spirits. There had been many farewells at the quayside and William had seen the ties to his friends on land break leaving them to gradually fade out of sight. He felt he had perhaps been rash to leave the Cape that he so loved but time would tell. Their Captain was a jolly Hampshire-bred former navy-man and he entertained his guests with his anecdotes about what things were like when he was a mere twelve year old on his first voyage.

The second course was being served when the ship hit the Cape Rollers, the mountainous swells with the brisk south-easterly gale sending the ship northwards up the western coast of Africa. The table-top in front of the diners tipped forward and then back again and immediately William had to excuse himself from the table as he feared he would be sick. He remembered he had felt ill in the Bay of Biscay on his sea journey to the Cape so many years earlier.

He took himself to the top deck and marvelled at the ingenuity of man as the steamer made headway through the squalls. The fresh, salty air was invigorating and he relaxed at the ship's rail as his sea-sickness abated somewhat.

He had left behind two loves of his life and they lay buried in the dark soil of Africa and he mourned them deeply. He would always remember Fanny, his patroness, dear friend and first love and Hugh, his faithful companion over four decades, with deep and abiding love. As he took stock of all the years including the peaks of success and the valleys of despair when plans failed to achieve the right results, he had to admit that on the whole going to Africa had been a blessing.

The rich variety of experiences throughout his life had stretched his mind and set his ambition and imagination in a steely resolve that had helped build the very fabric of the Colony. It was something to remember and feel some pride that one has been a force for good.

"Attorney General, old chap. Fancy seeing you here!" A man joined him and his voice was familiar.

William turned to look at his companion and a look of intense displeasure crossed his face, "You! What are you doing here? I had hoped never to set eyes on you again." William's blue eyes flashed and his mouth twisted angrily.

"More's the question, what are you doing here?" Roland Craven replied. "Seriously, old chap, I have made my fortune in Africa and I'm returning to dear old Ireland as a dutiful citizen. I hope to forge a new career and win friends and clear the path for myself to become an asset to society." He was dressed in fine suede breeches and a coat of fine wool with a shirt that tied neatly at the throat. He was still quite the dandy.

"There are two types that go to the far corners of the Empire," William spoke with deadly intent, "There are those who want to create a society with its economy, agriculture, parliament, logistical infrastructure and above all the morals and philosophy of tolerance and equality for all including the natives of the Colony, providing stable and enriching benefits. Would the natives have been better off left alone is a question for the future but surely learning and skills, religion and society will always enrich? I have seen a small town grow into a thriving Colony with industry and agriculture expanding in every part of it."

"Now, now William, remember the seven deadly sins. Pride will be your downfall," Roland sounded bored and unimpressed.

William with his grey hair blown about in the storm was not put off, "Then there is you. You came to Africa to plunder, steal and kill! You have taken the wealth from the unspoiled, innocent tribes. You have taken their treasures and abused them by offering worthless trinkets in return. An inequitable bartering never bothered your conscience. You have allowed me to wrestle with thoughts that you were possibly responsible for the murder of part of the Xhosa nation. It was almost as brilliant a story as the chants you say you fed a young sangoma which brought down an entire nation. I do not believe that even with your guile and selfish, unethical, thoughtless meddling with another people's religion, beliefs and way of living that you would actually stoop so low. You belong to the gangs of bandits who go to unexplored corners of the earth and slaughter the wildlife, destroy the flora and even rape the citizens so that those innocent people learn to hate the White man. But, the damage is done and chaos is the result. You give imperialism a bad name when at one time it was a means to create a world at one with itself where we all sing from the same hymn-sheet, where the law is clear and philosophy supporting fair distribution of wealth and a nurturing society is understood by all."

"What about you? You never informed on me. Why did the Attorney General keep the unholy secret of what I may or may not have done, to himself for all these years?" Roland sneered, still the repulsive snake with poison dripping from its fangs.

"Knowledge can destroy those one seeks to help," William spoke quietly, turned and walked away with a stoop to his shoulders. It was a burden he would carry with him for the rest of his days.

When he returned to the Captain's table he received an invitation to make an after dinner speech. Everyone at the table clapped as he stood up. He wasn't feeling in top form but warmed to his topic as he began to speak:

"I would rather you applaud the Colony than myself for what I have accomplished there as Attorney General. I arrived when there was considerable upheaval occurring in various parts of the country. This included the exodus of Boers from the Cape, the invasion of Xhosa and Basuto peoples entering the Cape, the Griquas finding a bolt hole in the north and the immigration of British settlers and people from Europe who sought to make new lives for themselves or to amass their fortunes. The rights of individuals on the whole were totally ignored. I have seen life-changing events that have turned the Cape of Storms into the Cape of Good Hope. We became self-sufficient with regard to food and we owe the eastern part of the Colony, Kaffraria, a gesture of gratitude as crops begin to yield and oxen and sheep are more than amply providing meat and wool for us all. In those years, many peace treaties were negotiated with kings and chiefs but now we don't require signed sheets of paper. There are displays of good will and tolerance. There is still one problem however as I believe much to my dismay that the Boer Republics to the north of our Colony may desire to either annex land northwards or to engage with us militarily to reoccupy the Cape. There is much bitterness in their hearts.

"I believe we must now engage our young people to bring their creativity and good sense to bear in order to protect the Colony and the new Parliament by showing a willingness to dedicate their lives to the wellbeing of all. I believe if the time is right those young men and women will lay down their lives for their country. With me are my ward, Amber and my protégé, Willem, and I will seek to immerse them in the current debates with British and European philosophers, ministers of religion and parliamentarians and when Willem is called to the bar and if he so desires, I will return him to my beloved Cape to continue what I had begun in 1839.

"A toast to the Queen. Long live the Queen!" William felt the love and admiration from the diners and as he sat down, Willem raised his glass, "A toast to William Ropert, to whom we all owe our gratitude and our admiration. To William!" Willem stood tall next to his father, still unaware of his mother's relationship with the man whom he had learnt to respect and even to love. He would be torn between the two of them. To whom should he dedicate his life? To the British Empire or to the young Boer republics north of the Orange River? What role would he assume in a few years' time when he returned?

-o0o-

That night while lying awake in the darkness with Nerina asleep next to him and the wind buffeting the steamship and towering waves crashing onto the deck, William mused that he was a migrating swan returning to his homeland in Ireland. In the realm of myths the wicked and jealous second wife of King Lir had cast a spell on Lir's children and turned them into swans and they flew far away to escape her wrath. When Saint Patrick arrived in Eire, he changed the evil stepmother into an ugly old crow banishing her from Lir's kingdom and the swan-children were guarded by a monk. When a prince and princess from two different counties in Ireland married the spell was broken just as Lir's evil wife had predicted and Lir's children regained their human form, but, they were no longer children. They had become old men and women so long had the spell ensnared them. He had been in his prime when the spell of the Cape captivated him and only when homesickness prevailed, the spell had been broken and like Lir's swans, he, too, was now old, his body ravished by time. He would return to Ireland no longer the man in his prime that he had been all those years ago when he had left Ireland's shores.

He had always likened Fanny to a swan for her beauty, stillness and dignity and when he had brought her to the Cape, the spell, the secret of their love for one another, that had turned her into a mute swan was broken and at last she was free to love him. The irony was that she couldn't remain ageless like the swan she had been, but had resumed her human form of a woman where the passing of so many years had left its mark and the time she had left to live had been heart-breakingly short. Yes, they were two swans and like the lifelong bond between a pair of gentle swans, their unconsummated love would endure beyond this life. It was different to the love between a man and a woman in marriage which he now enjoyed with Nerina. It was the love of wraiths, fairies and guardian angels…and as delicate as gossamer and as bright as sunshine and moonshine. He was certain those that he loved would welcome him in Heaven and he in turn, would open his arms to embrace those he loved who were yet to arrive in the place where God was omnipresent and he would humbly stand with them all equal in God's sight and he would be content that he had lived life to the full with God's blessing.

THE END

Notes

Printed in Great Britain
by Amazon